Copyright© 2025 by Brit Benson

All rights reserved.

No part of this book may be reproduced, distributed, or transmitted in any form or by any electronic or mechanical means, including information storage and retrieval systems, without written permission from the author, except for the use of brief quotations in a book review and certain other noncommercial use permitted by copyright law.

Any use of this publication to "train" generative artificial intelligence (AI) technologies to generate text is expressly prohibited. No generative AI was used in the writing of this work. The author expressly prohibits any entity from using this publication for purposes of training AI technologies to generate text, including without limitation technologies that are capable of generating works in the same style or genre as this publication.

This book is a work of fiction. Names, characters, places, and incidents are either the product of the author's imagination or are used fictitiously. Any resemblance to actual persons and things living or dead, locales, or events is entirely coincidental. Except for the original material written by the author, all mention of films, television shows and songs, song titles, and lyrics mentioned in the novel are the property of the songwriters and copyright holders.

Cover Design & Formatting: Kate Decided to Design

Photographer: Wander Aguiar at Wander Aguiar Photography, LLC

Editing: Rebecca at Fairest Reviews Editing Services, Emily Lawrence at Lawrence Editing, Sarah Plotcher at All Encompassing Books

Sensitivity/Authenticity Reading: Ashley Carey at Sunflower Studio

Author's Note

For Wrath and Redemption is the third book in *The Hometown Heartless series* and contains a crossover character from *The Next Life* series.

For Wrath and Redemption <u>DOES</u> contain spoilers for *The Next Life* duet and *The Hometown Heartless* series.

Reading the *The Next Life* duet and *The Hometown Heartless* series prior to *For Wrath and Redemption* will enhance your appreciation of this story as well as provide a better understanding of the depth of the character dynamics, personalities, and backstories.

For clarification, *For Wrath and Redemption* takes place chronologically as the next story in both *The Hometown Heartless* series and *The Next Life* series.

For the extended playlist, visit www.authorpritbenson.com/playlists

Playlist

BOTTOM OF THE BOTTLE - Jack Kays
Colorado - Reneé Rapp
I Don't Feel Alive - Chelsea Cutler
u turn me on (but u give me depression) - LØLØ
Hallucinogenics - Matt Maeson
(with Lana Del Rey)
Psycho - Taylor Acorn
run for the hills - Tate McRae
this is me trying - Taylor Swift
reckless driving - Lizzy McAlpine
(with Ben Kessler)
Landslide - Fleetwood Mac
Tattoos - Reneé Rapp
making the bed - Olivia Rodrigo
Blackbird - The Beatles
Close to you - Gracie Abrams
Meet Me in the Hallway - Harry Styles
Free Now - Gracie Abrams
Cover Me Up - Jason Isbell
Trouble - Ray LaMontagne
long story short - Taylor Swift
i am not who i was - Chance Peña
I Think I'm in Love - Taylor Acorn
hate to be lame - Lizzy McAlpine
(with FINNEAS)
I Found - Amber Run
Your Bones - Chelsea Cutler

note-2?

Content Note

Please be aware, For Wrath and Redemption contains some difficult topics that could be upsetting for some readers.

Topics that take place on page are: vulgar language, sexually explicit content, drug and alcohol use, graphic depictions of disordered eating and purging*, dubious consent*, sexual harassment, unplanned pregnancy, death of a loved one, detox, discussions of savior siblings

Topics that are referenced but do not take place on page are: overdose, suicide, emotional manipulation and abuse, domestic violence, organ transplant, cheating

*If you require a content-specific chapter guide for these topics, you can find one at www.authorbritbenson.com.

The healing journeys depicted in this book are unique to these characters.
If you are struggling with substance abuse or disordered eating, I encourage you to speak with a mental health professional.

You matter. Your health matters. Take care of you.

Mental health resources can be found at the back of this book.

*To the well-intentioned but misunderstood—
Even if they can't forgive you, forgive yourself.
You deserve your happily ever after.*

PROLOGUE

IT'S RAINING the day they move the hospital bed into the living room.

The ever-present tension that already saturated the house grows heavier, tighter. It becomes haunting, thickening the air until I wonder if I'll need oxygen, too.

Despite the rain crashing into my windows, I can still hear the monitors beeping through the floor and my mother's sobs through the wall. I can't close my eyes without seeing my older brother's face, swollen and pallid and suffering.

Dying.

Alone.

It makes my chest ache with guilt. He isn't used to being alone. Not like me.

Quietly, I climb out of bed and tiptoe down the stairs. I skip the ones that squeak, just like he taught me, and make my way on light feet to his bedside.

I stand inches from the hospital bed and run my eyes over him. His skin looks gray in the darkness, the circles under his eyes appearing crater-like. The outside light and the rain falling down the windows cast pockmarked shadows on his face. He looks like the moon, and he feels just as far away.

Then he opens his eyes, blue just like mine, and smiles. It's a tired smile. Pained. It's so different from the one in the photos hanging on the walls. I don't want this smile to replace the ones in my memories, but the change has already begun.

"Hey, bud."

"I didn't mean to wake you."

"You didn't," he lies, then winces as he scoots over and pats the mattress. "Climb up here."

I laugh quietly. "I'm too big. I don't want to hurt you."

"I'm dying. You won't hurt me." He pats the sliver of open mattress again. "Come on."

I hesitate, and then the doctor's words float into my mind.

Days. Two weeks, at most.

Carefully, I climb into the bed beside him. I lay my head on his chest and let him wrap his arm around me. I listen to his breathing. To his heartbeat. I don't know what a healthy heartbeat should sound like, but something tells me it's not like his. I don't think breathing should sound this shallow, either.

Dying.

Days.

He'll be dead soon.

I start to cry, silent tears slipping through my lashes. I try to control my breathing. I try not to sniffle or whimper, but my tears seep through the thin fabric of his hospital gown. He tightens his grip on me, and that makes me cry more. It's a weak hold. Too weak.

"Listen to me," he whispers. "This is not your fault."

I shake my head. He's wrong. It is.

"It's not. Do you hear me?"

"But Mom—"

"Forget what Mom and Dad said. They're wrong. This is *not* your fault. Sometimes bad stuff happens, and it's nobody's fault."

Dad said not to cry in front of him. Mom said he doesn't deserve to feel

PROLOGUE

like a burden. We're supposed to make his last days feel happy. We're supposed to lie.

I squeeze my eyes shut and try to stop crying. I try so hard.

"Everything will be okay. I promise."

It's not true. It won't be. He's lying, too. We're all liars.

"Can I tell you a secret?" he asks, and I nod. "I think they've had it wrong this whole time. *You* were *my* purpose. And I don't regret it. Not for a second."

I bury my face in his chest to stifle the sobs that wrack my body. His lips press into my hair, and the plastic from his nasal cannula feels strange against my scalp.

"Never let them make you believe differently, okay?"

I do what Dad said to do. I lie. I nod to pacify him because my parents are right. He doesn't deserve to feel like a burden. I wrap my arms around him and squeeze, careful not to hurt him, and I can't ignore how different his body feels. Frail. Disintegrated.

Dying.

"I love you, Theo." I choke out the words, gasping through tears, and swallow back the rest of what I want to say.

I'm sorry, Theo. I'm so, so sorry.

"I love you, too, Jo. Never forget that."

Six days later, my older brother slips into unconsciousness. Two days after that, I stand against the wall and watch him die while my parents hold his hands.

Then, eventually, I follow.

ONE

Claire

I RAP three times on the wooden office door, my trembling fingers held tightly in my fist even after I let my arm drop back to my side.

I count to sixty as I wait—he always waits a full minute before he answers—and do my best to keep my breathing calm. Just as I mentally get to sixty, his deep voice booms through the thick door.

"Come in."

I twist the knob, push the door open, and step into the large corner office. It's brighter in here than it is in the hallway, thanks to the floor-to-ceiling windows. The setting sun is filtering in, and the room is soaking up what's left of that golden hour glow. The office where I work is thirteen floors below this one and a fraction of the size, but that doesn't bother me. I've only been here for a year, and I'm confident that I'll work my way up. Not to the CEO's office, obviously, but executive creative director sounds really nice.

Eventually.

When my boss's boss glances up from his computer, his blue eyes crinkle almost sympathetically. "Ah, Ms. Davis. I was expecting you."

"Good evening, Mr. Henderson." I greet him with a professional smile, my voice only shaking slightly. "I was wondering if you had a minute to discuss the MixMosaic campaign."

The look he gives me is one of resignation. "You want to know why I gave Brandt Macy the team lead role."

I nod. Just hearing it makes my stomach twist in a knot of anger and disappointment. The wound is still fresh, the blow having only been dealt a few hours earlier. I worked my ass off on that campaign presentation, only for the team lead position to be given to Brandt Macy (yes, *those* Macys), the most mediocre of mediocre trust fund white boys. He had absolutely zero hand in any of the creative process. It was all me. And yet, one call from Mr. Henderson to my boss had Macy usurping a role with a huge brand that should have been mine.

It's upset me so much that I've vomited twice, and the only positive thoughts I've been able to muster have been gratitude that I keep a toothbrush at my desk and Xanax in my purse.

"I worked really hard on that branding presentation, sir. From conception to delivery, it was all me. I can recite MixMosaic's numbers in my sleep, and they loved everything I did. They said they were *extremely impressed* with my work. *My* work, Mr. Henderson. With respect, sir, I should have gotten team lead, and I'd like to know why you called my boss and told him to give it to Brandt."

He gives me a look like a father would give a daughter, and it's hard not to shrink back into my repressed memories. I hate when he does this. He has a handsome face. Strong jaw. Salt and pepper through his light brown hair. Piercing blue eyes. He's a very attractive man, but when he looks at me like this, all I see is my father. I have to practically beat back my impulse to submit. To go into people-pleasing mode.

But this is my career. My future. If I don't advocate for myself, no one will.

"Ms. Davis, you know why I had to make that call."

"I don't, actually. You usually have no hand in anything that takes place in the creative development department. Never once have you intervened in the year that I've been here. I deserve to lead this campaign. I earned it."

He sighs, but I refuse to back down.

I refuse until he stands, his six-one frame dwarfing mine, and he only seems larger as he closes the distance between us. When he's mere inches from me, I hold my breath. If I smell his cologne, I'll cave.

"Claire, I know you put a lot of time and effort into that presentation. I watched it, remember? Nights and nights of hard work. It was impressive. They were innovative and creative ideas, but you're still a junior in the department, and Brandt Macy has seniority."

I shake my head, a frown pulling at my lips. "That shouldn't matter when it was my work, and you know it."

"It's not fair. I agree."

"Then, why?"

He gives me a sympathetic smile, then toys with the collar of my blouse. "We're playing a dangerous game, my love. When this started, you said you didn't want me to interfere—"

"I didn't want you to interfere in my progress. I didn't want you to interfere with my success in the company. I didn't mean I wanted you to halt my chances of rising in the ranks. I wanted to do it on my own merit."

When he trails his knuckles over my jaw, my eyes flutter shut, and a sense of defeat starts to invade my mind. I'm going to lose this one.

"And what would people say if they found out? Do you want people saying you've received unfair advantages because of your connection to me? You don't want to be known as a woman who slept her way to the top."

I shake my head, and my heart sinks in my chest. My shoulders hunch forward. He's right. He's always right, but I try one last time.

"My work speaks for itself, Conrad."

He presses a kiss to my forehead. "It does. And it will. You just need to be patient."

He notches his finger under my chin and tilts my face upward. I open my eyes before he can tell me to, and then I'm locked onto his gaze, my resolve melting away with every soft breath fanned over my lips.

"You're too important to me, Claire. I need to be careful, so I don't lose you."

I release my exhale slowly, his words washing over me like a rising tide. There's enough time to save myself from drowning, but I don't. I could love him. I might already. So I stay and convince myself I'm a strong enough swimmer to survive.

"Okay," I whisper. "You're right."

When he brings his mouth to mine, I relent fully, letting him kiss me. I slide my palms up his buttery-soft bespoke suit and wrap my arms around his neck as he deepens the kiss, but then he pulls away. Too soon.

Once again, I'm left bereft and chasing a feeling that too often slips through my fingers.

"Will you be home when I get there?"

I force a smile and nod. "Yes."

I'm *always* there these days. He smiles back, his beautiful blue eyes crinkling at the corners in that way that bolsters my confidence, and then he turns and goes back to his desk without another word.

I've been dismissed.

A PHONE RINGS in the darkness, and it rouses me awake.

When Conrad sits up, so do I, clutching the duvet to cover my naked chest. His voice, deep and commanding despite the rasp from sleep, fills the quiet room, and I listen. I study his body language and his tone of voice. As always, his words are clipped, and he gives nothing away.

"Hello? Yes, this is Conrad Henderson. I see. No, it's fine. I'll be by tomorrow afternoon. Of course."

He hangs up without saying goodbye and places his phone on the nightstand. He lies down without acknowledging me, then turns his body so he's facing away from me. I watch as his back moves with each inhale and exhale. His breathing slows, and when I'm sure he's fallen back to sleep, I lie back down and attempt to do the same.

IN THE BATHROOM, I'm applying makeup when Conrad comes in to fix his tie in the mirror.

"I've made you coffee," I say with a smile.

He grunts. "I told you to let the house manager do that."

The house manager's name is Edward. He's essentially a live-in cook and maid. Conrad doesn't like when I call him Edward; Edward doesn't want me to call him Mr. Miller, and I refuse to call him *the house manager*, so I avoid talking about him entirely.

"I like making the coffee. It makes me feel useful."

I'd make dinner, too, if he'd let me. Anything to help feel less like a visitor between these pristine, million-dollar walls. Eleven months and all I've gotten is a phone charger I leave by the bed, a few silk nighties hanging in the closet, and a designated place for my toiletry bag under the bathroom sink. I was disgustingly excited about the phone charger.

I realize how sad that is.

Conrad walks to the side of the sink that I use and presses a kiss to the top of my head.

"I'll be leaving after lunch today and will be gone for a few days. I have some business."

I make eye contact in the mirror. "Is it about the call last night?"

"It is."

"Are you going to tell me what it was about? I'd like to help, if possible."

"There's nothing you can do, Claire."

I turn to face him and place my hands on his chest. He's already in his suit, and I'm back in yesterday's outfit.

"I want to help, Conrad. It must have been something serious to warrant a call that late at night."

He purses his lips as his eyes bounce between mine. I slide my hands around his neck and lift myself onto the balls of my feet so I can press a soft kiss to the corner of his mouth.

"Didn't you say you wanted to make us serious?" I say when I pull back, locking my gaze with his. Willing him to see how sincerely I mean every word. How much I want the dream he's crafted for me. "You said you care about me, right? We can't have a serious relationship if you don't let me in. I can help, even if it's just to share the mental load. Tell me, please."

Conrad sighs, his shoulders dipping before he nods once. "Elizabeth has died. I need to go upstate to make arrangements."

My eyes go wide. "Your ex-wife? What happened?"

"Her illness took a turn for the worse. It's nothing for you to worry about."

"I can come with. I know how stressful this must be. Let me come, and I can—"

"That's unnecessary. How would it look if we were both absent? I'll go alone."

"But, Con—"

"Claire, you will stay here. I just have to get ahold of my son so I can take care of the body, and then it will be done. I'll be back Sunday afternoon at the latest."

I blink. So he can *take care of* the *body*...

The. Not her body. *The* body. Detached and cold. She's nothing to him anymore. It makes me sad for her, but I push it away.

"What about a funeral?"

He chuckles, but it's a dead, hollow sound, and a chill runs down the back of my neck.

"I won't be funding a funeral. I'll carry out her after-death wishes and then finally wash my hands of the thing." He must see the horror on my face because his lips curve up into a soothing smile. "Eliza was unwell, and I'm glad she's not in pain anymore. Maybe now, without the constant stress of her presence looming over us, you and I will be able to go public soon."

I bite back the impulse to smile and stifle the spark of hope that ignites in my chest as shame washes over me.

Excitement over a woman's death? A woman whom I've never met? It's vile.

And anyway, Elizabeth Henderson's death still doesn't erase the main conflict shrouding my relationship with her ex-husband. Conrad is the CEO of the company where I'm currently employed, and I do not want anyone claiming I slept my way to the top.

He bends down and kisses me once more. It's a soft, sweet kiss, and it calms the self-loathing swirling in my empty stomach. When he steps backward, his smile is kind, but the words he speaks next deflate any confidence I'd started to feel.

"You should hurry if you're going to be at the office on time."

Right. Because I still have to go back to my apartment to change since I have no clothes here. Since I'm *not permitted* to leave clothes here.

"I'll see you when you get back." I force a smile and walk toward the bathroom door. "Travel safely. I hope it goes...well...as smoothly as possible."

"Thank you, my love. I will call you."

When he looks back at the mirror, I leave. I grab my purse and shoes by the door and let myself out of the apartment, grateful that Edward isn't around to witness my walk of shame. It doesn't matter that it happens almost every morning. It still makes me feel dirty.

My relationship with Conrad is unconventional, but these discomforts are the price I pay for falling for my boss. No one would believe that I didn't know who he was when we met. No one would care that I'm not using him to get ahead in my career.

I attempt to shove down my screaming insecurities. I try not to focus on what I used to want or see for myself. I tell myself that if I keep my head down and work my ass off, it will all pay off. I'm living in New York City and working my dream job. I tell myself that I'm fulfilled and happy. I tell myself it will be fine.

I say it, but I can't make myself believe it.

Then, because I deserve the downward spiral, I grab my phone, open a social media app, and go to the profile I know will make me feel worse. I spend my commute to work scrolling through photos of happy faces, faces that once used to be as familiar to me as my own, and I let myself sink deeper into darkness.

TWO

Jonah

I DROP my head to the cinderblock wall and close my eyes.

I need a cigarette, a shower, and my bed, but my smokes are in the fucking dressing room, and I'm locked out so Torren can fuck his girlfriend. The door beside me jostles, and I groan. They can't fuck on a couch like normal people? They gotta do it against the door so we all know what's happening?

When Callie starts to moan, my dick hardens in response, so I kick off the wall and storm down the hall. I need distance from this bullshit, but no matter what I do, they're in my fucking face.

When I spot Hammond, I stop in front of him and glare until he gets off the phone. As soon as he hangs up, I throw my demand at him.

"I need my own room from now on. I can't share any more suites with them."

Hammond's eyebrow arches slightly as his eyes scan over my face. He drops his attention down to my tightly balled fists, then back up to my clenched jaw. I know what he's thinking. It's what they all think.

Can we trust him alone?

Can we leave him unsupervised?

Jonah the ticking time bomb.
Jonah the live wire.

I cut into his thoughts with the truth.

"You want to keep me sober, Ham? Get me out of their suite. If I have to listen to them fucking anymore, I'm going to lose it."

It's a blunt, low blow, but it's the truth. I'm not exactly on the wagon, and everyone knows it. My position is a precarious illusion at best. But I know when I'm teetering. I know how it feels when my strength is faltering.

It feels like this.

"I'm keeping a key to your room," he says finally, and I jerk out a nod.

"Fine."

"And I'm giving one to Sav."

"She's not my fucking mom, Ham."

He doesn't respond. He just continues. "Torren and Mabel will also get one, and your security will obviously have one, too."

"So if I move out of the sex den, I'm losing my privacy?"

"No. No one will use it unless it's an emergency."

He doesn't reference the last *emergency*. He doesn't have to. I see the flash of concern in his eyes, and guilt lashes in my gut. The guilt is why I concede.

"Fine."

"If you need anything, at any point, you come to one of us."

Hammond's tone is one of sincerity, and the switch from all-business manager to caring father figure renders me speechless for a moment. I'm almost thirty, and Hammond is only ten years older than me, but once in a while, he'll say or do something that reminds me of what it might have felt like to have parents who gave a shit.

I clear my throat, shove back my mommy and daddy issues, then jerk out another nod.

"I won't do anything to jeopardize the tour, Wade."

"Fuck the tour, Jonah. We've talked about this. You're a priority. Everyone agrees."

That statement just makes the guilt churn more violently until it's creeping into my rib cage and making my heart race. I resist the urge to rub at my chest. Finishing this tour is crucial. It's our last obstacle to terminating our contract with our label. Knowing that everyone is willing to postpone that if I fuck up just increases my feelings of failure.

I breathe through my nose, inhaling deeply and exhaling slowly before laying myself bare for Hammond's scrutiny.

"We need to get through this tour. *I* need to get through this tour. The only time I really feel in control is when I'm on that stage. I just..."

I close my eyes and shake my head, chasing away the images creeping into my mind. The thoughts that plague me when I'm not playing music. The memories that always return, no matter how many toxins I pump into my bloodstream.

"Having my own room will help, and I will not do anything that will jeopardize this tour."

I can see the conflict in Ham's eyes. I know what he wants to say. I've heard it before. *My life is more important. The tour can be rescheduled. Everyone agrees.*

What they don't seem to get is how desperately my life might depend on this tour. I'm not exaggerating. Without it, I worry I'll spiral. I'll circle the drain without a call time or an adoring crowd to fish me out.

It's not healthy. I know that. I'm so aware of it that I haven't even mentioned it in my Thursday therapy sessions. But, for better or worse, it's what I've fucking got right now.

I don't break eye contact with my manager, and when he finally relents with a single nod, I feel like a brick has been removed from the pile of debris that's been holding space on my chest.

"Thank you."

"You'll have your own room by tonight."

With that, Hammond turns away while raising his phone to his ear, no doubt calling the hotel. Just as he disappears around a corner, I hear the door to the dressing room swing open and Callie's soft laughter filters into the hallway. My lips curl in disgust, and I point my feet in the direction of the exit doors. I can bum a smoke from a roadie. I don't feel like going back into the dressing room to retrieve mine. Not when I know it probably smells like sex.

Tonight, though, in my own room, I'll be able to sleep without her presence emanating through the walls and her scent permeating every surface in the suite.

My therapist says this road is best walked one step at a time. She says eventually, my steps won't feel like I'm on a fucking tightrope hovering above a cavern of jagged rocks.

I can do that. One step at a time, one foot in front of the other. I just hope to fucking God nothing new comes out and throws me off-balance.

Again.

I'M PICKING my way through my room service lunch when my phone rings.

I do the quick math. It's morning in New York, and while I'd much rather ignore the call, my curiosity overrides my better judgment. My father never calls. I don't think twice before I hit accept and put the phone to my ear.

"Yeah."

"Is that how celebrities are answering phones now?"

I roll my eyes. I didn't go through my rebellious phase until college. Despite the years and distance, it seems I'm not quite out of it. How cliché of me.

"Good morning, Father. How have you been?"

He doesn't acknowledge my question, which is fine. I don't particularly care about the answer. The words that do leave his mouth, though...

They hit me like a freight train.

I have to shake my head a few times before I can ask for clarification. There's no possible way I heard him correctly.

"I'm sorry, can you repeat that? I think I misheard."

He sighs. "Your mother has died. There will be no funeral. I've handled everything and she will be moved to the cemetery this afternoon. You do not need to come home as there is no will to review. I wanted you to know before it hit the news."

My mouth falls open twice, and I have to force a swallow before I can form words.

"When? How?"

He sighs again. This time there's a hint of sorrow. It's barely noticeable, but I hear it. As much as I hate to admit it, I'm still very attuned to his emotions.

"I learned about it yesterday. It was accidental. A misdiagnosis of medication...They believe she went in her sleep."

A wave of nausea rolls over me. I taste bile on my tongue as the lunch I just ate threatens to come back up. *Accidental.* I know what that means. It's the word families like mine toss out when they don't want to admit the truth. When they're in fucking denial.

It means it was anything but an accident.

"Were you with her?"

I ask the question despite already knowing the answer. It fuels my rage and redistributes my shame.

"You know she's been upstate."

"So she was alone. She died alone."

"Mari saw her three times a week. Your mother wasn't alone."

I scoff and shake my head. Mari. The housekeeper.

I bite my tongue at the urge to lash out at him. To tell him exactly what I think of him. To point a finger at him so I don't have to point it at myself.

"Anyway. Now you know. I have to—"

I hang up. Then I stand, shove my wallet and passport in my pocket, and head for the door. There's a security guard in the hallway, and I give him a casual nod.

"Gonna smoke. Be back in five."

He nods back, and the tension in my shoulders lessens when he makes no move to follow. Thank God we're not under twenty-four surveillance anymore. Instead of going to the roof to smoke, I push the button for the lobby and then hail a cab.

I'll text Ham from the airport and tell him to play the Paris shows without me. Rocky Halstrom, the guitarist from Caveat Lover, could do it easily. My band will be pissed that I left without talking to them first, but they'll understand. I've got to do this. Even if it fucking sucks, I have to be there. I'll deal with the fallout later.

I tip the cabbie, then buy my way onto the next flight to New York. It's not hard. I offer to upgrade a traveling college kid's seat to first class if he takes a later flight, and he jumps at it. I don't even have to play the dead mom card. I just sign his backpack, then take his seat in economy.

I shoot Hammond one text before I fasten my seat belt.

> ME
>
> My mom died. Heading back. Will text when I land. Have Rocky finish Paris for me.

Then I turn off my phone and shove it into my pocket, determined not to look at it until my feet are on American soil.

For the next eight hours, I try to ignore the buzzing in my ears. The tingling in my hands. The way each sound, each sensation, grows more intense with every mile of distance the plane covers. The memories invade, intrusive and persistent as ever. The left side of my stomach throbs. My heart races, and my vision blurs, but no attempt to sleep is successful.

The first time the attendant offers beverages, I turn it down because I try not to mix pills and booze anymore. I spend the next hour cursing myself for not bringing a book, or headphones, or some fucking nicotine gum. The second time the attendant passes, I ask for vodka, and she brings me three airplane bottles. I down them immediately.

It's fine, given the circumstances.

It's fine.

The liquor mixes with the anti-anxiety meds already coursing in my veins. It succeeds in dulling the ache, in quieting my mind, but it fuels my cravings.

When my fingers itch for another of the small glass bottles, I don't even bother fighting it. I play the rock star angle and flirt shamelessly with the attendant until she brings me four more. I drink these a little slower, spacing them out over the next two hours, attempting to force myself into a comfortable intoxication.

This isn't how I'm supposed to be dealing with my emotions. I know this. Conflicting arguments battle inside my skull. This is another failure. Another intentional fall from the wagon.

But my mom is fucking dead.

She's dead, and it's my fucking fault.

I grit my teeth and breathe through the age-old anger. The haunting despair. The guilt. It always comes back to the guilt. Even from the fucking grave, she has power over me. My mother, the puppet master. She's always played my emotions like a fucking marionette.

I almost wish I believed in hell just so I could imagine her burning in a pit of flames.

I drop my head into my hands and dig my palms into my eye sockets until I see white. I breathe deeply. I push my toes into the floor.

Nothing works.

I write a proposition on a napkin, and the next time the attendant walks by, I sneak it to her. Fifteen minutes later, we're crammed into the small airplane bathroom while I fuck her from behind. She's got her legs on either side of the toilet and her forearms on the wall in front of her face. Her flight attendant dress is pushed up on her hips, her pantyhose are shoved to her knees, and her thong is tugged to the side as I thrust as deep and fast into her as I can without making a racket. I reach around her body and rub on her clit until she comes, and then I spill into the condom.

We're quiet as she hurriedly fixes her outfit, taking a brief moment to glance at her reflection in the small mirror above the sink. She looks the same. No makeup smudges. No hair out of place. She gives me a wink, and with one last kiss, we both slip quietly back to where we came from.

Thanks to the orgasm, I manage to get a couple hours of sleep, but it's fitful and plagued with images I'd rather forget. None of it ever works for long. Sex, alcohol, drugs. The relief they provide never lasts. Temporary fixes are all I can rely on in a world like mine. One that lacks permanence in everything except pain.

I land at JFK airport around nine in the evening, but by the time I'm through customs and pulling out of the rental car garage, it's closer to eleven. I have every intention of getting on the interstate and driving straight to the cemetery, but the closer I get, the whiter my knuckles become from how tightly I'm gripping the steering wheel. After only twenty minutes, my leg starts bouncing. Twenty more minutes, and I'm clenching and unclenching my jaw. By the time I'm approaching my exit, my head is pounding, and sweat is dotting my hairline.

My body makes the decision before I have a chance to even think about it. Instead of turning toward the cemetery, I get back on the expressway and find the nearest liquor store.

Vodka. I need vodka.

"Just a little bit more." My words cut through the silence of the car, and I jump. I didn't mean to say them out loud, but then I repeat them. "Just a little bit more. Just to get through tonight, and after this, I'll dry out and stay sober."

I'll commit to the process this time. I will.

I just need to get through this.

THREE

Jonah

THE RENTAL JOLTS TO A STOP, my body bucking against the seat belt as the car hops the small curb and the bumper slams into the wrought iron fence.

Thank fuck I hit the brakes when I did.

I unbuckle and shove the door open, grabbing my vodka bottle from the floorboard before stumbling out into the grass.

"Fuck." I round the hood of the car and inspect the damage. I give the tire a kick and choke out a laugh. The front, right side of the Ferrari is dented and scratched. The headlight is busted. I should have asked for an SUV. "Fuck."

Despite an obvious tilt, the fence looks fine, though. I toss my vodka over it, and the bottle lands on the soft, manicured grass with a gentle thud. Here's hoping my landing is as gentle.

I'm unsteady as I climb onto the hood of the car, the metal denting under my boots. I consider how much this damage will cost me, but the worry flits away the moment my fingers wrap around the cool rails of the fence.

It's been years since I've climbed this fence. Twelve, at least. My hands are more calloused and weathered than they were back then, but the iron still feels familiar against my skin. The thought seizes my muscles as pain lashes in my gut. Of all the things to push me over the edge, I wouldn't have guessed it would be this. I squeeze my eyes shut and attempt to wrangle the inebriation-induced vertigo, to shut down the onslaught of unwanted memories, then get to work hauling my ass over the fence.

Unfortunately, my landing isn't like the vodka bottle's.

The air is knocked from my lungs as my back meets the hard ground, and I choke out a groan.

"Mother fuck, I'm too old for this."

I open my eyes and peer up at the dark sky as I catch my breath. It's a moody blend of blues and blacks. No stars. There never are here. It's fucking fitting.

Slowly, I roll onto my stomach, then rise onto my knees but keep my head resting on my forearms. I inhale deeply, the scent of soil and grass mixing with the scent of weed on my shirt. I wait for my head to stop spinning. It doesn't, but it slows, and that's as good as it's going to get right now. I sweep my hand through the grass beside me, latch on to the neck of my vodka bottle, and then slowly push to my feet.

Muscle memory leads me through the rows of headstones and monuments, and a new floral scent dances on every light breeze. It used to be my favorite thing about this cemetery. The variety of blooms left on the unforgotten burial plots. The people under that earth are loved. They are missed. They are visited often. It's not lost on me that the freshest flowers are often left on the most modest grave markers.

A frown tugs at my forehead. I uncap my vodka and lift the bottle to my lips. I tip it back, the booze filling my mouth and dribbling from the sides, and I swallow down the alcohol. It barely tastes like anything anymore. It may as well be water.

I screw the cap back on the bottle, then continue my walk, taking care to breathe through my mouth instead of my nose. I don't want to think about the flowers or about families mourning their dead. I don't want to think about the ones left behind.

When the white stone mausoleum comes into view, my steps slow. I squint, forcing the hazy glow around the building to lessen. I swallow back

THREE

Jonah

THE RENTAL JOLTS TO A STOP, my body bucking against the seat belt as the car hops the small curb and the bumper slams into the wrought iron fence.

Thank fuck I hit the brakes when I did.

I unbuckle and shove the door open, grabbing my vodka bottle from the floorboard before stumbling out into the grass.

"Fuck." I round the hood of the car and inspect the damage. I give the tire a kick and choke out a laugh. The front, right side of the Ferrari is dented and scratched. The headlight is busted. I should have asked for an SUV. "Fuck."

Despite an obvious tilt, the fence looks fine, though. I toss my vodka over it, and the bottle lands on the soft, manicured grass with a gentle thud. Here's hoping my landing is as gentle.

I'm unsteady as I climb onto the hood of the car, the metal denting under my boots. I consider how much this damage will cost me, but the worry flits away the moment my fingers wrap around the cool rails of the fence.

It's been years since I've climbed this fence. Twelve, at least. My hands are more calloused and weathered than they were back then, but the iron still feels familiar against my skin. The thought seizes my muscles as pain lashes in my gut. Of all the things to push me over the edge, I wouldn't have guessed it would be this. I squeeze my eyes shut and attempt to wrangle the inebriation-induced vertigo, to shut down the onslaught of unwanted memories, then get to work hauling my ass over the fence.

Unfortunately, my landing isn't like the vodka bottle's.

The air is knocked from my lungs as my back meets the hard ground, and I choke out a groan.

"Mother fuck, I'm too old for this."

I open my eyes and peer up at the dark sky as I catch my breath. It's a moody blend of blues and blacks. No stars. There never are here. It's fucking fitting.

Slowly, I roll onto my stomach, then rise onto my knees but keep my head resting on my forearms. I inhale deeply, the scent of soil and grass mixing with the scent of weed on my shirt. I wait for my head to stop spinning. It doesn't, but it slows, and that's as good as it's going to get right now. I sweep my hand through the grass beside me, latch on to the neck of my vodka bottle, and then slowly push to my feet.

Muscle memory leads me through the rows of headstones and monuments, and a new floral scent dances on every light breeze. It used to be my favorite thing about this cemetery. The variety of blooms left on the unforgotten burial plots. The people under that earth are loved. They are missed. They are visited often. It's not lost on me that the freshest flowers are often left on the most modest grave markers.

A frown tugs at my forehead. I uncap my vodka and lift the bottle to my lips. I tip it back, the booze filling my mouth and dribbling from the sides, and I swallow down the alcohol. It barely tastes like anything anymore. It may as well be water.

I screw the cap back on the bottle, then continue my walk, taking care to breathe through my mouth instead of my nose. I don't want to think about the flowers or about families mourning their dead. I don't want to think about the ones left behind.

When the white stone mausoleum comes into view, my steps slow. I squint, forcing the hazy glow around the building to lessen. I swallow back the lump that forms in my throat, then take another pull from the vodka bottle. I'm so fucking drunk, and it's still not enough.

I bypass the door—my key is in my safe deposit box in Los Angeles—and instead walk to the back of the building. I take a deep breath as I stare up at the colorful stained-glass window. Mary is cradling baby Jesus, with circular halos outlining both their heads.

Objectively, even in the dark of night, the art is beautiful.

I narrow my eyes as anger surges up my throat like bile, and I grit my teeth against the sudden desire to scream. I finish off the rest of my vodka, wipe my face with my forearm, and clear my throat.

"Sorry, Mother."

I hurl the bottle through the window.

The glass shatters, making a slightly musical sound, and my lips almost twitch into a smile. Then I'm plunged back into silence. Just my heavy breathing and the light, floral-scented breeze rustling through the grass.

I take my shirt off and use it to brush the glass from the stone windowsill, then pull myself through the opening. It's too high for me to enter feet first, and it's too small to allow me to turn around, so my forearms collide with the stone floor as I fall into the crypt, followed quickly by my body landing prostrate amongst the window remnants.

I hiss as shards of glass dig into my exposed skin—arms, hands, chest. Even the parts of my knees not protected by denim are assaulted, and I wonder which slices are caused by Mary and which by Jesus. The thought makes me chuckle as my blood smears on the white stone tiles, the red appearing black in the darkness.

I make my intoxicated, battered body stand, but it immediately wants to shrink. To crouch backward. This room feels so much smaller than the last time I was here. If I stretched my arms out, I could touch both walls. I don't attempt it. I keep my arms secured firmly at my sides.

This room feels smaller now because I was smaller then.

The thought draws out more memories, a nauseating blend of good and bad. I tip my head to the ceiling, and I clamp my eyes shut once more, but instead of forcing the memories down, I let myself feel them. I let them overwhelm me.

Every ounce of self-doubt. Of loss. Of feeling like an intruder in my own fucking home. It weighs heavily on my chest and makes it hurt to breathe.

Self-flagellation is my favorite pastime.

I clench my hands into fists as laughter echoes in my brain, loving and kind. More tender than anything I've ever known. And yet...it's tainted. It cuts deeper than the indifference. The disappointment. The neglect. How can you truly love someone if your life, your happiness, depends on their acquiescence? If it's conditional on their loyalty and obedience?

A sob claws its way up my throat, breaking violently through my lips. My body bows, and my hands clutch my head as hot tears break through the barrier of my eyelashes. They burn as they stream down my cheeks. I haven't cried in years. It's worse than I remember. I press my palms into my eyes, pushing until white flashes behind my eyelids.

I tried so fucking hard. Tried to be what they needed. Tried to do what was desired of me. What was *required* of me. No matter the pain. No matter the anguish. I tried, and I failed.

"Goddamn it." My voice is rough and strangled in my own ears. It sounds weak, and that fuels my anger. "Goddamn it!"

I turn to the wall and slap it with both palms, then press my forehead against it and pound with my fists. Choking back another wail, I push harder against the marble slabs.

I shouldn't have done this. I shouldn't be here. I fucked up.

The stone cools my heated skin as I rock my head back and forth. I breathe deeply, forcing my heart to calm. Forcing my tears to slow. Forcing the feelings back down into the dark recesses of my mind. Far away from my heart. Far away from my consciousness. No one can survive this way. I shouldn't have let myself forget.

When my emotions are manageable and my grief is masked, I straighten my spine. I make my six-foot-one frame fill the room and set my eyes on the gold frieze above the locked door. I count backward from one hundred until my body no longer has to fight the urge to fold in on itself.

I won't share space with the dead. Not anymore. Not in this room. Not in my head.

Turning to my left, I scan the memorials on the wall. Against my better judgment, I let myself focus on one. I know the dates by heart. The epitaph. I see it in my nightmares. My teeth grind, my jaw aching with the pressure as I fight back the sting of more tears.

"I won't share space with the dead," I whisper into the silence.

My gaze flits to another memorial. This one is new, and there is no sting of tears as I read the epitaph. My lips pull into a sneer. I almost want to laugh, but nothing about this is funny.

"NYPD. Come out with your hands up, or we're coming in."

The booming voice sounds through the mausoleum, making me jump, and a chuckle does break free. Just one.

Well. This is a little funny.

"I'm unarmed," I shout without looking away from the memorial plaque. "I'm coming out."

I take five more deep breaths, and before I surrender myself to the cops outside, I lower my voice and whisper into the room. To the crypts. To the bodies entombed inside. My voice is stronger than it was minutes before. There's no shaking. No weakness. Just pure, unadulterated hatred.

"I'm fucking glad you're dead."

FOUR

Claire

"YOU'RE LATE."

I glance toward the voice and smile. "I'm right on time."

"Exactly." Sasha makes a show of checking her watch. "On time is late for you."

"I got a later start than usual."

I give Sasha a shrug and drop my bag on the floor beside my desk. Days like this, I can't help but think of how much easier it would be if I could just leave for the office from Conrad's Upper West Side penthouse. Instead, my commute time is tripled because I have to go uptown to my apartment before I can take the train back down to Midtown.

I frown down at my computer keyboard as I kick off my tennis shoes and step into my pumps. The inconvenience makes me angry. Conrad tells me it's *safer this way*. He says it's to *protect me*, but on days like this…Well, it feels like disrespect. It feels like he doesn't value my time, and once again, I feel used. Dirty. And that brings me back to the thought that's been circling quietly in my head for weeks now.

Should I end it? But if I do, would my job be affected? Would he fire me?

The thoughts immediately fill me with guilt, and I give my head a little shake. I'm so fucking lucky that a man like Conrad—intelligent, kind, successful—would even look twice at me, let alone *want* me. He's good to me. I need to suck it up and stop being so whiny.

Patience. I know I need to have patience, but I've never been very good at that.

I drop my shoes into the bottom drawer of my desk and shut it more forcefully than I intended. The loud bang sounds through the office and makes me flinch.

"Damn. That bad?"

I flick my attention back to Sasha and force a smile. "It's fine."

She purses her lips, running her eyes over my face before leaning her hip on my desk and lowering her voice. "It's bullshit that Macy got the MixMosaic lead. We all think it."

"Apparently, seniority matters, and I've only been here a year."

"Claire, I got my first lead at six months."

I arch an eyebrow. "For a client like MixMosaic?"

"No. It was a much smaller client, but still. You did the work. It should have been yours."

I give her another smile, and this time, I try to make it believable. "It's fine, Sasha. Thank you for the support, but I'm fine. I'm just glad my presentation won them over. The MixMosaic account is good for the company. I'm going to go grab a coffee."

Without another word, I cross the floor of the office to the coffee station. After the third sympathetic expression from my colleagues, I keep my gaze fixed straight ahead and avoid eye contact. I guess Sasha wasn't kidding when she said *we all think it*. I suppose I should feel validated that everyone in my department believes I was fucking robbed, but I don't like the pity. I don't need everyone feeling sorry for me. Especially when I know that I'm the only one to blame.

I furrow my brow as I drop the espresso pod into the fancy coffee machine and run through all the pros of working at this company. It's arguably one of the best marketing firms in the country. Probably even the world. Not only does it look great on a résumé, but they promote from within, so there's a lot of opportunity to grow. It's also been named one of the top ten best places to work in the city every year for the last five years, and one glance around this office will tell you why. It's a bright, collaborative space full of motivated, happy people.

I absolutely love my job. But damn, I wish my personal life weren't so... *Constricting.*

I push the button on the espresso machine, and it whirs to life, then I drop my head back, tilting my face to the ceiling. My memories bring me back to a day in 5th Avenue Brew a year ago. I'd sit in that café every weekend with my double espresso and my laptop. I'd only been in the city for a couple of months, and I'd just accepted the position as a junior creative developer at Innovation Media. I was fresh-faced, wide-eyed, and full of hope.

Enter Conrad Henderson, with his salt-and-pepper hair, his pale blue eyes, and his charming smile. Every weekend, he found me in that coffee shop. Every weekend for a month we spoke, and when he finally asked me on a date, I was already half in love with him. I didn't care that he was twice my age or that I knew no real details about his personal life. All I cared about was that he wasn't wearing a ring, and he looked at me like I was the only person in the room. He was the most attentive listener. He complimented me. He made me feel important, and I was enamored.

Then, three months into our relationship, I had my first department meeting with the CEO. I felt sick to my stomach when my new boyfriend was the man standing at the front of the boardroom. I felt myself go pale. I nearly passed out.

But he...

Well, he was completely unfazed.

When he called me for a private meeting later that evening, I was furious. I was prepared to end it. But then he promised me that our relationship wouldn't interfere with my job. He said I was important to him. That he'd never felt for anyone what he felt for me.

I'll never forget what he said to me in his office that evening.

You make me want to fall in love again.

And then he fucked me on the couch in his office.

I can't help but laugh at myself now. I was so naïve, so blindly enamored with him that it took me a while to realize that Conrad had to have known who I was the whole time. When we'd met, I had my company-issued laptop and my security badge clipped to my bag. For three months, he'd lied to me. Omitted important truths. All while knowing I was a newly hired junior creative at his company.

And now it's coming back to bite me in the ass.

As if I need a reminder of my recent professional snub, Brandt Macy struts up beside me just as I'm tossing my used espresso pod in the trash. I greet him politely despite my urge to sneer. It's not Brandt's fault I was passed over for this position. He's not the one sleeping with the CEO. Brandt is actually a really nice guy, even if he is a card-carrying member of the nepotism club.

"Morning, Brandt. Congrats again on getting the MixMosaic lead."

"Thanks, Claire." Brandt returns my smile and shoves his hands in his pockets. "But you and I both know it should have been your position."

My brows shoot up, and he laughs. "Don't look surprised. You did great work."

I cock my head to the side and eye him suspiciously. "If you think I should have gotten the lead, then why did you take it?"

"The call came from Henderson," he says with a sheepish shrug. "I don't really feel comfortable going against the CEO. I hear he's kind of a dick."

I huff out a laugh, but I don't confirm or deny. I turn my attention to one of the brainstorming whiteboards and inhale the scent of my fresh espresso instead. I always feel so awkward when Conrad comes up in conversation.

"Anyway." Brandt drags out the word and then pauses nervously, drawing my eyes back to his face. "I look forward to working with you on it."

My hesitation isn't intentional. It just takes me a moment to sift through the conflict stirring in my mind. I'll still have to work on this campaign. Do I do my best work, knowing Brandt will likely get all the credit, or do I take a step back and let him fumble the job to make a point? From the uncertain expression on his face, it seems he's been worrying about it, too.

God, he looks so fucking pitiful right now. And the truth is that I probably couldn't slack even if I wanted to. I'm too excited. I have too many ideas. The realization makes my stomach twist into a tighter knot. It feels like a concession, like a surrender, but it also feels unavoidable. The MixMosaic campaign is going to be a huge success, and Brandt Macy will probably get a promotion based on my hard work. Hours and hours of planning, preparation, and some of my best designs will go toward boosting someone else's career, and I did it to myself.

I sigh.

"I'm looking forward to it, too," I say slowly. "We meet at ten, right?"

He nods. "Ten."

"See you then."

I make my way back to my desk slowly, but I keep my head high. I push down the jealousy and anger. I ignore the feelings of being used. Of being overpowered. I try to silence the chanting inside my mind. The thoughts that have grown louder recently. Reminders that I am not good enough.

Not good enough for Conrad. Not good enough for this job. Not good enough.

This time, I meet every one of my colleagues' pitying looks with a bright smile.

I'm fine. It's fine. It will all be fine.

This is what I say to myself, over and over, as I set my espresso on my desk and grab the small bag I keep in my top drawer. The one I haven't touched in months. I walk to the elevators, push the button for the lobby, and repeat the words until the doors open, revealing the large reception desk in the middle of the white and black tiled floor. The security guard nods as I pass him, and I return his greeting with a smile.

I'm fine. It's fine. It will all be fine.

I chant the words in time with my steps—thirty of them—until I'm pushing open a large wooden door and entering the lobby bathroom. Thankfully, it's empty. It usually is.

I close myself into the stall farthest from the door, tuck my hair into the back of my shirt, and empty the meager contents of my stomach into the toilet. I flush, then walk to the sink and wash my hands. I rinse my mouth from the tap twice. I take my toothbrush out of the small bag I keep in my desk and brush my teeth. Then I make myself look in the mirror, keeping my eyes on my face.

I clean up my eye makeup. I reapply my lip gloss. And then I force a smile.

It's robotic. Automated. It's all muscle memory. I ignore the guilt. I ignore the shame.

"I'm fine," I say to my reflection. "It's fine. It will all be fine."

I'VE MISSED spending time in my apartment.

It's much smaller in comparison to Conrad's. I don't have a chef or a maid or a smart house system. My door has four locks on it. I only have an old secondhand treadmill instead of an entire gym. And, of course, I'm alone, which has its drawbacks, but still. I love it here. I'm proud of it.

It's my first solo apartment. My first place that's just mine. In college, I had roommates until I moved in with my fiancé. After that relationship failed miserably, this apartment felt like a new beginning. My first real step in doing something on my own. I was in it for only a couple of months before I met Conrad, and then I started spending less and less time here. Conrad prefers his penthouse, and I don't blame him. I used to, but as I sink into my thrifted couch and curl my legs comfortably beneath me, I question whether I still do. Certainly, I'm more relaxed here. I don't feel like an imposter, and it's nice not to worry about how to *appear* like I belong.

I bring my cup of hot chamomile tea to my lips and take a sip. It's in a cheap tourist mug I got from a gift shop in Times Square. The tea warms me from the inside, and I close my eyes, relishing the feel of it pooling in my empty stomach as I sink into my thoughts. Everything in Conrad's kitchen is plain white and designer. Sterile and clinical. No character. No color. It might as well be a hospital operating room.

I prefer my tie-dye IHEARTNYC mug, even if I won't admit it out loud.

I worked on MixMosaic ideas all day, then came home and ran five miles on my treadmill. I showered in my postage stamp of a bathroom—in and out in five minutes before the hot water disappeared—and then I slipped into my favorite oversized, worn-out T-shirt and a pair of sweats that I stole from my ex-fiancé. Conrad would probably be appalled to see me in this outfit. The silk pajamas he bought me are by some Italian designer while this faded cotton shirt has a hole in the armpit. I can't help but snort a laugh at the contrasting mental images.

I drop my head back on the couch and cup my mug in my hands, listening to the traffic sounds filtering up from the street below my window and the music coming down from the floor of the apartment above me. Content for the first time in months, I sigh, welcoming the noise. You don't get noise like this from thirty stories up. It's the sounds of life, and there's nothing clinical about them.

I listen to the noise for a long time, my body relaxing with every passing car. Every siren. Every muffled laugh. When I finally fall asleep, I dream of a baby. A little boy with curly brown hair and hazel-green eyes. A baby I've only seen in photographs and short, thirty-second videos.

But I love him.

I love him so much it hurts.

A KNOCK on my door wakes me, and I shoot upright.

I blink rapidly in the dim light of my apartment. I must have fallen asleep on the couch. One glance at the clock on my stove tells me it's a little after 2 a.m., and my eyebrows furrow in confusion. Who would be knocking on my apartment door at two in the morning?

Another knock, this one louder, draws my attention back to the door. My heart speeds up, and fear prickles the back of my neck. This neighborhood is safe. I think. I guess I wouldn't know what goes down after midnight since I'm never here. Quickly, I dig around on the couch until I find my phone, but it's dead. I can't even call the cops. The thought heightens my anxiety. The one night I stay in my apartment in months and it's going to get me murdered.

When the person at the door knocks a third time, I shoot to my feet and rush into my bedroom to plug in my phone. I chew on my lip as I wait for it to power back on. I'll call the cops and ask for a drive-by or something. It's the longest fifteen seconds of my life. The moment my screen lights up, before I can even start to dial 9-1-1, the phone starts to chime with notifications. I have several missed texts and voicemails from—

"Claire, it's Conrad. Open the door."

The sigh of relief that leaves me escapes in a loud *woosh*. My body wants to collapse, but I manage to rush to the door and undo my four locks. When I swing the door open, Conrad doesn't wait to be invited in.

"What's wrong? I thought I wouldn't see you until Monday. Is everything okay?"

Conrad runs his hands through his hair, but he remains silent. He's more disheveled than I've ever seen him. No tie. No jacket. His shirt is rumpled, and the first few buttons are undone. His face, usually clean-shaven, is sporting a day's worth of stubble, and even in the dim light of the apartment, I can see the stress on his face.

"Conrad. What is it?"

When he finally turns to me, disapproval flashes over his face, no doubt at my pajamas, but it's gone in an instant, and his eyes go hard. His brow furrows, he sighs, and then he speaks.

"I have a job for you."

FIVE

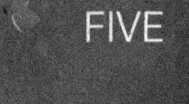

Jonah

I LIGHT my cigarette and take a long drag, deliberately ignoring the four pairs of eyes burning holes in my back.

My head is fucking pounding, and an intervention staged as a band meeting is the last thing I want to deal with right now. They should have stayed in Paris.

I close my eyes and tip my face to the ceiling. Christ, I really fucked it up this time.

When my cigarette is gone and no one has said a word, the silence becomes lethal, and I'm ready to lay my neck on the executioner's block just to put an end to it. Jeer. Pelt me with rotten vegetables. Celebrate as my skull falls into the dirt with an unceremonious thud. It would be better than the silence.

"Okay," I say with a tired exhale. "Can we just get this over with? I've had enough of the funeral atmosphere this weekend."

No one laughs at my joke. I guess that's the real test of the evening. When even the dark humor goes unappreciated.

I turn to face them and raise my eyebrows. "Get on with it."

"Get on with what, exactly, Jonah? I don't think you need me to tell you what a mess you've made. A Class E felony in New York State. Should I repeat for you what that means?"

I clamp my eyes shut so I don't roll them at Hammond's dry, patronizing tone. "No. That was covered, thanks."

Hammond *humphs*. "Then maybe you'd like me to *get on* with reminding you that we're supposed to be touring. Should I go over the schedule? Do you need me to tell you where we're all *supposed* to be right now?"

"No." I sigh. "I'm aware of that, too."

"Then what *exactly* should we *get on* with?"

"I don't know, *Wade*. You're the ones who decided to charter the jet and invade my hotel room at four in the morning. You tell me."

Hammond's jaw ticks and his nostrils flare as he tries not to lose his temper.

"Need I remind you where we picked you up from, Jonah? You're lucky we were already here. If we weren't, your ass would still be in a jail cell."

His voice quakes with repressed anger as he speaks. It's more emotion than we're used to seeing from him. Well, except Sav. She's been on the other end of some serious verbal ass-beatings from our manager. I don't know how I've managed to avoid one for this long.

I shake my head, but I don't have anything snarky to retort. I really don't need the reminder. It will be plastered all over the tabloids by sunrise, and he's right, anyway. I *am* lucky they were here. The fact that their first move after hearing about my mom was to cancel the shows and fly to New York...

It makes me feel even worse.

I finally let myself look at the other three people in the room. When I do, I immediately wish I hadn't. It's been a while since I've seen those expressions on their faces. Disappointment and anger laced heavily with concern. It bothers me more this time than it did last time.

Fuck.

I *really* fucked up.

I bring my fingers to my temples and rub, trying to lessen even a fraction of the tension in my head. I'm going to sleep for a week after this.

JONAH

"Look. I appreciate you p—"

A firm rap at the door cuts me off, and my eyebrows slant. I didn't make plans with anyone. I'm not expecting a visitor, but one look at the four other faces in the room tells me that they are.

"What the fuck did you guys do?" I say with a growl, and Sav scoffs, drawing my attention to her as Hammond moves to open the door.

"It wasn't us, dickhead, but it's the best option you've got right now, so I suggest you bite your fucking tongue. The angry, tortured musician act is overplayed and not doing you any favors at the moment."

Her words cut where she'd intended, and my defenses shoot back up.

"Oh, shut up, Savannah. I'm getting real tired of your high-and-mighty bullshit. You don't get to scold me."

I am grateful that they picked me up, but I don't need another fucking lecture right now. I'm a conflicted mess of emotions as it is, but Sav doesn't back down. She never does. She just smiles sweetly and bats her eyelashes.

"Stop acting like a petulant child and maybe I won't have to scold you."

I scowl and open my mouth to snap something back at her, but Hammond clears his throat, drawing my attention to him.

To him and the woman standing beside him.

My hackles rise. She doesn't look like another cop, but I can tell right away I'm not going to like why she's here. By showing up unannounced at my hotel room at four in the morning, she already has the upper hand, and I can't let her keep it. I'm outnumbered as it is.

Slowly, I drop my eyes down her body. I don't hide it. I check her out brazenly, but I keep my face blank. Making her uncomfortable is my goal. I linger on her breasts and subtle curves. I track her long legs from the hem of her pencil skirt to the heel on her understated designer pumps. When I leisurely arrive back at her face, I settle my attention on her lips before my gaze finally collides with hers.

She doesn't so much as flinch.

She narrows her eyes, lifts her chin slightly, and arches a delicate, perfectly-shaped eyebrow. Not intimidated. Not impressed. In fact, her perfect posture, fit figure, and disapproving expression piss me off and get my dick hard.

This woman is going to give me trouble.

"Well," I say smoothly, letting my voice maintain an edge of irritation. "Who do I have the pleasure of welcoming into my room this morning?"

The woman gives me a tight, forced smile before confirming my assumption.

"My name is Claire Davis." She drops her eyes down my body in an assessing manner before bringing them back to my face in a way that suggests she's found me wanting. It fuels my irritation, but when the next sentence leaves her mouth, I damn near crack a molar. "I'll be your PR manager for the foreseeable future."

When my eyes widen, hers flash with a challenge, and I grit my teeth. I was right. She's trouble. With a capital fucking T.

I turn my glare toward Savannah, then to Hammond. "Answers. Now."

Hammond sighs. "I might have been your first call from jail, but the cops called your father. Then he *also* called me."

I clamp my eyes shut. I should have known. The cops wouldn't have let me out without speaking to him first. It was his mausoleum I broke into, after all. But Conrad Henderson doesn't do things out of the kindness of his heart. If he's not pressing charges, there are definitely strings attached.

I take a deep breath, then open my eyes and look at Hammond. I intentionally ignore the woman in the corner. "And?"

"And, as you can imagine, he's not happy about the hoops he's currently jumping through to keep this out of the morning headlines—"

I scoff, cutting him off, but he raises an irritated eyebrow and continues.

"—and neither am I. You're still tied to the label until the European shows are finished, and if you remember correctly, there's a morality clause in our termination contract."

"Fuck." I drag a hand down my face, then reach into my pocket for another cigarette. "I forgot about the fucking morality clause."

Sav lets out a dry, tired laugh. "That actually makes me feel better."

I glance at her and raise my eyebrows in question. "You thought I would do this intentionally?" My exasperation increases when Sav gives me a shrug but says nothing. "I wouldn't, Savannah."

She looks away, dismissing me, and the fact that she doesn't believe me just proves the extent of the damage I've done. I light a new cigarette and take a long drag, closing my eyes from the disapproving faces and letting the toxins sit in my lungs before blowing it out slowly. This room is non-smoking. I've opened the balcony doors, but I'll still be paying a hefty bill to take care of cleaning and deodorizing after I check out.

Hammond speaks again.

"Headlines about you getting arrested for drunkenly breaking into your family mausoleum and desecrating the gravesite would put us in violation of the morality clause."

I nod and grit my teeth again, grinding them together and breathing through the guilt. I keep my eyes shut and focus just on the sound of his voice, the smoke in my lungs, and the feel of the nicotine coursing through my bloodstream. The help the liquor and the pills provided is disappearing by the minute.

No one is as disappointed by my actions as I am. Violating the morality clause would mean everything Hammond negotiated for leaving our label "amicably" after the tour would be void. The label would drop us, and we'd be forfeiting our cuts from the tour.

And while that sucks, it's not the worst part.

The worst part is that if we're dropped, we would be forced to abide by a non-compete. We couldn't put out another album as The Hometown Heartless for five more years. Not independently, and not with Rock Loveless Records, the label Sav is starting.

It would leash us creatively, and the despair that lashes in my chest warns that I wouldn't survive it. Heartless has been the only thing keeping me together. If I lose it because of my own fucked-up mistakes...

I'd have nothing left.

The thought is like a punch to the stomach, and I have to lean my body on the wall so I don't hunch over from the swirling anxiety. My life would be over, and not just metaphorically. What is there to live for if I can't write and perform music?

Nothing.

The reality makes me want to throw up.

I work to control my breathing as Hammond's voice waves about in the air around me, mixing with the sounds of my panicked heartbeat.

"Your father and I have *almost* successfully killed the story, but there are still likely to be mentions about it in the tabloids, and the label will probably find out eventually. Luckily, as of right now, they're just as eager to finish this tour as you are. They make more money that way. So your father and I have worked out a—"

"What's in it for him? What's my father getting out of this?"

"Having a son who isn't a felon isn't incentive enough?"

It's not Hammond who answers. It's the woman, and despite her obvious attempt to sound neutral, I hear the tension in her tone. Her voice is like warm honey over jagged glass. Sweet masking sharp. Husky, yet deceptively smooth and soothing. It calms my nerves before setting my teeth on edge.

Finally, I open my eyes and turn them toward her. Her face is blank as she stares back at me. Her head is cocked slightly to the side, and her eyebrow is arched as if her question wasn't rhetorical. She's waiting for me to answer, and when she blinks once, I do.

"No. It's not."

She purses her plump lips, and her forehead creases as she carefully considers her next words. When she speaks, it's slowly, and with a clarity that commands all my attention. Everything else in the room fades into silence until it's just her. The woman with the deceivingly honeyed voice and the cherubic blue eyes.

"Your reputation and well-being are important to Mr. Henderson, Mr. Hendrix. He doesn't want you or your career to suffer. This is why he sent me."

I walk toward her, closing the distance between us in only a few strides, until I'm only three feet in front of her. I tower over her, but she doesn't back down. She doesn't seem intimidated in the slightest.

"Sent you to do what?"

"To repair the damage to your public image and assist you in"—she pauses, and I watch her once again take measure of the weight of her words before continuing—"making less destructive choices in your daily routines."

My nostrils flare as I blink through the haze of fury. I can tell she's doing her best to avoid coming off as patronizing, but she fails. There's no

delicate way to tell someone they've fucked up so badly they've been assigned a babysitter. She calls herself a PR manager, but I see through the posturing. She's here because my father doesn't trust me to *behave* on my own. I've threatened the one thing he cares about—his image.

All my other fuckups pale in comparison to this one because this one connects me to him.

Shame burns my throat and fans the flames of my anger. Anger toward myself. Anger toward my father. Anger toward this woman for being his paid minion. I stare down at her. Her hair and makeup are flawless, despite it being almost four in the morning. Her designer clothes are without creases or wrinkles, and the expression on her pretty face is carefully constructed. It's all an artfully crafted façade for a single purpose. To deceive.

She's everything I hate about my father's world. Manufactured sincerity. Beautiful and calculating. Fake in every way.

I ball my hands into fists and squeeze tightly until my fingers ache from the pressure of my thick metal rings. A small voice in the back of my head tells me that this woman is not the enemy, that she doesn't deserve my wrath, but the chaotic vortex of my own emotions silences it.

She's here. *He's* not.

And focusing on her will hurt less than acknowledging the truth.

I curl my lip into a sneer. "My father sent you to babysit me."

"Those are your words. Not mine. I'm here to do a job."

I narrow my eyes. The surety in her voice pisses me off further. I don't like being a project. I don't like the idea of being manipulated into someone else for my father's approval. In this moment, I think I'd rather take the felony.

Bad press has followed Heartless around since the beginning, and while Sav has been able to somewhat repair her image, I've barely begun. Even attempting sobriety has done nothing to quell the rumors and gossip columns. As far as the public knows, I'm the volatile guitarist who will smoke, swallow, snort, or screw just about anything without pretense.

And honestly? They're not exactly wrong.

"Do you even know what you're getting yourself into?" I ask, my voice low and taunting. "You think being my shadow will come without trouble? It won't. This *job* won't be easy."

She lifts her chin defiantly. "I take my work very seriously. I am prepared."

"So staging a few photoshoots is supposed to reform the bad boy rock star in the public eye? Keeping me on a leash between shows will appease my father? You're working against a decade's worth of press. Shining me up and putting a bow on me isn't going to be enough. Do you understand that, *Ms.* Davis?"

She gives me a single nod, her prim and proper demeanor never wavering. "I'm aware."

"You're *aware*?"

"Yes. I am *quite* aware of the task before me. I have done my research, and I assure you I have a plan that's a bit more sophisticated than *photoshoots* and *leashes*."

I tilt my head to the side and study her. Her eyebrow is twitching slightly. It's the only tell that she doesn't like me questioning her ability to do her job. It makes me want to poke her again. It makes me want to see her composure break.

Then she surprises me by stepping closer, leaving only inches between us. She smells like lavender and sugar, and it has a soothing effect that throws me off-balance. I have the strongest urge to bury my face in her neck and breathe in, but I resist. Instead, I don't blink as she holds my eyes with her piercing blue gaze.

"Any moment you're not playing a concert will be managed by me. From the minute you wake up, to the minute you go to sleep, you will be adhering to *my* calendar. *My* plan. Call it babysitting. Call it PR management. Call it whatever you want. Either way, I can guarantee that if you cooperate, we will successfully reverse the public's opinion of you."

I scoff just to piss her off, but she arches an eyebrow.

"And here's something *you* should understand, *Mr.* Hendrix. Managing public relations is a lot like chess, and I am *very* good at chess."

My eyes flare at her words, and her lips twitch, almost as if she's fighting a smirk.

Chess.

JONAH

Managing public relations is a lot like chess.

The analogy isn't lost on me. I can read behind the lines. If this is chess, then I'm about to be her pawn. The anger that's been building in my stomach isn't enough to smother the spark of interest that she's ignited, and I think she knows it.

I bounce my eyes between hers. They really are a remarkable blue. Even in this poorly lit hotel room, I can tell. Her eyelashes, thick and long, brush against her eyelids as she looks up at me, staring me down. Refusing to concede.

Chess.

"How long?" I ask, and the question comes out quieter than I intended. An intimate whisper despite the four other people in the room. She lifts her shoulder in a small shrug before responding in kind.

"As long as it takes."

"And what's in it for you?"

Finally, she lets that smirk slip free, pink lips curving upward in a way that promises trouble. The most tempting kind.

"Let's just say I find fulfillment in a match well-played."

In this moment, I don't doubt her confidence. I believe her when she says she's good at her job. In fact, if there is anyone capable of cleaning up my abysmal image, I'd put money on her. I have a feeling I'm not going to like how she does it, but fuck me, it piques my interest anyway.

I nod once, then take a step away from her, clearing the air of lavender and sugar.

"Okay, Claire Davis. Let's see what you can do."

SIX

Claire

MY THOUGHTS ARE RUNNING rampant as I follow the rest of the band onto their private plane.

I had less than an hour to learn everything I could about Conrad's son before I was tossed to the wolves.

Or *wolf*, rather.

What I found spiked my anxiety higher than anything else since working at Innovation Media. Thank God for Xanax.

Jonah Hendrix is a PR disaster. Drinking. Drugs. Fighting. Random and indiscreet sexual relations. The stories are endless, and while I don't usually put much merit on gossip columns, the photo evidence was enough to make me blush. There was even a grainy photo of what I'm pretty sure was half of his ass while he screwed someone in a dark alleyway.

Curiously, the scandals have become less frequent over the last year or so. There was still the occasional "exclusive story" about sexual encounters from anonymous sources, or photos of Jonah getting wasted at clubs, but it hasn't been a daily occurrence for a while. It almost makes what he did last night—God, how was it only last night?—seem worse.

Something tells me he was trying to clean up his act on his own, but his mother's death derailed his progress. I can only imagine the pain he's in, and I'm probably just adding to it by being here.

The look on his face when I introduced myself...

Rage.

Rage and *shame*.

For a moment, I hurt for him. I empathized. I wanted to apologize and reassure him that it will be okay.

But then he became a condescending asshole, and all my concerns went up in smoke.

I can't deny that he's intriguing. I'm drawn to him in the way I would be drawn to the storyline in a mystery or thriller book. But if the tabloids hadn't confirmed it, the exchange in his hotel room did: Jonah Hendrix is going to be a pain in my ass, and I am in way over my head.

I don't manage public relations for celebrities, especially not defiant, uncooperative, infuriating rock stars like this one. I do digital marketing and rebranding for companies who've sought out my help. That's where my experience lies. That's what I'm good at, and the two specialties couldn't be more different.

Once on the plane, I take an empty seat with every intention of stewing in silence when the lead singer sits across from me with a welcoming smile.

"Hey. In all the commotion, we didn't get a chance to introduce ourselves properly. This is Mabel, and I'm Savannah. You can call me Sav."

Sav sticks her hand out just as Mabel plops down into the seat next to her. I give Mabel a nod, then take Sav's hand in a light shake.

"Hi. I'm Claire. You can call me Claire."

Sav laughs. It's husky and contagious, coaxing a laugh of my own to the surface. Then she leans closer and lowers her voice, flicking her eyes over my shoulder quickly before returning her attention to me. I mirror her posture, readying for a private conversation. Or as private as you can get on a sixteen-passenger jet.

"We're really grateful you're doing this. I know it was last minute and probably overwhelming, but if you need anything, you just ask."

Mabel nods in agreement. "Anything you need, we got you. Come to any of us. Me, Sav, Ham, or Torren. Hell, even Levi or Callie will be able to help."

"Levi and Callie?" Torren and Hammond, I know. Levi and Callie are names I don't recognize.

"Levi's my boyfriend," Sav clarifies, "and Callie is Torren's girlfriend. We left them in Paris, but they'll be meeting us in Stockholm."

"They're on tour with us, so you'll get to know them pretty well. No worries. They're great. We don't hang out with dicks." Mabel smirks at Sav. "Well, except Jonah."

Sav laughs again and gives me a shrug. "Yeah. Sorry about that."

"It's okay," I say with a sigh. "It's obvious that he's not happy with my being here, and I can understand that. But I meant it when I said I'm prepared. There's nothing he can throw at me that I can't handle."

My chest tightens when Sav's brow furrows, and she exchanges a cryptic glance with Mabel. "Just remember that you can come to us about anything. He didn't lie. It's not going to be easy."

"*Jonah* isn't easy," Mable interjects. "But know that you're appreciated and supported, and...well, as cliché as it sounds, there's a really good guy under all the..."

She trails off, so I finish for her. "Anger?"

Sav and Mabel both nod.

"Right. Well, thanks for the support and appreciation. I'll definitely come to you if I need anything."

Sav gives me a soft smile, then leans back in her seat. I take it as my cue that the conversation is over, rest my head on the seatback and close my eyes.

Jonah isn't easy, Mabel had said.

I'd gathered as much since learning that he was Conrad's son, but hearing it from a bandmate just adds to my fraying nerves.

I wanted to turn this job assignment down, but I couldn't do that to Conrad. He was desperate, and the promise of a promotion was too tempting. And I'll admit, I find challenge enticing, and Jonah Hendrix will definitely be a challenge.

If I can succeed here, it will do wonders for my career.

My career, *and* my relationship.

The last one has my heart quickening. The idea of proving myself to Conrad, of earning his affection, is intoxicating. Succeeding in this job will prove to everyone that I'm capable of climbing the ranks at Innovation Media on my own, and then Conrad and I won't have to keep our relationship hidden. Helping his son will show Conrad that I'm worthy of the title of girlfriend. I'm worthy of a place in the Henderson family.

I ignore the fact that Conrad doesn't want his son to know about us. He said Jonah can't learn of our relationship for *any* reason. I also ignore my own doubts about our relationship.

I push it away and tell myself that it's necessary. I'll sort it all out later. Right now, I have a job to do. I just have to work hard, and it will all pay off.

As the plane takes off, I mentally run through my to-do list. I sent several emails on the way to Jonah's hotel room this morning. I contacted the firm's lawyers, as well as non-profit organizations in every city along the tour schedule. When the plane levels out, I take out my laptop and get back to work crafting a volunteer schedule worthy of Saint Teresa.

If Jonah cooperates, I truly believe we can reverse the public's opinion of him.

If.

I'm not naïve. I know this man is a wild card. I know this won't be easy. He told me as much, and Sav and Mabel confirmed it. But I'm not backing down, despite my nerves.

I won't let him intimidate me, no matter how disarming I find him.

THE HOTEL in Stockholm is breathtaking.

It's a waterfront property with views of the Royal Palace and Gamla stan. The lobby itself is gorgeous, but the hotel also houses multiple five-star restaurants and a luxurious Nordic spa and fitness center. I've never stayed somewhere so elegant, and I get to be here for the next four days.

I must look like a starstruck child with how wide-eyed and impressed I am as we're escorted to our rooms. It's polar opposite from the rest of The

Hometown Heartless. The band members and their entourage are unfazed. They probably stay in hotels like this all the time, and I can't help but smile to myself because that means for the foreseeable future, I will be, too.

I follow everyone to the elevator, keeping a close eye on Jonah's back, and wait while Hammond punches in a code. Then we glide quickly to the top floor. We all filter into the hallway, then Hammond starts handing out key cards and rattling off room numbers. Sav, Mabel, and Torren all have their own rooms, but when he gets to Jonah and me, the room number is the same. I already knew about this, but Jonah didn't, and the way his bandmates have all halted in the hallway, I can tell they've been anticipating his outburst.

"Are you fucking kidding me? I'm sharing a room with her?" Jonah glares at Hammond while ignoring me. "She doesn't have to be up my ass, Ham. I'm capable of sleeping without her acting as a watchdog."

"*She* is right here," I say with a sigh, and he flicks his attention to me.

"*You* don't have to be up my ass," he repeats, then gives me a sardonic grin. "I'm capable of sleeping without *you* acting as a watchdog."

I roll my eyes. "I told you. Every moment you're not on that stage, you're with me."

His jaw pops as he sneers at me, and then he turns his wrath back on Hammond. I fold my arms and watch with everyone else as Jonah squares off against him. When Jonah's biceps flex, I worry that he'll throw a punch, so I drop my eyes to his fists and find his index finger picking at his thumb. A nervous tic? I store it away in my head, then look back at their faces. Hammond, to his credit, stays relaxed and unbothered. I can't tell if he loves his job or loathes it, but he has the patience of a saint.

"You said I'd have my own room," Jonah grits out.

"That was before you flew to New York, got drunk, wrecked a rental car, and committed a Class E felony."

"This is bullshit."

"I agree. I told you in Paris. You're the priority here, and since I can't trust you to take care of yourself, it's this or we call off the tour and you check yourself back into rehab."

"We're not calling off the tour."

Hammond nods, then his voice drops lower. It sounds concerned, and I'm taken aback by it. He cares, really cares, about Jonah.

"I know that's not what you want, and I'm inclined to believe it would do more harm than good right now."

I furrow my brow at the cryptic statement. More harm than good? Does he mean because of finances? Because of the label? When I glance at Jonah, he's lost some of his ire, and that confuses me further.

"Fine."

Jonah punctuates his concession by holding out his hand and letting Hammond put the key card in his palm. Hammond does, and then he returns to business.

"There are no two-bedroom suites here, but I've called ahead and had the hotel management erect a partition in the middle of the bedroom. The beds are separated, but you'll have to share the bathroom."

I glance at Jonah, expecting another outburst, but he gives a curt nod and turns silently toward the door.

"Thanks, Mr. Hammond," I say as I take my key card from him.

"You can call me Hammond, Ms. Davis."

I smile. "You can call me Claire."

With the show seemingly over, everyone starts to head to their rooms. I turn to Jonah, but a squeal of laughter has us both looking back down the hall, where we find Torren embraced by a woman with short red hair. It must be Callie, his girlfriend. My guess is confirmed when they start making out in the hallway, then she tugs him into the room and shuts the door. The whole scene has me wanting to laugh, but when I look back at Jonah, the humor dissipates.

He's glaring at the spot where Torren and Callie just stood, but it's not just anger I think I see pass over his face. It's longing, too. Jealousy. Just for a second, and then it's gone, wiped clean of everything except irritation.

I narrow my eyes at his back while he opens the door to our room and steps inside.

Was I mistaken? Did I imagine the emotions I just saw in Jonah's expression?

I don't have time to ruminate on it any longer because my mind goes blank the moment we step into the large, lavish suite. My jaw drops and all I feel is awe. It's beautiful. Larger than my apartment in Inwood. More stylishly decorated than anything I've ever seen before.

"Wow," I say on an exhale.

Jonah snorts but says nothing as he stomps through the suite and pushes open the door to the bedroom. I follow him into it, and sure enough, there's a wall of privacy glass set up between two fluffy, full beds. I don't ask his preference as I throw my purse onto the bed closest to the door, claiming it as my own.

"Is that to make sure I don't sneak out?"

I turn to Jonah, keeping my face blank as I shrug. "Do I need to be worried about you sneaking out? Are you sixteen now?"

His eyes narrow. "I didn't need a babysitter when I was sixteen."

"Hm. Regression, then." I bat my eyelashes, professionalism waning rapidly with my increasing exhaustion. "I hear that's normal as you age."

I know Jonah's only two years older than me. I learned that fact during my internet search, and while I always knew Conrad had children, it was still a shock to learn his son was my age.

Jonah doesn't acknowledge my comment. Instead, he disappears behind the opaque glass wall, and I watch as his outline throws itself on the bed. I wonder if he can see my outline as clearly as I see his. Honestly, for privacy glass, it doesn't feel very private, but I'm too tired to care. It takes all my strength not to fall asleep before the bellhops deliver our suitcases.

"I'm taking a shower, and then I'm going to sleep," I announce to the room.

Jonah *humphs*. All I can hear is indistinguishable chatter from whatever he's watching on his phone. I dig through my carry-on for my toiletry bag and a pair of my most modest pajamas. Then I head to the bathroom, take a Xanax, and shower for a long time. I imagine the hot water washing the stress from my muscles. Stress that has increased over the last twenty-four hours.

God, it feels like it's been months. A year. Definitely not a single day.

I want to laugh at how drastically my life has changed since yesterday. Playing the shadow and conscience of an unruly rock star is the last place

I'd ever expected to be. It wasn't even in the realm of possibility; yet, here I am. I drop my head back and let the shower spray on my face, standing there until I start to feel a little dizzy, and then I turn the water off and step out onto the heated bathroom tiles.

I avoid the mirror as I dry and get dressed. My head is in no place to see myself right now, but I do glance around for a scale as I brush my teeth. There isn't one, but I didn't think there would be. I'll check out the fitness center in the morning.

When I walk back into the bedroom, I find Jonah leaning on the wall wearing only a pair of boxer briefs.

"Took you long enough." He grunts at me, then shoves past and slams the door.

"What a child," I mumble to myself as I set up my phone charger and crawl into bed. "An absolute baby of a man."

Then I sigh because this is the most comfortable mattress I've ever lain on. I sprawl my hands and feet out like a starfish and snuggle my head into the soft down pillow. Thank God. I'm going to need beds like this if I have to deal with that man-baby every day.

My lips curl into a tiny smile, and they stay like that until the bathroom door opens. I don't acknowledge Jonah as he crosses the floor. I don't even open my eyes. I just listen as his feet pad on the soft carpet, his breathing steady and even. The sound of the duvet being tugged down accompanies the sound of his bed shifting under his weight. Then, just as I hear his head hit the pillow, his deep voice rumbles in the darkness.

"If you get lonely tonight, you're welcome to come over here. I'm told sharing a bed with me is an exhilarating experience."

His tone is suggestive, approaching seductive, and I frown when goosebumps erupt over my skin in response. I force out a single, tired laugh.

"There isn't a scenario in the world where I'd be desperate enough to climb into bed with you. Good night."

I turn my back to the partition, and his low chuckle sounds from the other side. The smile returns to my lips before I can stop it, but I don't force it away. I let it stay there, and I drift off into a dreamless sleep.

SEVEN

Jonah

NO ONE PERSON should be this loud in the morning.

Claire's alarm sounded at five thirty.

Five fucking thirty.

Then, it was followed up with *noise*. So much noise. Doors slamming. Suitcases banging. Terrible music at max volume. She's got to be doing it on purpose.

I groan and bury my face in my pillow, but I swear her music gets louder. Jesus Christ, I can't deal with this for the whole tour. I'll murder her.

"Can you *please* shut up? Some of us need to sleep off the jet lag."

"Oh, good. You're awake."

I turn my head toward the voice and find her standing next to my bed in a pair of bike shorts and a sports bra. The sports bra perks me up, but then she pulls the pillow out from under my head and tosses it on the floor. Fuck her great tits. She's annoying as hell.

"Get up. We've got work to do."

"Go. Away. Aren't you tired?"

"Jet lag is a state of mind." Her voice grows distant as she walks away.

"And anyway, shouldn't you be used to it by now? You're always jetting about the globe."

I pull the duvet over my head and try to ignore her, but she returns with the scent of coffee accompanying her. I hear her set the coffee mug on the counter, and it softens my mood a little. She brought me coffee. That's kind.

Then she tugs the duvet off my head, and I hate her again.

"You're annoying. Leave me alone."

"And you're acting like a surly, immature teenager." She huffs out a laugh. "I've got plenty of experience with *boys* like you. You have no idea how annoying I can get."

I lift my head and peek one eye open. "You have a kid?"

She rolls her pretty blue eyes. "I have an older brother, but my mother worked, and my father was a piece of shit, so my brother was my responsibility." She smirks. "Now get up before I dump ice water on your head."

I arch a brow. "You wouldn't."

"I've already got a pitcher ready." Her smirk transforms into an impish grin. "Don't underestimate me."

I met her less than forty-eight hours ago, and already I know not to underestimate her. I don't doubt she'd dump ice water on me, and she'd probably get a lot of joy out of doing it. I sigh and sit up.

"Are you going to give me this much trouble the whole tour?"

Claire shrugs. "Maybe. Depends on how you behave."

"Fine."

I throw off the duvet and stand, revealing my naked body to her. She doesn't even try to peek. Her eyes stay on my face, and she arches an unimpressed brow. Honestly, it's a hit to my ego.

"Drink your coffee. Get dressed. We have an appointment at the fitness center in thirty."

She turns swiftly and disappears behind the glass wall. I take a drink from my mug and watch her silhouette as she moves around on her side of the room. She's got a nice figure. Smaller than I usually go for, but her tits are a good handful, and she has this slender neck that I could easily wrap my hand around.

When my dick starts to harden, I break my stare and walk to my suitcase. No way she'd let me choke her, and I don't fuck people I have to see every day. I made that mistake once. I won't make it again.

"We getting a couple's massage?" I ask as I pull on a pair of jeans.

"You're meeting with a trainer."

I freeze. "Excuse me?"

"A trainer. You're meeting with one." She walks back around the partition and glances at my jeans. "Might want to wear something less restricting. Jeans aren't good for working out."

"Why the fuck am I meeting with a trainer, Davis?"

"You need a rage outlet that isn't smashing cars into fences or shattering stained-glass windows." She props her hand on her hip and grins again. This one is taunting. She's definitely getting joy out of irritating me. "And working out releases endorphins. You need more of those too."

I unbutton my jeans and shove them down my thighs, once again baring myself to her. Once again, she's completely uninterested.

"You don't know what I need."

She laughs and walks away. "I think I might know better than you do. Hurry. I don't want to be late."

I steal glances at Claire as we walk to the fitness center. Her face is glued to her phone, so I take advantage. She's got a head full of curls pulled back in a ponytail, but when I met her in my hotel room, her hair was stick straight. My attention zeroes in on the little curls at the nape of her slender neck. I bet they're soft. I bet they'd tickle my fingers if my hand was wrapped—

"Stop staring at me. You're being a creep."

"Your hair is curly."

"Observant when you're sober, huh?"

"It was straight in New York."

She sighs and looks up from her phone. "I'd straightened it. I'll straighten it again after my workout."

"Why?"

"Because I like it better straight."

I nod, but I don't say anything else. I also don't stop staring at her. I can be annoying, too, and I smirk when I see goosebumps appear on her neck.

FOR WRATH AND REDEMPTION

She goes back to her phone and continues to ignore me until we're walking into the fitness center.

Claire introduces me to my trainer. His name is Thor, and it fits him perfectly. I'm tall, and he still towers over me. He could probably bench me. He reminds me of Red, Sav's security guard.

As Thor takes me through the gym, I keep one eye on Claire. She's on a treadmill, and she's not jogging. She's sprinting. Sweat is dripping down her body. The exposed skin on her chest and stomach is glistening with it. When I get a mental image of licking it off her, I have to look away.

Fuck, I need to get laid.

I'm sure the last thing Thor wants is me sporting a hard dick during my training session. I try to think of things less sexy than a sweaty Claire Davis with tiny curls at the nape of her neck, but after ten minutes, it doesn't matter anymore.

Because Thor tries to kill me.

Squats. Bench press. Burpees.

Fuck burpees, man. That shit is the worst. Every one of my appendages feels like jelly. The exhaustion permeates all my muscles, and after a while, I can't even focus on my rage because I'm too busy reminding myself to breathe.

"How much longer?" Panting, I drop to the floor after my last burpee. "I'm fucking dying."

Thor chuckles. "Almost finished. Just stretching left."

His accent is thick, but I'm pretty sure I hear a hint of mocking in his tone. Probably. Hell, I'd mock me.

"How's he doing?" The toes of Claire's pink and white tennis shoes step in my line of sight, and I turn my head to look up at her. She's mocking me, too. "Damn, Hendrix. You look wrecked."

"Thor tried to kill me."

She shakes her head and nudges my body with the toe of her shoe. "Suck it up. We've got a full day before you have to be at the stadium."

I groan and sit up, dropping my head between my knees. She's a sadist.

Awesome.

. . .

JONAH

"HERE'S what I've got planned for Sweden. We'll go over Lisbon when we get there."

Claire drops a tablet on the couch beside me. I collapsed here the moment we walked into the room, and she's wasting no time.

"Look it over while I shower."

When she disappears into the bathroom, I shove the tablet away from me. It falls onto the ground, and I make no move to pick it up. The shower kicks on a minute later, and I close my eyes. The sound is soothing, and the image of her naked under the water...

Fuck.

I reach down and squeeze my dick through my shorts. I feel like I've been half hard since yesterday. That, paired with the ass-kicking Thor gave me, is making my head ache.

I need a joint or a drink. I need something harder. I need to get laid.

I clamp my eyes shut against the craving and tighten my fingers around my dick. Then I stroke. The shower is still on, so I shove my hand into my shorts.

Images of Claire in the shower, soaped up and washing herself, flash through my head. I imagine myself in there with her. I've got her pinned to the wall, both of us panting and surrounded by steam. I squeeze my dick and pretend it's her neck. I imagine her moaning, mouth open and pupils wide. It's so real, I can almost hear it. I can almost feel the vibrations from her throat on my palm. I stroke myself faster. Imagine sliding between her wet thighs. Pushing the head of my cock through—

"What the actual fuck are you doing?"

My body tenses in surprise, my muscles already aching from Thor's torture workout, and then I relax. I turn my head toward Claire. She's shocked and staring at my crotch. Now I'm mad I hadn't taken my dick out of my shorts. I arch a brow.

"It's not obvious? I'm trying to jerk off."

I start to stroke myself again, running my eyes over her. Her hair is in a towel, and she's clothed in another pencil skirt and button-down blouse ensemble. I never thought business attire would do it for me, but surprisingly, it does.

"Actually, Davis, stay right there..."

Her brows slant, and she glowers. "I'll be ready in fifteen. I'm sure it won't take that long to fuck your hand." She smiles. "Carry on."

When she closes the bathroom door, my erection starts to disappear, and I sigh. I'm not horny anymore. Being dismissed with my hard dick in my fist apparently fucks with my confidence.

Pissed, I take my hand out of my shorts and wait, watching the clock like a good boy. I sit idly on the couch until the blow-dryer cuts off exactly fifteen minutes later. Then I head into the bedroom to grab some clothes. I have every intention of kicking Claire out of the bathroom so I can shower, but when I approach the door, I find it cracked, and her whispered voice is filtering through the opening.

I can only make out a few words, but her tone is sweet. Sweeter than she's used with me. It's not how you'd speak with a family member or friend. It's how you'd speak to a lover. When she says *I miss you*, I frown. Then she giggles, and the surge of jealousy I feel surprises me. The giggle is melodic, tinkling like little bells, and I want to punch the person who drew it out of her.

Instead of knocking, I shove the door open and lean on the frame. She jumps, whipping her head in my direction with a scowl.

"I'm sorry. I have to go. I'll call you soon."

She's talking into the phone, but she's glaring at me. Her lover says something, a deep hum coming from the other end of the phone, and she smiles as she says goodbye. A cute smile. An attractive smile. Not at all like the snarky smiles she's been giving me.

She puts the phone on the counter and attacks.

"Ever heard of knocking?" She crosses her arms over her chest and narrows her eyes. "You don't just barge into the bathroom on someone."

"Sorry," I say flatly. I'm not sorry. "Boyfriend?"

"None of your business."

I drop my attention to her left hand. "No wedding band. No engagement ring. The voice sounded pretty deep, so I'm guessing male." I look back at her face. "You don't giggle like that for a grandfather or a sibling."

Her eyes flare, some flash of concern or worry, but then she schools her expression. Nothing but irritation once more.

JONAH

"It was a private conversation," she clips, shutting down further questioning, then she changes the subject. "I assume you want to shower?"

I don't answer right away. Her continued dismissals piss me off.

I stare at her, absorbing every detail. She's got a full face of makeup on now. The kind women do when they want to look like they're not wearing any makeup at all. It makes her cheekbones look sharper, her lips plumper, and her eyes bluer. And her hair is straight again, the little curls at the nape of her neck hidden from view. I don't like that I can't see those curls.

I bring my eyes back to hers and try to read her. I attempt to gather any sort of intel I can use, but just like in my hotel room, she gives nothing away. It's annoying, just like her.

I decide to give up for now. She'll let her guard down eventually.

I open my mouth to tell her that I do want to shower, but there's a knock on the door of the suite. I turn without saying another word to Claire and head to the door. When I open it, I find Sav waiting in the hallway.

"Hey. Can I come in?"

I stand aside and sweep my arm into the suite. She'd have come in, anyway. The fact that she asked for permission at all has my nerves sparking.

"What's up?" I ask, folding my arms over my chest as she takes a seat on the couch.

Instead of answering me, she turns toward the bathroom where Claire is watching from the doorway. Sav waves and gives her a smile.

"Hey, Claire. Is it cool if I talk to Jo alone for a bit?"

"Of course. I need to speak with Mr. Hammond anyway."

"Thanks," Sav says, and then we both wait in silence while Claire slips on some heels and leaves the suite.

Once she's gone and the door is shut, I face Sav.

"What do you want?" My defenses are up, and I'm prepping for a fight. The last time Sav asked to speak to me alone was when she'd staged the intervention that got my ass sent to rehab. "Spit it out so I can refuse."

Her brow furrows with concern. "I wanted to say I'm sorry."

Her tone is much softer than I'm used to. It's the opposite of the anger

I got from her in New York. I cock my head slightly, assessing her, and she laughs.

"It's not a trick, Jo. I'm sorry for how I spoke to you in New York. I was tired and worried, and when you seemed apathetic, I got pissed. I'm sorry."

I narrow my eyes. This is suspicious. "Sav, you'd just bailed me out of jail. I'd committed a felony. Anger is a reasonable reaction."

She shrugs. "Your mom just died, Jo. You didn't need anger. You needed support and empathy, and instead, I was a bitch."

I arch a brow. "When aren't you a bitch?"

Sav huffs out a laugh and rolls her eyes. "Whatever. I'm here to say I'm sorry. And...I'm here to say that if you don't want Claire here, we can send her packing."

I almost jump at the opportunity to get rid of the new ever-present thorn in my side, but I bite my tongue. This would be too easy, and it wouldn't take care of the other problems.

The label. My father. My *felony*.

"What's the catch?" I ask slowly, and Sav shrugs.

"No catch. What's the point of going along with it if it's just a smoke and mirrors act? It's a waste of time if it's not actually going to help. If you think rehab—"

"Rehab?" I bark out a humorless laugh. "Rehab will put us in violation of the morality clause, Savannah."

She shrugs again. "We all agree that—"

"I don't care what you and everyone else have agreed. *I* don't agree."

I drag my hands through my hair and start to pace, fury thrumming through my veins. Building in my head until the pressure aches. This isn't fucking happening.

"That's real great that you, Torren, and Mabel have discussed this without me," I spit sarcastically. "Awesome that being dropped from the label and unable to make music together for five fucking years is something you can live with, but *I* can't." I stop pacing and loom over her, glaring into her gray eyes as she watches me cautiously. "I can't live with that outcome, Savannah. I won't."

Her brows slant, and she takes a deep, steady breath before speaking.

JONAH

Her voice, calm as ever, grates on my nerves. "You're saying you want to keep Claire Davis, then?"

I close my eyes and grit my teeth.

"No. I don't want to keep her, but like you said, she's the best option we've got right now."

Sav's quiet for a long time. All I can hear are her even, measured breaths. She's silent for so long that, without realizing it, my inhales and exhales start to mimic hers. When my body has relaxed a bit, she speaks again.

"Do you really think it will help, Jonah? We just want you to be okay. Are you going to be okay?"

Suddenly, I'm grateful for the pause she enforced. I'm not stupid. I know it was an intentional tactic to calm me down. She probably thought it would make the conversation more productive. Make me see reason.

She was wrong.

All it did was put me back in control. It made it easier for me to mislead, and just like I've been doing for years, I lie to her.

"My mom's death tripped me up, but I'm okay, Sav. I'm okay. Promise."

She nods once and forces a smile. "Okay."

She doesn't believe me, not quite, but she wants to. Sav wants to see the best in everyone. She thinks that since she clawed her way back from rock bottom, I'm capable of it, too.

That's her weakness, and I'm a master at exploiting it.

Smoke and mirrors is what Sav called this arrangement with my new babysitter. An act of deception. If I can keep the upper hand over Claire Davis, I can ride this out. I can play this game. As long as I can control little Ms. Trouble, it will all be fine.

EIGHT

Claire

I SPEND the last half of the Stockholm concert sequestered in the dressing room with my laptop.

I was told I could watch the show from a VIP tent with everyone else, but I decided against it. I did some Jonah-related work at the start of the show, but now I've got to catch up on the MixMosaic rebrand. Conrad did say I didn't have to work on the campaign now that I've been assigned to his son, but I haven't been removed from the shared drive. There's no harm in helping. I refuse to let Innovation Media lose this account because Brandt Macy lacks creativity.

I'm eyebrow deep in design plans when the dressing room door opens, and the redheaded woman from the hallway last night comes walking in.

"Oh," I glance at the clock on my computer. "Is the show over?"

"Almost. They've still got encores. I just like to beat the mass exodus." She smiles and takes a seat in a chair across from me. "I'm Callie. You're Claire, right?"

"Yeah, Claire Davis." I return her smile and close my laptop lid. "You're Torren's girlfriend?"

She nods and a soft pink blush tints her pale cheeks, the color drawing my attention to a scar on the left side of her face. It's nearly three inches long, stretching diagonally from just under her eye to the corner of her mouth. I bring my eyes back to hers quickly, careful not to stare, but her tight smile tells me she caught me.

"Sorry," I say with a wince.

"It's okay. It's kind of hard to miss." Callie gives me a one-shouldered shrug. "I was in a pretty bad car accident. Got these, too."

She holds her left arm out between us, pointing to several more scars on her forearm, wrist, and hand. Then she reaches up and parts her short red hair, revealing another scar.

"Damn." The word slips out in a whisper. I immediately feel guilty, but Callie grins.

"Yeah. Damn. Got another on my stomach."

She pats her abdomen, and I shake my head. I'm at a loss for words. From the looks of it, she's lucky to be alive. I'm grappling with that realization, understanding just how bad the accident must have been, when I remember a headline from a while back.

"Was this in LA?"

She laughs awkwardly. "That's the one."

I have to bite my tongue on the impulse to say *damn* again. That accident made national news, but it was across the country, and I hadn't paid much attention to it. I do remember that there were several fatalities, though. She truly is lucky to be alive.

I tilt my head slightly and hold her eye contact. Her eyes are light green. My old best friend has hazel eyes with swirls of green the same color as Callie's. It makes my stomach twist and my heart ache.

"I'm glad you survived, Callie," I say honestly, and she smiles.

"Thanks, Claire. Me too."

The door to the dressing room opens, interrupting us, and a sweaty, shirtless Torren walks in. Callie jumps up from her seat and is immediately wrapped up in his tattooed arms. When he kisses her, I look away.

I glance toward the door and expect to see Jonah, but he's not there. I wait a while longer for it to swing open and reveal him, but after a few minutes, I start to worry. I turn to Torren and Callie and clear my throat.

"Where is Jonah?"

They break apart and look at me. Callie is blushing again, but Torren is completely unbothered.

"He probably went to smoke."

I sigh. "Where would that be?"

"End of the hallway, there's a door that leads outside. He's probably there."

"Thanks." I look at Callie and give her a small nod. "See you later."

Once in the hallway, I follow the EXIT signs to a large set of double doors. I push them open, letting in the night air, and step outside.

No cigarette smoke. No Jonah Hendrix.

"Goddamn it."

I groan and take out my phone, dial his number and wait while it rings and rings and rings. A voicemail doesn't even pick up. Of course this prick wouldn't have voicemail.

I dial again, each unanswered ring stoking my irritation as I storm back into the building. I open the door to the dressing room and check inside, even though I know he won't be there. He's not. I knock on the door to the girls' dressing room and then pop my head inside. He's not there, either.

"Have you seen Jonah?"

"Probably smoking," Sav says, and I shake my head.

"I checked."

Her eyebrows scrunch with concern, and when I glance at Mabel, her expression is similar.

"No worries," I lie. "He's just...testing me. I've got it under control."

I smile, wave goodbye, and escape back into the hallway.

"Goddamn it," I groan to myself. First full day on the job and I've fucking lost my charge. This is the last thing I need. "I'll kill him."

I have two options. The first is I can call Wade Hammond and ask for help, but this mistake will probably get reported back to Conrad. I'd look like I can't handle the job, and that's not acceptable. No. I have to go with option two, which is to find the fucker myself, then shove my foot up his ass.

I'm not worried about Jonah Hendrix. I know it's a challenge. He's feeling me out. Looking for boundaries he can toe. I just have to be firm. He'll see that I mean business.

I pull out my phone and send him a text.

> ME
>
> Where are you?

It's read immediately, but he doesn't respond, and that confirms my suspicions. This is a game to him. I hunt down one of the hulking security guards and ask them to bring me back to the hotel. It takes fifteen minutes to get there, and when I'm finally climbing out of the car, I'm so worked up that my hands are shaking.

"Do you need help, ma'am?"

"No." I shake my head. "I don't need help but thank you."

"Still, take my number." He pulls a business card out of the glove compartment and hands it to me. "Call if you need assistance with anything. I'm Damon. I'm Mr. King's security detail."

I read the card, then look back at Damon. Hammond told me that each band member has an assigned detail for public outings and events. He offered to bring Jonah's security guard on full-time, but I told him no.

I'm wondering now if that was the right choice.

"Why are you here? I was told concert security and bodyguards were two separate teams."

"They are, ma'am, but Mr. King prefers full-time security for himself and Ms. James. Ms. Loveless does as well. Mr. Hendrix and Ms. Rossi don't like bodyguards unless it's necessary."

I nod. It would make sense that Torren's protective of Callie, especially in the wake of her accident. Sav Loveless requiring twenty-four seven security makes sense, too. She's one of the most famous people on the planet.

I put the business card in my purse and look back at Damon.

"Thank you for the lift. I might need a ride in a few minutes to...somewhere."

Fuck, I have no idea where to start. If he's not in there...

"I'll wait for a bit."

"Thanks. If I'm not back down in fifteen minutes, just assume I'm good."

"Sure thing, Ms. Davis."

"You can call me Claire."

He nods and returns my smile, then I head into the hotel.

I ball my shaking hands into fists and try my best to take deep, even breaths as I walk quickly through the lobby. I step into the elevator and keep my eyes fixed on the door, avoiding the mirrored walls as I rocket to the top floor.

I don't know what I'll find, but I know I cannot let Jonah see me rattled. I can maintain control of a spoiled rock star. I'm a professional.

The elevator doors open on our floor, and I can already hear music thrumming from the suite I'm sharing with Jonah. The closer I get to the door, the louder it gets. He's having a party. He's having a fucking party in *my* room.

It takes me three tries to get the key card to work, and when it finally does, I throw open the door and march into the suite.

The loud, dark, *empty* suite.

What the fuck?

There's a Bluetooth speaker blaring on the coffee table, so I walk over and turn it off. Then I hear it.

Moaning.

Moaning, and squeaking, and...

Spanking?

The feminine yelp that follows the sound of a crack confirms it.

He certainly wasted no time. Bolted immediately after the show so he could come back here and get laid. Jonah Hendrix is no better than a horny teenager.

I march toward the bedroom with every intention of forcing an NDA and condoms on the participants, but when I step through the door and flip on the light, I see red.

Jonah is on my bed.

He's on my bed, and he's naked, with his dick shoved down the throat of an equally naked blonde woman. But that's not what freezes me in my tracks and steals the air from my lungs. No. It's the naked brunette woman the blonde woman is straddling that does that. The naked brunette who has her face shoved between the blonde woman's thighs.

He's having a fucking threesome on my bed, and all I can think about are the...juices...that are probably on my duvet. All that foreign DNA. It's going to be all wet and weird.

Just...ew.

I stare with my mouth gaping as Jonah looks at me lazily. Eyes hooded and lips swollen, hand fisted in the blonde woman's hair as she gags around him.

"Trouble. I've been waiting for you."

NINE

Claire

THE SHIVER his deep voice coaxes from my body is enough to snap me out of my trance, and my face folds into a scowl.

"Get your orgy off my bed!"

I screech the sentence, and the women jump at my intrusion, but Jonah grins. He reaches over the blonde's body and smacks her ass cheek. When she yelps, the sound is gargled, smothered by his dick.

"There's room for you," he taunts, then he pulls out of the blonde's throat and wraps his hand around what I'm sure is a very slobbery erection. "You can be next."

It takes everything in me not to trail my eyes down his sweaty, tattooed torso to his crotch. Barely two days and already this man has had his cock in his hand twice in my presence. The thought makes me lightheaded, and then my anger returns.

The eager expression that takes over his face as I walk toward him boosts my confidence. He actually thinks I'm going to take him up on his invitation. And he's *excited* about it.

Idiot.

I close the distance until my thighs are pressed to the mattress and I'm inches from his chest. He's kneeling on the bed, so he's got over a foot on me, but I tilt my chin up and meet his gaze. His full lips are curved in a wolfish smile that transforms his face. Jonah's an attractive man anyway, but this smile makes him deviously sexy. It's almost enough to make me forget that there's oral sex taking place a foot from where I'm standing and his bare dick is jutting between us coated in the blonde woman's saliva.

Almost.

I force a smile that mimics his, just so I don't sneer at him, then I hook my index finger in the leather necklace he's wearing. Slowly, I pull his face down until our lips are almost touching. He smells like alcohol, but there's also a hint of some expensive cologne that gives me pause. For a fraction of a second, I want to press my nose to his chest and smell him. I want more of it. When he wraps the hand not on his dick around my waist, I almost say fuck it and do it.

But then I blink away the disturbing thoughts and push forward.

"Jonah Hendrix," I whisper sweetly. His grip on my waist tightens, and my breath hitches just the slightest bit.

"Yeah, Claire Davis?"

I brush the tip of my nose against his, then speak to him like a lover would. Pillow talk.

"I find you absolutely repulsive. The only way you'd get me at the end of your dick was if I were dead, and you were committing another felony."

He chuckles. I drop his necklace, take a step back, and turn to face the women. Their eyes are already on me, and as weird as it is, I'm glad that I don't have to go out of my way to get their attention. Having to interrupt yet another sex act would be an inconvenience.

"Ladies. Did you sign a non-disclosure agreement?"

I try not to focus on the fact that the brunette's whole face is glistening with the blonde's arousal, and they're both completely naked. I can still see their big breasts in my periphery, and I hate to admit it, but it makes me self-conscious. So Jonah likes women with big boobs. Typical.

They look at each other, then back at me before the brunette speaks.

"Um...no?"

"For fuck's sake, Hendrix." I shoot him a glare and find him staring at me with narrowed eyes. "You don't have them sign NDAs?"

He shrugs. "Sometimes."

I take that to mean never. I look back at the naked women.

"Come with me, please."

Both women look at Jonah for permission, and he jerks out a nod. Arrogant asshole. I grab my tablet and pull up the premade non-disclosure agreements. Both women sign without reading them. I roll my eyes again.

"It says you're not allowed to talk about being here with Jonah Hendrix or any other part of your interaction with him this evening. That includes this conversation. If you do, you will be sued for an exorbitant amount of money. Do you understand?"

They both nod eagerly. I can tell they think they're going to get back in bed with Jonah. *My* bed. Too bad I have to crush that hope.

"Good." I point to the door. "Party's over. You need to leave."

Three jaws drop. Two on a gasp and one on a bark of laughter. The laughter grates on my nerves. He is such an asshole.

"Excuse me?" the brunette squeaks, looking between Jonah and me. I keep my face serious while Jonah looks amused. "You can't do that. He invited us up here."

"And I'm uninviting you," I say calmly.

"We came all the way from Virginia for this," the blonde argues. "You can't just kick us out."

Of course they came from Virginia. Wouldn't it be hilarious if they grew up near me? I have to bite my tongue on a laugh.

"Look..." I glance at the NDA for her name. "Danielle. I'm sorry you traveled all the way to Sweden just to suck Jonah Hendrix's dick." I flick disinterested eyes at Jonah and cringe. "I would be disappointed too since he's clearly not worth the plane ticket." I look back at the women with a sad smile. "I would recommend the Vasa Museum or Stockholm Old Town. I'm sure they'll be more satisfying."

"You're not in charge here," the brunette argues, then she looks at Jonah. "Tell her."

Jonah's eyes lock with mine, and I arch a challenging brow.

If I back down now, it will set the precedent for the rest of my time here. I need to put my foot down. I need him to take me seriously. I'm ready to fight tooth and nail to win this one, but just as I open my mouth to tell him as much, Jonah speaks.

"Get out." The command is spoken plainly, without emotion, and at first, I think he's talking to me. Then he breaks our stare and looks at the women. "Get out."

"But, Jonah—"

"Get. Out. Now. Or I'll call security."

I blink. It's surprising, to say the least. The last thing I expected was compliance from him. Or such harshness to the women he was about to fuck. I don't want to assume victory, though. I don't trust him not to have something else planned. Something cruel or annoying or challenging. I watch quietly as the dejected women hurriedly gather their clothes and rush out. I actually do feel bad for them. It's not their fault Jonah is an asshole who needs a babysitter.

Once the door closes, I turn back to him. "How much have you had to drink?"

"Not enough to put up with you."

I bounce my eyes between his, looking for the signs I know all too well. He's definitely on something, but it's hard for me to tell what or how much. I don't know his tolerance, and he's better at hiding it than the emotional, self-destructive teenager I used to know.

The thought threatens to pull memories I'd rather avoid, so I look away from him. His blue eyes are unsettling. In this moment, they're too similar to my brother's, despite the different shade of blue. The same troubled fog is there. The pain. And because I'm old enough to recognize it for what it is now, it messes with my head and my heart.

I take a deep breath and try to approach this professionally. This is a *job*. He is my *assignment*. He is not my older brother.

"Jonah, the only way this will work is if you follow my plan—"

"Fuck your plan. It's not going to work for me."

I grit my teeth, and my nostrils flare as my breathing accelerates. I hate being interrupted—especially when it's by an entitled, over-privileged manchild—but I try to ignore his attitude and press forward.

God, do I try.

"No more groupie flings without signing the non-disclo—"

"NDAs kill the mood."

"Too fucking bad," I snap, anger boiling hot in my stomach. "NDAs are going to save your dumb ass from more slutty tabloid stories, and you know it." I stomp around the room and pick up his clothes as I argue with him. "You're lucky I don't require all your conquests to provide medical records of their sexual health. You're lucky I don't badger them about birth control before they're subjected to ten minutes of subpar sex."

I turn and toss his pants at him. They hit his chest, then hit the floor. He makes no move to pick them up.

"Sober sex only from now on," I snap. "You *and* your partner. *Never* in my bed. And you're getting tested. Celibacy until we get the results back."

His brows rise. "That's a violation of my privacy."

"While I'm here, you have no privacy."

He takes a step toward me, humor giving way to something more sinister. "You're not in control here."

"I am. It's my job to—"

"Fuck your job and fuck my father."

The sudden vitriol in his tone makes me flinch, and for the first time since I walked in here, I'm actually worried about what he's going to say next. His biceps flex, and I have a feeling if I glance down, I'll find him picking at his thumb again. I don't, though. His hands are too close to his possibly diseased penis.

"I looked you up, Claire Davis. You know what I found?"

My eyes widen and sweat prickles the back of my neck as he continues. Every cruel sentence is a blow to my confidence.

"Just a poor, small-town girl from Podunk nowhere with big city aspirations, right? Majored in marketing at a throwaway university in a throwaway town. Graduated middle of your class. Rented a shitty apartment you couldn't afford in Manhattan because that's the dream. Now you're a little country bumpkin mingling with the rich city socialites in your second-hand Manolos. You want so bad to fit in, don't you, Davis?"

I keep my spine rod-straight and my face stone. I don't cry. I don't even blink. But every word out of his mouth makes me shrink down further inside myself, and I know he can see it. His sharp blue eyes are carving at my skin, exposing bone and muscle, hitting every nerve.

"Then you get hired as a junior creative developer at Innovation Media, one of the best marketing firms in the world, despite not attending a prestigious university. Despite not graduating with honors. Who'd you fuck, Claire? Was it your boss? Did your boyfriend make some calls? I bet he's some rich prick investment banker with a wife and kids at home. Bet you're his pathetic little side piece."

I hate him. My eyes sting. My chest throbs. I *hate* him.

He huffs out a laugh and tilts his head to the side as he runs his eyes over my face, then lowers his voice and speaks to me like a lover would.

"I bet you're the success story of your shitty little town. Bet your family just loves to show you off during the holidays. Do they know about the two-month stay at a 'wellness facility?' What about your hospital stay? Are you just a pretty little lie, Claire? Keeping up appearances for your married boyfriend?" He shakes his head, eyes dragging over my face in an almost curious manner. Collecting data. Testing a hypothesis. Studying. "I don't think you'd be so celebrated back home if they knew the real Claire Davis. Do you?"

I glare at him for what feels like hours, and he stares back. It's infuriating how unbothered he is. His face is placid with just a hint of amusement, and his muscles are relaxed and loose despite having just eviscerated my insides. He's standing here completely naked, and yet I'm the one who feels exposed.

I. Hate. Him.

I force my breaths to slow. I wait until I think I can speak without my voice cracking.

"Congratulations," I clip out, fury and pain licking up my insides, burning in my throat. "You know how to do a background check. You know nothing."

He shrugs. "I know you need this job. I know any position you'd get if you're fired from Innovation would be a serious downgrade."

"I won't get fired."

"You will if you fail to polish up the CEO's son into something shiny and presentable." He reaches toward my face, but I swat his hand away, and his cruel smirk returns. "Play it my way, or I'll fuck everything up for you."

I narrow my eyes and stay silent. When he realizes I'm not going to reply, he must think his threat scares me because he continues.

"You're going to take five giant fucking steps back. You're going to cancel every PR stunt that we can't fake. You're going to let me do whatever the hell I want, and after a month, you're going to lie. You'll tell Hammond and my father that I'm fine. That they never had anything to worry about at all. And then you'll disappear. Got it?"

The fucking audacity of this man. The absolute arrogance. I'm usually against violence, but I've never wanted to punch someone so much in my life. I clear my throat.

"Are you done?"

He fucking grins. "For now."

"Okay. My turn. Thank you for that riveting offer, but I'm going to decline."

His grin falls. "Excuse me?"

"I won't be doing *any* of what you just suggested."

"Do you realize that I can end your entire career with one phone call?"

"Do *you* realize that I know all about your deal with your label? The morality clause and how your stupidity put you at risk of violating it. How your selfish actions could screw over not just you, but your entire band. Remember that, Jonah? Because I sure do, and I read the whole contract. I know about every single consequence you're set to face if you don't cooperate. And here's the thing. I *know* that scares you. Who are you if you're not in this band? If you're not this cocky, broody, asshole rock star who gives zero fucks? Hm?"

I pause and watch his jaw pop. His eyes are narrowed to slits as he juts hit chin, telling me to go on.

"Without the rock star façade to hide behind, you're everything you hate. Just a spoiled little rich boy from upstate New York. Youngest of two sons. The baby. Set up for success by your parents in every possible way. Went to the best private schools on Daddy's generational wealth. Got a legacy acceptance to Yale. A trust fund, a mega yacht, a summer house in the South of France, and absolutely zero consequences for any of your bad behavior. The perfect little pride and joy. Until now."

I mimic his earlier gesture by reaching for his face, but unlike me, he doesn't swat at my hand. He lets me run my fingers over his jaw, then toy with a strand of his long blond hair.

"You're not the only one who can do an internet search, Jonah Theodore Henderson, but I have to say, I was surprised to see you with brown hair and glasses in your school pictures." I look back into his blue eyes. "Do you wear contacts?"

He swallows, and my attention drops to his Adam's apple. There's an anatomical heart tattooed on his throat, and it almost looks like it's beating with the movement. I drop my hand to my side and step back before I touch that, too. I make eye contact again, steeling my face to appear more resilient than I feel.

"I've watched women I love be manipulated and mistreated by men like you my whole life. I've watched them become husks of who they were, turning themselves inside out for selfish men who didn't appreciate them or see their worth. Men who couldn't see past their own wants or weaknesses. Their own addictions. You won't do that to me, Jonah. I won't let you. I'm here to do a job. I will do it *my* way, and I promise you, if I go down, I'm taking you with me."

While I'm talking, I watch Jonah's face grow devoid of emotion. It's just as fascinating as it is haunting. He goes from sinister to shocked, to pained, and then to...*nothing*. Indifferent. Completely shut down.

I wonder if this is how serial killers look just before they snap. Weirdly enough, though, I'm not afraid of him. Not even a little. Maybe my anger makes me stupid.

"Do you understand?" I ask slowly.

He nods.

"Sure, Davis." He takes a step toward me, and then a new smirk forms on his still-swollen, thoroughly kissed lips. It throws me so far off guard that my poker face slips, and I find myself frowning at him. "Now what do you suggest I do about this?"

His shift in mood is so disarming that it takes a second for me to

realize he's talking about his dick. We've just hurled insults and threatened each other's lives, and now he's...coming on to me? Is that really what's happening right now?

I give my head a shake. He wanted to shock me, and he succeeded. I'm momentarily speechless. I was so entrenched in the argument that I even forgot he was naked, but now I have to fight to keep my eyes planted firmly above his chin.

I don't want to know if he's still hard.

I don't care.

Instead of deigning to give him a response, I grab the phone and dial the hotel concierge. When they answer, I ask for two new pillows and for my bed linens to be changed as soon as possible. Then I hang up and move to my suitcases.

"I'm taking a shower," I say over my shoulder. I don't look at Jonah again as I roll my bag into the bathroom with me. "You have an appointment with your trainer in the morning. Good night."

The moment I shut and lock the bathroom door behind me, my body nearly collapses. I hadn't realized how fiercely I'd been fighting to stay upright, but now I'm exhausted. My fingers tremble, and tears form once again in my eyes.

I turn on the shower, leaving the glass door wide open so the water sound is louder, and sit on the edge of the tub. I drop my head between my knees and breathe. When I don't think I'm at risk of passing out, I drop to the floor in front of the toilet and empty my stomach into the bowl.

I flush. I rinse my mouth. I take a Xanax. I rinse my mouth again. I brush my teeth. Then I step into the shower and stand under the steady stream of hot water.

I force everything Jonah said in that bedroom out of my head—everything that was wrong, and everything that was not—and I focus instead on the task at hand. I visualize my calendar for tomorrow. I run over my mental checklist. I plan.

By the time I'm drying my body with one of the fluffy hotel towels, I feel better. I've successfully removed my past from my present, and despite very strong-armed attempts at devastation, I'm once again in control of my emotions.

I dress in pajamas, take a melatonin supplement, and climb into my freshly made bed. The hotel room is dark, silent but for Jonah's steady breathing, and just before I succumb to sleep, I steel my resolve.

I don't know if I'm going to succeed with Jonah Hendrix, but goddamn it, I will die trying. He's a brand. Nothing more. As long as I remember that, I'll at least get out with my sanity intact.

TEN

Jonah

"DO you want to shower first? We still have a lot to get through today."

I throw myself onto the couch and glare at Claire's back. I'm exhausted and can barely walk thanks to Thor, and she's expecting me to entertain her calendar? No.

"I'm starving. I'm not doing shit until I eat."

She huffs out a tiny laugh. "So order room service. I'll shower first."

She disappears into the bedroom, so I sit up with a groan. I open the hotel app on my phone and pull up the room service menu.

"Yo, come tell me what you want before you get naked."

The moment the sentence leaves my mouth, I frown. It's too nice. Too thoughtful. And I don't like the way my thoughts immediately go toward her standing naked in the shower. I haven't decided how to handle her yet, but being nice and picturing her naked was ruled out as an option even before she dumped a pitcher of water on my head this morning.

Claire steps back into the main room of the suite, a towel and clothes in her arms. From the way her eyes are narrowed, she's thinking the same thing I am. *Nice* is the last thing she expected. *Nice* is suspicious. *Nice* is not welcome.

She actually looks cute when she thinks I'm up to something—pert little nose all scrunched, full lips tilted downward. I almost smirk before I remember that she's an annoying, ankle-biting dog that needs to be muzzled.

"I'm fine. But thanks."

"You're *fine*?" My brows slant, and more thoughts bust through my filter before I can stop them. Fuck Thor, man. I can't be calculating when my body is in distress. "You did like a hundred squats and then full-out sprinted for half an hour. Aren't you hungry?"

She freezes for a fraction of a second, head jerking back in surprise before she catches herself and gives me an unbothered shrug.

"I had something this morning." She turns toward the bathroom and calls over her shoulder. "You could have, too, if you'd woken up with the alarm."

Then the door shuts, effectively ending the conversation. I stare at the spot in the hallway she just vacated. Her reaction has alarm bells going off in my head. There's a weakness somewhere. Something I can exploit. Something I can use. I just don't know what.

A knock at the door breaks me out of my trance. I haven't even ordered my food yet. I'm prepared to tell Hammond or whoever it is to fuck off and come back later, but when I open the door, my scowl vanishes.

"Boss," I greet, sticking out my hand so Levi's daughter Brynn can slap me a low five, then I glance over her shoulder and jerk a nod toward Sav's personal security guard. "Red."

Red nods but says nothing. I look back down at Brynn. She smiles up at me, so I give her a small smile in return.

"Hey, Jonah. Are you busy?"

Instead of answering, I swing the door wide and usher them in. I don't bother engaging with Red. I like him just fine, but knowing Sav sends him as a chaperone anytime Brynn comes over pisses me off. What does she think I'm going to do, snort something in front of the kid? Offer her weed? I've done a lot of dumb shit, but I have never and would never do anything to hurt Brynnlee. To hurt *anyone*. I've always kept my destruction contained so I'm the only casualty, and Sav knows it. Well, until now. The reminder that she doesn't trust me makes my ears ring, and I have to force away the urge to dig into my stash and take another pill.

I inhale slowly and focus my attention back on Brynn. "What's the word?"

"Ebullient," she recites as she takes a seat on the couch. "Adjective. Extre—"

"Extremely lively. Enthusiastic. Joyful." I drop to the couch next to her. "The young girl became ebullient when talking about science but hated her literature classes."

Brynn grins and rolls her eyes. "I thought I'd get you with that one."

"Gotta try harder, kid." I drop my attention to the paperback book and laptop computer in her lap. "Whatchya got?"

"*The Outsiders* by S.E. Hinton." She scowls at the book. "Have you read it?"

I arch a brow and take the paperback. "What do you think?"

"Good, because I need help with this dumb assignment."

"You don't like it? This one is a classic." Her expression flattens into one of disdain, and I chuckle. "For someone who loves words, you sure hate reading."

She groans. "Dictionaries are easy. Fiction books are dumb. Like...why do I have to know this stuff? None of it is real. I shouldn't have to analyze why these fake people do what they do in this fake story. It's a waste of time. I should be working on my coding project, not writing a book report about why this horsey kid is obsessed with sunsets."

"You mean Ponyboy?"

She groans again. "That's another thing. Why do they have such stupid names? Who names their kid Sodapop? It's dumb."

My lips twitch, and I have to bite my cheek to keep from smiling. I don't want to laugh at Brynn. She hates struggling with schoolwork, and English is her worst subject. It's been the hardest transition for her when she moved to online learning when the tour started. I can empathize. I used to be the same way. I refused to fail at anything until the anxiety became too much, and I stopped caring. I don't want that to happen to her.

"You're right. The names are weird." I tap her computer, then open the paperback to her bookmark. "Pull up the assignment. We'll knock it out together."

"OH. HELLO."

Brynn and I both look up from her laptop screen. Claire is standing in the doorway wearing another of her professional pencil skirts, and I take my glasses off so I can look her over. Straight hair. Light makeup. Confused, scrunched little nose. The sexiest, most deceptive kind of trouble.

"I'm Claire. What's your name?"

Claire walks to the couch, and Brynn grins up at her. "I'm Brynn. I'm with Savannah."

"You can call her Boss, Davis. She's Levi's daughter." Claire flicks her eyes to me and nods before turning her warm smile back on Brynn.

"Nice to meet you, Boss." When Brynn giggles, Claire's smile grows, and she darts her eyes between me and the kid. "What are you guys doing?"

"Jonah is helping me with an English assignment."

"He is?" The way her eyebrows rise with surprise has a smirk curving my lips.

"Thought I was illiterate?"

"No." When Claire smirks back, my heart picks up pace. "Legacy or not, you wouldn't have gotten into Yale if you couldn't read."

"Yale?" Brynn's jaw drops, and she whips around to face me. "You went to Yale?"

"For less than a semester," I answer honestly, without breaking eye contact with Claire. "Couldn't do Yale and Heartless, so I chose Heartless."

Brynn hums. "Makes sense."

There's a lot more to it than that. From the look on Claire's face, she can tell, but the answer satisfies Brynn, so I change the subject.

"Actually, Davis, I haven't ordered room service yet. Could you do that? Breakfast. Eggs and bacon. Some scones. And coffee. Black."

"Of course, Mr. Hendrix." Claire's answer is flat, no doubt unamused by my ordering her around, but when she turns to Brynn, she's nothing but sunshine and kindness. I roll my eyes. "Would you like something too, Boss?"

"No, thank you."

Claire pulls out her phone to order, and I go back to discussing *The Outsiders* with Brynnlee. The whole time, I can feel Claire watching me. It makes my skin prickle with unease, and suddenly, I don't want her to see this part of me. I don't even know why. I just keep replaying her words from last night.

Without the rock star façade to hide behind, you're everything you hate.

Fuck her for being right.

Fuck her for seeing me so clearly yet getting it so fucking *wrong*, too.

I keep my eyes off Claire and on Brynn's computer. I talk her through symbolism and character development. We discuss the importance of the sunsets. We hammer out an outline for her book report. We finish up just as the food comes, and when Brynn stands to leave, I can tell she feels more confident in her understanding of the book.

"Still hate it?" I ask, hooking my glasses onto my shirt collar and standing.

Brynn shrugs. "Nah, I guess not."

"Maybe we could watch the movie," Claire chimes in, and Brynn gasps.

"There's a movie?" Brynn turns accusatory eyes on me. "Why didn't you tell me there was a movie?"

I shoot Claire a glare, then point at Brynn. "The movie never covers everything you need, and we don't cut corners."

Brynn sighs. "Fine. But once my report is turned in, can we watch the movie?"

I nod. "Sure. Now get out."

Brynn laughs and says thank you, and I watch quietly as she and Red walk out the door, leaving me alone once again with Claire.

"How old is she?"

I turn and find Claire staring at the door, a tiny smile playing on her lips. It makes me want to smile too. Brynn has that effect on people.

"She's nine."

"Nine?" Claire shakes her head in surprise. "She's *nine*? I didn't read *The Outsiders* until middle school."

"Yeah." My smile slips, pride surging through me even though Brynn's not my kid. "She's fucking smart. Keeps Levi and Sav on their toes."

"Seems like she's keeping you on your toes, too."

I avert my eyes and shrug, then sit down at the table to eat. I try to ignore her, but she doesn't move. She just keeps staring. I sigh and look over at her.

"What do you want now, Trouble?"

She arches a brow at the nickname, but she doesn't comment on it. Instead, she nods to my chest. "Contacts?"

It takes me a minute to realize that she's talking about my glasses hanging on the collar of my shirt, her question from last night circling back into my mind. *Surprised to see you with brown hair and glasses. Do you wear contacts?*

I turn back to my plate, shove a forkful of omelet into my mouth, then answer while chewing.

"LASIK." I swallow and take a drink of my coffee. "I just need them for reading now."

We fall back into silence, but Claire still doesn't move. I can feel her eyes dragging over me, her attention scanning me for information like some sort of enemy agent. I sigh again, louder.

"*What*, Davis?"

"Nothing." She shrugs in my periphery. "You have twenty minutes to eat and shower. Then we get back to work."

ELEVEN

Jonah

WHEN I WALK into the bedroom, I'm surprised to see Claire messing around on my side of the partition.

With my towel around my waist, I round the privacy glass and watch her. She's got a tripod with a ring light set up, and she's laid a black silk sheet over my mattress. An image of fucking her on that silk sheet and recording it with that tripod pops into my mind so quickly that I flinch. I shake my head to clear it.

"What are you doing?"

Claire jumps and whirls on me, pressing a hand to her chest. "Christ, Hendrix. You scared me. You're too big to be that quiet."

I smirk and open my mouth to say something snarky, but I see one of my concert guitars and a portable amp next to the bed. My curiosity spikes.

"This isn't a sex tape, is it?"

She rolls her eyes at my question and moves to the tripod.

"Get dressed. Something normal. Jeans and one of your band tees." She looks up at me and purses her lips. Her attention drops to my collarbone and hands. "Put your necklace on and any rings you usually wear for concerts. Your watch, too."

I nod and let go of my towel. Her eyes snap shut before it even hits the ground, and I chuckle as I pull jeans and a T-shirt out of my suitcase.

"You know, some people would consider your inability to keep your clothes on sexual harassment."

I freeze, suddenly grateful she can't see me. I'd wanted to make her uncomfortable, but the idea of her feeling harassed doesn't sit well with me. It makes me feel guilty, and I don't need another fucking reason to feel guilty.

"Do *you* consider it sexual harassment?" I ask, trying my best to keep my tone disinterested. She huffs.

"No, I don't. I think you're an obnoxious, immature child who's trying to run me off in any way possible."

My muscles relax, and I blow out a slow, relieved exhale.

"I'm not intimidated by you, and you're not going to get rid of me by taking your dick out every other hour, so you might as well give up."

I smile to myself and do the button on my jeans, then pull the shirt over my head. I glance at her. Her eyes are still shut, and her hands are propped on her hips, but despite the frown on her pretty face, I don't miss the blush coloring her cheeks and neck.

I cross the floor on light feet until I'm standing inches from her. When I lean down and put my lips to her ear, she sucks in a sharp gasp that I feel in my groin.

"I've put my dick away, Trouble."

She exhales, her breath heating my neck. When she takes a step away from me, I almost want to pull her back.

"Thank God. Next order of business: curating your social media presence."

"My what?"

"Your social media presence. It's the first step in reversing the current public opinion of you, and we're starting with your fans. We'll use social media to show them a different side of you. A more positive one."

"I don't do social media."

"I know, and I don't blame you, but it's one of the best ways to take back your image. Fortunately for me, starting from scratch will be easier than trying to revamp something that already exists. In this case, we very much want to reinvent the wheel rather than try to patch up a busted one."

"Gee, thanks."

"I'm being honest. And it's a good thing, anyway. We're going to use social media to humanize you in the eyes of your fans. Show them what we want them to see instead of letting the tabloids decorate you in scandal."

"But they're *already* fans."

"Sure, they like you, but they're not particularly loyal. They eat up the drama and feed into it. We're going to remedy that."

I purse my lips. She makes a good point, and it's not lost on me that she keeps saying *we*. Not just me but her too. A team effort.

I study the setup she's constructed in the bedroom—dim lighting, silk sheets, camera tripod—and arch a brow. "But this *isn't* a sex tape?"

She gives me a fake smile. "You wish."

When I don't deny it, she shakes her head and forges forward.

"I've created an account for you on a popular social media site. We're leaning into the broody mystery that surrounds you, but we're going to provide fans little glimpses of 'the real' Jonah Hendrix. Of course I'll pick and choose what those glimpses will entail, but they'll all be delivered in a way that feels personal, almost intimate, while still maintaining your privacy."

"That sounds like you're setting us up for parasocial relationships."

"You're a celebrity, so we can't completely avoid that, but we've set boundaries. Your comments are off. Your direct messages are off. You won't be engaging with them, and you'll only follow your bandmates and close friends. You're not putting your whole personal life on display for strangers. You'll just be…giving them a peek behind the black, angry veil you've shrouded yourself in for ten years."

She taps something out on her phone, then hands it to me. I snort when I see the social media handle. "HeartlessHendrix? Really?"

She gives me an arrogant, one-shouldered shrug. No apology. No explanation. A smile forms on my lips before I can fight it off, so I look back at the phone.

"How do I already have this many followers? I haven't posted anything yet. I don't even have a bio or a profile picture."

"I followed Sav, Mabel, and Torren, and they've followed you back. They haven't shared anything, but fans have noticed. Everyone is hoping it's you."

I don't want to admit it, but I'm already impressed. It's such a simple fucking move, but it's brilliant. She must take my silence to mean I'm not convinced, though, because she starts pitching the idea again.

"Look. You've been playing defense for years. The whole band has, honestly. You've been reactive instead of proactive, and it's never truly helped anything. We're changing that today, and we're starting by conquering your fan base. We're going on offense, and when we succeed in this—and we *will* succeed, Jonah—you'll have millions of people across the globe on your side in this endeavor. Think of them as an international army fighting for your honor."

The more she talks, the more impressed I become. I bet she's a force in a boardroom. I said a lot of shit last night, but now I know how she got a job at my father's company—her own merit. It makes me feel like an asshole for suggesting otherwise, even if I'd only said it to piss her off. I'm not a misogynist. I don't think women *sleep their way to the top*. I lied and stooped to that level just to be a dick, and now I'm feeling like one.

I should apologize. I almost do. But then I don't. We're in a silent battle, and I still intend to win.

I change the subject. "So, *this* is PR chess?"

"This is chess, and our next move is a banger. En passant capture. No one will expect it."

I glance up and lock my gaze with hers. "This is a good idea, Claire. Thanks."

Her eyes widen and her mouth falls open before she folds her lips between her teeth to hide a smile. She shakes her head and looks away as another blush covers her cheeks.

"It's honestly a rudimentary tactic. Anyone would have started with it."

The way my simple compliment shocks her is almost sad. The confidence and attitude she exuded seconds earlier are gone, and now she's just an uncertain, insecure girl. Yearning for acceptance, but so unaccustomed to praise that she collapses in the face of it.

I ignore the shitty way it makes me feel and instead file the realization away in my memory. More intel. More evidence. More Claire Davis.

I snatch up my guitar, then sit on the edge of the bed with it. Having the guitar in my hands calms my nerves. It soothes the buzzing tension that's always running through my bloodstream.

"What now? You want me to smile for a picture? Post Heartless lyrics for the caption?"

She grins like I'm an idiot she finds amusing.

"I said we were showing glimpses of the *real you*, Hendrix. Sure, the profile will be heavily curated, but we want to be realistic, and something tells me you're not a *smile for the camera* kind of guy."

I nod in confirmation, and she continues.

"We're going to take the things the fans already like about you and infuse a little more personality. A little more *you*."

I nod again, and she gestures to the bed.

"Okay, sit on the edge of the mattress—you need to be able to play the guitar—and get comfortable."

I do as she says, and she attaches her phone to the tripod. She adjusts the height and shifts it around until she likes the positioning, and then she flips on the ring light.

"Fuck." I throw my hand up to shield my eyes. "That's bright."

"Sorry," she says, and she means it. "I just have to..." She adjusts the brightness of the light, then points it down a little so it's not burning my retinas. "How's that?"

"Much better."

She goes back to messing with the phone, and a thought pops into my head. I let myself say it without overthinking it.

"I'm the king in this analogy, right? If this is chess, then I'm the king."

"Not yet, you're not."

I can't see the features of her face, thanks to the ring light, but her tone is playful. I sit up straighter, my lips fighting the urge to turn up at the corners.

"So I'm a pawn," I say, my tone matching hers.

"For now. Until we make it across the board."

"I thought a pawn couldn't be promoted to a king?"

She waves her hand in the air. "It's not a perfect analogy, Hendrix, but you get the point. You let me get you across the board, and then you can take over the game. I hand you the crown."

I bite my cheek to keep from letting my smile free and look right at her face. I can't tell if she looks back, but I think she does. "Are you saying you're my queen, then?"

"Your words. Not mine."

"The queen's the most important piece on the board, Davis. Sounds to me like that's you."

There's a charged pause that stretches between us. I can feel her eyes on me, and I keep mine pointed in her direction. When her voice breaks through the silence, it's a challenge.

"Think you can handle that?"

I can't fight it anymore. I smile. "For now."

She hums. There's another moment of tension, and then after a few breaths, it disappears. Business again. Full speed ahead.

"Okay, so only your torso is in frame," she tells me. "Shoulders to knees. The camera is focused on the guitar. On your hands."

I nod. "Cool. Now what?"

"When I say go, you play."

"Play what?"

"Whatever. Something you like, but not The Hometown Heartless. Something *Jonah Hendrix*."

I think about it while I flip on my amp and tune the guitar. Then when Claire says go, I start to play. I've barely begun when she interrupts.

"Wait," Claire says, her voice cracking slightly. "Stop."

I stop. "What?"

"Is that... Are you playing Fleetwood Mac?"

"Yeah. 'Landslide.' Why?" I furrow my brow at her tone. It's confusing. It almost sounds sad. I wish I could see her face.

"Nothing. I just..." She forces a laugh. "I thought you'd play something more, I don't know, rock and roll, I guess."

I raise my eyebrows. "There are few things more rock and roll than Stevie Nicks, Davis."

"Right." Another awkward, breathy laugh, followed by a sniffle. "Of course. No, this is perfect, actually. Your fans will love it. Um, it's a, it's a nice surprise."

She almost sounds like she's crying, but then she clears her throat, and her next words are steady. Like I imagined the emotion seconds earlier.

"Sorry for interrupting. You can start whenever you're ready."

I don't question her. I just start over, and she doesn't interrupt me again. When I finish the song and the final notes fade out, Claire clicks something on the phone, then takes it off the tripod. She doesn't turn off the ring light. I know it's because she doesn't want me to see her.

"Great," she chirps. "I'll cut this down and post it. I'll...I'll be right back, though. I have to make a phone call."

She turns on her heel and leaves the bedroom. Seconds later, I hear the doors to the balcony open and shut, but I don't move. I just sit there, my eyes fixed on the floor behind the tripod where she was standing. I'm rarely stumped by people, but Claire Davis...

The woman has given me nothing but questions.

I don't like it.

She doesn't speak to me for the rest of the afternoon. We ride to the stadium separately, and she doesn't watch the show from the VIP tent. She's not in the dressing room after the concert, either. But when I pull up my new social media account later, I'm met with thousands of notifications.

Claire posted the video of me playing "Landslide."

It's not the whole video—just a clip of the first verse and chorus—but it's gotten almost a million likes in twenty minutes. With the moody lighting and the black silk bedsheets serving as a backdrop, it feels intimate, just like she said it would. And while you can't see my face, just my hands playing the guitar, she was right. It feels like *me*. More *me* than any music video or album photoshoot has.

I find myself smiling at the phone, but then I read the caption.

Can the child within my heart rise above?

My smile fades, my brow furrows, and I frown.

Exposed. I feel exposed.

And for the rest of the night, even after swallowing down my nightly cocktail of smuggled pills, I can think about one thing. *Only* one thing.

Trouble.

TWELVE

Claire

I FLIP through the photos on my phone and favorite the ones I think I can use.

They're all close-ups of Jonah on stage from the last two nights. From the wings. From the pit. I was everywhere. I got him from every angle. I even took a few of the crowd from backstage. I'm going to take some more tonight, and then I'll post a *Thank you, Stockholm* carousel when we leave for Lisbon. The fans will like that. Everyone wants to feel appreciated.

The video of Jonah playing "Landslide" got over four million likes in just under twenty-four hours. *The Star* called it "the video that broke the internet." I hate *The Star*, but I was surprised to see that their post was *almost* positive. They did question whether he posted it while high, or if it was recorded after a drug-fueled orgy, but Rome wasn't built in a day. I can't expect Jonah Hendrix's new glowing reputation to be either.

I go back to the video in my phone of Jonah playing and watch it again without sound. I've done this no less than twenty times since I filmed it. I don't have to turn the volume on. I hear the music just fine in my head.

My eyes start to sting before I'm halfway through the video, so I click out of it and shoot a quick glance toward Sav and Mabel. They're both engaged in their own things—Mabel is texting someone, and Sav is messing with an acoustic guitar and scribbling in a notebook—so they thankfully didn't notice my almost-tears.

Since I don't feel like having to avoid Jonah's dick again, I'm sitting through the opener in their dressing room. I'll be here after, too. I'm not worried about him taking off. I brought José back as full-time security, and he's promised to call me immediately if Jonah tries anything stupid.

So far today, I've had very little interaction with Jonah. It's his rest day with Thor, and he had therapy and his STI test this afternoon. I'm sure he needed a break from me, because I certainly needed one from him.

God, I hope we wrap this up soon. If I have to be here for the whole tour...

He's so confusing. One minute, he's cooperative, and the next, he's hurling insults. Insults that *really* hurt. Expertly crafted and dealt with lethal precision. I haven't been able to stop thinking about what he said to me the other night. The way he cut me down so effortlessly. Without any remorse or restraint. He wanted to hurt me, and he did. He magnified every insecurity. Pushed his fingers into every gaping, unhealable wound.

I've even dreamed about his comments. Ironically, the ones he got wrong are the ones that have haunted me the most.

I bet you're the success story of your shitty little town.
Bet your family just loves to show you off during the holidays.

I hate that I've given yet another man this kind of control over my emotions. I hate that it's sent me into yet another downward spiral. My stomach churns. Familiar hunger pains swirl with anxious energy in a way that makes me dizzy. I dig through my purse for some sugar-free mints and pop them in my mouth.

Then, because I'm a glutton for punishment, I close out of my photos and sign into my social media account. I don't even scroll through my feed. I just go straight for my ex-best-friend's profile.

The first picture is of my brother with my nephew in his arms, and my heart sinks. Macon looks so happy. So healthy. So *healed*. And the way he's looking at his son...Like he's the most precious gift. Photos like this always make me want to smile and cry. Smile because I never thought my brother would get here, and cry because I'm not part of it.

My finger hovers over the photo, and I consider liking it, but just like all the other times, I chicken out. I'm lucky I'm not blocked as it is. I don't want to push my luck.

The next photo is of my nephew with his face covered in something green. Some sort of vegetable. From his expression, he doesn't approve, and the caption confirms it.

Peas. 0/10. Do not recommend.

I laugh quietly and wipe my eyes.

"Oh, he's cute."

I jump and look up to find Sav behind me. She's standing in front of the mini fridge with a mineral water in her hand, but she's looking over my shoulder at the photo. She can probably tell that I've been crying because her smile drops.

"Sorry. I didn't mean to invade your privacy like that. That was shitty."

"No," I say with a forced laugh. "No. It's fine. He's my nephew."

"He's fucking adorable. His hair is the same color as yours."

I click off the phone screen and set it face down on the table. I force a swallow.

"Yeah, my brother has the same hair. Mine's curly like theirs too. I just straighten it."

"I bet they're missing you right now."

"No." I wince and give my head a little shake. "No. They're not."

Sav's eyes scan over my face. I don't know what she sees, but her smile turns sad.

"That sucks. I'm sorry."

I shrug, doing my best to breathe through the threat of more tears. "It's my fault. I have to live with it."

She furrows her brow. "Want to talk about it?"

I shrug again. I consider telling her no, but when I open my mouth, something else comes out. Something I've harbored in my chest for so long that it's taken up permanent residence around my heart and lungs. It's like letting air out of a balloon.

"It's simple, really. I made a shitty decision that hurt people. If I'd known it would do the damage it did..." I close my eyes and slump back in my seat. "I can't take it back."

I shake my head as a tear escapes through my lashes.

"When I finally realized how wrong I was…Well, it was too late. Now I'm dealing with the consequences of those choices."

Sav and I fall into silence. Even the sounds from Mabel's phone have stopped, and when I finally open my eyes, they're both looking at me. I'm afraid of what I'll see on their faces, but instead of judgment, I find empathy. I find understanding.

"Have you apologized? Explained?"

I look at Mabel and nod. "I've tried. Kind of. I don't blame them for not wanting to hear me out, though. I wouldn't forgive me either."

I haven't. I can't.

The admission brings on more tears, and my muscles sag with defeat. Then Sav puts her hand on mine.

"Can I say something? Unsolicited advice, kind of. It's cool if you don't want it."

I think about it for a moment. Do I want advice?

"There's nothing I can do that will make them forgive me, Sav. I don't want to force it."

She shakes her head. "I know. It's not about that."

I bite the inside of my cheek, then nod. "Sure. It can't hurt."

She smiles softly. "You have to forgive yourself, even if they can't."

I huff out a laugh before I can stop myself. My half smile is sardonic. Self-deprecating. "With respect, Sav, you don't know my story. You don't know what happened."

She shrugs. "Yeah, but I'm no stranger to shitty decisions, either. I've hurt a lot of people out of selfishness. I caused others pain because I was in pain. I'm not proud of it, and I know it's well within their right to never forgive me. Some of them will never speak to me again, and I've had to accept that." Her grip on my hand tightens. "I also know what remorse looks like. I know regret. I know how it eats at you, and no one can live like that. You're *allowed* to move on. It sounds like you've punished yourself enough."

I wipe at my cheeks, my hands coming back smeared with black mascara. I don't respond. I keep my eyes closed, grit my teeth, and breathe. I want to hear her. To believe her.

"She's right," Mabel adds, her voice closer now. "We're not perfect. We've all made mistakes. We're all the villains in someone's story. In Sav's case, she's the villain in a lot of stories."

Mabel says the last part playfully, and Sav snorts out a laugh that elicits a small smile from me.

"Thanks, Mabes."

Mabel giggles. "*Anyway*, Sav is right. You have to forgive yourself. Even if they can't."

I force a tight smile. "Sure." My voice cracks slightly, and I clear my throat again. "Thanks."

"Sometimes you have to cut away the worn-down parts of yourself," Mabel says. "The shit weighing you down. You've got to shed it so you can move forward."

I force a swallow and let myself ask a question that terrifies me. Something that's worried me for years. "What if there's nothing left?"

Sav squeezes my hand one more time. "You have to have faith that you'll grow back better."

Thankfully, I don't have to respond because the door opens, and Hammond pops in to let them know it's time to head to the stage. Sav and Mabel both leave me with smiles, and when they disappear into the hallway, I drop my head to the table and finally let the tears free.

Forgive yourself, even if they can't.

Have faith that you'll grow back better.

Simple sentences for insurmountable tasks. Forgive myself for ruining lives? Grow back better?

I can't. I won't.

I don't deserve it.

I GET BACK to the suite before the band.

I need a hot bath and a glass of wine, and I don't need to deal with Jonah Hendrix's mood swings.

I can tell I'm on the verge of a tailspin. That familiar refractory feeling is creeping out of the recesses of my mind, making my pulse spike and my stomach roil. I don't want to acknowledge it. It would mean failure. It would mean erasing all the progress I've made, and I can't accept that.

I sent a text to José after I finished taking photos and told him to let me know when they were heading back to the hotel, and then I preordered a glass of red wine from the guest services concierge. As soon as I'm in the suite, I take my wine straight to the bathroom. I turn the water as hot as I can stand it, use the hotel provided bubble bath, and do my best to clear my head as I sink to my chin in the luxury soaker tub.

I last five minutes before I'm mentally going over Jonah's calendar, and then I'm hauling myself out of the tub so I can get some work done on the MixMosaic account. Someday, I will learn how to relax without feeling guilty again.

I put on pajamas and throw my hair up into a towel, then crawl onto my bed with my laptop. I really wish I could be in the office to at least brainstorm with the team, but Brandt's been leaving comments on the shared drive for me. It will have to do while I'm stuck in Europe traipsing after Conrad's son.

Conrad.

I've only spoken to him once since I left New York. The time difference has made it difficult to talk on the phone, and he's not the best texter, so all my messages have received monosyllabic responses and the occasional emoji. It's cute when he sends emojis. I smile. Then I frown.

I wonder how he'd feel if he knew how close I've been to his son's penis. I wince. Or if he knew how hard it was not to look.

I shake my head and grab my phone. Conrad likely isn't working right now, and it would be nice to hear his voice. When my attempted video chat doesn't go through, I try a regular call. He answers on the third ring, his voice booming through the receiver against a backdrop of muffled conversation and classical music.

"Conrad Henderson."

"Hi! It's me."

"Ms. Davis." He clears his throat, and I hear something like cutlery clinking in the background. "What can I do for you? How is the job going?"

My smile dulls.

Ms. Davis?

How is the job *going?*

I haven't spoken to him in days, but he sounds less than thrilled to hear from me. And *the job*? As in *his son*?

"Um, *the job* is fine," I say slowly. "I don't need anything. I just called to talk."

"I see." There's a brief pause, and when he speaks again, the sound is far away. "I'll be right back. I have to take this. Work."

He's with someone, I realize. I check the time on my computer and do quick math.

"I'm sorry," I say quickly. "Are you busy? I can call back."

"Just a work dinner. It's not important."

I feel the creases in my forehead deepen as I frown into my lap. The restaurant sounds seem so much louder now. And the classical music...

My stomach cramps.

"Awfully late for a work dinner," I say carefully. "Where are you?"

"La Chateau." He says a muffled thank you, probably to a doorman or a host, and then the sounds are replaced with street noise and breeze. He's outside. "Is my son behaving?"

I ignore his question and focus on the statement. La Chateau is a Michelin star French restaurant in Manhattan. He took me there on our first real date. I'd never been somewhere so fancy, and I left with stars in my eyes.

"La Chateau? For work?" I force a laugh. "Isn't that a little intimate of an atmosphere for business?"

"It's close to the office."

"There are hundreds of places close to the office."

He doesn't respond, and I can practically feel his stern eyes on me, silently commanding me to back down. It's easier to ignore when he's not right in front of me. The distance makes me bolder. It makes me sit up straighter. I force myself to smile again.

"Who's the client?"

He sighs. "Claire, my love, don't do this."

"Do what?"

"You know what." He sighs. "How is Paris?"

"I'm in Stockholm."

"Ah, it's been years since I've been to Stockholm. Are you enjoying it?"

"I'm here for work. It's not a vacation."

He chuckles. "Of course. I picked the right person for the job. I knew I could trust you with this."

The sentence does what he intended. Teases that thing inside me that yearns for praise. To be appreciated. Even though part of me knows I'm being manipulated, I still smile. I do my best to ignore how much that disappointments me.

"I miss you," I say on a sigh.

"I miss you, too, my love. How about I—"

"Conrad," a woman's voice interrupts. "They brought out the food."

I know that voice.

"Ms. Davis, I'm going to have to let you go. We'll discuss the job later."

His tone has changed. He's no longer warm. No longer affectionate. He's business again. Cold. It makes me wince, and then it makes me angry.

"Is that Dierdre?" He doesn't answer, so I speak again. "I thought this was a business dinner. Why is Dierdre attending a business dinner with you? She never attends business dinners."

He clears his throat again, then hits me with a tone I've only heard him use with employees or staff when they've done something to displease him. Severe. Commanding. Superior.

"I'm glad to hear the job is going well. I will call you in a few days to check in. Will there be anything else?"

I blink, and it takes me a few breaths before I can speak. Almost four thousand miles between us, and I still feel like I've been slapped.

"No," I whisper, shaking my head slowly. "No...there's nothing else."

"Good."

He hangs up without saying goodbye. He gives me no chance to say anything in return. I pull the phone from my ear and stare at it as *call ended* disappears and the phone screen goes black. La Chateau on a Thursday night with Dierdre. I'm not an idiot. I know what this is.

"He out with his wife?"

My eyes shoot straight to the doorway. Jonah is leaning on the frame with his arms crossed, expression equal parts smug and sympathetic. He's still wearing the same distressed jeans and vintage band tee he had on for the show.

"When did you get here?" I snatch up my phone and click on the screen, finding a text from José. *OTW* sent twenty minutes ago. I look back at Jonah. "How long have you been listening in on my conversation?"

I run back through the phone call. I've been careful not to say Conrad's name. I'm usually good about hiding it. I've had a lot of practice recently. But did I let it slip...? I stare at him and wait for a sign. Is he fucking with me, or does he not know? Then he smirks.

"Long enough to know your boyfriend is cheating on his mistress with his wife. You're the mistress, in case you weren't sure."

I narrow my eyes at him. "I am not a mistress because he is not married, and he is not cheating on me."

The statement tastes like ash. Even I know it's a lie.

Jonah pushes off the doorframe and prowls toward me, looking me up and down in a way that makes me want to pull the duvet up to my neck.

"Who is Dierdre, then? Certainly not a *business* partner."

"I'm tired." I snap my laptop closed. "Don't stay up too late, please. We have a full day tomorrow."

He tilts his head to the side. "Are my test results back? I need to get laid."

I sigh, grateful for the subject change. "The doctor said five days."

"I'm not waiting five days to have sex, Davis. I wear condoms. I don't have any STIs."

"Sorry to break it to you, Hendrix, but that's not how it works." I throw the duvet off my body and climb out of bed so I can dig some ibuprofen out of my bag. "While I am beyond glad to hear you have at least one functioning brain cell in your head, condoms aren't one hundred percent preventative of anything." I throw the pills into my mouth and swallow them dry. "Not babies. Not sexually transmitted infections. Nothing."

"You're messing with my post-show routine. I play a show. I fuck a groupie or three."

I shrug. "You'll be fine."

He watches me with his arms folded over his chest, brows slanted slightly. Again, I feel like I'm being studied. A reminder that I need to mask any and all weaknesses. I stand taller, and he smiles.

"I get tested regularly on my own, and I know how condoms work. I'm not an idiot."

"Congratulations."

We fall into silence once more, and for some reason, I don't want to be the one to break our eye contact. It feels like a challenge, and between the dressing room conversation and the phone call, I really need to win something today. I take a step closer and peer up into his blue eyes. As much as it makes me want to vomit, I take a page out of his father's book.

"Is there anything else, Mr. Hendrix?"

I half-expect him to proposition me. Offer me a guest-starring role in his post-show routine or some other insufferable suggestion. I'm even prepared with a scathing retort, but then he surprises me.

"Why'd you pick that caption?"

"Excuse me?"

He arches a brow. "*Can the child within my heart rise above?*"

When it dawns on me, I huff out a laugh. "It's a lyric from the song you played, Jonah. Surely you know that."

"Why *that* lyric?"

He speaks calmly, almost indifferently, but something tells me my answer matters. It's more than artistic curiosity. That caption hit a nerve, and the realization makes my heart race. *This* is the win I need.

I shrug. "No reason. I like that lyric."

"Hmmm." He hums, eyes bouncing between mine. I don't back down.

"Why?" I ask innocently. "Is it a problem?"

The pause stretches, and I wonder if he finds comfort or protection in silence. Perhaps both. Or perhaps he wields it as a weapon—a way to control tone and direction. I smile softly. I am unbothered. I will not be manipulated.

"Well?"

"Nope. No problem."

He shakes his head once, then takes a step backward, attention dropping to my lips briefly before lifting back to my eyes. He doesn't smile, but there's a softness in his expression that gives me pause. When he speaks again, his voice is low, intimate, and chills once again tickle my arms and neck.

"I'll be ready for our full day tomorrow. Sleep well, Claire."

"You too," I say with a nod, and then he slips behind his side of the partition.

I watch his shadow move around his side of the room, and I pretend to busy myself with my phone until he disappears into the bathroom. The shower kicks on, and I release a sigh of relief as I crawl back into my bed.

Then I let myself smile.

Jonah's reaction to the caption I chose for that video boosts my confidence. It tells me I'm starting to figure him out. I'm one step closer to understanding him, and that's exactly the win I needed today.

I meant it when I said PR was like chess. It's a complex game, and to win, I need to stay several moves ahead. I need to maintain the upper hand.

The biggest threat to Jonah's public image is himself. To succeed in this job, I have to play *for* him while also playing *against* him. He's his own worst enemy, which means as long as I'm here, he's my enemy, too.

And what's the first step in defeating your enemy?

Understanding them.

I'm going to take you down, Jonah Hendrix, and you'll be thanking me after.

THIRTEEN

Jonah

"DO you have any questions before we get there?"

I turn my head on the leather seat to look at Claire.

She's got her straight, shiny brown hair pulled into a clip, a thin rose gold chain decorating her neck, and matching rose gold hoops in her earlobes. She's wearing a pair of designer sunglasses, but I can tell she's not looking at me. I've noticed that she keeps her eyes off me as much as possible. The only times she's looked at me—really looked at me—were when we were arguing, and she was sizing me up. Everything else can be compared to a cursory glance at best. I can't tell which I hate more—being seen or being ignored.

There's something eerily familiar about her blue eyes. Reflective in a way that feels revelatory. It's uncomfortable, but it's also intriguing. I find myself oscillating between wanting to hide from her and wanting to do something that attracts her full attention.

When I don't respond to her question, she turns her head toward me just as I knew she would. I can tell the moment her keen gaze lands on me. I dig my fingers into my thigh to distract from how my heart picks up pace.

"Jonah. Questions?"

"You're taking me to volunteer at a youth center." I shrug. "I assumed they'd instruct me on what to do when we get there."

Her lips curve down slightly, and I laugh.

"Are you shocked that I'm cooperating, Trouble? D'you expect me to throw a tantrum?"

Her eyebrow arches over the top of her sunglasses, but she doesn't say anything. She doesn't like when I call her Trouble, but she won't admit it.

"The video was a good call," I say honestly. "I'm intrigued. Figured I'd see what else you have up your sleeve."

I do my best to plaster sincerity on my face. I've fooled people with this look for years, but being scrutinized by Claire Davis is higher stakes. She's unbiased, and that will make her harder to convince. But if I can't scare or threaten her away, I have to try a different tactic.

I have to charm her.

The car pulls to a stop outside of a large brick building before she can respond, and I'm surprised to see a lack of flashing lights when we park.

"Where are the cameras?" I ask as I wait for José to open the car door. "We meeting them in there?"

"There are no cameras. We don't want it to seem like we set this up as a media stunt."

I furrow my brow. "But it *is* a stunt, and we need the media to know about it."

"They will, but we're controlling the narrative." Her lips quirk up at the side, then she hooks her finger in the cuff of her blouse sleeve and tugs. "It's all up here."

I can't help but chuckle as I follow Claire out of the car. It's all *up her sleeve*.

The moment I'm free of the car's cab, I inhale deeply, filling my lungs with air not tainted with lavender and sugar. I spent the entire drive taking small breaths through my mouth. Any longer and I might have passed out.

"Ms. Davis," a short, older woman with a Swedish accent greets us as we step up to large wooden doors. "Mr. Hendrix. Welcome."

"Hello, Mrs. Nilsson." Claire shakes the woman's hand, then turns to me. "Jonah, this is Ebba Nilsson. She runs the Stockholm Youth Center."

JONAH

I give the woman a genuine smile and take her hand in mine. "Nice to meet you, Mrs. Nilsson. I appreciate you letting me come in today."

"Yes, thank you," Claire says. "We're grateful you could accommodate us on such short notice."

"It's not every day the kids get to hang out with a celebrity. And don't worry, they've all been told the rules. Come on in. I'll bring you to them."

I follow Mrs. Nilsson into the building and give Claire's arm a nudge with mine.

"Rules?"

She nods. "They're allowed selfies and autographs but no live streaming, and I've asked that they don't post anything until after you've left."

My eyes widen, and she taps the sleeve of her blouse again. I huff out another laugh. *Controlling the narrative.* The media will be learning about my visit secondhand, so it will seem organic. It will seem *genuine*.

Another simple yet brilliant move.

Calculated, yes. Manipulative? Maybe. But brilliant just the same.

Mrs. Nilsson leads me into a large room full of kids, and then she introduces me in Swedish. She also introduces me to an interpreter who will shadow me while I'm here since I only speak English, and a lot of these kids don't.

The first fifteen minutes are just them asking me a ton of random questions. Where's my band? What's my favorite video game? When did I start playing guitar? Do I like kladdkaka? Have I seen the new superhero movie? What's Sav Loveless like? Can I skateboard?

The questions come in rapid fire. My poor interpreter can barely keep up, but it's the most fun I've had doing an interview in a long time. I even lose track of Claire for a while because I can't look away from the crowd of kids vying for my attention.

When the questions die down, they take me to a large table where they've been working on crafts. Paint, tissue paper, pipe cleaners, glitter, little googly eyes. Any craft material you can think of, they've got it on this table, but my attention zeroes in on a bin of small wooden baubles and figurines.

"What is this for?" I ask a little girl.

She waits for my translator to ask her in Swedish, then she answers me with a smile.

"Jewelry," my translator says. "They use it to make ornaments and jewelry. They were donated by a local woodcarver."

I nod and take a seat next to the little girl, snatching a small wooden figurine out of the bin. She scoots a tin of paintbrushes in front of me, so I grab one of those, too. I scan the paints on the table, then point to a few bottles in front of the girl.

"Can you pass me those blues, please?"

She does, and I get to work. The figurine is small. It doesn't take me long to cover it in a spiral of light and dark blue swirls. I set it aside to dry, thank the little girl, and let the kids pull me through a few other activities.

I win three games of tic-tac-toe, get my ass handed to me in a game of Wii Bowling, and am reminded just how out of shape I am when they force me into a game of basketball. Obviously, Thor is not a miracle worker. I'm a panting, gasping, pathetic mess. A walking billboard for the dangers of smoking and drinking. Don't be like me, kids. Just say no to, well, everything.

Then I'm mercifully brought a beat-up acoustic guitar and asked to play.

"Okay," I say as I throw the leather strap over my head and take a seat on the edge of a table. "Do we have any requests?"

I tune the guitar as the kids talk over each other excitedly. I glance at my interpreter, and he shrugs with a laugh.

"Just play what you like."

I nod and think for a moment, then my eyes catch on Claire. She's standing alone on the far wall, just outside of the crowd, but she's got her attention on me.

And she's smiling.

It's a small smile, lips curved slightly higher on one side, but she's definitely smiling, and it's not taunting or forced. It's happy. Playful, even.

It's beautiful.

My fingers freeze briefly before I catch myself, and her smile grows a fraction of an inch. She arches a teasing brow, so I narrow my eyes and give her a smile of my own before fingerpicking the opening chords to "Blackbird" by The Beatles.

It takes effort to tear my eyes from hers, but I make myself do it. I don't like the way my heart starts to race the longer I look at her. I don't like the way my neck starts to heat, or the way I can almost smell her lavender and sugar scent from across the room. I don't like the way my motives start to blur at the edges.

I don't like any of it.

I avert my gaze and don't look at her again until I'm handing the acoustic back to an employee and saying my goodbyes to the kids. Mrs. Nilsson asks if I would mind taking a group photo, and of course, I agree. That's why I'm here. It's a PR stunt orchestrated by my father's manipulative, evil-genius employee.

By my babysitter.

My babysitter who has a boyfriend who's probably cheating on her with some sidepiece named Dierdre.

Finally, I let myself look back at Claire, this time controlling the way my mind catalogues what it sees. A pleased expression. A keen eye. A need to succeed.

And a strong desire for acceptance.

I can use this.

I find fulfillment in a match well-played, she'd said back in that New York hotel room. Because this is a game to her. This is chess. I need to remember what a formidable opponent she is.

I smile at her again. I give her the same smile I give Sav and Mabel when I want them to believe I'm sober. The smile I give my therapist when I want her to believe I'm stable and improving. The smile I give Torren when I want him to believe I'm not harboring feelings of rejection and jealousy when it comes to his girlfriend.

I give Claire the smile I give everyone else when I need to get what I want, but because I don't expect her to buy it as easily, I throw in a wink. She blushes, and I mentally draw a tally in the Jonah column where I've been keeping score.

She's ahead, but I'll catch up quickly.

"Thank you again for having me, Mrs. Nilsson," I say, shaking her hand once more. "I had a great time."

"We did, too. Thank you so much. Feel free to come back anytime."

"Maybe next time we'll bring the rest of the band," Claire adds, and then we're climbing into the back seat and waving goodbye as the car drives away.

"I'm starving." I pull my phone out of my pocket and pull up the hotel app. "I'm going to order room service so it's at the room when we get back. What do you want?"

"I'm good."

My thumb hovers over the dinner selections and I glance at Claire. She's got her attention on her phone, and I can't help but wonder if she's texting her boyfriend.

Rich, cheating prick.

"You sure?" I bump her leg with my knee. "We were there for hours. You've got to be hungry."

She shrugs but still doesn't look at me. "I ate the cookies."

My jaw drops. "There were cookies? Why didn't you get me some?"

"It's my job to manage your PR, not feed you," she says dryly, and then she changes the subject. "You did great today, by the way. I think it went really well. And if all goes as planned, word of your visit should start trickling online within the next few hours. It will probably be global news before we leave for Lisbon tomorrow."

"You writing up a statement?"

She shakes her head. "No. We won't be making a statement."

"Why not?"

"Subtlety is key to making this seem organic."

I turn my head on the seatback so I can watch her fully. She's swiping and typing frantically, working nonstop and chewing on her lip anytime she's not talking to me. She's got these cute little lines between her eyebrows as she focuses, and a flash of her smile from earlier pops into my mind. Soft and sweet. Small, but so much more than I could handle.

Without overthinking, I reach into my pocket, pull out the wooden figurine I'd painted, and hold it out for her.

"Here, Trouble. I made you this."

She stops typing and looks down at the chess piece in my hand. Her forehead scrunches, and she lifts questioning eyes to mine. Instead of giving her an explanation, I arch a brow and wiggle the piece, drawing her attention back to it. Then slowly, she puts her phone in her lap and takes it.

I watch closely as she studies it, twirling it around between her delicate fingers, a myriad of emotions passing over her face. Confusion. Surprise.

As soon as I saw the small wooden queen, I thought of her. I grabbed it and painted it blue, like her eyes. It's strategy. It's a stealthy move.

I remember the way she reacted when I complimented her social media idea the other night. I saw the dejected look on her face when she'd finished that phone call with her cheating boyfriend.

Claire Davis is starved for praise, for attention, and that is something I can use.

She's too talented and smart, too beautiful, to be this insecure, but it is what it is. Insecurities aren't logical, and I have to calm the strong desire to pick her apart right here and now. To discover *why* she's like this. I want to crack her skull open and sift through her memories. I want to find every trauma. Every weakness. I want to know everything. What or who broke her confidence? A parent? A boyfriend? Something else?

Despite the protective surge I feel in my stomach—the yearning to find the people who hurt her and punish them for it—I can't deny that this discovery works in my favor. Women like Claire Davis just want to be seen. To be thought of.

This is strategy. This is chess, and I need to play the whole board.

When she sinks her teeth into her pillowy bottom lip—a move that goes straight to my dick—I let myself mentally draw another tally in the Jonah column. When she blushes again, my throat tightens, and I look away.

"Thank you," she whispers, putting the queen into her bag. "That was really...nice."

I nod, then pull out my phone to scroll on it as I speak to her. I don't know why, but I can't bring myself to look at her again. Not right now. I can't risk it.

"Yeah, well, I just wanted you to know I'm not going to fight you anymore. I doubted you and was an asshole, but you're proving me wrong. You're smart, and you're good at this, and I appreciate you. So..." I shrug. "Claire Davis, I'm glad you're my queen."

I hear her laugh, and I imagine that smile again. The happy one. The *real* one. And for the first time in years, I feel sleazy. I turn my body away from her and close my eyes.

"Wake me when we get to the hotel," I say abruptly.

I don't want to talk to her anymore.

"Okay."

Claire goes back to her phone, and I spend the rest of the ride listening to her breathe. I time my breaths with hers, each inhale like a knife to the chest. Filling my lungs with lavender and sugar. Taking hits of her like I need a fix.

I'm in control, I tell myself.

She'll be gone soon, and things can go back to normal.

FOURTEEN

Claire

"SO HOW'S IT GOING?"

I glance up from my phone to find Sav smiling at me. I hadn't even realized she'd moved seats. I smile.

"Good, I think. So far."

"I did an internet search this morning and everyone is buzzing about the youth center visit yesterday."

"I saw. Seems like it's going over well," I say with a nod, and then I flare my eyes. "I'm withholding judgment until the story's been out for forty-eight hours, though. You never know what kind of drama the tabloids will try to create."

Sav laughs. "Isn't that the truth." She glances down at her phone and starts to scroll. "But still...The headlines look promising. You did good."

My answering smile is tight, and I don't argue. She's right—early headlines are nothing but praise. Selfies from the kids have flooded social media, and news articles are circulating a quote from Ms. Nilsson that's saying how "wonderful" and "kind" it was that Jonah took time out of his day to visit the Stockholm Youth Center. So far, it's looking good, but I'm still waiting until I declare it successful.

"Are you planning to say anything?"

I shake my head and tell her what I told Jonah. "I've got a social media post scheduled for this afternoon, but it won't directly address the youth center. I think subtlety is key here. If we're going to do this and make it last, we need everyone to see it as authentic. If the media thinks we're only doing this for PR, we'll never win any of them over."

Sav smirks and arches a brow, but she says nothing. It makes me nervous.

"What?" I ask.

She shrugs. "You're good at this."

I laugh and shake my head. "No. Thanks, but no. Honestly, anyone with a background in marketing would have thought of it."

"I think you're being modest."

I laugh again, and it's even more awkward the second time.

"Seriously. There's a reason why Jo's dad trusted you with this. Give yourself some credit."

My face falls before I can catch myself, and I know my smile looks tight by the way her brow furrows.

"Thanks."

It's all I can manage to say, and the false cheer in my tone sounds so guilty in my head. I look away and rack my brain for a change of subject. If we stay on topic, I'm worried I'll spill what I've been thinking for the last few days. That I'm here just because I'm fucking my boss and not because I'm good at my job. On top of that, he chose me for this task not because he thinks I'm competent, but because he wanted to get me out of the way so he could fuck his secretary.

I can't help the way I flinch at the thoughts, and I have to give my head a little shake. Then I plaster a smile on my face and turn back to her.

"So do you guys always leave at the break of dawn?" I don't acknowledge the way she's studying me, eyes narrowed with concern. I just smile wider. "The private jet certainly made it easier, though. At least I didn't have to fumble through airport security at four in the morning."

Thankfully, she follows my lead on the subject change, even though I can tell she's still trying to puzzle out the previous one.

CLAIRE

"Sometimes we leave immediately after shows, and sometimes we leave early the morning after. We just do what Hammond tells us to do."

I sit up and turn around so I can survey the luxurious private jet. It has plush leather seating that can accommodate up to sixteen people. Several large chairs that recline into beds, two love-seat-type couches, and even two small private areas that can serve as bedrooms. There's also a small bathroom, a galley kitchenette, and two flatscreen televisions. Not even Conrad travels in this kind of luxury. It's only my second time flying with the band, so I'm still in awe, but everyone else is obviously used to it. To them, it's just another 4 a.m. flight in a forty-million-dollar piece of machinery.

Brynn is sleeping on a couch with her head in Mabel's lap while Mabel watches something on a tablet. She's wearing big pink headphones and pink pajamas, not a stitch of makeup on her face. Torren and Callie are curled up on another couch, while Levi and Jonah are sprawled out in two of the reclining chairs.

Jonah's chair is facing away from mine, so all I can see are his feet propped up on the footrest. I don't know if he's awake or sleeping. I don't know if he's reading or scrolling his phone. Briefly, I picture him with his glasses on with that serious expression on his face. Full lips tilted downward in a faint frown.

"Are you excited for Lisbon?"

I tear my gaze away from Jonah's feet and turn back to Sav. She's smirking again.

"Hm?"

"Are you excited for Lisbon?" she repeats, her tone playful. "You said you've never been, right?"

"Oh, yeah. I've never been out of America. I'm excited, but I'm here to work. I probably won't get much time to see anything."

Sav's smile turns mischievous, and it's got me sitting up straighter.

"What?"

She shrugs. "I know things were a little weird with Stockholm, but we usually get to the cities a few days early specifically to have the free time. You should have some fun. Get out and explore."

I shake my head. "No. Conrad—um, Mr. Henderson expects me to be working. I'll have the time off when the job is complete."

Sav snorts. "So, take Jo with you."

I frown and arch a brow, and she barks out a laugh. "Okay, good point."

As if I could trust Jonah not to be an asshole or run off and get wasted in a Portuguese bar or club or something. No. I'll stick with the hotel gym and spa. I open my mouth to say as much when the back of my neck prickles and my pulse picks up speed. Sav's eyes lift over my shoulder at the same time I'm hit with the scent of strong coffee and a faint, woodsy bodywash. The same kind I'd smell in the hotel bathroom after Jonah would shower.

Jonah doesn't say anything. He hovers behind me, and I don't bother turning to look up at him. I don't even know why. Something about his presence spikes my nerves, and I fist my hands in my lap. I'm working to steady my breathing when Sav drops her attention back to me. Her lips twitch as she purses them, trying to hide another of her smirks, but there is no ignoring the humor in her eyes.

"I'm going to go get some sleep," she says slowly, pushing to standing, then looks at Jonah once more. "Be nice."

She disappears behind me as Jonah steps in front of me. I force myself to tilt my head up, and my eyes run smack into his. Piercing blue and beguiling. It's enough to make my breath hitch.

"Double espresso."

He holds his hand out to me, and I look down to find a coffee mug. I take it, and he drops into the seat Sav just vacated. His legs are longer than hers, so when he stretches them out, they bracket mine. His boots dwarf my simple black ballet flats, and I find myself staring at them. I don't know why the sight captivates me, but it does.

I almost want to slide my foot closer to his and press them together. See what they look like side by side. The heel of my shoe beside the toe of his. The image of a pair of my heels sitting next to a pair of his boots in a closet flashes in my head, and I'm surprised by the excitement that stirs in my chest.

Then, as if reading my thoughts, his foot slides over and nudges mine. I snap my eyes back to his.

"Double espresso?" He leans forward and props his hands on his knees, then nods to the mug in my hands.

"Oh. Yeah. Thank you." I set the coffee on the small table beside my chair. "Did you need something?"

"Just needed a change of scenery."

He flicks his eyes behind me, and I hear a deep voice followed by a laugh. I just know it's Callie and Torren. I tilt my head to the side and narrow my eyes, studying Jonah's face. I know that expression. A familiar feeling stirs in my empty stomach, causing nausea and a slight buzzing in my ears.

"Are you jealous?"

He looks back at me, brief surprise passing over his face before he's stone again.

"No."

"You're lying. I know jealousy when I see it."

"Yeah? You're an expert, now?"

I jerk out a single nod. "When you're prone to jealousy, you recognize it in other people. You're jealous of Callie and Torren. But is it because you want what they have, or because you want what he has?"

Jonah scoffs a derisive laugh. It's not a confirmation, but it's not a denial, either. His jaw pops and his index finger starts picking at his thumb again. Such a subtle gesture that you wouldn't notice if you're not paying attention. I do. It's my job to pay attention. Then he turns that piercing gaze back on me, challenge and avoidance flashing over his face.

"Who are *you* jealous of, Trouble? Is it Callie?"

I roll my eyes. "You're so full of yourself I'm surprised you have room for food."

He shrugs and says nothing. I lower my voice, leaning forward so we aren't overheard.

"Having feelings for your bandmate's girlfriend is dangerous, Jonah."

His eyes bounce between mine, then he surprises me by reaching up and fingering one of the curls that has come loose from my clip. He gives it a small tug, then lets it bounce back.

"I was wondering if it would do that."

I shake my head with a sigh. "I'm serious. Have you talked about it with your therapist?"

His answering grin is sinister. "You're cute thinking I talk to my therapist about anything of importance."

"What?" My eyes widen with shock. "Therapy doesn't work if you're not honest."

I would know.

He tilts his head to the side and changes the subject.

"Why did 'Landslide' make you emotional? Is it connected to the men you mentioned? The ones who fucked with women you love?"

My heart stops, stealing my breath, and my eyes sting.

I feel…

I feel exposed. In an instant, I'm completely torn open and laid bare, and I hate it.

"That's none of your business." My whisper quakes. It contains none of the ire I try to fake but all the shock. All the fear and hurt. This is bad.

"Stop deflecting," I say, attempting to do exactly that. "Keeping things from your therapist is serious."

"You're going to make personal observations about me. It's only fair I get to do the same."

I grit my teeth and breathe through my nose, but I can't look away. I can't break eye contact as my stomach roils. My brain is so fuzzy that I don't think I could respond even if I wanted to. Then he shocks me again.

"I'm not jealous, but I'm struggling with feelings of abandonment, and I don't need a therapist to tell me that. I understand my emotions and actions perfectly. Callie chose Torren, and Torren chose Callie, and now I'm stuck with you."

I flinch, but I don't let myself dwell on that last sentence. I make myself take advantage of this rare moment of honesty. Not for leverage but for understanding.

"Did you and Callie date?"

His lips curl up slightly on one side.

"No. But we fucked. All three of us." My jaw drops, and he laughs quietly before continuing. "Unfortunately, I didn't realize how hard it would be to see someone every day after I'd fucked them. It was supposed to be casual—just a one-time thing—and she was supposed to leave. She didn't leave. Now I have to watch her with Torren, and I feel like I've lost my best friend to her. It's brought up a lot of repressed feelings of inadequacy, and I'm still trying to work through them."

I blink at him. He grins. "See? I don't need therapy. I need a lobotomy and a lifetime supply of Xanax."

The last confession rings in my ears, and I make a mental note to hide my prescription. I know his drug of choice now. Or one of them, at least, and it's the same as my brother's. But his explanation...I wasn't prepared to relate to him. I wasn't prepared for this version of Jonah.

I'm out of my depth. I shake my head to erase the thought.

"Your turn."

I look back at him and chew on the inside of my cheek. I shake my head again.

"I gave you something I haven't even given my therapist, Claire. Give me something back."

I frown. He's right. If this is going to work, he has to trust me.

"Okay. 'Landslide' triggered me because Fleetwood Mac was my best friend's favorite band."

"She dead?"

I fold my lips between my teeth while blinking away tears. "Might as well be. We don't talk anymore."

"Why?"

I stare at him and breathe slowly. His expression gives me pause. Curious and interested. I can't tell if he's looking at me like a person or a research subject. I think it's a little of both.

"That's more than I'm willing to tell."

"You still owe me more to make it even."

"This isn't the trauma Olympics, Jonah. It shouldn't be a quid pro quo."

"So it was traumatic?"

"Wasn't yours?"

He pauses, considering my question, and then he nods. "It shouldn't be quid pro quo, but it is. You owe me more. I don't want to tell my secrets to someone I don't know."

I turn my head away and grind my teeth. Nausea climbs up my throat. My forehead and upper lip dot with sweat. Then his index finger hooks softly under my chin, and he coaxes me to face him again. It's the concern flickering in his eyes that loosens my jaw and my tongue.

"The men who messed with the women I loved were also people I loved," I confess.

His eyes widen with surprise, and I grimace.

"My dad and my brother. My mom and my best friend. My dad was just a selfish, cheating asshole, but my brother struggled with addiction."

Now that I'm talking, I can't stop. It's falling from my lips like rushing rapids. Crashing through my throat and over my tongue like they're jagged rocks, relieving pressure yet causing pain just as strong. I close my eyes against the sting of tears.

I clench my fists in my lap.

"I was so tied up in my own mess...I was trying and failing to keep my own shit together, keep my mom from having a nervous breakdown, keep myself from self-destructing, that I ended up blaming him for everything. My dad wasn't there, but my brother was. He became my scapegoat, I guess. But my best friend...the only person I had... She loved him. She chose him, and it broke her, and I was *jealous*. Jealous and hurt and so fucking angry at them both."

His hands wrap around my fists. My attention falls to the contact, my eyes opening and releasing the flood of tears. The cuticle on his thumb is picked red, dried blood specked on the bottom corner of his nail. He hurts himself when he can't handle his emotions. I relate to that, too. I close my eyes again and force that realization to the back of my mind.

"I watched my best friend change. She started to act like him—careless and angry. And then..."

I breathe through my panic as memories flood my head. My brother and best friend, broken and bleeding in different ways. When I speak again, there's no hiding the waver in my voice. The weakness. The regret.

"I thought they were bad for each other. I thought if I could separate them, just for a little while, they'd see it, too." I lift my gaze back to his face. "I had an opportunity, and I took it, and I failed them both."

His eyes are narrowed, almost angry, and a chill skates over my skin. If I didn't know any better, I'd think it was protectiveness I see in his expression. But then he speaks, and it's toneless. Sterile. I'm a lab rat, and he sounds just like his fucking father.

"Neither of them has forgiven you?"

I shrug. "I don't blame them."

Sav's words from days ago come back in a rush. *You have to forgive yourself, even if they can't.* It makes me want to laugh. She's giving me too much credit.

"Where are they now?"

I give him a sad smile. "Together and thriving. They have a son. My nephew. Gabriel Christopher. I never see him."

Jonah blows out a slow breath and shakes his head. "That's rough."

I shrug again. "You know the funny thing? What you said about me being my family's pride and joy? I never go home. I spent Thanksgiving and Christmas working so I could avoid the discomfort and awkwardness of a family get-together. My mom married my best friend's dad, so not only is she with my brother, but she's my stepsister." I huff out a laugh. "Half of my family hates me."

"Wait...your brother married his stepsister?"

He's trying so hard not to look weirded out that I laugh again.

"One big happy family."

"Isn't that, like, kind of incestuous?"

I snort. "No. My mom didn't marry her dad until we were seventeen. And anyway, you don't have room to talk."

He arches a brow. "I never fucked my own stepsister."

I arch a brow back. "No, but this band is one tangled web of love affairs. Sav and Torren. Torren and Callie. You and Callie. You and Torren."

"I never fucked Torren," he protests with a grin. "I just fucked *with* him."

I laugh louder. "Whatever. My point is, this *band* is incestuous. Mabel's the only one who hasn't had sex with one of you, but maybe it's only a matter of time."

Now he laughs. "Nah. Mabes is bi, but she prefers women, and Sav is only about dick. And now she's only about Levi. Mabel's safe."

We fall back into silence, gazes locked, both smiling slightly despite ripping ourselves open. The tear tracks on my cheeks have cooled, and the longer I look at Jonah, the warmer I feel. Then I realize his hands are still clasping mine, his mangled thumb rubbing softly back and forth over my skin.

I release myself from him and sit back. He doesn't, though. He stays with his elbows on his knees, invading the space in front of me.

"Thanks for sharing that with me, Trouble," he says, his voice low.

Goosebumps prickle my arms and the back of my neck. I force a tight smile. "Ditto."

Finally, mercifully, he sits back in his seat. I take a deep breath, then stand. "Excuse me. I'll be right back."

"Your espresso is probably cold."

"It's fine. I'll still drink it."

Then I quickly make my way to the bathroom. I barely get the door shut behind me before I heave foamy bile into the sink.

FIFTEEN

Jonah

THAT WAS A MISTAKE.

I thought telling her something personal was a calculated risk to get ahead. I thought I could handle it. It wasn't supposed to humanize her. It wasn't supposed to make her relatable.

Understanding her was a strategic move. It backfired. It's been two days, and I'm still fucking rattled.

I stick my hands in my hair and pull. My knees bounce. My chest aches. I try to fend off the panic, but I fail. I've been failing a fucking lot lately. And because I apparently can't handle anything these days, I go to my stash and chase the pills with one of the airplane bottles I bought off a roadie. I swallow the self-loathing and anxiety with the liquor.

I drop onto my bed and listen to the shower. My current weakness is in there, washing the sweat off her body from our workout. She'll come out smelling like lavender and sugar, and I'll have to go back to surviving on shallow breaths. Oxygen deprivation is the only way I can tolerate being in confined spaces with Claire Davis. It's not surprising. Breath play has always been my kink, and she has such a pretty little neck.

We've got another partition in this hotel room. It's the same kind as the one we had in Stockholm. I can see her silhouette through it. It's such a strange form of temptation. I'm attracted to her shadow and captivated by her trauma. Drawn to darkness and pain. There's probably a song in there somewhere, but the creativity disappears as the chemical haze descends. I haven't written a song in years. I've resigned myself to the fact that I've lost the ability.

I pick up my phone and open my social media profile. Claire's posted more since the "Landslide" cover. There's a carousel of pictures from the Stockholm shows. *Stockholm, it's been real* is the caption. A smile forms on my lips. It sounds like something I'd post, but it's funny thinking of it in Claire's sexy voice.

I scroll through the carousel of photos. Most are of me, but there are a few of the whole band. I didn't even know she was taking pictures at every show. Something about that sends a wave of warmth over my body.

I tell myself it's the vodka.

The next post is a video of me playing the chorus of "Blackbird" at the youth center. There's no caption this time. You can only see the tops of the kids' heads as they watch, but my image is so clear that you can see the lines on my face and the strands of my hair. The audio is crisp, and a few times, you can hear the kids whispering. It's just enough to confirm the reports of my presence at the Stockholm Youth Center, but nothing more.

It's subtle, just like she'd said it should be.

Subtlety is key to making this seem organic.

I close my eyes and stifle a groan.

She's so fucking good at this, and it's already working. I think she might even believe what she's selling. We're lying to the whole world, and she doesn't even realize it.

I scroll to the next post. It's me on the plane ride here. I'm slouched in one of the recliner chairs with one of my legs thrown over the arm. Sprawled out and taking up space. The pose makes me look like an asshole, but I'm also wearing my glasses and reading a book. It almost seems to challenge the previous assumption. I'm sure this was Claire's intention.

JONAH

Strategic. Calculated.

Brilliant.

I don't understand all the thoughts spinning in my head or the emotions building in my chest. It's so opposite of what I'm used to, and it's scary. I haven't felt fear like this in a long time.

I fucking hate it.

I hate it because I'm not just starting to understand her, I've started to *like* her. To respect her. I'm a little in awe of her, to be honest, and that's probably the biggest problem. Developing feelings for my nanny could cause a serious fucking mess.

The plan was to charm her. Not be charmed.

My stupidity blends with my curiosity, and I search for Claire's social media profile. I find her easily. The excitement I feel when her account is public is embarrassing, but there aren't a lot of pictures.

Most of the photos are of her in sexy little dresses showing off that figure I've started seeing in my sleep. Sky-high heels flaunting her long legs. Lipstick that makes her look ready to be kissed. Her straightened hair pisses me off, though. I prefer the curls. I like how they look when she's freshly showered. How they coil at the nape of her neck when she's sweaty and running on the treadmill.

There are a few photos in Central Park. A latte in a quaint little coffee shop. A tiny Christmas tree in front of a rickety, old window. It must be in her apartment. It makes me wonder what the rest of it looks like.

Does she have pictures on the walls?

What color are her bedsheets?

Does she have a bookshelf?

The questions form rapid fire in my head, but everything goes silent when I scroll to the next picture. It's of a man's hand resting on her thigh, just at the hem of another of her sexy dresses. He's wearing a suit with gold cuff links, and I see the edge of a gold watch peeking out of his sleeve.

It's her boyfriend.

Jealousy flares hot in my chest and stomach. I can tell from the hand that the man is older, probably by a lot, and that pisses me off. In my head, he's this rich cheating asshole who preys on younger women. Women like Claire. Women who act confident but crave praise and acceptance. Women with daddy issues.

I tap the photo to see if there's a tag so I can stalk the fucker's profile, but there isn't one. I study the picture as if I'll find his name or social security number hidden in the blurred-out corners, but then my eyes fall on something else. Something worse.

His cuff link.

It's half in shadow, but I recognize the *C* engraved in loopy cursive font. I know for a fact there's an *H* next to it. No one else would notice, but I know these cuff links. I know them because my brother and I gave them to my dad for Christmas years ago. He thanked Theo but not me.

Accusations and assumptions crash into me, but I breathe through it. Instead of storming into the bathroom and demanding answers, I pull up the number for my father's office and dial his extension. I'll poke around for clues through him, first. He's always been easy for me to read. The phone rings three times before a woman answers.

"Conrad Henderson's office."

I clear my throat. "Who am I speaking with?"

"This is Mr. Henderson's office manager, Dierdre."

My heart stops.

What. The. Fuck.

I don't know what to say, so I hang up. The comfortable haze shatters. The awe and respect I'd felt for Claire moments earlier dissipate. The affection? Gone. I'm seething. Rage and jealousy and hatred thrash around in my skull. My head pounds as my heart slams into my rib cage.

I can't fucking believe this.

Claire Davis is fucking my father. She probably has been for months. And I've been dreaming of her naked. I've started fantasizing about her...

And she's fucking my father.

I click off my phone and throw it across the room. I stand from the bed and pace. I have to handle this. I have to calm the fuck down and think.

I have to fucking figure this out.

This is a good thing. This knocked sense into me. This isn't a game anymore. It's war, and the stakes are high.

And this new information? This is the fucking weapon I needed. This is the kill shot.

But before I pull the trigger, I'm going to punish Claire Davis. I'm going to make her feel my wrath.

I'm going to give her exactly what she deserves.

SIXTEEN

Claire

"YOU'RE OVERREACTING."

My jaw drops. I can't fucking believe the audacity of this man. And to say it in that tone. Like I'm annoying him. Like I'm a fucking child.

I take a deep breath, keep my voice low, and once again, defend myself.

"I'm not overreacting. I'm making a decision about my life based on my own observations. You've been avoiding me. I know you've been out with Diedre because, unlike me, she has no tact. It's been all over her social media. Apparently, she doesn't care if everyone knows and neither do you."

He sighs. "My love—"

"Don't," I say, cutting him off.

I hate that this is making me want to cry, but I won't let him hear it. I've wasted too much time and emotion on him. He's never appreciated it. It stops now.

"I'm not changing my mind. I've had a lot of time to think about it, actually. It was solidified by you not answering my calls or texts. The pictures on Diedre's social media were the cherry on top. I can't do this with you anymore. It's not good for either of us."

Silence.

He doesn't protest. Not right away. It makes me uneasy. It makes me worried for what he'll say eventually once he gathers his thoughts.

And then he speaks, and my fears are confirmed.

"The company will be sad to lose you, but I suppose it's for the best."

"What?" I choke out. It's all I can say. My voice is lodged in my throat.

"Claire, you have to understand the position this puts me in. I cannot see you at work every day—"

"You never see me. We're separated by thirteen floors."

"—and I cannot take the risk of you using this against me."

I gasp. "I wouldn't do that, and you know it. I haven't said anything—"

"Women do these things when they've been scorned."

I laugh. It's strangled, sorrow wrapped in fury, and it's honestly sad how not surprised I am. For as angry as I am at him, though, I'm more angry at myself.

I let this happen.

I let it get this far.

I should have ended it the day I saw him in that boardroom. I should have been more vigilant about learning who he was before I fell for him.

I should have been fucking smarter. I sneer even though he can't see me.

"Fine. I'll finish up this job, and then I'm done. I expect a glowing letter of recommendation, and then I don't want to hear from you again. If you attempt to blackball me, I'm taking this scandal to the tabloids."

He laughs.

He actually fucking laughs at me.

"It's your word against mine. No one will believe you."

It's a slap to the face. My cheek almost stings at the thought. And then I actually growl.

"I guess we'll have to wait and see, then. Fuck you."

I hang up before he can respond. I'm panting and sweating, adrenaline pumping through my body so rapidly that I feel dizzy.

I lied to him. It was a bluff. But I'll drag this out as long as I can. As long as I need to. He attempts to call me again, and I push ignore. I rush to my laptop and open the file for the MixMosaic campaign. He calls again, and I hit ignore again.

Then I delete every contribution I made for this campaign from the drive. Every design. Every idea. I remove it from the drive, then from my computer and cloud. It's done. The tech department may be able to retrieve it, but I won't worry about that now.

Just as I delete my company account, Conrad tries to ring through once more.

I answer it and say one sentence.

"Call me again and I'll get a restraining order."

I hang up and block his number. I wipe at the tears on my cheeks. I take deep breaths. I step off the balcony and make my way to the bathroom, but then the door to the suite opens. I check the time on my phone. Hammond said the band meeting would last an hour, and it's been exactly that.

I glance up at Jonah and force a smile, flattening my palm over my roiling stomach.

"How'd it go?"

He narrows his eyes. "Why have you been crying?"

I could say anything. Make any excuse. I'd watched a sad video. I'd read something upsetting. For some reason, though, I give him a sliver of the truth.

"They're angry tears."

His eyes slowly scan my face. His jaw pops. Then he takes two steps toward me.

"No one should have the power to make you feel like this. Especially not him."

My eyebrows slant. I flinch. Then I laugh awkwardly. I wave him off and turn away.

"Trust me. I know."

I turn my back to him and make my way to the bathroom. I can feel him staring at me. I'm steps from the door when his voice stops me again.

"We've got a change of plans today. Don't straighten your hair. Don't put on makeup. Wear tennis shoes. The car leaves in twenty minutes."

I turn around to look at him. "We have a full day, Jonah. We can't just cancel it."

He rolls his eyes. "Yeah, I saw the calendar. It's nothing we can't do when we get back. If it helps, you can use this as a photo op."

I tilt my head and study him. I don't trust him, not fully, but I'm excited anyway.

"Does it involve drugs, alcohol, or getting naked?"

He smirks in that way that makes my heart race. "No, no, and only if you're willing."

I ignore him and narrow my eyes. "What do you have planned?"

"You'll see," he says, his lips stretching across his face in a mischievous smile. He looks almost boyish. Playful. Damn if it doesn't make me cave. Then he checks his watch. "You've got fifteen minutes now."

I wait thirty more seconds just to draw out the ruse of my reluctance, and then I force an exasperated sigh. I bypass the bathroom and walk straight into the bedroom, closing the door behind me. Today was a workout rest day, so I'm still in my pajamas, and I change quickly into a tennis skirt, tank top, and sneakers. I pull my curly hair into a ponytail, avoid the mirror, and head back into the main room of the suite.

As I cross the carpet toward him, his eyes drag down my body, then back up. I don't comment on it. I don't snarl. I just...let him do it. I step in front of him, and he nods. He grabs a brown leather jacket from the couch and heads to the door. I follow.

We meet José near the elevator, walk to the car in silence, and just as I'm reaching for the car door handle, Jonah stuns me by opening it for me. I freeze, just long enough to give myself away, and the low chuckle that escapes him makes my nipples harden. I feel him move closer, his head hovering just above my shoulder, his woodsy bodywash invading my space, and his breath tickles the shell of my ear.

"Just get in the car, Trouble. We don't want to be late."

I narrow my eyes and do as he says. Then he slides in behind me.

"So where are we going?" I ask. Jonah doesn't look up from his phone. "Jonah." He doesn't acknowledge me. I scoff and look at José. "Where are we going, José?"

I watch him tilt his head up, and even though he's wearing sunglasses,

I know he's looking to Jonah for permission. I see Jonah's head jerk once in my periphery, and then José ignores me too.

I scoff again and resist the urge to stomp my foot on the car floor.

"Jonah, tell me where we're going."

Finally, he looks at me and arches a brow. "Relax, Davis. It's a surprise. You don't want to ruin the surprise, do you?"

I scowl at him. "What if I don't like surprises?"

He drops his attention back to his phone. "You'll like this one. Trust me."

Trust him? I don't even trust myself half the time. I fold my arms over my chest. Yes, I'm pouting—I truly don't like surprises—but the way he's smirking at his phone irritates me more. I don't like the way it makes me want to smile, too.

When neither Jonah nor José speak again, I sink into the plush leather seat and turn my attention out the window. A lush forest quickly replaces the buildings of the city of Lisbon, our multilane highway passing right through.

"What's this?"

"Parque de Monsanto," Jonah says. "It's a national forest."

"In the middle of the city?"

He nods. "Think of it like a much larger, more environmentally conscious version of Central Park."

"Hmmm." I look back out the window. "It's pretty."

He hums in agreement, and we fall back into silence. Soon, the dense forest thins, and buildings again join the scenery until José is slowing the car to a stop and pulling into a parking spot on the street.

"We're here? Where are we?"

"Belém." Jonah smirks and jerks his head toward his door. "Let's go, Trouble."

Jonah climbs out of the car, and I follow, with José stepping up behind us.

"What are we going to do?"

Jonah laughs, but he doesn't answer. I sigh and follow him toward a tall man wearing shorts and a polo. I can tell by his smile that he's been waiting for us, and that elevates my already sky-high curiosity. A friend? I didn't think Jonah had friends. Apart from the band, anyway.

When we stop in front of the man, he shakes Jonah's hand, then mine.

"Claire, this is Davi, our tour guide. Davi, this is Claire. She's my nanny."

I ignore Jonah and give Davi a smile. "Nice to meet you, Davi."

"You as well." He looks back at Jonah. "Are you ready?"

"We're ready."

"Great." He claps his hands together once and smiles. "We've got three stops today. *Mosteiro dos Jerónimos, Padrão dos Descobrimentos, Torre de Belém.* That's the Jerónimos Monastery, the Monument to the Discoveries, and the Belém Tower. We will be walking. It's a little over a kilometer, but there will be stairs. Are you up to it?"

Jonah laughs. "Claire's up to it. She runs treadmill marathons before breakfast."

I snort out a laugh and look up into Jonah's playful eyes. "We might need to carry Jonah, though. He's pitiful and out of shape."

"Hey, I've been training." He nudges me with his elbow. "But if I need a piggyback ride, I'll let you know."

"You'll let José know. There's no way you're getting on my back."

"We'll see."

His lips curl into a devious, sinful smile, and I know his comment was suggestive. My cheeks heat, and I look back at Davi. I clear my throat and then nod with a forced smile.

"Ready when you are."

Davi takes us to Jerónimos Monastery first, and it's fascinating. The Gothic architecture is beautiful, and as Davi tells us the history of the site, I become even more enthralled.

"This place is older than our entire country," I whisper to Jonah as we walk through the halls, and he laughs.

"Most places over here are."

"I never thought I'd be here, though. It's different experiencing it in person."

He catches me off guard by throwing his arm over my shoulders. I flinch and stiffen, his bodywash and deodorant engulfing me. I don't move away, though. I'm too stunned. It's taking all my focus just to put one foot in front of the other.

"Stick with me, and you'll experience a lot more."

A laugh bubbles out of me, so loud that it echoes off the centuries-old stone walls. His grip tightens around me as he stifles his own laugh.

"That line can't possibly work for you." I elbow him lightly, then shrug away. His arm drops to his side, but his smile remains fixed on his face.

"I'll let you know."

I shake my head, a blush once again creeping up my neck. My ears heat with the blood rush, and I look away. I don't speak to him for the rest of the monastery tour. Not even in the Church of Santa Maria, despite my desire to share my awe with someone.

With *him*.

I don't like how quickly he's disarmed me today. Am I that starved for affection that one kind gesture turns me into a blushing idiot? This man is horrid. He's repulsive, and I shouldn't be blushing over him. I must have lost my damn mind.

Jonah breaks the silence on the way to the Monument to the Discoveries, and it irritates me. While I don't want to experience all of this alone, it's easier to ignore my mixed feelings regarding him when I can pretend he's not here at all.

"So?"

"So *what?*"

I glance over at him. He exudes *cool*. Too cool for me. A pair of knockoff Wayfarers shields his blue eyes, his bleached hair is once again pulled into a bun, and his hands are shoved in his pockets as he walks. He doesn't take his eyes off the ground in front of him, and I find myself wishing they were on me. The desire crashes into me out of nowhere. It's so surprising that I rip my attention off his profile and stare at the sidewalk.

Goddamn it.

We need to go back to not speaking.

"What did you think? Did you like it?"

I nod and keep it curt. "I did."

"Belém is one of my favorite places to visit when we're in Lisbon."

"What?" The statement piques my curiosity, and even though I shouldn't, I engage further. "You've been here before?"

"This is my fourth time. I like history."

I shake my head, my brow furrowing as I let myself look at him again. "Why are we doing this, then?"

He smirks at the ground. "Sav said you'd never been out of the States. Thought you'd enjoy it."

I blink at him, the kind gesture shocking me into silence, and then he finally looks at me.

"Did I think wrong?"

"Oh." I shake my head. "No. No, this is great. Thank you."

I love it, actually, but I don't tell him that. I can't. I shouldn't. Then he hits me with a smile so wide, it gives me chills. I have to look away again.

"Good. I appreciate what you're doing, Trouble. Even if you are a pain in my ass."

I laugh, but I don't respond. I don't say anything. I don't trust myself not to let my errant thoughts loose into the universe if I open my mouth. Every smile he sends me keeps me buzzing, though. Every time he nudges me with his elbow or throws his arm over my shoulders, my chest tightens, and it takes all my strength not to reach for him. Not to sink into his hold.

This is bad.

I just broke up with his father, and now I'm...I don't even know. Crushing?

Am I *crushing* on Jonah Hendrix? On my ex's son?

No. No way.

I cannot stand this man. He is a liar. An addict. A slut. He's spoiled and full of himself, and he thinks rules don't apply to him.

He is quite literally *the worst.*

I do not have a crush.

I'm just feeling dejected from the termination of my almost year-long relationship. That's all. It's off-centering to see Jonah not just cooperating but being kind. Being thoughtful. I'm vulnerable, and it's nice to have someone paying attention to me.

It's all surface-level bullshit, but it's nice, even if it is coming from an asshole rock star with an attitude problem and an inflated ego.

I'm stewing in my thoughts—scolding myself and explaining away the stupid butterflies that keep trying to erupt in my stomach—when Jonah takes my hand in his. I narrow my eyes at him.

"What are you doing?"

He smiles down at me, then nods to the road we're about to cross. "Safety first."

I roll my eyes, even though he can't see it through my sunglasses, but I don't break the hold. His hand is warm and dominates mine. The calloused pads of his fingers reach almost to my wrist, and I can feel them pressing into my skin. Holding me close.

Safety first.

He doesn't let go when we're safely across the road.

Neither do I.

Not during the tour of the Monument to the Discoveries, and not during the walk to Belém Tower. Even when he points out a stone rhinoceros-shaped gargoyle carved into one of the tower's turrets, he doesn't release my hand. He just lifts mine with his, pointing briefly with his index finger before dropping our hands back down between us. Why he doesn't just point with his other hand, I don't know, but the gesture makes my stomach flip and my brows furrow. I'm excited and confused. It's dizzying.

I have well and truly lost my damn mind.

He doesn't break our connection until it's necessary for ascending the narrow spiral staircase to reach the top of the tower, and when he does, I feel the loss immediately.

I fold my hand into a fist, wishing I could imprint the shape of him into my palm, then wishing to lobotomize myself, because what the actual fuck is that thought? I shove it out of my head, but then we start up the stairs, and he places one hand gently on my waist. He leans over my shoulder and puts his mouth to my ear.

"So you don't fall."

I can't suppress the shiver he elicits, and when I force a laugh, it's shaky and breathless. The whole climb to the top, I can only think of his hand on my waist. The heat it produces, seeping through my Shirt. The thought of his calluses on my bare skin.

I'm grateful when we reach the top, and I step out of his hold. Then my breath disappears for a different reason.

"Oh wow," I whisper. "It's...It's..."

"Beautiful."

I nod. "Yeah. It is."

It's a sweeping, 360 view of the area, made even more breathtaking in the golden glow of the late afternoon sun. My eyes follow the Tagus all the way to where the river meets the Atlantic, and the water seems to sparkle. When I spin around, I can see Belém.

I walk to the far wall and peer over the stone. I take in the picturesque coastline and breathe in the salty air. When a cool breeze makes me shiver and causes goosebumps to rise on my skin, I wrap my arms around my chest. Then, without warning, the scent of leather and bodywash engulfs me as Jonah wraps his leather jacket around my shoulders. I had been so distracted by him that I'd forgotten José had been carrying it.

I look up into Jonah's face with wide, curious eyes, and he winks at me.

"It gets cooler at night this time of year. I brought it in case you needed it."

I blink, words escaping me, and unexpected tears sting my eyes. I quickly turn my head back toward the water.

He's being too kind. Too thoughtful.

Too much like what I've always looked for and never found.

Jonah traces his fingers over the nape of my neck, making me shiver again, and he tugs on a strand of my hair. I know he straightened it just to let it coil back into a curl.

"I love how it does that."

I fold my lips between my teeth in an attempt to tame my smile. I try, but I fail, and I'm grateful he can't see it. I snuggle down into his jacket, though, and I tell myself it's just for the warmth. It's not the smell or the sentiment. It's not because of him.

I tell myself this, but I know it's a lie.

I also know I'm totally fucked.

SEVENTEEN

Claire

WE GET BACK to the hotel around nine.

We stayed at the tower until sunset, and then he took me to dinner.

I've tried so hard not to stress over the dinner, but the cuisine was unfamiliar, and now I have no idea how many calories I need to burn off. Jonah wouldn't let me order anything simple. He insisted on dessert. I've been fixating on it since, and that anxiety only spikes my feelings of failure. One unplanned meal, and I'm teetering on the edge of panic.

Eight weeks of treatment up in smoke, and I let a man unworthy of me light the match.

No. That's not true. He may have handed me the match, but I'm the one who struck it and set everything ablaze.

The realization only makes my stomach roil. It only makes everything worse. My throat burns. My teeth ache. My bones and limbs grow heavy, and I feel everything I worked for slipping away.

I never should have stopped seeing my therapist.

I never should have—

"You okay?"

I shake my head and whip my attention toward Jonah. His eyes are on me, assessing me as if peeling back my carefully constructed layers and seeing every flaw underneath.

"Yeah. Fine. Just tired."

"You've been off since dinner."

I look away and busy myself with kicking off my shoes and pulling my hair from the ponytail.

"I'm not feeling well. I'm going to get ready for bed."

He hums, his stare never leaving me, and I feel like he knows I'm lying. When I walk into the bedroom to gather my toiletries and pajamas, he follows, and I can feel his gaze on my back.

"I'm sorry I didn't take any pictures today," I say into my suitcase. "I forgot it was supposed to be a photo op."

He doesn't answer right away, and when I stand and look at him, he's still staring at me. His eyes are narrowed in thought, and he's picking at his thumb again.

"It's fine," he says finally. "I didn't do it as a PR stunt, anyway."

The soft smile that forms on my lips is an honest one. It momentarily quiets the screaming in my head.

"Thank you again, Jonah. I really, really enjoyed today."

He nods, then moves toward his side of the room. He waits until he disappears behind the partition before he answers.

"So did I."

I watch his shadow as he changes. His arms rise as he pulls off his shirt. His back bows as he kicks off his jeans. I can hear the clothing fall to the floor, and I swear the jangle of his belt echoes through the otherwise quiet room. When he finally drops into bed, I turn and walk calmly into the bathroom.

I go through the motions of my nightly routine. I change into pajamas. I carry out my six-step skincare regimen. The whole time, I work to keep my eyes on the sink until they're pulled to the mirror, and I spend too long staring at my reflection. I focus on the way my face has filled out, but instead of cringing, I tell myself it's a good thing. It's what I wanted. My eyes are brighter. My hair is fuller. I look healthy. I haven't ruined that. Yet.

My attention falls to the curls at my hairline. Out of curiosity, I reach up and finger one. I tug on it, pulling it straight and letting it bounce back. My lips curl into a small smile.

I love how it does that.

Jonah's voice echoes in my head once more as I walk to my bed. I pull back the duvet and climb onto the soft mattress, then I do what I always do. I grab my phone, log into my social media, and go to my ex-best-friend's profile. There's nothing new, so I go to my brother's profile. I know he never posts, but I'm still disappointed when I find nothing.

I decide to check the follower count on Jonah's profile. It's been growing by the thousands every day. He'll be to one million soon if it keeps going this route. When his profile appears on my screen, though, my eyes don't go to the follower count. They go straight to the most recent photo. It's not one I scheduled, and it makes my entire body tingle.

I click on the picture to enlarge it and blink several times before I'm convinced it's real. There's no caption, but it's time-stamped only fifteen minutes ago. He must have posted it when I was in the bathroom.

The photo is of me on the roof of Belém Tower. I'm not tagged, and my back is to the camera as I look out toward the ocean. You can't see my face, just my curly hair in the ponytail and Jonah's large leather jacket draped over my shoulders. The like count just keeps rising. Thousands and thousands of likes, and I'm grateful that the comments are turned off. I don't know how this will affect my PR campaign, but in this moment, I don't care.

I'm just...warm. Warm and blushing, and trying like hell to stifle a laugh.

I close my eyes and drop my phone onto the bed beside me. It means nothing. It's just a picture. But...

I slap my hand over my face and swallow back a groan.

But *fuck.*

I fall asleep grinning, replaying scenes from the day in Belém. At some point, my dreams turn heated. Stolen kisses. Possessive stares. Sensual caresses. And just before it becomes full-on X-rated, reality crashes through.

Jonah turns into Conrad. He says terrible things. He belittles me. Berates me. Beats me down into myself until my own insecurities are crashing over me, stealing my breath and my power. Drowning me in guilt.

Women do these things when they've been scorned.

He's right. I have done terrible, terrible things. Broken hearts. Ruined lives. My best friend flashes in my head. My brother. Their son.

And then I wake up.

Jonah's deep breathing is the only sound in the dark room, and quietly, I climb out of my bed and tiptoe into the bathroom. I empty my stomach into the toilet with tears streaming down my face. I rinse my mouth twice, swishing for at least thirty seconds each time, and then I brush my teeth with my eyes closed so I don't have to see my reflection in the mirror. I take a Xanax, lie back down in bed, and take comfort in the familiar feeling of emptiness.

I tell myself that I'll call my therapist in the morning.

THE FIRST SHOW in Lisbon is a good one.

Just like every show in Stockholm, this one is sold out. The energy in the stadium is palpable, and I find myself buzzing along with it. The excitement becomes contagious, and for the first time, I watch the entire show. I, of course, take photos for Jonah's social media, but I pay more attention to the show outside of the viewfinder this time. I let myself really *see* The Hometown Heartless perform, and the experience is unlike any live show I've ever seen.

Sav's stage presence is legendary. She plays the crowd like she plays her guitar. She laughs and it vibrates through the audience. I feel every ounce of emotion she puts behind the songs she sings, and I know without a shadow of a doubt that she'll go down in history as a music icon. She's larger than life, and everyone in this stadium knows it.

It's not just her, though. The whole band has a visible, almost tangible, chemistry. They're so in sync, so tapped into each other, that I suddenly understand how they've made it this long. I get how they managed to hold on through all the challenges and dark times. I get why they're fighting so hard for Jonah. They're a family, and I'm envious.

A feeling of sadness washes over me. What would it be like to have something like that? Where every flaw is known and your family loves you, anyway. Where you're not alone when you're hurting or struggling. Where people fight for you when you can't fight for yourself. I can't even fathom it. Even in the best friendship I've ever had, I still kept secrets. I still spent every day pretending to be something I wasn't. And when it mattered the most, I let down the people I loved.

I'm so lost in my thoughts that I don't even realize the show is coming to an end. The crowd roars so loud that I have to put my hands over my ears, but I can't help but laugh at the smirk on Sav's face. She always looks like she's about to pull a prank or tell a secret. Her charisma is unmatched.

"Lisbon, you've been beautiful. This is a show we won't forget."

Sav's grin grows as she pauses, and it feels like the crowd takes a collective inhale. They're waiting for something, and I don't understand it until Sav leans in to speak once more.

"Now, Lisbon, even though this is good night..."

"It's not goodbye," the crowd shouts back in unison, and Sav's laugh booms through the stadium.

"But just in case, so you don't forget us, back there is Mabel on drums, over here is Jonah on guitar, that's Torren on bass, my name is Sav Loveless, and we're The Hometown Heartless. Thank you so much, Lisbon! We love you! Have a great night."

The audience cheers as the lights dim, then one by one, the band members walk off stage. Then the crowd starts to stomp and chant *encore, encore*, and I swear I can feel the stadium shake. I wouldn't be surprised to learn in the morning that it registered as an earthquake.

The chanting and stomping don't stop until the lights come back up just enough to show four shadowy figures moving back to their instruments. The chants turn into cheers, the stage lights brighten, and The Hometown Heartless launch into another song. This one is the only song I recognize, and I'm excited to be able to sing along on the chorus.

I understand fandoms now. There's something to be said for loving something so fiercely and bonding with millions of people over that love.

It's a connection unlike any other, especially on a scale this massive. When the final notes of the encore song fade out and the stadium lights come on, I'm actually sad that it's over. Sad and already looking forward to tomorrow's show.

Because I was standing behind the barricade, I'm able to avoid the mass exodus of bodies as everyone pours through the exit doors. Instead of going to the dressing room, though, I have one of the security guards take me back to the hotel. As amazing as that show was, I need just a little longer before I have to see Jonah again. With any luck, I can pretend to be asleep before he gets back to the suite.

He's messing with my head. I can't tell if he's playing me, or if he's really just accepted me being here. I don't like not knowing. It's an obstacle I don't know how to tackle. Worse, I don't know if I want to.

This morning, he made my double espresso and was ready for the gym even before I was. He was not only cooperative during our guitar video session, but he complimented me multiple times. And then there was the touching, the smiles, the eye contact...

It just...

It just made my brain go a little fuzzy, and that's the last thing that needs to happen. It's not a good idea to fall for Jonah Hendrix, but I'm not an idiot. I know I've got a crush. It's hard to avoid when he's being so...

I don't even know.

Attentive? Kind?

Suggestive...

But the part that messes with me the most? I know for a fact that if I wanted something to happen, it could happen. Jonah Hendrix is a slut, and no matter what his motives are, if I wanted to fall into bed with him, he'd be all for it. The little comments he makes? The invitations? They're not just jokes. There's truth behind them.

If I wanted him to fuck me, he'd gladly do it.

And unfortunately, just the thought of it makes my body hot. I have to press my palms into my eyes to force away the images of his naked, tattooed chest. He hasn't been naked in front of me since we recorded "Landslide," and truth be told, I'm disappointed. Disappointed but also grateful. If it happened again, I'd probably let myself look. My imagination is running wild, and it's almost too much to bear.

EIGHTEEN

Claire

THE SECURITY GUARD drops me at the hotel, and I make my way to the suite on my own. I open the door, flip on the light, then go straight for the bathroom to take off my makeup. I go through my nighttime routine, then walk back into the suite to grab a water from the mini fridge.

I stop in my tracks.

There is a small teal gift bag on the table. The excitement that surges through me is embarrassing, and even though I'm alone, I blush. Would Jonah have gotten me a gift?

No. That's ridiculous. He wouldn't do something like that. This probably isn't even for me.

But then my thoughts turn to the little chess piece. The wooden queen that he painted for me after our visit to the Stockholm Youth Center. I have it safely tucked away in my carry-on luggage. Jonah can be sweet. He's surprised me a lot lately. So maybe...

I reach inside the bag and pull out a small white box with a card. The card has my name on it, so I open it carefully. Then I frown.

I miss you.

- C

CONRAD. A plethora of conflicting emotions floods my mind. I'm barely able to begin sifting through them when the door to the suite swings open, and I whip around to find Jonah. I quickly hide the card behind my back, then shove it into the band of my pajama shorts.

I must look guilty as hell because Jonah's eyes narrow with suspicion, and then they drop to the bag on the table. His responding smile is sinister as he stalks toward me.

"Did the rich prick send you expensive jewelry?"

I don't answer, and he laughs.

"Can you be bought, Trouble?" He reaches past me and grabs the white box. "Do you think he bought something similar for Dierdre?"

He pulls the lid off the box and drops it to the floor. Then he breaks our eye contact to survey what's in the box. I haven't even looked yet, but when he smiles once more, I know I won't like it.

"Yellow gold? If he's going to drop this kind of money to buy your loyalty, he could at least get you something you'd like."

I grit my teeth. "You don't know what I like."

"Your earrings are rose gold. That delicate little necklace you wear is rose gold. The little diamond pave ring you wear on your middle finger is rose gold." He drops the box onto the floor next to the lid, then pulls the neck of my pajama top down. He traces my collarbone, and I suck in a harsh breath. Then, he hooks his finger into my necklace. "Rose gold, Davis. This fuck doesn't know you at all."

My brow furrows, and I tear my eyes away from his to glance at the floor. A chunky, gold, chain-link bracelet encrusted with diamonds lies on the carpet. It must have cost Conrad over ten thousand dollars, but Jonah is right. I hate it.

"See? You'd never wear something so ostentatious." Jonah's voice is gloating, but his tone is intimate. "No. Claire Davis, you prefer classy and elegant. Understated." He hooks his thumb under my chin and tilts my face back to his. He smiles. "How does it feel to know your boyfriend will spend twenty grand to dress you like a cheap slut?"

I slap him. And then I gasp, my hand coming up to cover my mouth. I have to swallow back the impulse to apologize. I watch, eyes widening, as his cheek blooms red from where my hand connected.

And then he fucking laughs. He takes a step toward me, backing me against the table until I can feel his panted breaths ghosting over my lips. He pins me with his blue eyes, and like prey cornered by a predator, I freeze.

"You can take it out on me if you need to, Trouble. You give me all your anger. I can handle it." He slides his hands into my hair and cradles the back of my head. "You want to slap me? You want to call me names? Do it. I fucking want you to. He doesn't pay attention to you, and that pisses you off. Good. It should. It pisses me off for you. But you know what?"

When I don't answer, he tightens his grip on my hair. The sting shoots straight to my clit, surprising me, and I press my thighs together. He pulls just a little more, and I have to swallow back a whimper. My nipples harden. If he looked down, he'd see it.

He repeats himself slowly.

"Do you know what, Claire?"

I swallow roughly. "What?"

"I. Pay. Attention."

Jonah leans closer, invading my space completely, and puts his lips against my ear. My eyes flutter shut. I breathe him in when I know I shouldn't. I revel in the way his cheek feels against mine. The way his heat sears my skin.

"I pay attention to every single thing you do, and it's driving me fucking crazy."

I shake my head, but I can't speak. He moves his hand from my hair and wraps it around my neck. I want him to squeeze. Just a little. The thought shocks me, but now that I've thought it, I can't get rid of it. I want it. I want it so badly that I have to bite my tongue against the need to tell him. To beg.

When he presses his forehead to mine, his lips ghost over my lips, and I want to kiss him. I don't care what he's saying. I don't care about the consequences. I want his lips on me so badly that I feel dizzy.

"I pay attention. The way you blush. The way you think. The way you fucking smell. You're all I can think about, and I want you. I want you, Claire, and it's going to get me in so much fucking trouble. But you want to know a secret?"

"Yes," I whisper, and I feel him smile.

"Trouble is my weakness."

I don't know who moves first, but our lips collide. My hands fist into his shirt as his hand not wrapped around my neck grips my waist. He groans when my mouth opens for him, his tongue tangling with mine.

"Fuck, you taste better than I thought you would."

His hand leaves my neck and moves to my ass, then he lifts me. I wrap my legs around his waist, and he starts walking to the bedroom. I know where this is going. I know what a terrible idea it is. I can't bring myself to care.

I pay attention, and I want you.

I want you, Claire.

He sets me gently on my feet in front of his bed, but his mouth doesn't leave me. My lips, my jaw, my neck. He unbuttons my pajama top and pushes it down my shoulders, then shoves my shorts down my legs. The card falls with the shorts, but thankfully, my shorts cover it.

Once I'm in just my panties, my thoughts wander to my body—what he sees, what he thinks. I'm grateful the lights are dim. I fist my hands against the urge to cover myself, but when he hitches at the waist and takes one of my nipples into his mouth, my attention zeroes in on that feeling, and only that feeling.

I gasp and tug on his shirt. I want it off him. I want to see and feel and taste his skin. In one swift motion, he pulls his shirt over his head, then his hand wraps around my neck once more.

"You have no idea how much I've thought about this pretty little neck, Trouble. I knew it would feel good against my palm. I knew you'd fit perfectly between my fingers. I want to wrap my hands around this perfect little neck and fuck you nice and slow."

His grip tightens just a little, and I whimper. I sink my fingers into the band of his jeans to pull him closer. He chuckles, but it almost sounds pained.

"Of course you'd like it. Of course, you fucking would. You just had to do it, didn't you?"

"Do what?"

My voice is hoarse, and I can feel my throat vibrating against his palm. From the way his eyes flash, he likes it. He leans in close, bites my lower lip, and slips his other hand down the front of my panties.

"Be fucking irresistible."

Jonah shoves two fingers into me, making me groan and thrust my hips forward. His palm presses on my clit as he pumps into me, and I'm overwhelmed by the different sensations. He's fucking me with his fingers as his mouth ravages mine, and he hasn't taken his hand off my throat.

I moan into his mouth and shove my hands into his long hair. I don't even know what I'm grasping for. I've never been a hair puller. I just know I need to hold on to something. My hips start to move of their own accord, chasing the erotic pleasure his fingers bring, and he groans again.

"Jesus Christ," he pants out, pulling back and running his eyes over my face. He drops his attention between us, watching as he fingers me. "Goddamn it, Trouble. God-fucking-damn it."

I don't have a chance to consider his words before he's dropping to his knees, pulling my underwear down my thighs, and putting his mouth over my pussy.

"Oh, fuck," I gasp out. "Oh, God."

Jonah digs his fingers into my ass cheeks and pulls me closer to his face. He sucks hard on my clit, swipes his tongue over me three times, then stands up.

"Lie down."

I don't move. His talented, tattooed hands undo his pants, then work to push them down his slim hips.

"Trouble, lie down on that bed right fucking now."

Slowly, I do as he says, but I don't take my eyes off him. I stare shamelessly as his jeans hit the floor and his erection springs free.

"Oh my God," I whisper, my eyes going wide.

He wraps one of his hands around his hard cock and laughs.

"You sure you want to feed my ego like that? You think I'm an arrogant asshole now? The way you're staring at my cock is about to make me insufferable."

I tear my eyes from his large erection—like *intimidatingly* large—and look back at his smirking face. He sinks his teeth into his lower lip and runs his eyes over my naked body. I'm flushed and panting. My breasts are heavy and aching. My thighs are sticky with my arousal. I'm sure I look ready to be fucked, and God help me, I totally am.

"Tell me you're going to let me have you, Claire."

It almost sounds like a plea. He climbs onto the bed and prowls toward me slowly until I'm lying flat and he's hovering above me. His body is positioned perfectly between my thighs, and I can feel the head of his cock brushing against my wet, throbbing pussy.

"You've seen my medical records. You know I'm clear." He leans down and growls against my lips. "Tell me you're going to give me exactly what I've been wanting since I first saw you in that hotel room."

Reality hits me.

The hotel room.

The one I was in because I was assigned to be his PR manager.

Fuck.

I squeeze my eyes shut, and he freezes.

"Trouble..."

I feel the space between us grow as he pushes himself back up on extended arms. I shake my head again, and then he groans and throws himself onto the bed beside me. When I finally open my eyes and turn my head to look at him, he has an arm thrown over his face and his dick is standing straight up, rock-hard as ever.

"I'm sorry," I whisper. "I just—"

"You don't have to apologize, Davis. I get it. Honestly, I'm surprised you let me get as far as we did."

I stifle a smile at the misery in his voice, then push myself into the sitting position. My pussy is still throbbing, so I understand his disappointment. In fact, I have to mentally beat back the urge to say fuck it and climb on top of him. Instead, I grab a pillow and hide behind it.

"It's not that I don't want to."

He slides his hand down his abdomen. The movement catches my attention, and I look just in time to see him wrap his hand around his dick and stroke. My mouth waters. I can't stop staring. He strokes again, and I have to bite the inside of my cheek to keep from moaning.

"You staring makes me think you want a show."

I jump at his voice, then turn to look at him. His grin is equal parts taunting and tempting. He's still just as turned on as I am. I nod.

"I do want a show."

"Fuck you." He squeezes his eyes shut and groans. "Fuck you, Claire Davis."

I open my mouth to ask what he means, but then he starts pumping his cock, and my voice vanishes. I can't take my eyes off him. He squeezes and jerks himself, and I can feel myself dripping. I've never been so turned on in my life.

He reaches up with his free hand and grabs the pillow, tossing it on the floor.

"Spread your legs for me." His voice is strained, his eyes flicking between my breasts and my pelvis. "Spread them. Show me that swollen little cunt. Torment me with what I can't have."

I don't hesitate.

I lean back, propping myself on my extended arms, and bare myself to him. His expression is ravenous. Ravenous and almost angry. His lip curls into something resembling a sneer, and it gives me pause. Briefly, I wonder if he hates me, if what he sees disgusts him, but that thought is erased when he slides his fingers inside me once more.

"Jonah," I moan, clenching around him as he curls his fingers. "Oh my God."

He pumps his cock faster, and he doesn't take his eyes off my pussy as he finger-fucks me. I gasp when his thumb presses on my clit, and as much as I want to watch as he plays with my pussy, I can't take my eyes off his cock. The way he works himself. I want to touch him like that. I want to taste him. I want him inside me.

The thought almost sends me over the edge. My pussy clenches, and Jonah chokes out another groan.

"You're going to come when I come, aren't you, Trouble." He starts to thrust harder, his thumb circling my clit faster, and I moan in response.

"You're going to come with me. You're going to soak my hand with your cum, and you're going to fucking ruin me. Every time I come, I'm going to think of this tight, perfect fucking cunt, and this tiny, swollen little clit, and your sexy, strangled moans. Is that your plan? Is that what you want?"

I don't know what to say. I don't even know if he's talking sense. I shake my head and open my mouth, but all that comes out is a breathless plea.

"Please, Jonah. Please."

My orgasm comes with all the subtlety of a freight train. My breath leaves me in a whoosh and my body bows, but I force my eyes to stay open. I don't look away from Jonah's swollen cock.

"That's right. Squeeze my fingers like you'd squeeze my cock."

I choke out a moan just as Jonah's body starts to tense up. His muscles contract, his fingers curl inside me and stop pumping, and then he's shooting his release all over his abdomen, painting his tattoos in streaks of white, glossy cum.

He pumps his cock until there's nothing left, and then I bring my eyes to his face. He's already looking at me. He's not smiling, though. He's studying me again. I give him a tight smile.

"Are you going to, um, remove your hand?"

He shrugs and makes no move to take his fingers out of me.

"I'm committing your pussy to memory."

He states the words plainly, no humor at all, but I force a laugh anyway. It shouldn't feel like a compliment, but it does. I look away and my attention falls back to his stomach and chest. At the glistening cum dripping down his sides.

And then I notice something else. I squint, then lean closer.

"Is that a scar?"

At the question, he releases me and gets off the bed. I grab a pillow and shield myself with it once more.

"Yeah." He bends down and grabs his shirt, then uses it to wipe off his stomach.

"What's it from?" I ask, and I don't miss how Mr. Intense Eye Contact is refusing to look at me.

"Kidney transplant."

"What?" I breathe out. "You had a kidney transplant?"

His answering laugh is dark. "I was the donor."

He doesn't say another word as he walks to the bathroom and shuts the door behind him. Minutes later, I hear the shower kick on.

I wait for him until it's clear that I'm being avoided, then I stand and pick up my clothes from the floor. I tear up and dispose of the card from Conrad, then put on a new pair of pajamas and crawl into my own bed. I curl my body into a ball. I picture myself growing smaller and smaller, disappearing under the duvet.

For the briefest of moments, I felt beautiful. I felt desired. That moment is over now.

I fall asleep before he returns to the bedroom.

NINETEEN

Jonah

I'M OBSESSED WITH HER.

There's no other way to explain how she's invaded my mind, tormenting me with her presence while I'm awake and asleep. Nearly two weeks of nothing but Claire Davis in my head. Taking up so much space that I can barely see straight.

I spend half of my free time plotting how to make her pay for fucking my father and the other half thinking of ways to get her back into my bed.

And the thing I don't want to admit, even to myself, is that I want to keep her. I want her to be mine. I just don't know in what capacity.

Sex slave? Soulmate?

At the moment, my brain can't identify a difference.

I spend the rest of Lisbon trying like hell to get her out of my fucking head, but after the plane ride to Madrid, I resign myself to riding it out. Fucking her might be a successful way to satiate my cravings, but I doubt it. It would probably just make me more ravenous for her, if that's even possible. My chess game is so fucked.

I get no peace from Claire Davis. I am in so much fucking trouble.

Fuck her for being so fucking tempting. Fuck her for being everything I dream about.

But fuck, do I want to fuck her.

I bounce my eyes between her ass and the sweaty little curls at the nape of her neck as we walk back from the hotel gym. Her husky voice punctures my bubble, and I swallow back a groan. Why is her voice so goddamn sexy?

"What?" I snap, and she turns just enough to glower at me.

"I asked if you'd had a chance to look at the schedule for today."

"Yeah. Volunteering in the kitchen at a homeless shelter. Photo op. Another guitar cover video if we have time."

She nods. "Good."

I roll my eyes at her back like a petulant teenager, and we don't talk again until we're back in the suite. I know my attitude isn't helping anything, but if being an ass gives me space, I have to try it.

"I'm showering first." I push past her and don't give her a chance to protest. "Order me breakfast."

I slam and lock the bathroom door behind me, then suck in lungsful of clean air. I can't shower after her anymore. It becomes a sauna of lavender and sugar, and it gets me so fucking hard that I could black out. It's difficult enough sleeping in the same room as her. Watching her silhouette through the glass partition. I could throw a blanket over it, but I'd just end up pulling it off again. Claire Davis's shadow is my new porn.

Despite the lack of her scent in the shower, I still have to jerk off to relieve some of the tension. I'm not interested in anyone else. One word from Claire, one invitation, and I'd bend her over any surface possible and fuck her until her pussy squeezes every last ounce of cum from my body. I will fill her fucking up with it. Until it drips down her thighs. Until she can't—

"Hey. Can you hurry up? We need to leave in an hour, and I still have to get ready."

I tilt my head to the ceiling and groan. This woman.

I turn off the water and climb out of the shower. I dry off, then wrap a towel around my waist before heading to the bedroom. Just as I round the corner, I run smack into Claire.

The way her eyes widen and that red tint colors her cheeks bring a satisfied grin to my face. Affecting her is my current drug of choice. It's too bad she can't replace the pills completely.

I take one step forward, and she takes one step back.

"I had my fingers in your pussy while you watched me jerk my dick, but me in a towel surprises you?"

She schools her face into a scowl. "I'm not surprised."

"I know that blush, Trouble." I take another step toward her, but instead of stepping back again, she stands taller. "I bet I know what you're thinking, too."

"You've been a moody, irritable asshole for two weeks. I'm not thinking about anything other than finishing this job and getting the fuck away from you and The Hometown Heartless."

It makes my gut twist and my blood boil. I don't want to admit the fear that overcomes me. The panic. But why? Because I haven't made her pay yet? Or because I can't stand the idea of losing her?

I push my conflicted feelings away and force another smile. I know it looks like a sneer. I don't really care.

"Is this how you deal with your feelings, Davis? You run from them?"

She scoffs. "You're one to talk. You've been drowning your demons in vodka and chasing it with Xanax. Newsflash, *Hendrix,* that shit is a temporary fix. It does nothing but make things worse, especially if you only have one fucking kidney."

I can tell from the flinch of her eyebrow that she regrets saying it, but it's not the sentence itself that pisses me off. It's the truth behind it. I never should have mentioned the transplant.

"Don't think just because you've been up my ass for weeks that you know anything about my demons."

"I know enough."

"You know shit."

"I know you're never sober. I know you can't make it through a single day without taking something. Did you not hear me before? I know the signs, and yours might as well be flashing neon. You might have everyone else fooled but not me. I see right through you."

I feel like I'm being stabbed. I feel like we've regressed back to that night in Stockholm when she tore me up and left me to bleed out.

My teeth grind. My jaw aches.

I want to spit what I know at her. I want to slice her open in retaliation, but I know there will be no coming back from that. Any chance I have of winning this game, in any capacity, will crumble. So instead of lashing out, instead of hitting her with every last thing I've discovered about her own demons, I bite my tongue.

I bite my tongue, I play on her guilt, and I pick at her unhealed wounds.

"Fine." I nod and step away from her. "Fine, Claire. You're right. And if you want to leave, do it. I won't stop you. I've been dealing with this alone, and I can do it again. I don't need you."

I watch her face go from anger, to regret, to concern, just like I wanted. My strategic move worked, and I feel like a complete sleazeball. I feel like my father. I don't trust myself not to take it back, so I say nothing else. I walk to my side of the room and get changed. And when the bathroom door closes and the shower turns on, I drop my head between my knees and breathe.

"Play the whole board," I whisper to myself. "This is chess, not checkers. Play the whole fucking board."

As much as it kills me, I mentally add another tally in my column. I'm winning. That's all that matters now.

"HEY."

Claire flicks her eyes up to me briefly before training them back on her laptop.

"Hey."

"You coming?"

She shakes her head. "No, thanks. I have to finalize our next few events, and I'm not eager to jump out of a plane. Have fun, though."

Sav's using our last day in Madrid to go skydiving. She tries to do it in every country we play in, and she tries like hell to get all of us to go with her. Everyone else usually does, but I've skipped all of them since Paris.

I head back into the bedroom, grab my book and my glasses, then take them to the couch and drop onto the cushion beside her. Claire turns her head toward me and arches a brow.

"Sav said you were leaving at ten. It's nine. Don't you have to meet them? You can't be late if you want to be back before soundcheck."

I put on my glasses and open my book. "I'm staying with you."

"Why?"

"You're my nanny, Claire. I can't go anywhere without you."

"That's ridiculous. You'll be with your entire band, your manager, and at least three security details. I'm not worried about it."

I sigh and make eye contact with her. "Maybe not, but I'd rather be here with you."

Her head jerks back slightly. She runs her eyes over my face. Then, without another word, she goes back to her laptop.

We sit in the quiet for the next hour. The only sound in the room is her clacking on her keyboard and me turning my book pages. I hate how much I enjoy it.

Then the energy shifts. I'm too fucking tuned into her. I watch her body go rigid out of the corner of my eye. I feel her breathing stop, then quicken. When I turn to look at her fully, she's staring wide-eyed at her computer, her mouth gaping open in disbelief. I lean closer to look at the screen. She slaps it shut, but not before I see the signature on the email.

"An email from my father?" I ask slowly, working to keep the anger from my voice.

"Yeah."

"What did he want?"

She blows out a slow breath, then shakes her head. "It's work-related."

"I'm your work."

"Other work. Nothing to do with you."

She stands from the couch, her movements stiff, and walks into the bedroom. My ire for my father burns in my chest. I don't know what he's said to Claire, but it's hurt her. I'm certain she lied. It's not about work. It's about their relationship. That pisses me off even more.

At him and at her.

I place my glasses and book on the coffee table, then follow her into the bedroom.

"You're taking the rest of the day off," I say to her. "We both are."

"No."

"Yes, Claire. Grab your swimsuit. There's a heated saltwater pool on the roof. It's closed to the public while we're here."

"No, Jonah."

I close the distance between us and put my hands on her shoulders. Pride surges when she doesn't push me away. I hold her gaze, then I smile.

"You're coming with me. I need someone there if I drown."

Claire rolls her eyes and shrugs me off her. "You can swim fine."

"It's been a while." That's not a lie. It's been years. When she doesn't respond I poke again. "Did you bring a swimsuit?" Her lack of response tells me she did. "Put on your suit. Come swim with me on the roof of this luxury European hotel. If you do, I'll behave for at least the next two countries."

She looks up at me through her lashes. Her face is blank and unamused. I sigh and go with the truth. She responds best when I give her honesty. She doesn't have to know it's heavily filtered and carefully chosen.

"You're still mad at me. I deserve that. I was a prick. It's hard for me to deal with my feelings for you."

Got her. Her eyes widen. "*Toward* me, you mean?"

"I said what I said. I told you in Lisbon that I want you. Almost having you has only made it worse."

She shakes her head. "Sex will complicate our working relationship."

"I know. But I can't change what I feel." I reach up and pull one of her curls, then smile. "I told you that I pay attention, Trouble. I like what I see. As long as you're here, it's going to fuck with me. But..." I shrug. "I need you here, so we're at a stalemate."

Her eyes soften. Her lips twitch at the corner. And then she turns away.

"Fine. Get out while I change."

"I'll meet you on the roof."

JONAH

I leave the bedroom and shut the door behind me. I smile the whole way to the pool. A small voice in the back of my head whispers to be careful, but just like every other reasonable warning my subconscious has tried to send me, I squash it. Hedonism is the word of the day, and I plan to embrace it.

"THOSE ARE UNDERWEAR."

I glance up from my lounge chair and almost swallow my tongue. I've seen her completely naked, but this simple black one-piece is sparking carnal urges. And her hair? Those dark curls are thrown up into a messy bun on the top of her head, the antithesis of everything she pretends to be every other day.

This look. This casual, carefree, disheveled look...

It will star in my fantasies for years to come.

I breathe slowly and shrug. My boxer briefs won't hide an erection.

"I said it's been a while since I've swum." I push up from the chair and cross the pool deck until she's within arm's reach. "Why would I pack a swimsuit if I never go near a pool?"

She shakes her head, then slaps a bottle of sunscreen on my chest.

"Put this on. You don't want to burn."

"You want to do it for me?"

She tilts her head up and smiles sweetly, my smirk reflected in her mirrored sunglasses. I know what she'll say before she says it. I still wait for her answer.

"You're a big boy. Do it yourself."

I laugh and do as she says. She's right. I don't want to burn. There's nothing sexy about a rock star who looks like a lobster. When I'm finished, I toss the sunscreen onto one of the chairs and walk to Claire. She's laid a towel out on a lounge chair, along with a couple bottles of water and an e-reader. No laptop.

"Together?" I nod toward the pool. "One, two, three, jump?"

She laughs, making my chest tighten. "That's juvenile."

"One..." I say slowly, walking toward her.

She shakes her head. "Don't you dare."

I don't miss the laugh in her voice. I don't miss how she's failing to hide her smile.

"...Two..."

A giggle bubbles out of her, and she throws her hands up between us. I don't stop prowling toward her.

"I swear to God, Jonah Hendrix, I will murder you."

My smile stretches wide. I like when she's sassy and playful. I'll take any threat she throws at me if she says them in that tone, with that smile.

When she tries to back away from me, I snatch her by the waist and lift her bridal-style into my arms as she shrieks.

"Three, jump!"

Her arms tighten around me, and she buries her face in my neck just as we hit the water. She doesn't let go as we submerge and sink to the bottom. She holds on as I kick us back to the surface. She stays wrapped around me, even as we break through the water and gasp for breath.

"Asshole," she pants out. "You're such a dick."

She finally releases me and swims to the other side of the pool, but I can't take my eyes off her. The water sluicing down her cheeks and chin. Glistening on her neck. I'm hard in an instant.

"Shit, I lost my sunglasses."

Her voice is only half-irritated, but I dive to the bottom and get her sunglasses for her anyway.

"Here," I say, tossing them to her.

She barely catches them but slips them back on her face and then purses her lips at me.

"You're not going to drown. You're a good swimmer. You lured me up here on false pretenses."

Slowly, I swim toward her. "Are you mad at me again?"

"I'm always mad at you."

I don't know why that makes me happy, but it does. It might have something to do with her teasing tone of voice or the tiny smirk playing at her lips. If she's mad at me, she's still feeling something. She's thinking of me. Anger is better than apathy.

When I'm close enough, I put my arms on the pool's edge on either side of her, caging her in. We can touch the bottom here, so I tower over her. Again, she doesn't push me away. Again, excitement threatens to overrule my good sense.

"I like when you're mad at me," I whisper between us.

"Yeah?"

I watch a water droplet slide to her lips, tracing the seam. I want to lick it off.

"Mmm. I like when you sass. I like when you challenge me."

She lets out a breathy laugh. "Why's that?"

"It's sexy. Turns me on. But I fucking hate it, too."

"Why?"

I take her sunglasses off and set them on the pool deck, then rub my thumb over her lower lip, smearing the water droplet like lip gloss. Like cum.

"Because it just makes me want you more."

Her slow exhale is shaky. It tickles my lips and nose. I want to put my mouth on hers and breathe her breath. I want to swallow her.

Her eyes drop to my lips. My hard dick strains against the soaking wet fabric of my boxer briefs. My plan was to play it cool, but my plan was incinerated by one heated look from the little pain in my ass in front of me.

"Let me kiss you. Put me out of my fucking misery."

"It's a bad idea."

I smirk, then move to grip her throat. I stare at the way my fingers wrap so perfectly around it. Trachea. Carotid arteries. Jugular. All right here in the palm of my hand. I slide down to her collarbone and apply pressure. Not a lot. Just enough to test her. To give the illusion of being pinned. Her eyelashes flutter, and her white teeth sink into her pillowy, pink lower lip.

Fuck me, she's fucking perfect.

Of all the women I've met, why does this one have to be the one who fucks with me? Why here? Why now?

Supreme temptation. It's my punishment.

Claire Davis could be my penance, but I'll be damned if I admit my sins out loud. They're mine and mine alone to contend with.

No atonement, then. Just pain.

"I disagree," I say, my voice rough and desperate. "I think it's the best idea I've ever had." I run my nose over hers, our lips centimeters from touching. "Let me kiss you, Claire. Let me have you. I swear I'll—"

Her mouth presses against mine and opens immediately. I groan and palm the back of her head, sliding my other hand to her ass. I hold her against me as I coax her to wrap her legs around my waist. She gasps when I press my hard cock against her hot pussy.

"See? You see what you do to me, Trouble?" She starts to rub on me. The sensation makes starbursts appear on the backs of my eyelids. "Fuck, you make me fucking crazy."

When she moves her tiny, delicate hand to my neck, I picture it splayed over my tattoo. Holding that heart in her palm. *My* heart.

It's too much. Any more, and I'm going to fuck her in this pool. I pull away.

"You have three minutes to get to the suite before I come after you. If you've changed your mind by the time I catch up, we'll go back to how we were before. But if you haven't..." I put more distance between us. "If you want this, I'm going to fuck you."

She stares at me. Her chest heaves up and down with her labored breathing. My eyes drop to watch her cleavage strain against the swimsuit, imagining exactly what I know is underneath.

I nod to the door of the roof.

"Clock's ticking, Trouble."

She gasps, and then she moves. I close my eyes so I don't stare at her wet body. That black suit suctioned to her skin. Nipples visible through the thin fabric. Ass cheeks peeking from the bottom. I grab my cock and squeeze to relieve some pressure.

When the door slams shut, I start to count. I force myself to go slow, but as soon as I get to one-eighty, I'm springing out of the pool and darting for the door.

Fuck, please let her want this. If she's changed her mind, I will die.

It takes a year to get back to the suite. I fling the door open and head straight for the bedroom. Claire whips around to face me, a towel clutched to her naked body. I grin.

"Well?" I ask, the need obvious in the single syllable. She doesn't

JONAH

answer, so I take three more steps toward her. "You're usually such a mouthy little thing, Trouble. Did you lose your voice between here and the pool?"

Her eyes narrow just like I knew they would, then she tilts her head to the side and drops her gaze to my hard cock. The wet boxer briefs do nothing to conceal it. I keep my attention trained on her face so I can see that blush creep up her neck. It only makes me harder.

"Words, Claire. Words."

She flicks her eyes back to mine. "Take them off."

I grin and do as she commanded, kicking the sopping wet cotton to the side of the room. I place my hands on my hips and watch as she surveys my whole body. Then she drops her towel.

I've never known temptation like this.

Standing in front of a naked Claire Davis, wanting her like this, but forcing myself to remain still. I'm a bull at a bullfight, waiting impatiently for the gate to open, and she's my red flag. I'd charge her right now if I could.

"I've never..." Her lips purse as she glances back at my face. "I've never been with someone that...size."

Pride surges inside me before it's extinguished by jealousy. By rage. I don't know all of her exes, but I know one. It makes me want her more just to fuck them both up. My head is such a mess, a cage fight of conflicting emotions battling out inside my skull.

I want her. I want to hurt her. I want to hurt my father. I want to light our pasts on fire so I can keep her for myself, knowing damn fucking well that it's impossible.

I force my expression into placidity and give her another truth. "I'll be gentle."

She nods, then walks backward until her thighs bump the mattress. I grit my teeth and watch as she slides onto the bed, stretches her legs out in front of her, and lies back on the pillow. Then she raises her arm and crooks her finger at me.

I charge.

"Spread your legs," I command as I kneel on the mattress.

The words bring memories of Lisbon. When she obeys, all I can think about is the way she tasted on my tongue. The way she felt squeezing my fingers.

I lower myself between her thighs and inhale. Lavender and sugar and sex. I take her tiny clit between my lips and suck hard just to hear her gasp. Her hips lift off the bed, so I reach around her legs and press my arm to her pelvis, pinning her into the mattress. The only way I'm letting her free now is if she asks me to.

I lick her up and down, reveling in her taste, in the way she tries to pulse her pussy against me. She's whimpering and squirming. It's so fucking hot that I flex my ass and press my cock into the mattress.

"I will dream about this pussy." I pull back as I watch my fingers slowly push inside her. "Fuck, the way you're swallowing me up." I crook my fingers, rubbing that spot inside her that makes her moan. "You have no fucking idea what this does to me, Claire. You have no fucking idea."

"More." She tries to move on my hand. "More, Jonah."

"More? Yeah?"

"Yes. More."

My grin doesn't leave my face as I flick my tongue over her clit. I graze my teeth on it just to hear her cry out. When I look up her body, her eyes lock with mine, and my tongue moves faster.

"Oh, Jesus. Oh my God." Her hands are clutching at her tits. She's trying so hard to move, to fuck my face, but I pin her down harder. "I'm so close."

I suck one last time on her clit. I wait until I feel her pussy pulsing around my fingers. Then I release her and rise back onto my knees. I leave her wanting. Her brows scrunch, full lips turning into a pout, and I laugh.

"You've got to earn it." I wrap my hand around my cock and stroke. "How will you earn it, Trouble?"

She sits up and crawls down the bed toward me. The way she arches her back, sticking her ass into the air. She's doing it on purpose. I know it. I reach over her body and smack one perfect ass cheek. She gasps, and I laugh.

"Are you going to suck it or stare at it?"

She snarls up at me before wrapping her hand around my cock.

Finally, she licks up my shaft and takes the head into her mouth. When she swirls her tongue around my ridge, I groan.

"Oh, fuck. This hot little tongue." I fist my hand into her curls, but I let her lead. I let her test me out. She slides my cock farther into her mouth, breeching her throat, and I see fucking stars. "That's it. That's my girl. Just like that."

Slowly, she takes more of me, laving her tongue on the underside of my cock and using her hand to work the rest. It's erotic as fuck watching more and more of my cock disappear into her mouth. I picture it sliding into her throat, cutting off her air supply.

"Jesus Christ, Claire." I tighten my grip on her hair and pulse into her. "Yes, baby. Fuck, you're doing so good."

I push more of myself into her. She doesn't even gag. She just takes me until I pull out to let her gasp for breath. She looks up at me with her eyes watering, her mouth covered in spit, and I could come now. I could fucking come right now from half a blow job.

"I want to fuck your throat," I say roughly. "Will you let me?"

She hesitates. I hold my breath as she considers. Then mercifully, she nods. "Yes."

Fuck, the way her voice rasps around the word...

"If it's too much, tap my thigh twice."

She nods again. "Okay."

"Do it right now. Tap it twice. Show me you understand."

As soon as she does what I ask, I move. I start slow, sliding in a little deeper each time. I fill her up, then pull out so she can breathe. So she can gulp in a lungful of air around my cock, cooling the skin on my shaft, before I push back in.

When she taps my thigh, I pull out. I stroke her hair and swipe a thumb gently over her cheek. "Are you okay?"

"I'm okay. I just need a minute."

She closes her eyes and breathes slowly through her nose. Deep, calming breaths, like she's trying to settle herself. I start to worry. Did I hurt her? Did I scare her? I'm seconds from backing off entirely when she takes my cock into her mouth once more.

Her moves are confident, eager. I let her lead for a moment just so I can watch her, and then I take over. I start slow, pushing in farther and farther each time, until I'm as far down her throat as she can handle. Until she gags. And fuck, the way she gags. The way she pants. The way her eyes water, tears streaming down her cheeks. The way she fucking takes me...

I move faster, shoving down and pulling out quickly, until I'm fucking her like I said I would. She's a mess of spit and tears, and I'm in fucking heaven. I pull all the way out and use her hair to tilt her face to mine. Her eyelashes are matted as she blinks up at me. Her cheeks are flushed and glistening.

"This time, I want you to swallow around me. Can you do that?"

She nods, and I smile.

"Of course you can." I reach down and rub my thumb over her jaw, then rub the tip of my cock over her lower lip as she opens for me. "Tap twice if you need a break, okay?" She nods again. "Stick your tongue out." I slap the head of my cock on her tongue. "You're too fucking perfect," I whisper, then I shove into her mouth again.

I bring my hand to her neck, feeling her throat contract with my cock inside, feeling her muscles move when she swallows. Choking me while I choke her.

"Fuck me. Goddamn, you're doing so fucking good. Swallow just like that." I groan. "I could fuck your throat forever. You're so fucking good at this. I could do it for-fucking-ever, Trouble. Look at me. Look up at me while you swallow my cock."

She obeys. She obeys, and my chest aches with need.

Fuck her. Fuck Claire Davis for being the only woman I've ever wanted to keep.

I pull out and tug her hair, so she rises back onto her knees.

"Lie down, spread your legs wide, and shove your fingers in your pussy."

She blinks twice, then does exactly what I told her to do. I watch her finger-fuck herself as I climb off the bed and grab a condom from my suitcase. I don't take my eyes off her as I rip open the package and slide the latex down my throbbing cock.

I position myself between her legs once more. I let myself watch the show long enough to regain a semblance of composure. Long enough to set my head straight. Then I look back at her flushed, desperate face. Her mouth is red and swollen. Her cheeks are flushed and tear-stained. And her eyes...they're so fucking needy. Her pupils are blown wide and begging for me.

I reach down and pinch one of her nipples.

"Have you earned it, Trouble?"

She nods. "Yes. I have."

"You're such a fucking good girl." I swipe the head of my cock through her pussy lips, and then I slowly push inside.

TWENTY

Claire

I STRETCH and mold around him.

The most exquisite kind of pain.

But he's gentle, just like he said he'd be. He's careful with me. I didn't know it was possible for someone to be soft while also being rough.

I didn't know I could feel so safe, so respected, so *beautiful*, while being used. I want to chase those feelings. I want to capture them. Beautiful. Respected. Safe. I want to please him just so I can keep them. So I can feel these things for as long as possible.

I've never been with a man like this. He's commanding and forceful and *filthy* but still so very gentle.

I don't have time to piece together the puzzle that is Jonah Hendrix.

I barely have the brain capacity to feel anything other than extreme, debilitating euphoria as he slides in and out of me. Each time, he sinks a little deeper, stretching me a little farther. It feels...

"Fuck, you're squeezing me so tight, Claire."

Jonah groans, then puts his hands on my pelvis and uses his thumbs to spread my pussy lips wider. I can feel the extra stretch, his thumbs and his cock reshaping me both outside and in. He spits on my pussy and rubs it into me, onto his cock. He slides his spit over my throbbing clit, and I cry out. A high-pitched, wailing sound. I sound absolutely inhuman. I'll never recover from this. I'd be embarrassed if I could think straight.

"Look at you. You just keep taking me. God, you're fucking greedy for me. You just keep sucking me deeper."

I can't handle it. I can't handle him. I'm going to explode.

"You're driving me mad," I rasp out, and he laughs.

"You have no fucking idea."

Suddenly, he's hovering over me, my breasts pressed to his sweaty, tattooed chest, and he's kissing me. His tongue darts in and out of my mouth in time with his cock thrusting into my pussy. It's too much. There's no room left, yet I want more. I want more, but he pulls away every time I try to take control.

I sink my hands into his blond hair and pull at the root.

"Stop making me chase you," I pant against his mouth.

"But I like you like this."

He tries to pull away again, but I take his lower lip between my teeth and bite. He groans and starts to pump faster.

"Fuck, I really like you like this."

He crooks his hips to the side and hits a different spot inside me. It makes me cry out and clutch at him.

"Baby, did I just find your sweet spot?"

I move my hips with his, hitting that spot again and again.

"I fucking did, didn't I? You're the one in trouble now, Davis." He fucks me harder, and I groan, low and desperate. My chest vibrates with it, and he growls. "You're in so much fucking trouble. You'll never fucking forget me."

His words flutter in and out of my head briefly. I register them, clock the strangeness of his tone, but then it disappears. It's gone the moment he presses my thighs together and shoves them against my chest.

"Oh my fuck, Jonah."

"That's right. Say it again."

He fucks me harder, bottoming out deeper than I thought possible. Until his hips slam into my ass and the backs of my thighs. The sound of skin slapping onto skin, of his hard cock moving in and out of my soaking wet pussy...

"Fuck, it's so, it's so..."

"Say my fucking name, Claire."

"Jonah. Jonah. Jonah."

I chant it like he wants. Like an incantation. More. More. More.

His palm splays on my collarbone, and my excitement increases. I wait for him to move it to my neck, but he doesn't. He just applies pressure to my collarbone, pinning me into the mattress. Maintaining control.

I wrap my hand around his wrist and try to coax him to my throat, but he doesn't budge.

"Please," I beg.

"Please what?"

I squeeze my eyes shut, willing the request to fall from my lips, but I can't bring myself to say it. Even after all he's done, all *we've* done, I can't say it. His answering laugh is dark. He knows, and he doesn't remove his hand from my collarbone.

He moves my legs apart and presses my knees to my shoulders, lifting my ass from the bed until I'm arched and folded. I mentally thank myself for yoga because who the fuck bends like this.

Then he spits again and rubs his thumb on my clit.

"Oh God." I groan.

"You close, Trouble?"

His voice is strained and breathless. He's holding back. He's ready. I nod.

"Good."

He pulls out of me, pulls off the condom, then pumps into me twice more. It drives me fucking crazy, skin on skin, heat on heat. My pussy clenches around him, so close. So close.

Then he pulls out of me completely, lets go of my legs, and pumps his dick until he's coming all over my pelvis and stomach. I watch breathlessly as his mouth drops open on a long groan, his eyes never leaving my body. Fascinated by his cum covering my skin.

When he's finished, I wait impatiently. I wait for him to return between my legs and bring me to orgasm in some way. With his fingers or tongue. But then he stands beside the bed, looming over me, and hits me with a glare.

My brows furrow and a chill skates down my spine. I close my legs, sit up, and cover my chest, ignoring the way his cum smears against my skin.

"What?" I say quietly.

He says nothing, so I repeat myself more forcefully. I snap at him and quickly start throwing on armor. Fortified steel for whatever he's going to say. I can tell from the look in his eyes that it won't be good.

"What?"

A sinister grin stretches over his face, and my heartbeat sounds like warning bells in my head.

"How does it compare?"

My heart stops. My stomach drops. I open my mouth and force out only one word. The only one I can actually form, and even then, it's a ghostly, shaky whisper.

"What?"

The hatred that flashes over his face, the pain that I see in his eyes, guts me. And then in a blink, it disappears.

"I have to admit, when I said you fucked your way into Innovation, I didn't even consider the CEO. Great work, Davis. Bang up job. My dad usually likes them a little younger, but..."

I shake my head. I want to protest, to defend myself, but I can't breathe. It's made worse when he tilts his head to the side and scans my body. I'm again a lab rat. A cadaver to a med student. A case study.

He sneers.

"I guess I'm not surprised. That was probably some of the best pussy I've ever had. I came so hard I saw fucking stars. Maybe I should fuck more homewrecking whores."

I flinch. "I'm not... I didn't..."

"What do you call women who fuck married men, Davis? Because I usually call them homewreckers."

"I'm not." I shake my head again. I lean forward. I want to plead with him. "He's not married. I didn't—"

Jonah cuts me off with a laugh. Loud and sharp, slicing me from neck to navel.

"He was married, Davis. Married right up until my mother killed herself."

I feel the color leech from my face. His voice dulls because of the pounding in my head, the blood whooshing in my ears.

"No..."

"Yes. Married. Mother was living upstate *for her health,* but depression is only manageable with constant treatment. Why treat your depression when your husband is fucking a junior creative developer at his company?"

I feel like I've been slapped. I don't even realize I'm crying until the tears reach my lips.

"That's not fair...I didn't...It wasn't my fault."

He can't put that on me. He can't blame his mother's death on me. I can't carry that guilt on my shoulders. I know without a single shadow of a doubt that it's not my fault, but everything is blurry. Everything. My vision. My memories. My logical thinking. I'm a raw nerve.

"No, it wasn't." He shrugs. "You didn't force the sleeping pills and red wine down her throat. You didn't make her give the housekeeper the week off." He reaches down and pinches my chin between his thumb and forefinger. "But you sure fucking didn't help."

I jerk myself out of his grip. He tries to smile, but he can't. It's a frown. Sad and pained and disgusted, but it seems directed inward. Disgusted not with me, but himself.

I can't help but feel like a murder-suicide was just committed.

He sliced me in half, then fell on the same sword.

He takes two steps backward, his own chest heaving as his eyes turn glassy.

"Checkmate, Trouble. Pack your shit and get out of my life."

He turns and walks out. I don't go after him. He's still completely naked, but I can't bring myself to care at all. I stare at the place he vacated for a long time. Minutes or hours. I don't move until my heartbeat returns to normal and my tears stop falling. Until my mind goes utterly silent.

Numbly, I walk to the bathroom and step into the shower. I turn the knobs to scalding. I sit in the corner on the tiled floor and watch as the steam fills the glass enclosure. I close my eyes, rest my head on the natural stone wall, and breathe it in. I imagine dissolving into it. Condensing myself into a water droplet on the glass, then slipping back down into the drain. Down, down, down. Away from here. Away from this.

What have I done?

I try like hell to employ the healthy coping mechanisms I learned during my stay at the treatment center. To wrangle the extreme anxiety clawing its way up my throat into something more manageable. But...

How could I have been so stupid?

There were signs. There we so many signs. Did I really not see them? Did I ignore them?

Rationally, I know Jonah's mom's death isn't my fault. But anxiety isn't rational. My insecurities aren't, either.

"Fuck." My voice is swallowed up by the stream of water from the shower. I lift my head and drop it back on the stone wall, then raise my voice. "Fuck."

What am I going to do? What the fuck am I going to do?

The whole scene with Jonah muscles its way back into the forefront of my mind. Every touch. Every feeling. Every praise and every insult. It makes my stomach cramp, and I pull my knees to my chest.

Then I think of Conrad's email. Of the veiled threats he made through the company server. Anyone else would see it as a professional message from the CEO to a subordinate. But I spent almost a year with that man, so I know better.

It's just another stupid fucking decision to tack on to my long list of regrets.

I stand and step under the showerhead, letting the hot water cascade down my body. I let the tears building in my eyes fall and stream down my cheeks. They mix with the water, blending together, cleansing me. I am the steam. I am the condensation on the glass. I am the droplets swirling down the drain.

I breathe. I breathe. I breathe. One inhale and exhale at a time.

When my head is clear, I turn off the water and step out of the shower. I dry off my body, put on pajamas, and pack my suitcase.

I have a plan, and it doesn't involve bending to the commands of any man.

TWENTY ONE

Claire

I'M out of the suite before dawn.

Jonah didn't come back after the final show, and I didn't want to be there when he came to pack his shit before leaving for Scotland. I'm sure he thinks I'm gone for good. I'm sure he thinks he broke me.

He hurt me. He devastated me, in fact. But he didn't break me, and I'm not going anywhere. Even if I wanted to, I couldn't, anyway.

I'm waiting in the lobby as, one by one, every member of The Hometown Heartless and their entourage start to join me. It's time to go to the airport and board the jet, so I steel my spine and wait.

Mabel, Sav, Levi, Brynn, and Red arrive first. Hammond next, along with two more security details. I recognize one as Damon, which means...

Torren, Callie, and Jonah are last, with José bringing up the rear.

José is on my shitlist right now. I'll deal with him later. Jonah is my focus. He doesn't see me right away, but I keep my face neutral and stare at him until his eyes meet mine. I rejoice in the way his expression shows shock before he's able to muscle it into anger.

That's right, asshole. You're not getting rid of me that easily.

I want so badly to smile, but I refrain. I don't want to provoke him right now. Not when it would be so easy to make a scene and fuck up all the work I've done these past few weeks. No. I keep my expression blank, and I hold his eyes as he crosses the lobby floor. His jaw pops, but I don't look away. I refuse to be the one to break eye contact. I will stay right here in this stare off until sunset if I have to.

When Jonah steps in front of me, towering over me in that way he does, I lift my chin.

"Davis."

"Hendrix."

"Goin' to Edinburgh?"

I arch a brow. "Where else would I be going?"

His eyes drop to my lips, his nostrils flare, and then, surprisingly, he turns away. Pride washes over me. A victory, albeit a small one. I'm not stupid. I know this isn't over, but I release a slow, relieved breath anyway.

Jonah stands beside me, our shoulders touching, as we wait for the cars to pull around. When we climb into the SUVs, he sits right next to me. He spreads his legs, taking up space, but I don't shrink for him. As much as it kills me to be swamped in the scent and heat of him, I sit up straight, keep my shoulders wide, and face forward.

The ride to the airport is silent, and when we board the jet, I take a seat at the front of the cabin. Jonah takes one at the very back. This loosens another band of worry from around my chest. He's not going to fight me on this. Not yet at least. But he's stewing, so I close my eyes and prep myself for yet another battle. This three-hour plane ride is just a respite. The moment we're in his new suite, I'm sure he'll explode. That's fine. I've got shit to say to him, too.

I'm roused from a very light sleep when someone takes the seat in front of me. My eyes pop open, and I sit straight up. Mabel laughs.

"Oh, shit, did I wake you?"

I rub my eyes and shake my head. "No, you're fine."

"You sure? It's not important."

I give Mabel a smile. I like her. I like all of them. She, Sav, and Callie have been kind and welcoming since I crashed into their lives five weeks ago. God, how has it been five weeks? It feels like it's been an eternity.

"No, you're good," I reassure her. "I was just resting. Honestly, I don't know how you guys do it. I'm exhausted, and I'm not playing sold-out shows every Thursday through Sunday. And you do this for how long?"

Mabel smirks. "Eighteen weeks total, but we get three weeks off in the middle, so only fifteen weeks of shows."

I do the math in my head. Four shows every week for fifteen weeks...

"Sixty shows, Mabel."

"Well, we only play two shows in Munich, Zürich, and Milan, so fifty-four."

I huff out a laugh. "You're superhuman."

"Nah. It helps that we love performing and our fans. For a long time, we were lucky to have two consecutive days off total, so this is cake in comparison, and it's a hell of a lot easier than some bands get."

I hum, but I don't respond. I've heard Sav and Mabel talking about how rough it was before Hammond renegotiated their contract. It sounded miserable. Like star-studded hell. It makes me feel bad for all of them. No wonder they struggled for so long.

The thought makes me want to turn in my seat to check on Jonah.

I don't.

Then I lower my voice. "So what comes after?"

"After what?"

"This tour."

Mabel's eyes scan my face, and I can't help but feel like she's deciding whether to trust me with something. I sit up straighter, but I don't push. She flicks her attention behind me quickly before sitting forward.

"After, if all goes as planned, we'll take some time off, and then we'll do it all over again. Only..."

I arch a brow. "Only?"

"Only we'll do it under Sav's label."

My jaw drops. "Sav's starting her own label?"

"Yeah. It's still hush-hush. It's not illegal or anything, not violating any clauses, but she wants to wait to launch until after we're out from under this contract."

"Right. Which is why you need to keep Jonah in line."

Mabel purses her lips, then glances over my shoulder once more.

"You're doing a great job, actually. I just wanted you to know that. He's doing a fuck ton better than he does on his own. He's less pissy. He's got more energy on stage. Hell, he even spoke in our last band meeting. Plus, Hammond's been really happy with the buzz you've started in the press. You're crushin' it."

"Thanks."

"I should be thanking you. Truly. Jonah...I don't know. He's better than he was two years ago, but we still kind of tiptoe around him. He's always been really good about keeping his feelings hidden from us."

I flare my eyes. "Yeah."

His feelings are the least of it. I don't know if any of them realize that.

I lay my head back on my seat and once again resist the urge to turn around. It's nice to hear that Mabel thinks I'm doing a good job. And from a strictly professional standpoint, I am. I'm doing a great job, actually, considering what I started with. But if she knew the whole truth...

Well. If she knew, she wouldn't be thanking me at all.

"I wanted to check on you, though. Are you okay after last night?"

My muscles go rigid, and my chest tightens. Last night.

"What do you mean?"

"Jonah said you weren't feeling well. You skipped the show, and then Jo crashed in Tor and Cal's suite. But then he looked kind of shocked to see you this morning, so I thought maybe you were sicker than he let on."

"Oh. Yeah. I mean, no. I'm okay now. I'll be fine. Thanks for checking."

I make a mental note to get a refill on my anxiety meds. Then, maybe that won't be a total lie.

"I TOLD YOU TO LEAVE."

Jonah's words are hissed at me the moment the suite door shuts behind him. I prop my hands on my hips and scowl.

"And I told you I'm here to do a job. I'm not leaving until it's finished."

"Have you seen the tabloids lately? They fucking love me. Job's over. Go home."

He brushes past me, so I turn and follow him into the bedroom. He stops abruptly, probably noting the absence of our glass partition, but I ignore his reaction.

CLAIRE

"*Some* of the current headlines are great, sure, but every single article still questions you. They still feed into the rumors and speculations about your inevitable downfall. I know. I've read every single one of them. I have your name on an internet alert. I read everything right after it's posted."

Jonah laughs and turns to face me. His smirk is infuriating. I hate it even more now that I recognize the emotions he's trying to mask. Cruelty to hide his pain. Snark to cover up his jealousy. I recognize it because I've lived it. I want to tell him that I get it. I want to give him kindness and understanding, but he opens his mouth and pisses me off again.

"Sorry, Davis, but your perfectionist ass is going to have to take the L on this one. If eliminating all tabloid rumors is your measure of success, this is one project you're not going to get an A plus on."

"This isn't a *project*, Jonah. It's a commitment. I don't bail on commitments. I see them through."

He drags a hand down his face and groans again. "For fuck's sake, Claire. You will *never* get me to a point where I'm portrayed as an angel in the tabloids. It's impossible."

"I know that, but I can tip the scales in your favor. I want more praise than insults, and I know I can get it there. I know I can succeed in this. I know it."

"If you're worried about your job, don't be. Lie." His words are low and hissed, as if trying to keep from shouting. I almost wish he would. "Tell my father I'm fixed, and I'll back it up. We can all just pretend like your little chess game panned out, and you can go back to playing dumb while he fucks you on his office desk."

I grind my teeth and fist my hands. I want to slap him. I want to shake him. He's so fucking angry, and he's holding a goddamn grudge. He *hates* his father, and now he hates me, too. No amount of logic or truth will change that.

But I'm so fucking sick of being walked all over.

I can't fight fire with fire, so I'll throw some water on it and try again later.

"I'm going to refresh your memory since it's been a long five weeks. I've been assigned to do a job. I will complete this job. If you make me leave now, you will regret it."

"Right." Jonah laughs. "Because if you go down, you're taking me with you."

"Fucking right, I will."

Jonah wipes his expression of all emotion. Every feeling and thought, gone. A clean, blank wall has been erected, shutting me out entirely.

"You're so fucking stubborn. You're a stubborn pain in my ass."

I don't acknowledge the insults. Instead, I follow his lead. Emotions gone. Wall up. I hope he feels just as cold and dejected as I do.

"I've wiped the calendar this week. We need a break from each other, so I'll stay out of your way. I only ask that you don't do anything that will unravel the progress we've made. It would be more detrimental to you than to me."

I don't say another word. I just turn and leave. The moment I step into the hall, I nod at José, signaling it's safe for him to enter. He nods back as he walks past me with his suitcase in tow. I don't wait for the door to shut before I head down the hall.

Hammond opens the door before I have a chance to knock. He extends his hand, offering me the key card to my new room.

"Thanks for this." I put the key card in my back pocket. "Sorry it was such late notice."

"You gave me almost twelve hours. I've worked with much less."

"Well." I shrug. "I'm still sorry."

He narrows his eyes slightly. "You're sure this is a good idea?"

He's skeptical. I don't blame him. I am, too. But I also think it's necessary. Jonah and I need a bit of space to reset our priorities. He needs to check his wrath, and I need to check my...well...lust.

And anxiety.

And guilt.

And lust.

What a mess.

I nod and give him a reassuring smile.

"I do. It's much needed. I think Jonah will be fine, actually, but he's got José with him just to be safe."

"Very well. I assume I won't be seeing much of you?"

"Probably not, but you have my number if you need it."

CLAIRE

I say my goodbyes to Hammond, then take the elevator to my floor. I specifically asked to be as far from the band as possible when I called him yesterday. I worried that I'd overreacted all day, but when Jonah didn't return after the show, I knew it was the right call.

I'm not abandoning him like I did my brother. I won't make that mistake again. Not now. Not when I'm so close to redemption—to actually *helping* someone. I'm seeing this to the end.

Jonah Hendrix is my penance.

I meant it when I said he would regret it if I left.

What I didn't admit was that I would regret it, too.

TWENTY TWO

Jonah

"WHAT THE FUCK is up with you?"

Torren tosses a french fry at my head. I was zoning again. Spiraling.

"What do you mean?"

"You've been throwing silent tantrums all week. Why don't you just call her and apologize?"

I arch a brow. "Who?"

"Don't be an idiot."

"What makes you think I did something to apologize for? Fuck, what makes you think it's about her at all?"

Torren looks at me like I actually *am* an idiot. Then he smirks.

"You check her social media profile multiple times a day. You log into your own, too, and I know it's just to see if she's posted anything new. And..."

There's a pause, and I sigh.

"And what, dick?"

"And this is the first time in weeks that you've been a moody bastard. Doesn't take a rocket scientist to put two and two together. She's gone MIA, and you've regressed back into an asshole."

My lip curls and my eyes narrow. I don't like that I've been so easy to read. I don't like it at all. Then his eyes widen.

"Did you sleep with her?"

Warning bells sound in my head. *Danger! Danger! Danger!*

I hide a lot of shit from Torren, but I'm usually open about who I fuck. This time, though...

This time it's different.

Telling the truth would do nothing to me. Everyone knows I'm a slut, anyway. But it could seriously fuck shit up for Claire. If it got back to Hammond, he'd fire her. He'd probably tell my dad. If my dad found out, I don't want to think about what he'd do to her career. My dad is a vengeful, heartless bastard. It's one of the few things we have in common.

"No."

The lie rolls off my tongue smoothly. I keep my tone flat, but a hint of disappointment creeps in, and I realize it's not fake. Torren probably takes it to mean I want to fuck her and can't. But it actually means I did, and I'm disappointed I'll never get to do it again.

I drop my head to my basket of fish and chips. I sprinkle more vinegar on what's left of my fries, just so I have something else to do, then stick my hand under my thigh so I stop picking at my fucking thumb.

I wonder if she's having fun. Is she exploring Edinburgh or is she just chilling in her hotel room? Is she eating? Has she met someone? The chain of thought makes my chest ache, but then my phone rings. The number on the screen just makes me angrier.

"I gotta take this." I wave my phone as I slide out of the booth. "I'm finished, so I'll just meet you outside."

I don't let Torren respond. I head straight for the door of the pub with my head down. Once outside, I glance at José.

"You can give me some space, José. It's just a phone call."

He nods, and I walk down the street away from him. When I'm at a safe distance, I answer.

"Yeah?"

"Jonah."

"Dad." I take my cigarettes out of my pocket, place one between my lips, and light it. "What do you want?"

"I'm calling in regard to Ms. Davis."

My spine snaps straight. My defenses on high alert. "What about her?"

"I'd like to speak with her. I've been unable to get through to her phone."

I take a drag from my cigarette. "Huh. Weird."

"Yes." He sighs. "I would like to speak with her."

If my mind weren't a chaotic mess of thoughts, I'd be pleased that I've annoyed him. Instead, as usual these days, my focus is on Claire. Is she okay? Is something wrong?

"Jonah."

"Hm?"

"Ms. Davis. I need to speak to her."

"Hold."

I take the phone away from my ear and pull up my text thread with Claire.

> ME
> Hey. You alive?

I watch as my message goes from delivered to read within seconds. Her reply comes immediately after.

> TROUBLE
> Are you in a PR crisis?

> No.

> Then no, I am not alive. I will be dead until Sunday.

I smirk and bite my lip to stifle a laugh. It's been four days since I've talked to her, and Tor is right. I've been a miserable asshole.

> I've already written a eulogy.

> Fuck off.

I bark out a laugh. Then, because I'm flooded with dopamine or some bullshit, I send another text. A stupid one. An *honest* one.

> I miss your sass.

The message is read, and I wait for her reply. Chat bubbles pop up, then disappear. Pop up, then disappear again. My father's voice sounds again from the receiver, and I grit my teeth.

"Jonah, what the hell is—"

"I said *hold*. I know you're not accustomed to waiting, but you're going to have to—"

> My sass or my ass?

Claire's message comes through and momentarily shocks me. I read it three times before my brain comprehends, and then I'm grinning. Like all out ear-to-ear, lip-splitting grin.

> Do I have to choose?

More chat bubbles. Another seconds long wait that seems like years. The way I'm feeling at this moment is embarrassing. It's a fucking text conversation, and here I am panting impatiently for my next hit.

> Go do something productive, Hendrix. I'll see you Sunday.

I'm still smiling when I put the phone back to my ear.

"She's busy."

"Jonah, for fuck's sake. Tell her I need—"

"Tell her yourself."

"Then give her the fucking phone."

There goes my good mood. Now I want to light something on fire. Some*one*.

"No can do, Dad. She's busy. She's here to *work*, remember? You should know that since you're her boss. Send her an email. I'm sure she'll get back to you expeditiously."

He grows quiet, but I can picture his face. Scowling. Jaw hard. Nostrils flaring. Eyes condescending and freezing fucking cold. It's been years, but it still gives me the worst kind of chills. I take another drag from my cigarette.

"Yes, Son. She is there to *work*. Any other behaviors will be cause for termination. Do you understand?"

"I don't, actually. Please explain."

"Wearing your jacket on the rooftop of *Torre de Belém*, Jonah? Posting her on your social media?"

My heartbeat thuds loudly in my head. My blood boils, singeing my skin. I speak slowly, calmly, but inside I'm raging. How fucking dare this man.

"What exactly are you suggesting?"

"She's a beautiful girl. A good worker. But she's not for you."

"Excuse me?"

"She's not one of your little fans. Ms. Davis is...*ambitious*. You need to be careful."

I laugh so I don't explode on him.

"I'm sorry, Dad, but are you pissing on her or protecting me from her?"

"Don't be glib, Jonah. I am saying do not fuck Ms. Davis. Women like her cannot be trusted, and that one's wily. I wouldn't put it past her to tr—"

"Shut the fuck up," I force through my teeth. I'm seething. "You don't get to tell me shit about her. Not a single fucking thing."

"She will use you to get to me. To get to your money. Trust me, I know women like her."

"Jesus Christ. Spare me a lecture about your past fucking mistresses."

And his current *fucking mistress.*

I press my palm into my forehead. Hot ash from my cigarette falls onto my wrist, but it doesn't stop the visions. Him and Claire. Claire and him.

He's fucked her. Christ, she thinks he's her fucking boyfriend, and I can't get a handle on my jealousy and rage. I hate him for having her. I hate her for making me want her. I hate myself for falling back into this place I always swear I'll never return to.

Then I see my mother. My brother. I see a younger me standing against a wall, observing. Always fucking observing. Never part of the family. Never wanted. Only needed.

Needed until I was no longer useful.

Something inside tells me that what my father is saying about Claire isn't true. She's not a user. She wouldn't sleep with me for personal gain. *I* seduced *her*. There's something between us. I fucking feel it. I fucking know it.

But goddamn it, my head is such a mess.

I'm so fucking used to being used.

"Women like her know how to play a man. She'll lure you with charm. Get you to let her into your bed. And then she'll pounce. One night of fun could—"

I hang up.

I crouch down and put my forearms on my knees. Thank fuck this pub is in an alley, and I don't have to worry about pedestrians. Thank fuck Edinburgh is more chill than LA. It's almost safe to have a mental breakdown in public.

"Shit, Jo. You okay?" Torren's hand lands on my back, and he crouches beside me. "What's up? Do I need a medic or something?"

I bark out a dark laugh. "More like a contract killer."

"For who?"

"Conrad Henderson."

"What did he say?"

I laugh again, then push myself to standing. Torren follows.

"More bullshit. Gave me such a fucking headache that I had to take a moment." I avert my eyes from Torren's as I take out another cigarette. I check my watch as I spark it up, trying like hell to hide the trembling in my hands. "Almost soundcheck. Let's go before we piss off Sav."

The sooner I get away from him, the sooner I can turn my mind off.

I just need it to shut the hell up for a while. Then I'll be fine.

IT'S TOO easy to score prescription drugs when you're a rock star.

Everyone has them. Everyone wants to share them with you. It's a wonder how anyone ever gets sober in this industry. I could walk out into the audience now and come back with a fucking pharmacy in my pockets within minutes. If I wanted, I could call no less than twenty people who would hook me up with their doctor, and I'd have a bottle of painkillers by the end of the show.

I know how to be subtle, though. I've been doing this for years.

Roadies and groupies are my suppliers. You just have to know what you're looking for. They've got tells, and I can recognize all of them. I hit up my go-to roadie after soundcheck for Xanax. He's reliable and discreet, and at this point I don't even have to ask. I just nod to an exit door and meet him outside five minutes later.

"Been a minute," he says as he hands me a generic Ibuprofen bottle.

I take it and shove it into my pocket, then hand him a wad of cash.

"Yeah. My stash stretched."

It's not a lie. It's not uncommon. I've had periods where I use less. I trick my brain into thinking it's healed. I give my therapist a sliver of truth and pretend it works. I use the music as a crutch. It never lasts, though. I either can't handle the comedown or something sets me off. So after my mom died, I doubled up. I thought I'd need more to do the least.

I got Trouble instead.

I take the bottle back out of my pocket and take a pill.

"Thanks," I say, and then I walk out.

I clock the groupie during the third song, but I don't make the decision right away. I scan the wings for Claire first. If she's here, I can't see her. No *Thank You, Edinburgh* photo post, I guess. I ignore the way my stomach twists.

Right before the encore, I flag José over.

"Floor. Third row. Blonde hair. Fake tits. Got my name written on her chest in black paint or marker or some shit. Go now."

"Dressing room or hotel?"

"Hotel." José nods and starts to turn away, but I stop him. "Vodka."

He doesn't even question me. He just nods again and disappears. I go back onto the stage for the encores, and I expect to feel better. There's always guilt. There's always a feeling of failure. But usually, I can ignore them. Usually, the Xanax dulls the noise enough that I can look forward to a fuck and a fix.

Tonight, that doesn't happen.

Tonight, I just hate myself, and I let myself wallow in it.

The groupie is waiting on the couch holding a bottle of expensive vodka when I get back to the suite. Her red glitter bra and jeans are already discarded on the floor. I'm surprised she left her thong on, honestly.

"You want to party?" she asks the moment the door shuts behind me. It's a confirmation that I chose correctly. I'm never fucking wrong about this shit.

"What you got?"

She giggles and reaches into a red glitter purse at her feet, then wiggles an orange prescription bottle at me. "Benzos."

I shake my head. "Got that covered. Painkillers?"

She purses her lips and dives back into her bag, then pops back up with six small, white, oval pills in the palm of her hand. I take one, check the imprint, then grab another.

"Now we can party, sweets."

I chase two painkillers with a swig of vodka, then kick off my shoes before falling onto the couch next to the woman. She tries to climb onto my lap, but I hold up a hand. I'm not high enough for this yet.

"Wait." I take my phone and turn on some music, then close my eyes. "I need a minute."

I feel the couch cushion shift beside me. "Can I take off your shirt?"

I sit up and raise my hands above my head. She takes my shirt off, then goes for the button on my jeans. I let her undo that, too. She rubs on my thigh, then my dick, and I want to laugh at how *not* hard I am. I could blame it on the pills, but I know it's not that. It's because the hand is wrong. The scent is wrong. The woman is wrong. And anyway, if I was *really* wanting to fuck, I'd have gone with a different drug cocktail.

I sink further into the couch cushion. My head swims. She straddles me. I don't bother pushing her away, but when she tries to kiss me, I turn my head. Her hands are in my hair. Her tongue is in my ear. I feel nothing but disgust.

Then, because I'm fucking addicted to trouble, I grab my phone and snap a pic.

Naked fucking blonde straddling me, tits in my face, lips on my neck. I even manage a smirk. I don't second-guess it. I pull up her text thread and shoot her the photo.

Then I turn my phone off and wait.

TWENTY THREE

Claire

I'LL KILL HIM.

I will fucking murder him and burn his stupid body.

Not this bullshit again. Not again. It's Stockholm déjà vu, but this time it's not just anger I'm feeling. It's jealousy. It's so much jealousy. It's bubbling and boiling, filling me with rage, making me stupid.

He's going to fuck everything up. All of it.

I don't even bother changing out of my pajamas or putting on shoes. I just bolt into the hallway and slam my hand into the elevator button. I'm in front of his suite and swiping my key card in a matter of minutes. Sure as shit, the moment I step into the suite, the photo comes to life right before my eyes. His pants are still on, and while there is lipstick all over him, there is none on his lips.

It shouldn't make me feel better, but it does.

"Well, I'm here." I stand in front of Jonah with my hands on my hips. I go for annoyed, but irate is what he gets. I couldn't hide it if I wanted to. "I don't know what you need me for. Your tests were clear. You can fuck whomever you want."

He looks up at me with a scowl, and my jaw drops. He's high. I turn to the woman.

"Get out." She opens her mouth to argue, but I don't let her. "I said get the fuck out before I throw you out." I snatch her bag and shoes, then open the door and toss them in the hall. "Get out now, or I swear to God, I will drag you out by your hair."

The calm I've cultivated is gone. The decorum, gone.

"Okay, fine, you crazy psycho."

She rolls her eyes and starts to climb off Jonah slowly. Too slowly.

"Hurry the fuck up," I snap, then I open the door and kick her jeans and bra with the rest of her shit. My eyes land on José, and from his expression, he knows I'm going to murder him, too.

"Did you make her sign an NDA?"

José nods. "Yes, Ms. Davis."

I point at him. "Don't move."

I turn back to the woman and shout at her, clapping my hands with each word.

"Move your ass! My patience is fucking shot!"

As soon as she has a foot in the hallway, I slam the door on her back. She yelps, but I whip around and glare at Jonah. He's standing now, watching me with that blank fucking face. I cross the floor, shove at his chest, and unleash every ounce of my rage on him.

"What the actual fuck were you thinking? Do you want to self-sabotage, you fucking idiot?" My voice quakes, my throat straining with my raised voice. I don't care who hears me. I'd shout louder if I could. "Sober sex only. Sober sex only, Jonah! I leave you alone for four fucking days, and this is what you decide to do?"

I pick the vodka bottle up from the table and throw it in the kitchenette sink. It shatters. Then I march back to him and pat down his jeans. I choke out a sad laugh when I find a pill bottle in his pocket.

I snatch it and take it into the bathroom. It says Ibuprofen, but I'm not an idiot. Jonah follows and watches as I flush the pills down the toilet. I expect him to fight me, but he doesn't, which is just more infuriating. Then I throw the empty bottle at him. He doesn't even flinch.

I am so fucking mad, and I lean into it. I lean into it, so I don't have to admit how much this also hurts. I shove at his chest again.

"Do you have to fuck everything up? Do you? The rules are simple. They're simple fucking rules, Jonah! It's not that hard. You're a grown fucking adult, so why is it so fucking hard for you? Just be an adult and control yourself!"

He snatches my wrists and holds them against his chest. "You're a hypocrite, Davis."

I snarl at his even tone. I'm a raging bitch, and he sounds unaffected. I want to rip his stupid head off and shove it down his throat.

"I'm not getting blitzed and fucking strangers, you moron."

His nostrils flare and he tightens his grip on my hands.

"No, but I watch you. You pretend like you're so composed, so superior, but I see you. Have you eaten today, Claire? Or did you run five miles on double espresso and chewing gum?"

My head jerks back. It's a low, unexpected blow. "Shut up."

"I watch you counting calories in your head."

"Shut *up*, Jonah."

"Why do you carry a toothbrush everywhere, Claire? Why are you so obsessive about your workouts? You think I don't notice? I fucking do. You talk about controlling myself as if you're any better, but you're not, Claire. You're no fucking better."

"I *am* in control."

I rip my wrists out of his hands and take a step back. The bathroom is big enough that I can get several feet between us before I hit the shower. When I shout at him, though, the sound bounces off the walls. I still don't lower my voice.

"I am in control, Jonah. So what is it you want to do? You want to punish me? You want to prove that I'm just as fucked up as you are? Will that somehow make you feel better?"

"Yes!" Finally, he shows some emotion, raising his voice to match mine. "Yes, Claire. Yes, I want to punish you. Yes, I want to know you're just as fucked up as me. It does make me feel fucking better."

"Why? What the hell is that solving? *Why*?"

"Because I can't get you out of my fucking head! Because I'm fucking tormented with thoughts of you naked and moaning my name and driving me fucking mad, and then I have to picture you with *him*."

Jonah presses his palms into his eyes and groans.

"God, I hate you for it. I hate him. I hate you. I hate myself for not being able to stop thinking about you." He drops his hands and takes a few steps toward me. "I look at you and I see me. I see us. And then I fucking see *him*, and I want you to hurt like I do."

I scoff. "You were going to get high and sleep with a groupie to hurt me? Do you realize how fucking stupid that is?"

"No, I was going to get high and sleep with a groupie to get you out of my fucking head. Make you hate me in the process, and I couldn't fucking do it. I couldn't even pretend that I wanted her, and I hated every single minute of it. But, Christ, I'm powerless. Don't you get it? I'm fucking lost and losing, and I don't know what your next move is. I don't know how to win this one—"

"This isn't a game, Jonah. This isn't—"

"You said it was a game! You did! It's chess, remember? Play the whole fucking board. Every move, calculated. Everything strategic. Queen of manipulation. But who are you playing? Me? My father? Yourself? Because fuck me, Claire, I really can't tell, but I need to know. I need to know."

I shake my head. I don't understand what he's saying. I don't get it.

"What are you talking about? What does that even mean?"

He takes another step forward, close enough now to take my wrists again. This time, though, his grip is soft. He places my hands on his chest, holding me to him. So gentle, but desperate, too. His heart thuds under my palms, his pulse throbbing in his neck. That heart tattoo quivers with each panted breath, and I'm speechless. He's completely unraveled, and I have no idea how to handle it.

"Tell me you feel it. I know I'm not imagining this. I know it. Tell me you feel it, too, whatever this is."

I press my fingertips into his chest. "You're high, Jonah. You're going to regret all of this in the morning."

"It's not the drugs, Claire. It's fucking present all the time. I can't make it stop." He presses his forehead to mine and laughs. "I already regret it."

My mouth drops open, but I have nothing to say. I almost want to say something to soothe him, to walk it back, but I don't know how. I can't because, as usual, I understand him. I get it. I feel the same way. We've messed this up so badly.

"I know," I whisper. "I know."

He pulls back and hits me with those striking blue eyes. There's hope swirling in them. Hope and sadness, and it makes me want to cry.

"I'm sorry for messing everything up. I never should have—"

"No. No, Claire. It wasn't a mistake."

"It was, Jonah. It *is* a mistake. You just said you regret it."

"I regret it because you fucking own me now. I regret it because you consume me. But God, I want it. I want it even if you'll just trap me and take all my money."

I gasp, cycling through emotions. It's insulting and ridiculous and so fucking wrong, but for some stupid reason, I also find it endearing. I slip my hands from his grip and hold his gaze.

"I'm not going to trap you, Jonah. I'm not interested in your money."

He gives me a small, lopsided smile. "I wouldn't mind."

I sigh and close my eyes. "You need to sleep this off."

"I'm not that fucked up, Trouble."

"Yeah, well, after all that, I am." I tilt my head to the ceiling. Fuck, I can't even begin to process all of this. "Go to sleep. We have a lot to talk about tomorrow."

He doesn't say anything, so I take a giant step back. He's looking at me, studying, as always, but this time, he looks sad. Sorrowful. He looks like he thinks he's just made his last move and lost.

"Every time I think I've got you figured out, you throw something else at me."

I give him a small smile and shrug. "Check?"

He huffs out a laugh. "Maybe. For now."

My brow furrows, concern flooding me. He shouldn't be alone, but I can't be the one to stay with him. It would only make things worse. I force a smile.

"I'll see you in the morning."

He nods. "In the morning."

I turn and walk out. I send one text to Torren, asking him if he will stay with Jonah tonight. When he doesn't answer within fifteen seconds, I shoot one off to Callie, too. She answers immediately.

> ME
>
> Hey. Can you tell Torren to check his phone? I need someone to stay with Jonah tonight.
>
> CALLIE
>
> Everything okay?
>
> I think so, but I'd feel better if someone stayed with him. It just can't be me.
>
> He's on his way.
>
> Thank you.
>
> Anytime. Seriously.

I shove my phone back in my pocket, then scan the hallway for José. When I find him, all my anger returns. His eyes grow wider as I stomp my way toward him. He's over six feet tall, so when I'm in front of him, I have to tilt my head up to meet his eyes, but he doesn't scare me. He should be the one who's scared.

"How fucking dare you," I growl, my voice low. "You're supposed to be looking out for him, not enabling—"

"I'm not—"

"I'm talking," I shout. He flinches. "I know you're helping him get fucked up. If you're not supplying it, you're turning a blind eye to him buying it. It might have been okay before, but it's not okay now."

The fear that passes over this giant man's face. The concern. José doesn't want to hurt Jonah. It's possible he doesn't know how bad it is. I don't think anyone does. It's obvious he cares about him, but as far as I'm concerned, he doesn't care enough.

"He's my boss, Ms. Davis. I've been with him for over a year now. I do what he says."

"*I'm* your boss now." His brows furrow. When he doesn't respond, I say it louder. "Do you hear me? I am your fucking boss now. From now on, you answer to me. You do as *I* say."

"Respectfully, Ms. Davis, he hired me. Not Mr. Hammond. Not Ms. Loveless. Mr. Hendrix did."

I close my eyes and blow a frustrated breath out my nose. Then I inhale, willing my pulse to return to normal.

"When he hired you, did anyone tell you about his overdose?"

"I knew he used sometimes. I knew he'd been to rehab, but that's the norm in this industry. My previous employer did, too."

God, I want to scream. "And I suppose your previous employer referred you to Jonah."

"Um...yeah, actually."

"José, listen very closely to what I'm about to say. You are a very nice guy. I know you care about him. But Jonah hired you because he knew you wouldn't interfere. It's why he didn't tell you how bad it can get. He's an addict, José. He can't just *use sometimes*. Frankly, I'm fucking baffled that no one prepped you on it."

"Well...I was hired during a chaotic time. Everyone was pretty stressed, and Mr. Hammond was preoccupied."

I laugh. It's no excuse. Jonah must have everyone so fooled, and it breaks my heart.

"Things are changing right now. If you don't want to tell him no, then get me, and I'll do it. You run everything by me. You do what I tell you. If you don't, I will have you fired."

"You can't do that."

"The fuck I can't. Jonah is my responsibility, so from now on, you answer to me. Are we clear?"

José's eyebrows scrunch, the lines in between them growing deeper. He looks young. Younger than me. It makes me angrier with Jonah than I am with José. Jonah took advantage of him. There's no way around it.

"José, I need an answer."

Finally, he nods. "We're clear, Ms. Davis. And for what it's worth, I'm sorry. The last thing I want to do is harm him."

I sigh again. "I know. Have a good night, José."

TWENTY FOUR

Jonah

"WHAT THE FUCK?"

I jolt out of bed, freezing. Freezing and wet. I wipe the water from my eyes, then open them to find Claire standing at my bedside with an empty glass and a smirk.

"Oh, I'm sorry. Were you hoping to sleep off your stupidity?"

I scowl, but my lips twitch with the need to smile.

"You're supposed to be dead until Sunday."

"Yeah, well, some demon resurrected me early, so here I am." She turns around, giving me a great view of her ass in her bike shorts. "Get up. We've got an appointment at the gym."

I groan to mask my excitement, then roll out of bed and get dressed. I find her waiting by the door, tapping her foot. When she sees me, she checks her watch.

"That was fast for you."

I grin. "I can be fast."

"Ugh. Spare me the innuendo. It's too early."

I don't bother fighting my laugh. I don't bring up last night, either. I didn't know how she would handle things in the light of day. I still don't. I was worried when I saw her that it would be awkward. I'm grateful for the guise. I'm even more grateful she didn't make me wait in suspense until Sunday.

I'm nervous, and I'm fucking embarrassed, and truth be told, I'm scared. Years-old abandonment issues are stirring. They were already restless, thanks to the change in my friendship with Torren, but this shit with Claire has me teetering on panic.

I'm not proud of how I reacted last night, but I know from experience it could have been worse. So much worse.

The gym is empty when we walk in. It's always cleared out for us, but when I search for another giant, ripped trainer, I don't see one.

"Where's the Scottish Thor?"

Claire huffs a laugh. "It was too late to book someone. I'm your trainer today."

"We going to get sweaty together, Trouble?"

She arches a brow. "I'm going to run you ragged, Hendrix. I'm going to work you so hard, by the time I'm done with you, you won't know which way's up."

Fuck, I'm going to get hard. "You might want to watch what you say, Davis. I'm going to get the wrong idea."

She ignores my comment entirely, then proceeds to do exactly what she said she would. Her workout might even be more difficult than Thor's, but she keeps up with me.

Fifteen minutes in, and I'm ready to call it quits. Not because of the squats, though. Because of her. Sweat drips down her chest, sliding into her cleavage. Her lower back glistens. Her cheeks and neck flush the sexiest pink. When she does squats, I try so fucking hard not to stare at her ass. At the way her muscles flex with each motion.

I try and fail. And when my dick gets hard, I turn around and groan.

"I can't do this anymore, Trouble. I have to tap out."

"What?" Her question is breathy, panted. It just sends more blood to my cock.

"We have to stop."

"We're almost done. You can't quit yet."

I push my palms into my eyes and shake my head.

"Trouble, if I do anything else, I will pass out from lack of blood to my brain. I'm so fucking hard that it hurts."

She snorts. "Working out turns you on?"

"*You* turn me on. You're all sweaty and breathless and bossy. Every time you bend over, I remember how it felt being inside you. When you lay down for crunches, I replayed how you looked lying beneath me. My hips between your thighs." I groan again. "Fuck, I'm fucking worthless. This is pointless. I can't do this with you."

She goes quiet, just her labored breathing getting lost in the '90s rock playing from the gym speakers. I worry I went too far. I should have kept my fucking mouth shut. I should have just said I was tired.

"Forget it. I'm wiped and talking nonsense. I need a shower and some ibuprofen. Forget everything I just said."

I will her to agree and let it drop. I need her to just pretend I didn't say any of what I just said. It's a lot. After last night, it's too fucking much.

"I'll see you at soundcheck," I say to the wall, then take a few steps toward the door. I need to get the hell out of here. Then she speaks, and I stop in my tracks.

"I want you, too, Jonah."

Her whispered confession makes my heart stop, and my ears go on high alert.

"What did you say?"

"I said I get it, okay? I'm attracted to you. I think about it a lot. This is hard for me, too, Jonah. But..."

Fuck. There's always a fucking but. The pause stretches. My patience wears thin. I can't take any more suspense.

"Just say it, Claire."

She sighs. "But you said a lot of shit that hurt me. You got me in a very vulnerable position, and then you turned on me. You called me terrible things. You tried to make me feel guilty for your mother's death. That shit had to come from somewhere. You had already been thinking it, fuming over it, and your goal was to hurt me. I can't just forget that because we're attracted to each other."

I squeeze my eyes shut again. She's right. And even though it's more than just physical attraction for me, she's right. I fucked up.

"I know," I say finally. "I'm sorry. I was so out of line, and you didn't deserve that. You shouldn't have been the target of my anger."

"No, I shouldn't have. Had you talked to me like an adult instead of talking yourself into a grudge, I'd have told you the truth. *And* I would have told you that I'd already ended things with your dad. I'd been thinking about doing it for a while, actually."

My brows slant, then I turn around and face her. "When?"

"The day you took me to Belém."

"Fuck."

She laughs. "Yeah."

"Was he fucking his secretary?"

"Probably." She shrugs. "But it was more than that. That was just my breaking point. If I'm being honest, I'd been thinking about ending things since around the three-month mark. That's when I found out he was my CEO."

"You didn't know."

I'm such a fucking prick. She didn't know.

"No, asshole, I didn't know. I told you I wouldn't sleep with someone just to get a job. I never would have agreed to the first date if I'd known. He knew who I was, but I had no idea who he was. I should have done it then, but...I don't know." She rubs her forehead and closes her eyes. "I have an aversion to failure, I guess, and ending things seemed like a failure. It messed with my inferiority complex or something, and I think a small part of me was also worried that if I ended things, he'd have me fired." She groans, then laughs. "Guess my instincts were right on that one."

"What? He fired you?"

He's a fucking asshole. He's such a fucking asshole. And I'm exactly like him.

"He tried, but I quit before he could officially do it. Sent a resignation letter that I'd already had drafted, then deleted all my files from a campaign I was working on."

"You already had the letter drafted?"

"Yeah. Told you, I'd been thinking about it for a while. I like to be prepared."

I give her an amused half smile. "Is that chess, too?"

"My life is a chessboard." She smirks, then rolls her eyes. "Now he's actually trying to get me to come back just to finish that campaign. Said if I don't, I'll *never work in this city again*."

She drops her voice low, reciting my father's threat with a menacing air of superiority. I can actually hear him saying it.

"Is that what that email was about the other day?"

She nods, and I feel like an even bigger asshole. That's what tipped the scales for me. That's when I let my wrath take over. The whole time, she'd just been threatened by my own father. She'd been fucked over by both of us in the span of twenty-four hours.

I go back to my father's phone call yesterday. It all makes fucking sense now.

"He called me yesterday and asked for you."

"I blocked his number and marked his email address as spam. Did he tell you what he wanted?"

"Not why he wanted to speak to you, no. But he told me to be careful of you. He said you'd use me. Trap me."

She scoffs. "*That's* what set you off? You thought I was going to, what, get knocked up and take you for all you're worth?"

"No." I shake my head. "Fuck, I don't even know. I know you wouldn't do that. I know it, but my head is such a mess, Claire. I don't know how to explain it."

"I do. You'd already expected the worst from me, and he just confirmed your suspicions."

She sounds so hurt. She sounds betrayed. I did this to her. I took my own insecurities and used them against her. She's right, but she's also wrong.

"I expected the worst so I wouldn't hope for the best," I confess. "You've gotten under my skin, Trouble, and I like it. I like it too fucking much. And I just kept thinking, *when she leaves*..." I hesitate. The words are scary. Too honest. Too raw. I force myself to say them anyway. "I kept thinking, *When she leaves, she'll go back to him, and she'll take my heart with her*."

Claire shakes her head and takes a few steps toward me. "I told you. I'm not leaving."

"You have a job to do. I know."

"I'm not leaving because I care. I'm not leaving because you matter." She gives me a sad smile. "And anyway, you're technically not my job, anymore."

My heart stutters. My breath catches. "I'm not?"

"I quit, remember? Conrad doesn't even want me to be here. I've been given an order to leave, but I've chosen to stay. I made the decision even before…"

She trails off, but she doesn't have to say it.

Even before I fucked her, then tried to break her. My eyes clamp shut. I want to reach for her. I want to hold her against me and never let go, but I keep my hands fisted at my sides.

"I'm so fucking sorry, Claire."

"I know." I wait for her to say more. When she does, it's not what I want to hear. "Let's go back to the room. You've got to record a new video before soundcheck."

"Okay. Let's get on with it."

She walks past me toward the door, and I follow. I don't know what to do moving forward, but I do know that I'm going to do my best not to hurt her again.

I'm not leaving because I care. I'm not leaving because you matter.

I replay her words over and over in my head. She cares. I matter to her. She chose to stay. I hold on to that. I let it propel me through the rest of the afternoon. Through the whole show. I sink my teeth into it and refuse to let go as I lie down to sleep.

She matters. She fucking matters. And I can't lose her.

"DID YOU GET IT?"

José nods and hands the bag to me. I open it and check inside, then hand it back.

"Put it in the suite, yeah? I'll handle the rest."

José takes the bag, but he hesitates before turning around. He looks at me cautiously, so I arch a brow as I light my cigarette.

"You need something else?"

He swallows. "You sure this is a good idea?"

I blink at him. He's never questioned me before. "You think it's not?"

"No, it's not that. It's just...It sends a message, is all. I want to make sure you're okay with that."

I take a drag from my cigarette and blow the smoke out the side of my mouth, careful not to hit José. "I know it sends a message. That's exactly what I want it to do."

"Okay."

He turns and leaves without saying anything else, and I head back inside. The music from our opening band is pounding out into the stadium. Instead of going into the dressing room, I throw my hair into a bun and make my way to the front.

The moment I set foot on the floor, the fans standing on the other side of the barricade start to scream. I wave. I touch a few hands. I sign a hat and a tour shirt. Then I zero in on Claire and close the distance between us.

"Hey," I say into her ear, and she jumps. The expression she turns on me is one of shock, but it's quickly replaced with a smile.

"Hey. What are you doing out here?"

I nod to the stage where Callie's band, Caveat Lover, is playing.

"What do you think?"

"They're so good! I had no idea Callie could sing and play like that."

I nod and turn my attention back to the band, but I lean into Claire until our arms touch. I can feel the heat from her skin against mine, and I breathe. I'm so fucking obsessed.

"When did they get here?"

Claire rises on her toes and shouts the question to me. I crouch down so I'm closer to her ear, then I throw my arm around her for good measure. It's absolutely not necessary, but I do it anyway.

"Rocky, Ezra, Becket, and Crue got into Scotland a few hours after we did. They'll be opening for us this weekend, then next weekend in Dublin."

"That's it?"

"Yeah. The guys will probably stay with Callie for a few weeks, though. They're finishing up their album. I think Sav got them some studio time in Italy."

She smiles and turns back to the stage, but I don't remove my arm from her shoulders. When she leans into me, swaying a little to the music, I pull her closer. I close my eyes and tell myself not to read into it. Not to get my hopes up.

I don't listen.

By the time Caveat's set is over, I'm resisting the urge to kiss Claire goodbye in front of all these people, consequences be damned. I don't do it, but fuck, do I want to.

I'm hyperaware of her for the whole show. She moves around, taking pictures, but I always know where she is. I feel her. I smell her.

It's fucking ridiculous, but I don't care anymore.

I want her. It's as simple as that.

AFTER THE SHOW, I text Claire to meet me in my suite.

We're leaving for Dublin in the morning. I thought I could wait until then, but I can't.

I pace back and forth, wearing a hole in the carpet as I wait. My thumb starts to bleed, so I shove it into the pocket of my jeans. Nerves and excitement swirl in my stomach, making me nauseous. What if she hates it? No. She won't. I know she won't.

But what if she does?

I'm running through scenarios when there's a knock at the door. It makes me laugh. I cross the floor and swing the door open.

"Don't you have a key card?"

Claire rolls her eyes. "I don't want to invade your privacy unless I have to."

I move to the side and gesture for her to enter. "That's a lie, and you know it."

"Shut up. I'm trying to give you a longer leash."

I grab her by the arm and spin her to me, then hold her eye contact.

"I don't want privacy, Trouble. I don't want a longer leash. You could tether me to your leg, and I'd fucking love it."

Her cheeks pinken, and she flutters her lashes. She drops her eyes to my chest, almost shy, so I drop my hands from her arms and give her some space.

"I have a gift for you," I say, forcing as much confidence into my tone as I can. "Go sit down." She arches a brow. "Go sit down, *please*."

When she's perched on the couch, I grab the large velvet bag that I got from José. I could have wrapped it or put it in a gift bag. I should have.

"Sorry," I say quickly as I hand it to her. "I probably should have wrapped it."

"No, it's fi—whoa."

"Oh, careful. It's heavy."

She laughs and sets the bag on her lap. Then she flicks her eyes up to me.

"You can sit next to me. I won't bite."

I'm so nervous, I can't even crack a sex joke. I just plop onto the cushion next to her.

"Do I get any hints?"

I shake my head. "No. Just open it. I'm dying over here."

She huffs out another laugh, but she mercifully opens the velvet bag, and I hold my breath.

She gasps when she pulls out the thick wooden board inside. She sets it on the table carefully, then runs her fingers lightly over the top. The rose gold border shimmers in the overhead light. It's the perfect accent to the black polished wood and black and white tiled squares.

I watch intently as she opens the drawer on the board, her fingers trembling as she pulls out the stone chess pieces. Each one has a band of rose gold along the bottom, and as she places them on the board, she sucks in a shaky breath.

"Do you like it?" I whisper.

She looks up at me with tears in her eyes. She nods but doesn't speak.

"It's not custom. I didn't have the patience for that. But I had it overnighted from Italy, and your name is engraved on the back. I, um...I thought you'd like it. I wanted to get you something to show how much I appreciate you."

Her tears fall faster as she turns the chess board around, sees the engraving, then she laughs. "Trouble? That's not my name."

I grin, but I stay quiet, and her smile softens.

"Thank you. I love it."

"Yeah? Are you sure? Because I can send it back."

"No. Don't do that. I love it. It's honestly...It's honestly the most thoughtful gift I've ever been given. I just..." She shakes her head and hiccups on a sob. "I don't know what to say."

I cup her face and wipe the tears on her cheeks with my thumbs. Then I drop my forehead to hers.

"I'm so fucking sorry, Claire. I really am. I hate that I hurt you. I hate it. I need you to know that. I see you. I appreciate you. I'm fucking in awe of you half the time, and I'm so fucking sorry."

I feel her cheeks move under my hands. A smile. She's smiling.

"What about the other half?"

Now I smile. "The other half you're a pain in my ass."

She laughs and shakes her head. I caress her skin with my thumb. "I'm so sorry, Claire. I've never been more sorry."

"I believe you."

Then her mouth is on mine, gliding smoothly, wet with tears. I hold her closer, but I let her lead. It's soft and tender. It makes my chest hurt. It makes my heart thud hard into my rib cage. It's everything I've ever fucking wanted.

Words I've never said form in the back of my mind. Powerful words. Terrifying words. I've never felt anything more fiercely. I've never been so sure of anything. I want to say them. I want to set them free and relieve myself of this soul-deep ache. I want to, but I don't.

I let myself revel in this kiss. A kiss I'm so fucking grateful for from a woman who's too good to be true.

I don't deserve her. I'm sure of it.

But fuck me, I'm going to keep her.

TWENTY FIVE

Claire

"THIS MIGHT BE MY FAVORITE YET."

Jonah runs his fingers over a row of books, tracing each spine before moving to the next one. I smile.

"We were lucky to be here when it was going on."

"Bullshit. You could have chosen anything. Another food pantry. An animal shelter. Youth center. You chose this. Take some credit, Trouble."

I roll my eyes, but I don't argue. He's right. I've grown mindful of the events I plan for him now. I search for things I know he'll enjoy.

Doing inventory at the food pantry was a bust because he was bored out of his mind, so I canceled anything with rote tasks. He's enjoyed working with kids and anything that can involve music. He's always reading, so when I saw that the local library was hosting their yearly book sale the same week we were in Dublin, I jumped on it.

We spent all yesterday helping the other volunteers organize the used books by genre and author. It was no small task. There are hundreds of books in this room. At the beginning, I was anxious that we'd mess up the system. We wouldn't get it done in time. The books wouldn't be alphabetized correctly. But every time I looked at Jonah, he seemed...not happy, exactly...but unburdened. At peace.

I was agonizing over a section of mystery books when he stepped beside me and nudged me with his arm. Leaning down, he whispered in my ear, *Relax, Trouble. It doesn't have to be perfect.* I smiled for the rest of the afternoon.

So did he.

"Doors open in fifteen." He looks at his watch. "You worried?"

I arch a brow. "About what?"

"Dunno. That I'll make a scene or cause some sort of chaos."

I shake my head and narrow my eyes playfully. My lips twitch with the need to smile, but I try my best to hold it off. I shrug. "Not at all. You'd never disrespect the books like that."

For a moment, I think I see a blush color his cheeks. It makes my pulse pick up speed. I want to touch my hands to his face and feel the soft heat on my palms. I almost do, but he turns away and starts fiddling with the books in front of him again.

"You going to get anything?"

He keeps his eyes on the books as he replies.

"I already have a stack."

Of course he does.

Jonah glances over his shoulder at me. "You?"

"Probably not. I'm not much of a reader."

"That's a shame, Trouble. I don't fuck girls who don't read."

I bark out a laugh. "That's the biggest lie I've ever heard. You don't even ask their names. No way you know if they can read."

He lets out an exaggerated sigh. "Don't be jealous, Trouble. I'll get you something."

He walks away, leaving me smiling stupidly while I stare at his back.

"Hey!"

I turn and find Mabel grinning at me. She's with Brynn and two guys I recognize from Callie's band.

"Hey! You're here! Anyone else make it?" I glance around for some familiar faces, but I find none.

"No. Sav can't really go anywhere public, so Levi stayed with her. Callie and Tor are doing their own thing. And Rocky and Becket are..."

Mable trails off and looks to the guys with her. They exchange a quick glance, then one of them grins at me.

"They're making music. Obviously."

The other one tries to cover up a cough with a laugh, and I narrow my eyes.

"*Obviously.*" I flick my attention between the two of them. "I apologize. I don't think we've met. I'm Claire."

The taller one smiles wider and sticks out his hand. I take it, and he shakes wildly.

"I'm Ezra. This is—"

"I'm Crue." He bats Ezra's hand away and replaces it with his. "I'm English, if you can't tell."

I laugh. "The accent gave it away."

A heavy, tattooed arm is thrown over my shoulder and instinctively, I sink into his familiar body.

"Back off, wanker. Not every chick wants to fuck you just because you have an accent." Jonah glances at Brynn. "Sorry, Boss."

"It's fine." She shrugs. "It's true anyway."

Crue sticks his tongue out at Brynn playfully, making her laugh, then looks back at Jonah.

"You Americans sound like arseholes when you try to use British slang."

"You sound like an arsehole all the time."

"Okay, this is boring," Ezra cuts in, giving Crue's shoulder a shove. He turns an impish smile on me. "My bad, Claire Bear. He's still a pup. Hasn't been properly socialized yet."

Crue barks out a laugh and lets Ezra push him away. I arch a brow and look at Mabel.

"Are they always like that?"

Mabel laughs. "Yes."

"No," Brynn chimes in. "They're usually worse."

"Okay, yeah, that's true. Wait until you see all four of them together. I don't know how Callie does it. If I didn't have Sav, I'd have put Jo and Torren down years ago."

Jonah scoffs, but it's playful. "We're not dogs, Mabel."

I can tell from Mabel's face that she's a little shocked. I'm certain she doesn't get playful Jonah very often, if ever. She smiles, then looks at him with faux innocence.

"Aren't you?"

Jonah laughs, a deep, genuine sound, and I feel his body quake with it. It excites me. It makes me downright giddy, and when I look at Mabel, I can tell it excites her, too. Then he turns his attention to Brynn.

"What are you doing here, Boss? Don't you hate reading?"

"Yeah, fiction." She puts a sassy hand on her hip. "I hate reading fiction, but there are a lot of books here that aren't fiction."

"That there are." I feel rather than see him nod since he still hasn't taken his arm off my shoulder. "How much money did you swindle from everyone?"

"I did not swindle," she says with a gasp. Jonah must give her a look that says he thinks she's full of shit, because she rolls her eyes. "Okay, fine. I got twenty from Dad, twenty from Sav, ten from Red, and Ezra gave me five."

"Nothing from Crue?" Mabel asks, and Brynn shakes her head.

"He said he was broke."

Jonah snorts. "Cheap wanker."

I roll my eyes at Jonah's comment, then look at Brynn.

"Most of the books here are under five pounds. Fifty-five pounds is going to get you a lot of books."

Brynn bounces her eyebrows. "Yeah, but then we're going to get ice cream and go souvenir shopping. I want one of those little stuffed Highland cows."

Just then, the doors to the large room open and people start filing in.

"Let's go, kid. We'll get you some books."

When Jonah removes his arm from my shoulders, I have to stop myself from frowning. Instead, I smile as he and Brynn walk toward the non-fiction set of tables and leave me with Mabel.

"Thanks for inviting us," Mabel says, pulling my attention once again from Jonah's retreating back.

"Yeah, of course. I'm glad you came. I think it's good for...well..."

I shrug, not knowing how to explain it, but Mabel nods.

"Yeah, me too."

Jonah needs to remember that he has people who love him. People who have always been there for him and who care about the person he is behind the rock star persona. He needs to remember that he has, at the very least, three people who have not and will not abandon him. I'm going to do everything I can to remind him.

As more and more people filter into the room, I sink quietly into the shadows. Instead of helping, I track Jonah and take photos. He signs a few autographs and takes some pictures, but for the majority of our time at the book sale, he talks to people about books. He helps them find books. He gives book recommendations. At one point, while speaking with an older man about a classic fiction novel, I get to witness Jonah actually smile and laugh. A real smile. A genuine laugh.

For a moment, I'm jealous of the older man. I want those smiles from Jonah. I want to draw those laughs from him. But then I'm overwhelmed by a sense of gratitude. This is exactly what Jonah needed. A day in his element with kind, like-minded, normal people. Not fans. Not other celebrities. Just plain, everyday, regular people.

It's amazing to watch, actually. I knew there was charisma hiding underneath all that anger, but I never could have guessed it was this powerful.

He's enchanting, is what he is. It's the only word I can think to describe it. Jonah Hendrix is fucking enchanting, and I've been enchanted.

"Ten years ago, when we were just starting out, this was him."

I look over to find that Mabel has joined me. I nod, then return to Jonah.

"What changed?"

I see her shrug in my periphery.

"He's always been a nurturer. He looked out for all of us. But he also has this deep, powerful sense of empathy, and I think..." She sighs. When I look at her, she's watching Jonah with her eyes narrowed. "I think it was too much for him. I think he broke when he learned that he can't save everyone. Rather than feel the disappointment, he just...turned off."

"I see that."

"Yeah."

"I also get the feeling he was a perfectionist."

Mabel laughs. "He still is, actually. I mean, I was surprised when I learned he'd dropped out of Yale, but it makes sense now. Yale was to please his dad, and his dad, well—"

"Is an asshole?"

"Yep. A big, hairy asshole. Honestly, if I was that man's kid, I'd have dropped out of college just to piss him off, too. He's a prick." I nod in agreement, and then she shakes her head. "But the music? Jo's meticulous about the music. It's the only thing he's never wavered on. Relationships. Himself. Everything else, he's let go. The music? Never."

The statement hits me right in the chest.

"Because it's the only thing he can control," I whisper. I get it. I understand it so viscerally that I have to breathe through the sudden sting of tears. "No wonder this tour is so important to him. Why he doesn't want to violate the morality clause because he would lose the music as he knows it."

"Yeah. And I...um...well...not to put any more pressure on you...because this is in no way on your shoulders, but..."

"But what, Mabel?"

She shrugs. "Well. I don't think he believes he can survive without it."

My heart sinks. I want to rush to Jonah and hug him. I want to shake him, tell him he has so much to live for until he believes it. My feet yearn to run in his direction, but I stay put.

Just when I think I know Jonah, something else is revealed. Something new and heartbreaking. I feel like I'm sifting carefully through sand just to find another hidden, forbidden piece of him. I know I shouldn't. I should leave it alone and walk away, because with everything I learn, I relate to him more. I understand him on a deeper level.

And that is so very dangerous.

. . .

CLAIRE

ON THE WAY back to the hotel, Jonah sets his tote bag of books on the seat between us.

"So, what all did you get?"

He gestures to the bag. "You can look if you want."

I lean over and peer into the bag. "Jesus, Jonah. There's like twenty books in here."

I pull them out one by one, reading the titles as I do. A lot of novels, which is no surprise. He's always reading some thick, beaten-up paperback. There's also a collection of short stories, a variety of biographies, autobiographies, and memoirs of famous musicians. There's a book about world religions. And then...

"Auden?" I flip the book to read the back cover. "I've never seen you read poetry." I shrug. "I guess it shouldn't surprise me. Music is poetry, after all."

"That one's for you."

I glance at Jonah. I wish he'd look back, but he's scrolling through his phone.

"For me?"

"Yeah, Trouble. I told you I'd get you something." He puts his phone in his lap, then rests his head on the seat back with his eyes closed. "I got you a collection of poems by W.H. Auden."

"Oh. Well, thank you. That was really kind."

I slide the book into my bag, then mimic his posture. Leaned back. Eyes closed. Slow, even breathing to hide the emotions swirling under the surface.

Later, after we've both gone to bed, I roll onto my side, turn on my phone flashlight, and thumb through the poetry book. I scan the titles of a few poems, and then I come to a folded receipt stuck between two pages like a bookmark.

My pulse speeds as I look over the receipt. It's from today, and it lists a seventeen-book transaction. My fingers start to tremble. Jonah put this in here, I know it, and he never does anything without reason. When I inhale, it's shaky and shallow. I'm afraid to read what's on the page, but I'm also curious. So damn curious.

I close my eyes and try to wrangle my emotions, but I can't. It's a failure. So, I give into temptation.

The poem is titled "The More Loving One," which is enough to bring tears to my eyes. But the rest of the poem...

It's beautiful and heartbreaking. Not just a poem, but a confession. Teardrops fall as I blink, dotting the pages of the book. I wipe them away, but I read it again. I read the poem over and over, my body absorbing every word, and each time I fall a little harder. I sink a little deeper. I lose more and more of my good sense until it's gone. Until I'm no longer thinking but feeling. Until I'm nothing but adoration and awe. Then, despite all the reasons not to, I let go, and I give in. I can't ignore these feelings anymore.

I have never met a man like Jonah Hendrix.

I know I never will again.

TWENTY SIX

Jonah

OUR LAST MORNING IN LIVERPOOL, I'm awoken by ice cold water.

I jolt upright, ready to pretend I'm pissed, but my threats evaporate. Instead of finding Claire in her usual bike shorts and sports bra, she's standing in front of me in blue, lacy lingerie. That's all it takes for me to get hard. I haven't even touched her.

I start to move toward her, but she throws up a palm.

"Stay right there. I'm in charge now."

My grin is immediate. I love when she's bossy. I nod.

"Okay, Trouble. You're in charge."

"Lie back down."

I do. She smirks. "Good boy."

Fuck me, I'm going to come. How embarrassing.

"This is what we're going to do, Mr. Hendrix. I've been thinking about this, and I think you're right. I think we should test things out."

I arch a brow. "Test things out?"

She nods once. "We should see if we can be something without committing murder."

Excitement wraps around my chest and squeezes while my stomach does flips. This might be butterflies. I think I've got fucking butterflies.

"Okay." I speak slowly. I don't want to spook her. If this is a dream, I don't want to wake up yet. "So...what are you doing?"

"First, we need to even the score." She takes two more steps toward me and runs her finger over my erection tented in my boxer briefs. "I believe you owe me two orgasms. One with your tongue, and one with your cock."

I nod, my mouth watering. "I do. I do owe you two orgasms."

"We're going to do it my way."

"Trouble, I'll do it anyway you want me to. You just say the word."

The smile that stretches over her face is sinful. I want to bite that bottom lip.

"Good." I try to touch her, but she smacks my hand away. "Ah, ah. None of that."

I pout. I fucking pout, and she laughs.

"Spread your arms." I do. "Wider." I do. "Good boy. You're doing so good."

I watch as she pulls something from under the bed. At first, I think it's rope, but when she wraps it around my wrist, I see that it's nylon. Pantyhose.

She ties some kind of advanced knot, and when I try to move my arm, I realize she's tied it to the bed frame. Then she walks slowly to the other side of the bed. Leisurely. Like she's got nothing but time. She does the same thing to my other arm. When she's finished, I tug at that one too.

"Were you a Girl Scout?"

She huffs out a laugh. "No, but you can learn anything on the internet." She faces me. "Are you okay with this?"

I nod rapidly. "Absolutely. More than okay. I'm 100 percent okay with anything. Everything."

Another gloriously salacious grin. "Good."

She takes off her bra, and I groan. I ball my hands into fists. I want her nipples in my mouth. I want to fucking lick her. Then she turns, gives me a perfect view of her ass, and pulls her panties down.

"Fuck me, Claire." I drop my eyes to her swollen, wet pussy lips and groan again. "Fuck, baby."

She faces me again, and I run my eyes over her. Naked and gorgeous. Skin flushed. Nipples peaked. Those dark curls cascading over her shoulders. My dick is so hard. It's painfully hard. I need her. I need her like air.

"I'm going to blindfold you now, Mr. Hendrix. What is your safe word?"

My eyes widen. I blink a few times. I don't want to lose this view. I want it imprinted on my brain.

"Mr. Hendrix."

I flick my eyes back to her face and force a swallow. When I speak, the words are rough.

"I won't need a safe word."

"Pick a safe word."

"Elephant."

She sinks her teeth into her bottom lip and tries to fend off a laugh. "Elephant?"

"Because I will never fucking forget this."

She rolls her eyes then climbs onto the bed. She crawls toward me, pulls something off the head of the bed, then pulls it down over my eyes. I can't see. I can't move my arms. It's the sexiest fucking thing I've ever experienced.

"I'm going to ride your face, now."

"Oh, fuck yes."

"Impress me."

The bed dips with her movement as she climbs on top of me. I can feel her knees by my ears and her shins on my biceps. And her scent...

"Jesus." I inhale. "Jesus Christ."

I raise my head, wanting her pussy on my tongue, unwilling to wait, but she pushes me back down.

"Bad boy, Mr. Hendrix. I'm in charge."

Her fingers slide into my hair, and she pulls. Mercifully, she tugs my head up and lowers her body at the same time. I groan against her, and then I attack. I cover her pussy with my mouth. I fuck her hole with my tongue. I suck hard on her clit. She whimpers and moans.

And then she starts to move. Dragging her wet pussy over my mouth, covering my face in her juices. I love it. I fucking love it. If my hands weren't tied, I'd pull her down more. I'd smother myself with her pussy, but with the way she's moving, all I can do is let her ride me.

It's the single greatest moment in my life until this moment.

"Good boy. Good. Good. Just like that."

Claire's voice is so breathy and sexy and, *fuck me*, she's perfect. Her fist tightens in my hair, and she pulls me closer. I shake my head, my nose and lips and chin coated with her while I do my best to get her off. Then, because she's amazing and she wants to fucking ruin me, her delicate little hand wraps around my cock. All I can do is groan with my mouth full of her. She gasps.

"You're not allowed to come yet." She squeezes harder, and I groan again with her clit in my mouth. "You can't come until I tell you to."

I can't respond. She fucks my face faster. She pushes down on me more. This is as close to heaven as I will ever get. I will die with her pussy in my mouth and her arousal dripping down my chin, and it is fucking heaven.

"Oh my God. Suck it. Suck it."

I do as she says. I wrap my lips around her clit and suck until she's jerking and moaning. Until she's coming on my face. Thank God she lets go of my dick because I'm on the brink of coming with her.

Her hands leave my hair as she finishes. She pants and rubs herself slowly over my lips, riding out the last of her orgasm, then she's climbing off my face and sitting on my abdomen. The heat and wetness from her pussy send a current of electricity straight to my dick, and I flex my abs. I want to see it. I can picture it in my head. My abs shining with her cum and my spit. Her naked pussy pressed against my stomach. Rubbing on it. Dripping on it.

"Jesus Christ, Trouble. You're killing me. You're killing me."

She trails her fingers down my chest and goosebumps break out over my skin. The blindfold is heightening my other senses. Her touch. Her sounds. Her scent. Her taste. It's all more powerful. More potent. I fucking love it, but it might *actually* kill me. I'm going to combust.

"You did so good, baby," she whispers. "So, so good."

I didn't think I'd like being called baby, but hearing it in her sweet tone? I'll take it. I'll take her any way I can get her. Her fingers trace my jaw, then run over my lips.

"Are you ready for me, or do you need a break?"

God, it kills me to say this, but...

"If you want me to last more than thirty seconds, I'm going to need a minute."

She climbs off me, but her lips press to mine, and I kiss her. I welcome her tongue. I suck on her lips. I know she can taste herself. The way she's humming into my mouth tells me she likes it. But when I try to take more, she leans away. I'm so frustrated, I growl.

"Come back here."

"Time's up." Her tone is teasing, and I hear a crinkle of plastic right before she rolls a condom down my cock. Shit, even that feels good.

The bed dips again, she straddles me, then grabs my cock. Her tiny hand squeezes me, then runs the head of my dick through her wet, swollen lips. I can picture it. I know how it looks from above, but I'd kill to see it from this angle.

When she slides down my cock in one steady motion, flexing those inner muscles the moment she's fully seated, I choke out another groan.

"Fuck, Trouble, I'm—"

My words halt when she starts to move. She rocks back and forth, grinding her clit into my pelvis as her pussy pulses on my dick. Then she props her hands on my thighs and rides me faster.

This would be the most amazing view. I try to see through the blindfold, but I don't even get an outline, so I close my eyes and try to imagine it. Claire with her thighs spread around me. Tits up, pussy on full display while impaled with my cock. It's fucking erotic, but I know the vision in my head doesn't do the real thing justice. And then she's making these strangled, whimpering sounds.

I can't take it. I dig my heels into the mattress and thrust up into her.

"Oh my God." She moans the words and falls forward, digging her fingers into my chest. "Oh shit, Jonah. Oh fuck."

"You like that, Trouble?" I grit out the words as I move faster, trying my fucking hardest not to come too soon. "Yeah, you do. You fucking love it."

Fuck, so do I. Up and down. Up and down. My pelvis slaps into her ass, the noise like a drum beat inside my head. My cock hits her so deep that she cries out, chanting my name with every flex of my hips.

"That's right, baby. Even with my hands tied, I can make you scream."

When her inner walls start to quake and spasm, I quicken.

"You're so close. Rub your clit and come on my cock, Trouble. All fucking over it."

Just as I'm certain she's going to detonate, she pulls off me. She's gone. I'm stunned silent, but before I have a chance to even ask her what happened, she's back on me.

Skin on skin. Heat on heat. Nothing between us.

She fucks me hard and fast, and I let her lead. I let her use me. I let her drive me out of my fucking mind waiting for her to squeeze my cock as she comes so I can follow behind her.

But then she pulls off me again. She sits on my pelvis, my hard, wet cock pressing up against her back. I can hear her fingers working her clit, and she whimpers and moves on top of me. I know exactly what she's doing, and I need her to stop. I need her.

"No." I growl. "No, Claire. Get back on my dick."

Her wetness once again coats my skin, making it slick. This is punishment. She's punishing me.

"Claire Davis, I swear to fucking God—"

She lets out a low moan that I can feel in my stomach. Her body jerks, the hot, sweaty skin of her back vibrating against my erection, and she comes. Not around my cock where I want her—where I *need* her—but on her own fucking fingers.

"Are you fucking kidding me?"

She laughs. I know I sound desperate. The shock and disappointment are evident in every syllable. And she laughs at me.

Her hand pats my cheek, and her lips press against mine. I open my mouth. I try to kiss her deeply, but, once again, she pulls away.

"Thank you, Mr. Hendrix. You were stunning."

The weight of her is gone from my body. I'm panting. I'm fuming. I'm so fucking hard that I could cry.

"This isn't funny, Claire. Finish what you started."

JONAH

"I did."

Something strange—cool and waxy—glides over my chest. Like writing or a drawing. I don't have the sanity to focus on it.

"Then untie me so I can finish."

Another small laugh. She's not going to untie me. Lips wrap around the head of my cock and I groan.

"Fuck yes." I thrust into her, hitting the back of her throat twice before she once again leaves me. "God damn it, Trouble."

There's rustling. My phone dings. And then—

"See you at soundcheck."

The door to the bedroom closes, followed by the door to the suite.

She's gone.

She's gone, and she's left me blindfolded and tied to the bed with a rock-hard erection. I try to get my hands free so I can at the very least jerk off, but I can't. I can't turn over, either. I'm fucking stuck here. I don't know if I want to laugh or scream. I end up doing an odd combination of both.

I can't even be angry with her. I deserve this. Hell, I deserve far worse. When she said she wanted to even the score, any number of punishments went through my head. Tying me up, fucking me, then leaving me hard and wanting wasn't even in the realm of possibility.

Now, all I can do is wait here.

Claire wouldn't allow me to miss soundcheck, so I know she has a plan to release me.

I do everything I can to keep from replaying the entire erotic experience that just took place because when I think of it, I get hard again, and I don't need that. Instead, I think about the plot of the novel I'm reading. I go through tonight's set list. I decide on the next song I'll play for our social media videos, and by the time I hear the door open, my fingers are tingling from being tied for so long.

"What the actual fuck?" Torren barks out a laugh. "This is the best thing I've seen in a long time."

"Shut the hell up and untie me."

"I don't know, man. I think I need photographic evidence that this took place."

I groan. "I'm sure that tiny pain in my fucking ass took some."

I listen as Torren crosses the floor then grabs the pantyhose tied to my wrist. He starts to cut, and I realize he's using scissors. The minute my hand is free, I rip off my blindfold and sit up. Torren moves to my other hand, and without looking at me arches an eyebrow.

"So how did this happen?"

The question gives me pause. "What did she tell you?"

He frees my other hand, and I stand from the bed.

"She just texted and said you'd gotten yourself into trouble and would appreciate some help."

I sigh. "Trouble is right."

I make my way to the bathroom, and he follows. As soon as I see my reflection, I bark out a laugh.

ASSHOLE is written across my chest in red lipstick, standing out against the more muted colors of my tattoos.

I can't help my wide grin. She is such a fucking pain in my ass.

"This was Claire, wasn't it?"

I glance over my shoulder and find Torren watching me. His head is tilted to the side, his lips twitching around a smile. I shrug.

"Yeah. It was her."

He shakes his head. "I fucking knew you fucked her."

I turn to face him and lean on the sink. I smirk. "Actually, Tor, I think *she* fucked *me*."

Now he laughs. "Not that I'm the poster child for good decisions, but do you think this is wise? I mean, she works for your dad. She's literally hired to help you. Could be risky."

I shrug and brush past him. I don't bother telling him everything. I haven't quite processed the whole thing myself, and some of it doesn't feel like my story to tell. But he's my best friend, so I give him as much as I can.

"It might not be wise, but it's happening. I don't want to stop it."

I walk back into the room and step into a pair of boxer briefs. No way I'm washing the scent of her off now. I'm keeping it until I can have her again. And God help her, it had better be soon.

TWENTY SEVEN

Claire

JONAH MAKES IT TO SOUNDCHECK.

I knew he would. I'm not ready to see him, though, so I hide out in the girls' dressing room. I half expect him to come looking for me, but he doesn't, and I'm grateful.

Truth be told, I'm embarrassed. I've never, ever, done something like that before, and I'm shocked by how much I enjoyed it. I also feel a little remorseful for leaving him like that. I have to keep reminding myself that he did worse to me. I could have done so much worse to him. At least I didn't say cruel things to him. At least I didn't break his heart and leave him to sit in his own self-loathing. At least I didn't—

I shake my head. I can't do this. If I'm to really try with Jonah, I have to be able to move past what he did and said in Madrid. People do cruel things when they're hurting. Jealousy and anger are a volatile combination. I should know. I believe him when he says he's sorry. I've chosen to believe him.

I sink back into the couch and close my eyes. The muffled music from soundcheck filters through the door, and instinctively I try to pick out the lead guitar. Then I groan.

I've always been one to fall hard, and always for the wrong reasons. For the wrong *men*. Admittedly, in the past, it hasn't taken much to gain my affection. A well-timed compliment. A small thing in common. A perceived hint of the promise of forever.

Every single time, I've been wrong. Every single time, I ended up used and discarded.

The boy I loved in high school only wanted me for my body. The man I loved in college only wanted me for my connection to my best friend. And Conrad…Well, with Conrad, deep down, I knew he wasn't who I wanted him to be. I gave him almost a year of my life, anyway.

I can't help but wonder what I'm missing with Jonah. I can't help but anticipate the moment it's revealed what a naïve decision it was to give in to this connection. I didn't make the choice to fall for him. I have, however, made the choice to pursue it.

I try to revert my train of thought toward work. I reach for my phone and pull up Jonah's social media. The last thing I posted is a carousel from Dublin that includes two pictures from the book sale. It's gotten millions of likes, and it's been reposted in dozens of media articles online. A quick search of Jonah's name brings a smile to my face, too. My personal life might be a shit show, but I am succeeding with this job. It boosts my confidence just enough to make me stupid.

Out of habit, damn near muscle memory, I pull up my ex-best friend's profile. The very first post makes me gasp. My hand flies to my mouth as my eyes fill with tears. Happiness and sadness. Loss and longing. A deep, deep sense of self-loathing, and a reminder of the worst thing I've ever done.

It's a pregnancy announcement. Nothing flashy or over the top. Just a photo of my brother's and nephew's hands resting atop Lennon's small belly bump.

Family of four coming soon, the caption reads, followed by two blue hearts and two pink hearts.

A baby girl.

With tears streaming down my cheeks and a pained smile on my face, I scroll through the dozens of comments. Well-wishes and congratulations from people in my hometown. There's a bunch of heart emojis from my mom. My brother's best friend Chris has posted *ready for babysitting duty*. And then I see a comment that halts my scrolling and steals my breath.

It's from Samantha, a girl we went to high school with. A girl who is now my ex-best friend's new best friend. A girl I used to both hate and envy for how comfortable she seemed in her own skin. For how brave and unapologetically *her* she was.

Her comment stabs me right in the chest.

Auntie Sam can't wait to snuggle her!

Auntie Sam.

I bet my nephew calls her auntie. I bet the new baby will when she starts talking. I'm sure Lennon and Macon reinforce it. My mom and stepdad probably do, too.

In every single way, she's replaced me, and I have no one to blame but myself.

I sigh and press my hand to my stomach as it starts to roil and twist. It always does this when thoughts like these threaten to overwhelm me. Guilt and loss and regret.

And jealousy. Always the fucking jealousy. Always the anger.

It's toxic.

I am toxic.

My anxiety swells like bricks being stacked quickly on my chest. Crushing me. Burying me. Reminding me that I'm not enough. That I never will be. I'm ugly and twisted inside. I'm full of hate. I'm defective. It's all my fault.

I fist my hands and squeeze them, trying my best to breathe through the maelstrom of insults swirling violently in my head. Ugly. Twisted. Evil.

Shut up.

I flex my toes into the floor.

Shut *up*.

I train my ear to the muffled music in the hallway.

Shut up!

Inhale and exhale. Picture a chess board. Dig my nails into my palms.

Shut up! Shut up! Shut up!

I try so fucking hard, and like so often these days, I fail.

Slowly, I stand from the couch and walk to the bathroom. I kneel, tuck my hair into the back of my shirt, then make myself vomit into the toilet. I feel better knowing my stomach is empty. I calm just picturing a caloric deficit.

And then I hate myself even more.

I know what this does to my body. I know the dangers. I've always known. But reminding myself of them only makes it worse. It just fuels those feelings of failure. It shines light on my inadequacies.

How can I be expected to care about long-term damage when I hate myself?

I stand. Wash my hands. Rinse my mouth in the sink. I rinse it two more times. I grab Sav's toothpaste, then curse myself for forgetting my small toiletry bag in the hotel suite. My toothpaste is gentle on enamel. Sav's is whitening. I squirt some on my finger and rub it all over my tongue, shoving as far back as I can reach. I fill my mouth with water from the tap for a fourth time, gargle with it, then spit it out. Then I make myself look into the mirror.

I keep my eyes only on my face.

I force a smile.

I run my tongue over the backs of my teeth.

I'm still paying off the dental work I had done last year. I don't want to ruin it. Then I swallow twice and bring my hand up to push on my throat. It doesn't hurt. It's not sore, at least not in the way that causes concern. Not in the way it did last time. I bend over and gulp down some more water from the sink. I stand, squeeze my eyes shut and breathe again.

It's not out of control. I can handle this. I've gotten better before. I can do it again. It's not as bad as it was.

As long as I start now, it won't get that bad again.

I walk to the fridge and take out a bottle of water, then grab an electrolyte package from my bag. I pour the package into the water, give it a shake, and drink it. I try not to picture the cool liquid pooling into my empty stomach. I try not to fixate on it.

Then, because I'm feeling particularly bold, I grab something from the food display on the counter and make myself eat it slowly. Bite, chew, swallow, bite, chew, swallow, over and over, until it's gone. I try not to think about the caloric intake of a medium-sized blueberry muffin. I try not to add it to the green smoothie I had earlier despite the fact I just emptied my stomach into the toilet.

It's all going to be fine.

I'm going to keep this muffin down. I won't think about how many calories I have to burn in the morning. I won't obsess over my size, or my appearance, or my façade of perfection. I won't tell myself that it affects my worth as a fucking human being.

I'm a human being with a body. The body does not define me as a human being.

But what if the inside—

Shut up.

I squeeze my eyes shut and shake my head.

"Shut up!"

Inhale. Exhale. I'm going to be fine. Inhale. Exhale. I have this under control.

I *need* to be in control.

I open my eyes and grab a banana.

I'm halfway through the banana when the door to the dressing room opens, and Ziggy barrels in, followed by Brynn, Levi, and Sav's security guard, Red.

"Claire. Hey. Sorry. Would have knocked if we knew you were in here."

I put the banana down and smile at Levi. "Hi. It's okay. I'm just hanging out until it's time to get to work." Ziggy sits down in front of me and nudges my leg with her nose. I pet her head, then give her a cheese cube from the food tray on the counter. "You're all in a box tonight, right?"

"Yep." Brynn steals a strawberry and takes a bite. "All of us. The Caveat boys, too." She rolls her eyes and sighs. "I hope they behave."

Red laughs and gives Brynn's shoulder a nudge as he reaches over her and snags a few grapes. "Not everyone can be as mature as you, Boss."

"They're in their twenties. It's annoying."

I flick my eyes to Levi with a grin. He shrugs. "She's not wrong."

"Are you going to sit with us?"

I turn my attention back to Brynn and shake my head. "Probably not. I need to get pictures for Jonah's social media."

"His page looks awesome."

"Thanks." I arch a brow. "You have social media?"

"No. I saw it from Sav's." She huffs. "Dad and Sav say I can't get my own until I'm thirteen."

"That's smart. There are a lot of weirdos out there."

"Yet I have to go on tour with Ezra, Crue, and Rocky."

Red and I bark out a laugh, and Levi ruffles Brynn's hair. "Not the same kind of weirdos."

She huffs again. "Yeah. I know."

Brynn trudges to the sofa and dramatically throws herself on it, then Ziggy jumps next to her and lays her head on Brynn's lap. I look at Levi, and he flares his eyes, making me laugh again.

"She's right, though. Jonah's socials look great. Seems like the press is liking what they're seeing, too."

"Yeah, thank you. I'm happy with how we're progressing."

"Do you think you'll be finished up, soon?"

It's a normal question. Completely harmless. But it bothers me in a way that it shouldn't. *Finished up* is synonymous with *leaving*. Will I be *leaving* soon. I shrug and force a smile.

"I'm not sure. I'd like to be a little more confident in the stability of the branding before I close it out."

The words turn my stomach. They're so impersonal. So *professional*. Jonah is a human. He's so much more than a brand. He's become so much more to me...

"That makes sense." Levi grins. "Though, your work does seem to be influencing more than just the media."

"How so?"

He flicks his eyes to Red, then back to me.

"I'm used to Jonah being a lot more...isolated, I guess. Reserved. I'm not used to seeing him smile, let alone laugh. He's been doing that a lot recently."

I nod and ignore the conflicting emotions swirling in my head and chest. I try not to think about the *stability of the brand* or what comes after I've *finished up*. I try not to question if this change in him is because of the actual work I've done or the other things.

"Mabel and Sav have said something similar."

"I obviously don't know him as well as they do. I only came into this world a few years ago, and by then, Jonah had already..."

Levi pauses, brows furrowed, and then shakes his head. Whatever he was going to say, he's decided against it. But I know. Jonah had already succumbed to his demons. The thought hits a little harder right now. I wish I'd stop relating to him in these ways. These *painful* ways.

"Anyway, I did meet him once a long time ago. Right when the band was starting out. And... I don't know. He seems...a little more like that guy, and a little less like the guy I've come to know."

"Well..." I nod and force cheeriness into my tone. "I'm glad to hear it."

Just then, the door swings wide, revealing Sav and Mabel. Soundcheck is over. The show will be starting soon.

"Well, I'm going to head out to the floor," I say to everyone. "I want to get some fan photos before the opener."

I leave before Sav or Mabel can try to convince me to stay. I didn't lie. I do want to get fan photos. It's something I've been doing since night one in Edinburgh. Admittedly, it started because I had to watch the show from farther back, so Jonah wouldn't see me, but it's gone over well with fans.

I take pictures of the crowd until the opening band takes the stage, and then I snap a few of them, too. I get into a groove. All of my thoughts are focused on work. No images of Jonah naked and tied to the bed. No thoughts of Lennon and Macon's new baby. No guilt. No embarrassment. Just work.

Until The Hometown Heartless takes the stage, of course. Then I'm hit with a wave of images and memories from earlier.

When Jonah takes his place by his guitar, my cheeks heat. My pulse picks up speed. I have to fold my lips between my teeth to keep from smiling. I'm torn between wanting to sink into the crowd to hide and wanting to wave my arms until I finally have his eyes on me. He makes the decision for me, though. The moment he glances up from his guitar, he finds me. He doesn't even have to look. Our eyes lock, he gives me a subtle smirk, and he...takes off his shirt?

Everyone around me starts to scream. This move is very out of character for him. His on-stage outfit is the same as his off-stage outfit. Jeans and a band tee. As far as I know, Jonah Hendrix has never played a show shirtless.

For a moment, I'm confused, and then I see it. The ASSHOLE I'd written on his chest with bright red lipstick is still there. It's a little faded and smudged, and it blends a bit with his tattoos, but it's there. I bark out a laugh before my jaw drops. If the ASSHOLE is still on his chest, then that means he hasn't showered. And if he hasn't showered...

His grin grows sinful. He knows exactly what I'm thinking. When he licks his lips slowly, it's confirmed. He's still covered in me. His stomach. His face. His dick. I'm all over him.

And from the look on his face, he wants to keep it that way.

TWENTY EIGHT

Claire

"YOU THINK YOU'RE FUNNY."

I look up from my laptop and arch a brow. "I assure you; I take myself quite seriously."

Jonah walks toward me. I work to keep my expression bored, but my chest rises and falls with my quickening breaths. His attention drops to the movement, and his jaw pops. When he looks back at my face, his eyes are heated. It sends a shiver through me.

"Are you proud of yourself, Trouble? Tying me up. Using me to come. Then leaving me hard and horny?"

I smirk. "I am, actually."

"Hm." He kneels in front of me, and my excitement spikes. He taps on my laptop screen. "Is your work saved?"

I narrow my eyes. "Yes."

"Good."

Carefully, he closes the laptop and sets it on the table beside the couch. Then he leans in, putting his hands on the back of the couch and bracketing me between his forearms. His scent overwhelms me. Woodsy bodywash and sweat. I inhale slowly.

"Are we even now?"

I shrug. "I don't know. Are we?"

I don't understand the emotion that passes over his face. I want to run my fingers over his lips, but I don't. His blue eyes bounce between mine like he's searching for something, and then he shakes his head.

"No. We're not even. But I'll make it up to you. I promise."

My chest warms from the inside. He's not talking about orgasms. He's not talking about sex at all. It's so much more. My next breath is shaky, and for some reason, I want to cry. I nod.

"Okay," I whisper, and then his lips are on me.

He kisses me slowly, tongue caressing mine as we move in time with each other. His calloused hands cup my face. I wrap my arms around his neck. He doesn't take it further. Doesn't try to turn things heated.

He doesn't, so I do.

I slip my fingers in his hair and deepen the kiss. I scoot forward, leaving no room between us. I press my breasts to his chest. I widen my legs so I can pull him closer. When I bite his lip, he groans into my mouth.

He pulls away, so I move my lips to his neck, and he groans again. "We don't have to do this, Claire."

"I know."

I try to pull him onto the couch with me, but he pulls back again and grabs my wrist. He brings my hand between us, opens my fingers, then presses a kiss to my palm.

It's the softest, most gentle gesture I've ever received. The intimacy makes my heart squeeze. It makes my chest ache. I feel cherished. I feel important, and I don't understand it. I don't understand *him*.

A quiet, terrified part of me prays that this isn't another trick. If it is, it will break me. There will be no coming back from this for me. Mentally, emotionally, I don't think I could handle it. I don't know when it happened. I don't know how. But I've fallen so fucking hard for this man, and if he doesn't feel the same, it will ruin me.

It will ruin me completely.

He traces calloused fingers over my jaw, then cradles my face with both hands. When he presses his forehead to mine, my eyes flutter shut. He brings his lips to mine, then whispers so quietly, it's barely more than an exhale. His words pass between us like a shared breath. I breathe them in, down my throat, to my lungs, and into my bloodstream. I feel them in my body. In my heart. In every organ. Part of me.

Permanent.

"I promise."

I kiss him. I kiss him fiercely. I want to breathe him in with those words. I want to make him permanent, and the thought scares me.

The last time I told someone I loved him, he broke my heart. I wasn't who he wanted. I wasn't enough, and it sent me spiraling downward at such a rapid pace that I couldn't recover. I lost control. I almost lost everything.

I pull Jonah closer. I want him on top of me. I want the weight of him to force the past from my memories. He's here. It's him. It's not the same as anyone before him.

"I want you," I say. "I want you now."

In one swift motion, he stands and lifts me into his arms. He carries me to the bedroom without breaking our kiss, then lays me gently on my bed. He stands again and takes off his shirt. I do the same. When he undoes his pants, I follow suit. I match his movements step for step, until we're both naked, and I'm reaching for him.

When his body covers mine, I sigh with relief. I press myself against him, wrapping my legs around his waist. I want to merge us together. Melt him into me. I want his cells to be my cells. *Permanent.*

I snake my hand between us and grab him. I squeeze his hard cock, and he grunts into my mouth. I guide him through my pussy lips until he's where I want him, and then I press my hips up as he pushes down.

We both moan when he enters me. He stretches and fills me, then he moves. He pulses slowly, hinging his hips and curving his lower half so he hits me deep. I don't stop kissing him. I don't let our bodies separate.

"You're perfect," he murmurs into my mouth. "You're perfect, Claire."

It brings tears to my eyes. My impulse is to protest. To tell him I'm not perfect. I'm dark, and angry, and messed up. *I'm not who you think I am. I'll never be.*

I don't. I keep the confessions inside. I shove them far away, because this moment *is* perfect. Right now, with him, I *feel* perfect. I feel fresh and clean and new. *I love you*, I want to say. *I love you. Please don't leave.*

Please don't hurt me.

I won't survive it.

I won't survive him.

I DREAM OF JONAH.

Of his arms wrapped around me. Of his breath and lips on my neck. His hands on my body. Cupping my breasts. Splayed across my stomach, pressing me into him.

Jonah, I whisper. My lips move, but there's no sound. Just breath. *Jonah.*

His cock pushes into me from behind. A whole new sensation. A whole new angle. I moan and pulse against him. His hand slides down my stomach to my pelvis. His fingers rub on my clit. I moan louder.

Yes, yes, yes.

"That's right, baby." His voice is in my ear. Low and strained. "Come for me, Trouble. Come for me."

His hand grabs my throat, his fingers pressing in the sides of my neck lightly, and my orgasm startles me awake. My eyes fly open, and I cry out, the soft dawn glow streaming through the windows, but Jonah is still here. Still inside me. Still wrapped around me.

"Oh my God," I say on a gasp, and he hums in my ear.

"Good morning." He pulls out and I roll over, taking his lips in a desperate kiss. "You're so soft. So eager for me even when you're sleeping."

"I'm always eager for you." I climb on top of him and waste no time sliding down onto his cock. "Fuck."

"Always?" He punctuates the question with a thrust up, making me gasp. "Even when you're mad at me?"

"Yes," I cry out as he starts a punishing rhythm. "Especially when I'm mad."

"Good." He wraps his hand around my throat once more, squeezes once, then slides to my collarbone. His gives me a light push. "Now lean back and put your hands on my thighs. I need to see it for real."

I blush. He's referring to the blindfold. I rode him shamelessly when he couldn't see me and his hands were tied, and he wants me to do it again.

I do as he says. I support my weight on his thighs and his eyes go straight to my pussy. To where his cock is sliding in and out of me.

"Fuck me, it's the sexiest thing I've ever seen."

I'm emboldened. I move my body faster. I rock back and forth. I bounce up and down. It feels so good that my mouth falls open with heavy, panted breaths. I want to drop my head back and close my eyes, but watching him is too captivating. Jonah's blue eyes are full of heat. His expression is hungry and awestruck.

"You like this?" I ask, already knowing the answer. "You like watching me fuck you?"

"Fuck, yes." I swirl my hips, and he groans. "I want to fucking film it and watch it over and over. You're a fucking goddess."

In this moment, I feel like a goddess. Worshipped and powerful. It's enough to make me come. When he lifts up on one forearm and uses his free hand to rub my clit, my orgasm hits like a tidal wave. He barely touches me, and I'm digging my nails into his thighs and screaming.

"Jonah, oh my God."

I'm sure the others can hear me. The whole hotel, maybe. Right now, I don't care.

I fall forward and wrap my hands around his neck.

"Fuck, Trouble. You're going to make me come."

His Adam's apple bobs under my thumb, that tattooed heart rising and falling with every labored breath, every rough swallow. His throat vibrates with his groan. I think I can feel his rapid, thundering pulse under my fingers.

"Yes. Like that." His encouragement eggs me on, and I squeeze slightly. Just a little. Mimicking what he did to me. "Fuck, Claire."

He wraps his hands around my wrists. His eyes penetrate mine. That same rapturous expression. Begging me silently. A supplicant.

Then I ride him.

"Jesus." He chokes out the word with his teeth gritted, and I grin.

"No, Jonah. Claire."

He lets out a pained laugh. His heart tattoo throbs under my thumbs.

"Fuck, Claire. Just like that. Fuck."

I pulse around him. I make him moan and chant my name. I make his face twist up and his mouth gape open. I squeeze him until he releases my wrists and grips my hips. Then he pounds into me.

"Oh my God," I say on a low moan. "Yes. Yes. Harder."

Quickly, I'm flipped onto my back, and he obeys, thrusting into me hard and fast. My whole body quakes with the impact as he fucks me, but I want more. I need more.

"Choke me."

He freezes and his eyes jump to mine. There's no hiding the excitement in them.

"What did you say?"

"Choke me, Jonah." I grab his wrist and move it to my throat. "Choke me, please."

His chest heaves, and his eyes fall to his hand. He flexes his fingers around my neck slightly, then bites his lip.

"Are you sure?"

"God, yes."

He hesitates, bouncing his attention between my eyes and my throat.

"I'm not going to restrict oxygen."

"No."

"Yes. It's that or nothing. I don't want to risk hurting you."

"You won't."

"Claire, please. That or nothing."

I want to protest. I want to tell him I don't want gentle. I want everything. But the look in his eyes stops me, and I nod.

"Okay."

"What's your safe word?"

I arch a brow. "Elephant."

His lips curve into a smirk. "Smartass."

I clench around his cock, and he grunts, then hits me with a sinful grin.

"Careful. You're going to get yourself in trouble."

"I can handle it."

Slowly, he lowers himself back over me, keeping his hand around my neck and bringing his face inches from mine.

"I want you to use your safe word if you're uncomfortable or if you feel me applying pressure any heavier than this."

I swallow, my throat expanding and contracting in his hand. "You're applying barely any pressure at all."

"Exactly." I scowl, and he chuckles before taking my lower lip between his teeth and biting lightly. "Quit pouting. We can work up to more, but not now. Any discomfort. Any pressure. Use your safe word."

I nod, and he flexes his hips, hitting me deep with his cock and making me whimper.

"Say you understand, Claire."

"I understand. Any discomfort or pressure, I say elephant."

He grins and presses another kiss to my lips.

"Thank you," he says, and then he starts to move again.

He tries to go slowly, but I don't let him. I buck up into him and make him fuck me faster. He groans and drops his forehead to mine. His fingers flex around my neck.

"I've had dreams of this. Fucking you with my hand wrapped around your pretty little throat." He cants his hips to the side, and I gasp at the new sensation. "You fit so perfectly in my hand, Trouble. I can feel your heartbeat. I can feel your breathing. Everything I need right in my palm."

"I love it," I rasp out. "I love having your hand around my throat."

"Fuck."

His groan is almost pained, and he speeds up. He flexes his fingers again, pulsing them around me. I can breathe. I'm not lightheaded. But it's so sensual and erotic. I'm so turned on that my skin is buzzing.

"Just think of all the ways I'm going to fuck you."

His forearm puts pressure on my collarbone, pinning me into the mattress, while he pushes up on his other arm so he can peer down at me.

"Every surface. Every position. Every country. I'm going to own every fucking orgasm from now on, Trouble. Until my cock smells permanently like your pussy. Until your cum is all I taste. Until every time I make a fist, you feel it around this pretty little fucking throat, and it makes you wet."

Every word is rasped and gritty, and I picture everything he says. It pushes me closer and closer to the edge. My pussy throbs and clenches around him rhythmically. His body starts to quake. His movement grows frantic.

"Fuck, Claire. Fuck."

"Are you going to come with me, Jonah?"

"God, yes."

He drops back down and wraps his arm around my back, holding me against him just as his muscles tense. Our sweaty bodies collide, connected from sternum to thigh, and it's still not close enough. He jerks and curls around me as we come together. His low groan matches mine and vibrates through me. He pants into my neck, then buries his face into my hair.

He doesn't let go of me. He doesn't slide out of me. He just holds me closer, then presses kisses to my head. My ear. My shoulder and jaw. Then, finally, my lips.

"You're mine, Claire Davis." He growls the words into my mouth possessively, almost angrily, with his hand still wrapped around my throat. "Do you understand what I'm saying? You're mine."

I nod and take his lips again.

I understand.

I don't think he does, though. Not the true extent of it.

He might mean I'm his right now, but my heart will be his forever.

Checkmate, Jonah Hendrix.

You've won.

TWENTY NINE

Jonah

I WATCH her when she doesn't know it.

When she's working. When she's sleeping. When she's exercising. When she's eating.

Especially when she's eating.

I keep tabs on her like I've never done with anyone. Not even my brother. Claire Davis owns me. Body, mind, heart. All of it. And it's terrifying.

I dream of losing her. Of her seeing me for what I am. Of her not needing me anymore.

Of something worse.

My thoughts keep cycling back to Theo. He was the only person I ever trusted completely. The only person I really, truly loved, and who loved me in return.

It's different, of course. The love I had for my brother is nothing like what I feel for Claire, but the vulnerability feels the same. It's a physical, consistent ache in my chest. A rubber band of worry just tight enough to remind me that opening my heart to anyone makes me open for pain. And even with Theo, there was the underlying truth of the matter. The ever-present question. How pure was that love? How conditional?

Losing him still fucked me up. Set me on a path to destruction. It was delayed, but inevitable. I tried so hard to redeem myself. I tried to be someone my parents wanted after Theo died. It was useless. Theo was the one who mattered, and without him...

I shake my head.

I recognize this. The heightened anxiety. The headaches. The trouble sleeping. I'm pissy and jumpy. It happens every time I try to stop using. It was worse when I went to rehab. At least I'm not vomiting and shaking on the bathroom floor in a puddle of my own sweat. Yet.

Fuck.

I feel too much without the pills.

I blink and bring the room back into focus. I bring *Claire* back into focus. She ran five miles again this morning. She still hasn't ordered breakfast.

"How about we go out to eat?"

I meet her eyes in the bathroom mirror, then step up behind her and wrap my arms around her waist. I kiss that little dip where her neck and shoulder meet. She hums and leans into me. She smells so sweet. The lavender calms my mind. The sugar makes my mouth water.

"We can find a cute little café. Have some tea. Eat a scone with clotted cream and jam."

I do my best to fake a British accent. She laughs, then turns and throws her arms around my neck.

"You sound like Crue when he's trying to mimic Ezra's American accent."

I grin. "That bad?"

She flares her eyes playfully, then kisses me. It's chaste, and when I try to deepen it, she pulls away. I chase her and kiss her again. She just got out of the shower, but I'm ready to dirty her up again.

"Mmmm, back up." She pushes on my chest, so I sigh and give her space. Her lips curve up into a small, suggestive smile. "We have work to do today. We can't put it off anymore."

"But you've never been to Wales." I fold my hands under my chin. "*Pleeease*? I want to show you around Cardiff."

Claire rolls her eyes. "As much as I would love to, we have things on the calendar. I still have a job to do, and we don't want anyone getting the wrong idea."

She brushes past me. I frown and follow her into the bedroom.

"And what exactly is the wrong idea?"

She doesn't look up as she puts on a pair of socks, then grabs her laptop.

"You know. That I'm not taking this seriously. That I'm...I don't know...*Sleeping* on the job."

She huffs a laugh at her joke, but I don't think it's funny.

"What if we just tell them?"

She stops in her tracks, then turns to face me. Her expression is shock. Shock and concern.

"We can't do that, Jonah."

"Why not?"

"Because. I'm still here to work. I'm still—"

"I'm not your job anymore, remember? You're not employed by Innovation."

"Yes, but I still need to maintain some semblance of professionalism. Do you know what will happen to my career if it gets out that I'm sleeping with you?"

That she's *sleeping* with me. Not dating. Not even "seeing."

Just *sleeping with me*.

I try to ignore the shitty way that makes me feel, but I can't. It echoes in my head. I scan my eyes over her face, realization hitting me in the gut and making everything worse. I breathe through my nose. I try to stop grinding my teeth before speaking.

"This is about my dad, isn't it."

"Has he stopped calling you?"

"No."

"Then yeah, he has a lot to do with it."

"Why? He's not your boss anymore. It's not like he can fire you again."

My words come out harsher than I intend. I snap instead of state. My usual calm, unaffected mask is no match for these emotions. No match for Claire Davis.

Her nostrils flare. I've pissed her off.

"First of all, he didn't fire me. I quit. And secondly, you know how influential your father is in the marketing world. Jonah, if he finds out about this—about us—he could seriously tank any chance I have of working in this industry again."

"So, what? We just never tell anyone?"

She closes her eyes again. "That's not what I'm saying."

"Then let me at least tell the rest of my band."

"The *rest* of your band?" Her eyes fly open, then narrow at me. "What do you mean the rest?"

I sigh. "Torren knows."

"How does Torren know?"

"You called him to come untie me from the bed, remember? He's not an idiot."

"Right." She blows out a slow breath. "Right. I should have known that would happen."

"So let me tell the rest of them."

"No." She shakes her head. "It's too risky."

"Claire, I don't want to hide this."

"I'm not asking you to. Now just isn't the right time."

I scoff. "When will be the right time, exactly? When the *job* is finished? Because I'll still be his son, Claire, and he'll still be the CEO of Innovation Media. None of this is going to change."

"I know." She sighs and tilts her head to the ceiling. "I know."

She's stressed. It's evident in every muscle in her body. This is weighing heavily on both of us, but I hate seeing her upset, and I know what stress does to me. I'm learning what it does to her, too.

My anger calms. My insecurities quiet enough that I can ignore them. I close the distance between us and pull her into a hug. Claire wraps her arms around my waist, and I feel the rest of the tension leave my body. My mind is a mess. My heart is overwhelmed. But as long as she's in my arms, I can relax.

"I'm sorry," I whisper into her hair. "Let's order room service, and then we can get started on your to-do list, okay? We'll table this conversation for later."

"Thank you." She lifts onto her tiptoes and kisses me. "Thank you."

Later. We'll worry about it later. Fine. I've got plenty of other things to worry about right now, anyway. So, we order breakfast, and I try like hell not to make it obvious that I'm tracking her every move. Her every bite. I pay attention to every chew and swallow. It takes everything in me not to encourage her to eat more when she says she's finished.

She disappears into the bedroom, and I stay in the main room. I barely breathe as I wait for her to head into the bathroom. Every sense is trained on her. My thumb is picked raw. I listen and listen.

Finally, when she doesn't come out of the bedroom, I stand and follow her in. I find her messing with the ring light, and I let out a slow, relieved breath.

"So, what's it going to be today?"

I sit on the side of the bed and glance around the room. She's got the black silk sheet spread out already and my guitar and amp in the corner. Her sexy little social media setup.

"Ray LaMontagne," I tell her, and she hums.

"Folk rock. I like it."

"Well, emphasis on the rock." My lips curl into a small smile.

"I'd expect nothing else. Alright, you ready?"

"Ready when you are, Trouble."

"Okay...Let me just...Yep. Go."

I launch into the song the same way I've been doing all the others. Opening chords, then moving into a solo instrumental version where it sounds like my guitar is "singing" the vocals. I add my own flourishes, but I stay true to the vocals. It makes it easier for my followers to identify the song.

I want to laugh at myself.

My *followers*.

It still sounds asinine, but Claire was right. The social media move is paying off. Even the paps have been affected. Lately, they shout out questions about my various volunteering events instead of my impending rehab visit. Claire is brilliant, and I can't deny that anymore.

I think about it, about her, the whole time I play. About the influence she's had on my life. The way she holds my emotions in her fucking hand. She consumes my thoughts, and I'm grateful for it. She's a lot better than the trouble that usually invades my head.

As the song fills the room, I hope like hell she recognizes it. Because just like all the others, it's for her. This one isn't subtle, though. "Trouble" by Ray LaMontagne is so obvious, I might as well have the lyrics tattooed on my forehead. I wish I could see her face, but that fucking ring light makes it impossible.

When the last notes fade, we sit in silence. She doesn't turn off the ring light, and I don't speak. I turn off my amp, put my guitar back on the stand, and wait. I wait until the anticipation gnaws at my insides. I pick at my thumb until it bleeds, so I fold it into my fist. Then I break.

"You're killing me over here."

Silence.

"Claire."

"Yeah?"

"What did you think?"

"It was great. They're always great. You're a talented musician."

Her tone is forced. Fake niceties. I blow out a slow breath and nod. "Right. Thanks. Send me the video, yeah? I'll post it."

"You sure? I can—"

"I'm sure. Send it."

"Okay."

I can feel her looking at me, so I cross the floor and turn the ring light off myself. What I find when I look in her eyes takes my breath away. My hands cup her face, my thumbs wiping her silent tears.

"What's wrong, baby? What did I do?"

Claire shakes her head. "Nothing. Nothing is wrong."

She snakes her arms around my neck and lifts onto her tiptoes. I bend down to meet her and press my lips to hers in a soft kiss. I taste her tears. I feel her heat. I pull her closer.

"Why are you crying?"

She huffs out a sad laugh. "I don't even know. I don't even know anymore. You just keep...You just keep...The queen. The chess set. The book. And now this..."

She buries her face into my neck, her breath skirting over my heart tattoo. When she speaks, her lips tickle the thin skin there, and I swear I feel it in my chest. A direct line from the tattoo to the real thing. I'm a goner.

"I just feel...I just feel *everything*."

I laugh into her hair, then press a kiss to her head. "I know. Me too."

Fucking *everything*.

When Claire goes back to work, I step into the bathroom, shut the door, and count my stash. I won't buy more. This is it.

Then I tell myself to brace for the comedown.

"ARE YOU COMING WITH ME?"

"No." Claire looks up from her laptop with a smile. "I don't want to encroach on your dude time."

I snort out a laugh. "It's just brunch, Trouble. Torren and Levi won't care if you come."

She smirks. "It's so funny to think about you and Torren, all tatted up and intimidating, eating *brunch*."

"I can crush some eggs bennie, baby."

She shakes her head with a laugh. "Go have fun. I'll be at the stadium before the show starts. I've got to make some calls and finalize your plans for Amsterdam. Have you had a chance to look at the calendar?"

I grin. "Nope."

"Jonah. I want your feedback."

I cross the floor until I'm directly in front of her, then bend down and cup her face.

"I trust you, and it's fun to be surprised." She fights a smile and narrows her eyes. She's not angry, but it's cute that she's pretending. I kiss her once, then pull back just enough to make eye contact. "I'll be watching for you on the floor. You better be there as soon as the stage lights go up."

Finally, she lets the smile slip. "I won't be late, Mr. Hendrix."

I stand up and run my eyes over her. She hasn't eaten breakfast yet, but she's still in her pajamas. At least I know she won't be running five miles on nothing but espresso today. I open my mouth to suggest she order room service, but then my phone rings.

Claire flicks wide eyes to me. We both know the only person who would be calling. Everyone in the band texts except Ham, and Ham has no reason to be calling me right now. I've been a good boy lately.

I let the phone ring out, but it starts right back up again. Claire sighs. "Just answer it, Jonah. He won't stop until you do."

I grit my teeth and take the phone out of my pocket. I should just block his number, but that will just make it worse. At least this way, I can fend him off. Make excuses. Tell him Claire is, in fact, still doing the job she was assigned, even if she's technically no longer employed by my father.

I hit accept and bring the phone to my ear.

"Father."

"Jonah. I need to speak with Claire."

I don't bother hiding my smirk. He's past frustrated. He's irate. "She's busy. She's finalizing my events for Amsterdam."

"She needs to get her ass back here and work on this campaign. We are going to lo—"

I hang up. He calls right back.

"Father."

"Jonah! Stop fucking around!"

I flinch at the volume, and so does Claire. He's so loud, even she heard it. And the concern, the borderline fear that shows in her eyes, has me turning to walk out of the suite. She doesn't need to hear this, but she jumps up and grabs my arm. She shakes her head, so despite my instincts, I stay put.

"Claire is working here, and she isn't going back to Innovation."

"If we lose this campaign, it will ruin her career. She needs to finish what she started. She needs to—"

Claire snatches the phone out of my hand, her face flushed red with anger. "You gave the MixMosaic campaign to Brandt Macy, Conrad. It's not my responsibility. If you lose this campaign, that's on him, not me."

Whatever he says next, I can't hear it. His volume is lowered, and for a moment, I'm shocked at the immediate change. The furious version of my father is gone. With Claire, he's become soft. Intimate.

I want to stab him.

Claire clamps her eyes closed. Her brows slant harshly.

"It's Brandt's campaign. It has been from the beginning. If it needed me, you'd have let me have the lead position."

Another pause. Her jaw pops. Her nostrils flare. And then her shoulders drop.

"I don't have the energy for this, Conrad. I made a commitment to help your son, and that's what I'm doing."

Your son, she called me. Not Jonah. *Your son*. I understand why, but it still makes my stomach churn. It makes my hands shake as I ball them into fists.

I've had Claire Davis in my bed every night. I've tasted every inch of her body. There's not an inch of her skin I haven't touched. She's the last person I see when I close my eyes. She's the person who stars in every dream. She's the first person I see when I wake up.

But I'm still *Conrad's son*.

"My resignation still stands. I'm not leaving until this job is done. I'm not coming back to Innovation."

She flinches. I don't know what he said, but I can tell it's bad. A threat, probably. It makes me hate him even more, and I didn't think that was possible.

"You do what you feel you need to do, Conrad."

She hangs up and hands me back my phone. "Well?"

She huffs a laugh, then mimics my father. *"This isn't over, Claire. This isn't over."*

Mother fuck, I hate him. I pull her into a hug.

"Are you worried?"

She shrugs, then steps away from me. "I don't know what I am, honestly. But I'm not going back to work for him. I don't care how much money he offers me or how many threats he makes. This is about my dignity. It's about my integrity. I'm not going to compromise either of those things."

I force a smile. "You're not good at compromise."

Finally, she smiles back. It's small and tired, but it's there. "I'm really not."

"I'm going to text Torren and bail."

She puts her hand over my phone before I can even type out a text. "No. Go. I'll be fine. I have work to do, and I refuse to let that asshole derail me."

"Are you sure?"

"Yeah. I'm sure." She kisses me once. "Thank you, though."

"If you need me, call Torren. I'm turning my phone off in case my dad tries to call again."

"Okay. I'll see you tonight."

THIRTY

Claire

I'M PUSHING the button for the elevator when Mabel steps up beside me.

"Hey. You heading to the gym too?"

I smile at her. She's holding a bright pink water bottle and wearing leggings, a tank top, and a pair of pink sneakers. I nod. "You going to join me today?"

"Looks like it. Don't you and Jonah usually go early?"

We step into the elevator together, and she pushes the button for the gym.

"Yeah, but it's our rest day. He went to brunch with the guys."

"You don't look like you're resting."

I laugh. "I had a very stressful phone call and need to burn off some frustration."

"Ah." She nods and flares her eyes. "Same, actually."

We step into the gym together and both head to the treadmills.

"Want to talk about it?" I ask as I throw my towel over the bar and put my water bottle in the cup holder. "I'm a good listener."

Mabel flashes me a sardonic grin. "It's just relationship stuff. My girlfriend..." She shakes her head and shrugs. "She's not exactly out, and it's hard for me keeping things on the DL."

I train my eyes on my treadmill screen and nod slowly.

"I can understand that," I tell her. "I've been there. Not with someone who wasn't out, but just in a relationship that had to be kind of secretive. Kind of fun at first, I guess. But it loses the appeal pretty quickly."

"Yeah, and this is definitely losing its appeal. But what can I do? I love her. I'd rather be with her in secret than not at all."

I bite my cheek on the urge to cry. I can hear the sadness in Mabel's tone despite her attempt to sound upbeat. I hear it, and I recognize it. I hate that I was ever that person. I hate even more that I still am. Out of one dirty little secret situation and right into another one.

Fuck, what am I doing?

What can I do? I love her.

What can I do?

Do I love Jonah? Do I even know what love is? I thought I felt it in high school, and I was wrong. I thought I felt it in college, and I was wrong. I tried to force it with Conrad, and that was the worst decision I've ever made.

Who can I trust if I can't even trust myself?

"Well. Just remember your worth," I say, the words tasting like bile.

Jonah was right. I'm a hypocrite.

Mabel says something else, but I don't hear her. I put my headphones in and start my warm-up. Once I'm through that, I go full out. I break into a run, but instead of quieting my thoughts, they just get louder. They spiral faster with each rotation of the tread under my feet.

Conrad offered me three times my salary to come back. When I turned him down, he once again threatened to blackball me.

I punch the button on the screen, increasing the speed.

I'll have to change careers. Moving out of New York won't even work. Conrad Henderson has connections all over the world. I could attempt to freelance, but I would have to move back to Virginia. I'd probably have to take on a second job, anyway. I'd have to go back to a place where I don't belong, and I'm not wanted. A place that has never, truly, felt like home.

And Jonah...

CLAIRE

God, how could this even work? I guess if Conrad does ruin my career, he'd have no other moves to play. There would be no reason to hide my relationship with Jonah. My insides churn.

I turn the speed higher. My head starts to swim.

What do I want? What is even possible? And does what I want even matter?

What do I deserve?

I grit my teeth on that question. I blink the sweat out of my eyes, reaching up quickly to wipe it away. My stomach roils.

I glance at the treadmill screen again. Five miles. I can make it to six. I ignore the familiar lightheadedness. I've pushed through it before. It happens when I work out on an empty stomach, and despite myself, I visualize my stomach shrinking. My body using every fat cell. Every calorie. Every flaw.

Burning them all up until they're gone.

One more week until the band takes their three-week break. I just have to make it through Amsterdam. Then I can take a breath and clear my head. I'll call my therapist. I'll get myself back under control. Then I'll figure out what to do.

I max out the speed until I'm full-on sprinting. I blink away the spots in my vision.

Just another half mile, I tell myself. *Push, push, push.*

Then it all goes dark.

"YEAH, just tell them I might be late to soundcheck when they get back. We're pulling into the hospital now."

I blink my eyes open. The underside of Mabel's face is the first thing to come into focus. I'm in her lap. There's a pounding in my head. I move my hand to my forehead, and she looks at me.

"Oh, thank God," she says to me, then she goes back to her phone. "She's awake. I'll keep you informed."

Mabel drops her phone on the car seat, but when I try to sit up, she puts her arm across my chest gently.

"Girl, just stay down, okay? You've got a nasty gash on your head."

"Shit."

I lie back and close my eyes. That's when I realize there's a towel being held to my forehead, just along my hairline. It's Mabel. She must be holding something over my, as she called it, *gash*.

"So, that's why my skull feels like it's been cracked open."

Mabel snorts out a laugh. "Yep. Kinda has been."

"What happened?"

"I don't know. One minute you were running like you were being chased, and the next minute you were unconscious and bleeding on the ground. Scared the shit out of me."

"Sorry."

I groan, and she pats my shoulder. "We're pulling into the hospital now. I think you're going to need stitches. You just hang tight."

I do as she says. Sav's security guard opens the car door, and I take over holding the towel to my head. The guard helps me into a wheelchair, then pushes me toward some sort of private entrance where two medical professionals are already waiting.

I close my eyes again. The movement of the chair nauseates me as we rush through some double doors, then down a hall and into an empty private room.

The nurses introduce themselves as they help me onto a hospital bed. They ask me some triage questions. They take my vitals. They take my blood. They hook me up to an IV.

And then they disappear.

I lie back on the pillow and close my eyes once more. "That was fast."

"Yeah. Ham called ahead. He tried to make me stay at the hotel so he could take you—he said it would be less likely to draw attention—but I told him to fuck off."

I laugh, and then groan, because it makes my head throb. "Thank you. I'd rather you be here than him."

"Right?" I can hear the playfulness in Mabel's tone. "Obviously I'm much better company." I hear her phone ding, and then I listen as she types something out before she speaks again. "Sorry. It's just Sav wanting updates. Red texted her."

"Oh, did you not tell her?"

"Wasn't really time, honestly. I just flagged down the nearest security guard and called Ham as Red was hauling you to the car."

The image of me cradled in Red's giant arms makes me want to laugh before her words sink in. "So, who all knows I'm here?"

"Well, Ham and Red, obviously. Now that Sav knows, I'm sure Callie knows. The guys will probably know soon."

I nod my head slowly, careful not exacerbate the ache. I don't want Jonah to see me like this. I don't want his searching gaze on me. He sees more than I want him to, and this would be much more than I want to share.

"Can you send Sav a message and ask her not to tell the guys? Just not until I'm out."

"Oh...Sure." A pause. More typing. "She said no problem. Callie doesn't even know."

I let out a slow sigh of relief. "Thank you."

Mabel and I sit in comfortable silence until the door to the room opens and a doctor steps in. She's an older woman with brown skin and short, curly hair. She smiles softly and greets Mabel and me.

"Hello, I'm Doctor Shirazi."

I smile back. "Hi, Doctor Shirazi. I'm Claire."

"And I'm Mabel. It's nice to meet you."

"You as well. Mabel, are you family?"

"Oh, no," I cut in. "She's not family, but she's fine to be in here."

"Okay, sounds good." The doctor turns her attention on me. She consults a chart, then zeroes in on my forehead. "So, I hear you've had a bit of a fall."

I laugh. "Yeah. You can say that."

She examines the cut on my head, then shines a flashlight in my eyes.

"Well, you don't have a concussion. I know you said the head wound bled quite a bit, but that's not uncommon for head wounds. Your cut is actually quite minor. Two staples and some extra strength ibuprofen should take care of that."

"Oh, that's great news." I look over at Mabel and she flashes me a thumbs up. "So, no real down time, then?"

"Not for this." Doctor Shirazi looks down at a chart on a clipboard.

"But you're extremely dehydrated, and your blood sugar was very low. You said you passed out while exercising?"

I nod. "Yes, ma'am. I was on the treadmill."

"Have you eaten today?"

"No, but I usually don't before I work out. It gives me cramps."

I force a smile and try to hide how my defenses rise. *Look innocent*, I tell myself. *Look healthy.*

Act like you're in control.

I know I shouldn't, but I make excuses anyway.

"I adhere to a pretty routine diet and exercise program, actually. This is the first time this has happened."

I don't elaborate by saying I know exactly how many calories I consume and exactly how many I have to burn off every day. And while I'm sure the return of certain *habits* has put a strain on my body, I don't admit to them. I just smile and shrug. The sooner I get out of this hospital room, the better.

"Maybe it's from all the traveling? I'm not used to so much time on a plane."

Doctor Shirazi runs her eyes over my face, and the hairs on my arms and the back of my neck rise. She turns to Mabel.

"Ma'am, can you step out for a moment, please? I'm going to close the head wound."

"Oh, yeah, of course. I'll just be out here."

I can hear the concern in Mabel's voice. I can feel her eyes on me as she leaves, but I don't take mine off Doctor Shirazi. A prickle of awareness skirts down my spine, triggering my fight or flight response.

She knows.

I try not to panic. I work to keep my breathing regular. She's going to prod me with questions. She'll want to know about my eating habits. My medical history. My mental health. I'm already formulating the lies. The excuses. But when she speaks, they all disappear from my mind, leaving me speechless.

"Ms. Davis, when was your last period?"

I'm stunned. I shake my head. I blink and try to recall it. I close my eyes and think. My periods have always been irregular, and that's only been exacerbated recently. I can't think of my last period. I have no idea when it was.

"I'm on birth control."

"What method?"

"The pill."

"And do you take it regularly? Same time every day?"

I start to nod, but then I stop. I do. Or I did. But I haven't. Not with the traveling and the time zones and the stress. And not only have I not been consistent, with the vomiting...

I clamp my eyes shut.

"Shit."

"Ms. Davis, is it possible you could be pregnant?"

I shake my head. *No. No. No.* It's not possible. It cannot be possible. Then, slowly, I nod.

"Yes," I whisper.

"I take it this wasn't planned."

"No."

"I'm going to close your head wound, and then I'll send a nurse in to take a urine sample. We'll also run your blood. Just to be sure."

I nod. "Okay."

She numbs my head with some sort of gel, but it's unnecessary. I feel nothing except dread. She closes me up with two staples and explains how I need to care for it. She tells me that I'll have to see a doctor in two weeks to get them removed. I nod through all of it, but barely hear any of it.

My thoughts are elsewhere, cycling over and over on the same things: I should have made him wear a condom. I should have made him pull out. I should never have slept with him in the first place. I cannot have a baby with Jonah Hendrix.

How can they tell so soon? How can this be possible?

I drop my head into my hands.

I'm so stupid. I'm so fucking stupid.

"Should I send your friend back in, or do you need a minute?"

I breathe in and out. I open my eyes and count the tiles on the floor. I don't know what to do. I don't know what to do. I can't leave her out there. She's going to know something is wrong. Do I tell her the truth? Do I lie?

I don't know what to do.

"You can send her in."

"A nurse will be back to collect the urine sample, and I'll call with the blood test results. I'll put a rush on it, so it should only be a few hours."

"Thank you."

Doctor Shirazi's shoes clack across the floor. The door opens. She mumbles something to Mabel. Then Mabel walks in, shutting the door behind her.

"Oh my God, Claire. Are you okay? Did it hurt that bad?" Her hand comes down softly on my shoulder, then she rubs my arm. "You need me to get you anything? Some water? Did they give you anything for—"

"I'm pregnant." When she doesn't respond, I sit up and look at her. Her eyes are wide. Her mouth is open. "Mabel. I'm pregnant."

"Okay." Slowly, she nods. "Okay. Yes. How do we feel about this?"

"Shitty."

"Right. Do you know...Not that it matters, of course. But...do you..."

"It's Jonah."

"Shit."

I snort out a sad, pathetic laugh that sounds more like a sob. "Yeah." I drop my head back into my hands, careful not to catch my staples. "God, what the hell am I going to do?"

Mabel squeezes my shoulder. "Anything you need, let me know. I'll get you anything you need."

"Thanks."

It gets quiet again, but the air is charged. It's not a comfortable silence. I know she has questions. I sit back up and give her a tight smile.

"You can ask, if you want. It's fine."

She winces, then shrugs. "Was this, like, a one-time thing, or..."

"It's...*or*."

"How long?"

"Not long."

"What kind of relationship is this? Like...Do you think he'll be happy about it?"

I groan. "It's the kind of relationship where my first thought was how to keep this from him."

"Shit."

I laugh again. I can't help it. One syllable, yet it encompasses everything perfectly.

"It's just..." I sigh and shake my head. "Mabel, we're such a mess. Him and me. Together and individually. We're a mess, and this was not the plan, and I can't even—"

A knock sounds, cutting me off, and I tell the nurse to come in. They give me a little plastic cup and tell me how to use it. Then they gesture to the bathroom door. Even with having to wheel my IV bag into the bathroom with me, the whole ordeal still takes less than five minutes. Less than five minutes to decide the rest of my life.

When the nurse comes back with the results of the urine test, I'm not shocked. I knew it would be positive.

When the doctor calls with the results of the blood test, though, my heart drops into my stomach. According to the test, I'm around five weeks pregnant.

I do the mental math. Five weeks pregnant means the date of conception would have to be...

Madrid.

I almost want to laugh. Of course. Of course, the most humiliating and heartbreaking sexual experience of my life would result in a pregnancy.

It certainly doesn't bode well for whatever is yet to come.

Shit.

THIRTY ONE

Jonah

"WHAT DO you mean she went to the hospital?"

Mabel flinches, then scowls at me. "You don't have to yell, asshole. She's fine. It was just a minor injury."

An injury? She's fucking injured? I start to pace. My already splitting fucking headache intensifies.

"Why am I just learning about it at fucking soundcheck? You didn't think you should let one of us know?"

"Did you not hear me? It wasn't a big deal. She's fine, Jo."

"What happened?" I snap the question as I pull my phone out of my pocket and turn it back on with shaking fingers. No missed texts pop up, but I'm kicking myself for ever turning it off.

She was in the hospital, and I didn't know.

She was in the hospital, and I wasn't there for her.

"Nothing. She just got a little dizzy on the treadmill."

I whip my head back at Mabel. "A little dizzy?"

"She passed out."

"She passed out?" I shout again. I can't help it.

What the fuck was Claire doing on the treadmill? She was in her pajamas when I left. It was supposed to be our rest day. I pull up her contact and call her. A thousand thoughts swirl through my head as it rings. Did she eat? Is she overtired? Is she sick?

Then I see Theo.

Theo with his head shaved.

Theo with his face swollen.

Theo's grave marker in our family mausoleum.

Images of Theo change to images of Claire. Claire, injured. Claire, sick and dying. Claire's headstone.

Her phone goes to voicemail, and I want to fucking scream. Instead of leaving a message, I stick my phone back in my pocket and turn to leave.

"Where are you going? We've got soundcheck!" Sav calls after me. I wave a hand in the air, but I don't stop walking.

"Do it without me. I'll be back for the show."

José takes me back to the hotel. I absently reach into my pocket twice for pills and come up empty. By the time I'm stepping into the elevator, both of my thumbs are bleeding, and my chest aches with panic.

Claire's words from the other day hit me hard. *I feel everything.*

The moment I'm in the suite, I call her name. She doesn't answer. I rush to the bedroom—maybe she's sleeping—but I hear the shower running, so I change course. I don't think. I don't knock. I just open the bathroom door and walk in. Seeing her outline through the fogged-up shower door calms me slightly, but it's not enough. I open the door and step right into the shower with her.

"Oh my God." She whips around, eyes wide. Her hand splays over her chest and she pants. "Jonah. What are you doing?"

I look her over quickly, surveying every inch of her body. I ghost my hands over her wet skin. Looking for injury. Feeling for pain. She's wearing some sort of shower cap, so I reach up and take it off her. There's a small cut with two silver staples on her hairline. I try to touch it, but she wraps her hand around my wrist, stopping me.

"Careful. I'm not supposed to get it wet yet."

I step closer, pressing her back into the tile wall. The shower hits my back, but she's out of the stream. My clothes are soaked. My boots. I don't care. I can't take my eyes off her. Her face. The cut. The staples. I wrap my free hand around hers, just to keep myself from trying to touch it again.

I just need to feel her. I just need to know for sure that she's unharmed. That she's alive.

I feel everything.

"Does it hurt? Are you alright? What happened?"

Her brows furrow as her eyes bounce between mine. "It doesn't hurt." She reaches up and puts her hand on my cheek. "It's okay. I'm okay."

I hate that word. *Okay.* What does it even fucking mean? Again, I flash back to Theo. Sick and dying in our living room.

Everything will be okay. I promise.

It wasn't okay. He lied. It's one big fucking lie.

I lean into Claire and close my eyes. I breathe in the hot air. It smells like lavender and sugar. Like her. Slowly, my muscles start to relax. I grab her hip and pull her into me. I run my hand up her back so I can cup her neck.

Questions dance on the tip of my tongue. Accusations. *How did this happen? How could you be so reckless?* But when I open my mouth, I give her the rawest, most vulnerable truth. She's always pulling the most painful truths out of me. She doesn't even have to try.

"I was scared. Mabel said you went to the hospital, and I panicked."

My voice is strained with exhaustion. Less than an hour and I feel like I've run a marathon. The longer I hold her, the longer I breathe her in, the more my muscles relax. Tension bleeds steadily from my body, and all I have to do is hold her close. *I feel everything.*

"I'm sorry." She rests her head on my chest. "I'm okay. It was nothing."

"Did you eat before you ran?"

I feel her body tense. There's a charged moment of silence. She doesn't have to tell me. I know the answer already.

"I was just dehydrated from all the traveling. I need to remember to drink more water."

I force a swallow, clamping my eyes shut. She lied to me. She doesn't trust me with the truth, and I know what that means. I know because I lie all the fucking time.

I was right. I was right about the calorie counting, and the toothbrush, and the obsessive fucking workouts. Something is wrong.

And if she's ashamed, it's probably bad.

Pressing the issue will make it worse. Prodding her with questions will only lead to more lies. I know it, because I fucking live it. If I push, she'll retreat further into herself—further away from me—and that's not acceptable. Not when I need her close.

"Okay," I murmur into her hair. "I'm just glad you're okay."

Okay.

It's all one big fucking lie, and I feel *everything*.

OUR OPENING BAND is halfway through their set, and she's still not here.

I keep cycling from the dressing rooms to the stage wings. I take out my phone and text her once. It's delivered, but it stays unread. I start thinking about all the things that could go wrong. She has a head wound. She could have a concussion. She could have internal bleeding. She could—

I shove my hands in my hair and pull. I try to breathe. I reach into my pocket and come up empty.

Empty.

I pace.

I head out the exit and chain-smoke two cigarettes in a matter of minutes. When I'm still wired, I find my guitar case, rip open the liner and pull out my other cigarette case. There are pre-rolls in it, but no pills.

Like a fucking burglar, I steal back outside. I've never tried to hide smoking weed from anyone accept Brynn. Now, it feels like a deception, and I don't even know why.

No, that's not true. It's because of Claire. Her perfectionist, bossy ass. I don't want to disappoint her. I want to be worthy of her.

I light the pre-roll and suck until the end glows red. I hold it in my lungs until it burns, and I cough. I feel like such an asshole that the first hit only serves to make me feel more like an asshole. Like a liar and a failure.

JONAH

I take another hit.

I drop my head on the wall and blow the smoke through my nose. I wait and wait. I check my phone. My text still says unread. I finish the pre-roll. A false-calm settles over my limbs. I feel heavier, but my thoughts are still loud. Spinning slower now, but still loud enough that I can't handle it.

I've fucked up.

Inside, I find José.

"Vodka. Something small. Put it under my bed in the suite."

I don't wait for him to say anything. I just turn around and find my roadie. I nod to the exit, then go into the bathroom to wait. I splash water on my face, then look in the mirror. My eyes are bloodshot, and I don't even have eyedrops.

"Fuck me."

At five minutes on the dot, I walk slowly to the exit. He's already waiting for me.

"I don't have cash on me, but I'll get you after."

He nods and hands over the ibuprofen bottle. "I know you're good for it."

"Thanks."

I shove the bottle into my pocket, head back inside, then stop in my tracks.

"Claire."

She looks from me to the roadie behind me and back.

"What were you just doing?" Her question is whispered, her voice shaky. And Jesus, she looks so sad. She's not even angry. She's just sad.

This is exactly what I didn't want to do.

When I don't answer her, she closes the distance between us, reaches into my pocket, and pulls out the ibuprofen bottle. Her eyes flutter shut. When she opens them, I expect to see anger. I don't.

I wish it was anger. I'd take that over the disappointment I see.

Claire takes my hand and shoves the pill bottle back into my palm. My fingers close around it on impulse. I don't know if I want to whip the bottle against the wall or put it back in my pocket. I do neither. I just stand there and stare at her.

"I have a headache. I'm going back to the room. Have a good show."

I watch her leave, and I say nothing. I don't try to stop her. When she's gone, I turn to José.

"Why didn't you stop her?"

His brow furrows. "I'm sorry."

I huff and shove past him. A familiar emotion flares in my chest. It's comfortable. I prefer it, and I feed into it. It grows until everything else is consumed. Sadness. Dejection. Disgust. It's all gone.

Incinerated by rage.

MY BODY IS tense when I step into the suite.

My jaw aches from clenching it through the whole concert.

I go straight to the bedroom and find Claire in bed with her laptop. When she sees me, she snaps it shut. She runs her gaze over my face, no doubt noting my mood. Her brows slant and her eyes narrow. Even before I speak, the air seems to spark between us. Frenetic energy. Unfettered chaos. It's dangerous, but I don't bother trying to stop it.

"You have no right to be disappointed in me." I go for calm, but every word quakes. Simmers. Threatens to boil over. "You take the same meds. I've seen you do it."

"I have a prescription from a psychiatrist. I'm not buying it from a roadie like some back-alley crack addict."

I grit my teeth. "No. But the way you deal with your shit is so much better, isn't it?"

She shakes her head. "Don't. Don't you dare."

"That two-month stay at a wellness facility was for your eating disorder, wasn't it?"

She doesn't answer. She just glares at me with her nostrils flaring. Good. At least our emotions match now. I'm so fucking mad. I'm so angry at myself for letting her down, but she's no better. She's just as fucked up as I am. We're the same. We deserve each other.

She just refuses to see it.

"It was." I press, even though I know I shouldn't. I know it will do nothing but harm. I do it anyway. "Just admit it. You went to rehab for an eating disorder, and now you've relapsed. You're not perfect. Admit it, Claire. Admit it."

She stands abruptly from the bed. Her fists are balled tight. Her chest is heaving. I know immediately I've made a mistake.

"Fine," she shouts, and I flinch. "Fine, yes, you're right. I spent two months going through treatment, and I've fucked it all up. Does that make you feel better, Jonah? Is that what you want to hear? That I'm fucked up, too?"

I shake my head as tears stream down her furious face. I feel worse. I regret everything.

"Stop." I shake my head. "Stop. I don't want to hear anymore."

She doesn't. She keeps going. Crying and sneering. Hateful and hurting. I did this.

"Oh no, you wanted this." She takes two steps closer and glares up at me. "You wanted to rip me open, so you could feel better about your own shit, right? You want to hear about how I let it get so bad, I had ulcers in my throat? You want me to tell you how I permanently ruined my teeth? I had to take out a fucking loan to get them fixed because I'd emptied my entire savings and maxed out my credit card paying for rehab and hospital bills."

She takes two more steps. Her body is vibrating. I wouldn't be surprised if she takes a swing at me. I'd fucking deserve it. I brace myself for it, but then her face falls. Pain swallows the anger, and I feel it in my stomach. In my chest.

"See, unlike you, Jonah *Henderson*, I had to do it all alone. I didn't have my daddy's money or my rock star royalties to pay for it. I didn't have a band of people who cared about me to send me to rehab. I didn't have anyone. No support. No encouragement. I had to pay for it myself. I had to go through it myself. And yeah, now I've fucked it all up. Are you happy now? Does that make you feel fucking better?"

"No." I shake my head, blinking away my own tears. "No, it doesn't."

I drop to my knees in front of her, wrap my arms around her, and rest my forehead on her stomach. She stiffens, but she doesn't push me away.

"I'm sorry. God, I'm so sorry, Claire." I breathe her in and hold her tighter. "I don't want to hurt you. I'm just...I'm so fucking angry all the time. I'm so tired of being angry, but I don't know how to feel anything else. I *can't*. I can't be anything but angry."

Everything else hurts too much.

The room goes silent. She doesn't move, doesn't speak, but I don't let her go. I can't. I won't. When her hands slip into my hair, I let out a shaky exhale. I tremble under her touch. When she moves her hands to my wrists and steps back, though, my heart plummets. She's walking away. She's going to leave me, and I don't blame her. She should. She should walk away and never look back.

But then she kneels on the ground with me.

Her hands cup my face. Her blue eyes shine as they hold mine.

"I don't know what to say to make you feel better. Tell me what to do, and I'll do it. Tell me how to help."

I'm stunned for a moment, and I have to blink against the rush of more tears. I open my mouth to speak, but nothing comes out. I force a swallow. I shake my head. I put my hands over hers, hold them to me, and try again.

"I don't know how to handle this," I whisper. "You just came in here and ripped me open. I feel like I've been skinned. Everything is bloody and raw and exposed, and nothing is working. Nothing."

"What do you mean?"

Her thumb rubs my cheek, wiping at my tears. Her touch is so gentle. It's *loving*. I'm so fucked.

"I don't know how to feel all of this," I rasp out. "I conditioned myself to be numb to it. That part of me is off. It's supposed to be off. I've protected myself from it for so fucking long because it hurts. It fucking hurts, and it's consuming, and it's changing fucking everything."

"Jonah, I don't understand."

Her eyes peer into mine, searching, and it's too much. Too vulnerable. Too open. I close mine, cutting off that connection, but I don't let go of her hands. I still need something. I still need her...

"I'm sorry. I don't want to hurt you. I want to help, Jonah, I just don't—"

"I love you, Claire. I'm fucking in love with you."

She says nothing. It's complete, utter silence, and my heart aches. I crack open, and I fucking bleed out. She doesn't feel the same. I knew she wouldn't. How could she? But fuck, the confirmation is killer.

I open my eyes and scan her shocked face, then choke out a laugh.

"See? I knew from the jump you'd give me trouble. I just didn't think it would be like this."

Her face falls as a new wave of tears floods her eyes. I brace myself. She delivers my death blow on a shaky whisper.

"I can't be with an addict."

I wince, then nod. "I understand."

"I care about you so much. I do. I want to—"

"No." I shake my head. "Don't say anything else. I don't want you to. I just...Fuck, I'm sorry. I shouldn't have said it."

I let go of her and try to pull away, but she doesn't release me. She slips her hands to the back of my head, holding me in place, and there's something in her eyes I can't identify. Something that gives me hope but cuts deep. Whatever she might feel for me, she doesn't want it. That's worse than her feeling nothing at all.

"I'm sorry for causing you pain. It's the last thing I want to do. If you want me to leave, I will."

It's not at all what I want to hear. I feel pathetic and desperate. But for the first time in a long fucking time, I don't feel angry.

"I don't. I don't want you to leave." I force a smile, then give her a shrug. "We have a job to do, right?"

"Right." Something passes over her face, then she gives me a flat, sad smile. "Let's just make it through Amsterdam. Maybe a break is what you need."

I swallow and nod, then pull away. She lets me go this time. I push to standing and offer her my hand so I can help her up.

"Yeah, Trouble. I think I just need a break."

THIRTY TWO

Jonah

I SLEEP ALONE. We speak in formalities. I avoid her.

I spend the flight to Amsterdam with my back to her seat, so I don't spend the whole trip staring at her. I take long, frequent smoke breaks just so I don't have to be in the suite with her more than necessary.

I feel low.

I feel so fucking low that I long for the anger. I want to be mad. I want to hate someone. Something. I can't.

When Theo died, he was gone. I wasn't reminded constantly of what I'd lost. The grief, at times, was unbearable, but losing Claire is different. The guilt is still present. I still dwell on my mistakes. I'm still filled with regret. But this is a whole new kind of pain.

It's anguish. It's torture.

She's right here in front of me, and I feel like I've carved my heart out and given it to her. She has it in the palm of her hand; I have to watch every day as she holds it. I don't even want it back. She can keep it. It never did me any good, anyway. It made me want her when I couldn't have her. It made me think she could be mine. It lied.

Death would be better.

"Have you looked at the calendar?"

I don't glance up from my book to lie to her. "Yes."

"Good."

I can tell from my periphery that she goes back to staring out the car window. I don't care where we're going. I'll smile and be a good boy. I'll play my part, and in six days, Claire and I will go our separate ways. She says it's just for the band's break. I know better. That three weeks will never end. Even if she wants to come back, I won't let her. I can't do this anymore.

The car stops, and Claire gets out without a word. I finish the page I'm reading, dog ear it to hold my place, then switch my eyeglasses for my sunglasses before climbing out after her.

I step beside her with my head down. When she starts to walk, I follow. I zero in on the click-clack of her heels, but I keep my eyes off her legs. I stare at the pavement instead.

"They already have your acoustic guitar, and I sent ahead a bag of gifts with it. Small stuff. Dolls and cars and things. You have three rooms you'll have to visit and play for privately, so you'll have to wear a mask for those patients."

My body tenses, and my breathing speeds up. My feet slow, but she keeps talking.

"For the rest, the nurses have set up like a little party. Snacks and your gifts. You'll put on a concert of sorts, I guess. I told them absolutely no press, and I've already had the whole ward set up with extra security. It's peds. Mostly young kids, but there are some teenagers. I think the oldest is seventeen, and he's a huge fan."

I stop. My thumb starts to sting. I keep my eyes on the pavement.

"Did you forget something? We've got—" She must pause to check her watch. "—ten minutes."

I don't move. I hear a small gasp, and then she walks closer and grabs my hand. She cups my hand in between hers and rubs at my thumb. The one I've already picked raw.

"Jonah, what's wrong?"

Slowly, I bring my eyes up to survey the building in front of me. As soon as I read the words on the side of the building, I can't breathe.

JONAH

They're in Dutch, but I don't have to be able to read them to know. I know it in my bones. This is a children's hospital.

I feel dizzy. I blink twice to clear my vision, and then I shake my head.

"I can't go in there. I'm sorry. I can't."

I close my eyes again, pull my hand from hers, and turn back to the car. The click-clack of her heels gets louder as she chases after me. The sound blends with my rapid heartbeat.

I need to get out of here. I need to get out of here.

"Why? What can I do?"

I reach the car and pull on the handle.

"Unlock it," I shout to José. As soon as I hear the car beep, I yank open the door and get back in.

"Jonah." Claire leans into the back seat and gives me a concerned, confused glance. "What is going on? This has been on the calendar for weeks."

I rest my head on the seat back and try to calm my breathing. I squeeze my eyes shut and grit my teeth, trying to force away the visions.

"I'm sorry," I tell her. "I didn't check the calendar. I should have. I'm sorry. I can't do this."

Another pause. I drop my head between my knees and jam my hands into my hair. I pull. I should have kept the pills. I should have read the calendar. I'd have been prepared. I should have kept the pills.

"Okay. Just let me make a couple calls, and then we can go back to the suite."

I don't answer. The car door shuts. I hear the hum of her voice as she talks on the phone. I count backwards from one thousand and pick at my thumb. *I should have kept the pills.*

The car door opens, and she slides back in.

"Okay, Sav and Mabel are coming to fill in. If anyone asks, you have the food poisoning. Hey." She grabs my hand again, halting my picking. "Stop it. You're bleeding."

I ignore her and start on the other thumb. *I should have kept the pills.*

"Jonah, stop." She grabs my other hand. Both of mine are in hers. Then she's so close, I can feel her breath when she speaks. "What's wrong? What's happening?"

I shake my head. "I can't be here. I'm sorry." My heart is beating so loud. I can hear my blood rushing through my veins. I might have a heart attack. My chest is going to burst. "I can't be here. I can't be here."

"We're going back to the hotel now." She brings my hands to her lips and kisses them. "We're going back. Just breathe, okay?" She inhales, then exhales slowly, her breath dancing across my knuckles, cooling and warming. Calming. "Breathe with me. Just breathe."

I do. Breathe in. Breathe out. Focus on Claire's hands wrapped around mine. On her body beside me. On her scent.

She's here.

She's here, but she's not mine. Theo's dead. I've fucked everything up.

I should have kept the pills.

I JOLT UPRIGHT, my chest heaving.

I rub at my eyes, but I still see him. I still see him dead and gray in that hospital bed. Head shaved. Face swollen. My mom's voice echoes in my ears. The sound is so real, she might as well be standing beside my bed.

It should have been you. It should have been you.

It should have been me.

I press my palms into my eyes until I see white, but the images don't leave. They mold and blend, adding Claire. Claire laughing. Claire crying. Claire dead. Claire fucking my father. Claire standing over my dead brother's body. Claire's voice chanting over and over.

It should have been you.

I fist my hair and yank on it. The voices just get louder. The images get brighter.

I roll out of bed and, on instinct, go for my stashes.

I rip through my clothes. I check every pocket. Every pair of socks. *Nothing.* I unzip the liner of my suitcase. *Nothing.* I tear open the liner of my guitar case. *Nothing.* I dig through my toiletry bag. I dump out every ibuprofen bottle I have. *Nothing.* I lift the mattress. I pull back the sheets. I take the cases off the pillows. *Nothing.* The drawer in the bedside table. *Nothing.*

I check every one of my usual hiding places, and I come up empty.

JONAH

I'll call a friend. I'll text the roadie. I grab my phone and head out of the bedroom, but I halt at the foot of Claire's bed.

Claire.

I scan her side of the room in the darkness, zeroing in quickly on her suitcase. I rush to it and rummage through it. When my fingers wrap around an orange prescription bottle, my body almost collapses with relief.

"Jonah?"

I freeze. Slowly, I turn and face her. She's in her pajamas. Her hair is mussed from sleep, and her face is creased with worry.

"What's wrong? Why are you crying?"

I wipe at my face. I didn't even realize I was crying.

She scans my face, and then drops her gaze down my body. Her posture stiffens when she sees the prescription bottle.

"Jonah, are you...?" She lifts her eyes back to mine. "Are you trying to take my medication?"

I clamp my eyes shut. I fist my hands against the tremble and shake my head. I don't even know what to say to her. I can't even apologize. In this moment, I'm only sorry that I got caught.

"Yes."

I brace myself for anger. I'm ready for her to scream at me. To call Hammond or Sav. To leave me. But then she crosses the floor, and her hands cup my cheeks.

"You're sweating."

Her voice is soft and sweet. No anger. Just concern. She slides one hand to my heaving chest and rests it above my heart. I'm sure she can feel it racing.

"Is this about today? Did you have a nightmare or a panic attack or something?"

I open my eyes and hold her gaze. I inhale shakily. "Yes."

The hand she has resting on my chest slides to my shoulder, then down my arm, stopping at my wrist. When she tries to take the prescription bottle, I let her.

"Are you having withdrawal symptoms?"

I force a swallow and nod. "Yes."

"Okay. I'll call Hammond to get a doctor."

"No." I grab her wrist before she can step away. "No. Don't tell him. It's just..." I close my eyes again and try to slow my breathing. "I can do it. I've done it before. The hospital just..."

I shake my head. My voice is hoarse and strained. It doesn't sound like mine, and I can't find the words. I just see Theo in that hospital bed. I see *me* in that bed. I can feel the IVs. I can hear the monitors. There are too many memories. Too many.

My pulse picks up speed again, but she moves her hand back to my cheek.

"The hospital triggered you."

I nod. "Yes."

When Claire urges me forward, I open my eyes and follow her to her bed. She sits on the mattress, so I sit beside her, and she takes both of my hands in hers.

"How long have you been off of it?"

I know she means the pills. I clear my throat. "Been tapering since Scotland. Completely off since Sunday."

She stiffens. "You've been detoxing this whole time?"

I huff out a laugh that makes my battered body hurt. The headaches. The irritability. The increased anxiety. All compliments of the comedown.

"Yeah. Sexy, right?"

"Jesus, Jonah. You should have told me. You're not supposed to do that without medical supervision. Does your therapist know?"

I huff out another laugh. My therapist didn't even know I was still using.

"I'm fine, Trouble. I've done this before. The hospital just..."

I groan, then squeeze her hands just to make sure she's real. I turn slightly so I can rest my head atop Claire's, and she leans into my chest. I inhale lavender and sugar, and I don't let go of her hands. When I speak again, my voice is steadier.

"Everything is louder when I'm clean, anyway, but withdrawal amplifies things. Feelings. Worries. Fears. Everything is sharper. Stronger. The hospital would have bothered me no matter what, but right now..."

"Because you're detoxing, it was worse."

I hum. That's putting it lightly.

"You're supposed to manage your stress levels during detox. I picked one hell of a week to get clean."

I say it as a joke, but I can tell from the way her body slouches that she doesn't take it as one.

"I'm sorry. First my fall, and then the children's hospital. God, I'm supposed to be helping, and all I'm doing is making things harder for you."

"No. This isn't on you." I release her hands and wrap my arms around her. "You're here. It helps more than you know. Just be here."

"Okay. I'm here."

Claire presses a soft kiss to my throat that I feel in my chest, then we sink into silence. I listen to her breathe. I imagine my heartbeat thrumming with hers. Our bodies syncing completely. Until every function of hers is in time with mine. She calms the storm in my head. The blood in my veins.

I love her. The thought makes my eyes burn with tears.

"Hey." She leans back and looks up at me. "Want to play chess? I have this gorgeous new board I'm dying to break in."

I give her a small smile and nod. "Yeah, Trouble. I do."

"Good." She stands, then gives me a smirk. "But put some pants on first. You're naked."

I laugh. I'd forgotten I was naked.

I walk to my side of the room and pull on some athletic shorts and a T-shirt while Claire sets her chess board up on her bed. I take some ibuprofen and try not to think about where Claire hid her Xanax. I don't want to know. I don't trust myself yet.

I can't be with an addict.

Her pained words have been circling around in my head since she said them.

I've never considered myself an addict. Not even after almost dying from an overdose. When I was in rehab, I lied. I said what I needed to get released. I told myself I didn't belong there. I thought just because I'm able to taper off and go a while without using that means I'm in control.

I'm not.

Something always brings me back to the pills. Anything to blunt my emotions. Anything to fog up my memories. Anything to dull reality.

Even after weeks of tapering, after wanting so badly to get sober and stay sober, I'd have taken those pills tonight without a second thought.

I'm not in control.

The truth is, I *am* an addict, and that truth just makes me want to turn the room upside down in search of Claire's Xanax.

THIRTY THREE

Jonah

"I'M WHITE?" I take a seat across from Claire on the bed, careful not to jostle the chess board between us. "Is that because after my detox, I'll be pure as the driven snow?"

She rolls her eyes. "I thought you'd want the first move advantage. But if you don't want it, fine."

"I'll take it." I move my rook pawn up two spaces. "Your turn, Trouble."

Claire smiles sweetly, then proceeds to hand me my ass in seven moves. Then she beats me in two more consecutive games just as swiftly. I rub my forehead and inhale slowly.

"You're only winning because I can't focus."

She glances up at me as she sets up the board again, this time making herself white. "How bad is it?"

I drop my head into my hands and huff a pained laugh. "Not as bad as it could be."

Meaning, I'm not vomiting or seizing or having thoughts of jumping out of the window just to make it all stop. In rehab, I was under constant supervision during detox. Thankfully, it's never been that bad since. I don't tell her that, though. I don't want her to have that visual of me.

"My head pounds. My body aches. I haven't fully calmed down from the nightmare. And to be completely honest, it's taking a lot for me not to tear the room apart just to find your script."

She folds her lips between her teeth and nods. "I learned to play chess when I was in rehab for my eating disorder. It was a good distraction."

My eyes widen, then I whistle. "The only thing I learned in rehab is how to be a better liar."

Claire's brows furrow, and she forces a laugh. My stomach twists. I am an idiot. I squeeze my eyes shut and give my head a shake. I never should have said that, but my brain is so fucking fuzzy. I start to spiral, but then she speaks again, and all my attention focuses back on her.

"I started purging when I was fifteen. I had a therapist in college who said it was a maladaptive coping strategy for my anxiety disorder." She laughs. "I thought it was just because I hated myself, but I was wrong." She moves her king pawn two spaces, then looks at me. "Your move."

I want to comfort her, but I don't know what to say. So instead, I move my piece and give her one of my truths.

"My older brother Theo died when I was ten. He had a brain tumor. Cancerous. Inoperable. The hospital triggered those memories."

"I'm sorry. I knew you had an older brother who'd passed. I didn't know how. How old was he?"

"Seventeen."

"Wow, you really were the baby." Her eyes bounce between mine, and I see the moment she makes the connection. "Your middle name is Theodore."

Yep. My parents weren't even subtle.

"He was the favorite," I say with a shrug. "They'd never wanted a second child."

Her lips purse, and then she drops her eyes to the board to make her next move.

"My father used to hit my mom and my brother, but never me. He'd hit them, then tell me I was the only one who never let him down."

"What a prick."

She laughs. "Yeah. And after he and my mom split, he'd cancel plans or break promises, then blame my brother for it. I was young and didn't see it for what it was. Really hurt my relationship with Macon."

"Macon's your brother?"

She nods, and I shake my head. "Are all dads assholes?"

"I hope not."

"I'm glad I don't have kids. I don't want to think of all the ways I could fuck them up."

"Right." Her answering huff of laughter is forced, and she wipes at her eyes. When she smiles, it's almost mournful. "Your turn."

I consider the board as I speak.

"After Theo died, I basically did, too. I worked my ass off for a few years. Graduated high school early with honors. Got accepted to Yale. Thought if I was perfect, I'd earn my way back into my family. Realized halfway into my first semester at Yale that I was wrong."

"Your brother died when you were ten and your parents just...abandoned you?"

I smile at the protectiveness in her voice. "They didn't *abandon* me. They just...stopped talking to me or looking at me or acting like I existed, unless it was to tell me something I did wrong."

"That's disgusting."

I move my piece and shrug. "I asked them to send me away for school my sophomore year of high school. They said it was too expensive."

Claire's jaw drops. "Your dad is a multi-millionaire."

"C'mon, Trouble. That money is for the people they care about. *Themselves*."

She bites her lip, looks at the board, then looks back at me. "Your mom, too? I mean...I know your dad is terrible, but I guess since he cheated on your mom, I thought she wouldn't be as bad. I had her positioned as a victim in my mind."

I laugh. "Everyone is a victim of Conrad Henderson, but my mom was definitely a villain, too. When Theo died, something broke inside her. She went from tolerating me, to resenting me. She just kind of shut down. That's when Dear Old Dad started taking mistresses." I smile. "Once I caught him with my classmate's older sister."

Her eyebrows slant, and she averts her gaze. Shame. She's feeling shame. I reach over and take her hand. I give it a squeeze.

"He's the asshole. Not you."

She doesn't respond, and her attention goes back to the board. She's quiet for a long time before she finally speaks again. This time, her voice is quieter. Sadder.

"My brother overdosed at a party when I was a senior in high school. I didn't know until months after."

She sniffles, and when a tear rolls down her cheek, she swipes it away with the back of her hand.

"I didn't understand his struggles when we were younger. I was crass and cruel. I had no compassion. Then he almost died, and I had to hear about it from some random guy on the football team."

Her eyes stay on the board, but she doesn't move one of her pieces. I get the feeling she's not thinking of chess anymore.

"You were struggling too, Trouble. Trust me. When you're ear deep in your own shit, it's hard to have compassion for anyone. I would know."

She shrugs and wipes away more tears. "Macon and Lennon were the two most important people in my life, and I..." She scoffs and tilts her head to the ceiling. "When I actually tried to help, when I tried to step out of my own mess long enough to help them, I just made things worse."

"What do you mean? What did you do?"

She hesitates, chewing on her lip and dropping her eyes to the floor. Then she blows out a slow breath and nods.

"At the end of senior year Macon got beat up pretty bad. Dealers. Someone he used to sell for, too. They beat Macon up and left him for dead, but not before threatening Lennon's life. It was a big, convoluted web, honestly, but the guy who did it was untouchable in our town. Lennon's dad decided to send her away, but Macon wrote her a letter and put it in her suitcase. It explained everything. Said he would wait for her. Begged her to wait for him." She closes her eyes and shakes her head, her voice dropping to a whisper. "I took the letter. I kept it. So, she went away thinking everyone had abandoned her. I thought it was best for both of them, but it...it had so many repercussions that I never could have predicted. When the truth came out..." She shrugs. "Well. Now you know."

She takes a deep breath, looks back at the board, and makes her move. Then she forces a smile and looks back at me. "Your turn."

I hold her gaze, shimmering blue with the tears she's trying to hold back, and all I want to do is pull her to me. I want to hold her.

Instead, I look back at the board.

"The first time I used was after we'd signed our record deal. It was celebratory and experimental. Everyone else was doing it."

I close my eyes and picture Sav and Torren. High and in love. Seemingly unburdened. I wanted it. I wanted to feel less heavy. I wanted to be carefree, too.

"It was like cutting a brake line. I went from never touching anything harder than extra strength NSAIDs to a full-out druggie in a matter of a month. It just got worse when I realized that coming down meant contending with reality, so I just...never came down."

Claire sighs. "I understand that. The brake line part, I mean. With the purging...well...I don't know. It felt like the only thing that I had full control over, I guess. It was more than just wanting to be perfect, or my fucked-up self-image. It was about control, but in the end, all it did was make me spiral out of control. Ironic, right?"

I laugh. "Yeah."

Ironic, but so fucking relatable. We're the same, her and me.

"I OD'd on the anniversary of my brother's death. I'd been through many of them, so I don't know what it was about that one that set me off. I just wanted to quiet everything down. I just needed some peace. It wasn't a suicide attempt, but I didn't care if I died."

I move my piece, then make eye contact. "Your move, Trouble."

She surveys the board, moves her knight, then smirks at me. "Check."

"Fuck." She laughs, and I quickly move my king. Then I arch a brow. "How many times have you passed up a chance to win?"

She doesn't answer, and I frantically search the board. "Could I be in checkmate right now?"

She shrugs coyly. "I'll never tell."

I shake my head and fight a smile. She's brilliant. She's brilliant, and I'm in love with her. I'm in love with her, and it fucking hurts. I nod back to the board.

"Your move. Again."

She purses her lips and taps her chin. She's pretending, I realize. This whole time, she's been pretending to play. She's probably seen ten different paths to victory, but she's drawing it out just to distract me.

"My eating disorder hit an all-time low just after college. The truth about the letter came out. I'd kept it to myself for years because I was scared and misguided, and after it came out, my fiancé left me. I found out later he was only with me because he was still in love with my stepsister."

A pang of jealousy overwhelms me. She was engaged. She'd said yes to someone once. Accepted their love only for them to leave her.

I'd never do that. I'd never leave her. But...

I can't be with an addict.

I breathe through the need to scream and instead make a joke.

"This is the stepsister who is also your ex-best-friend and your brother's baby mama?"

Claire scrunches her nose playfully and nods.

"That's the one."

"Your fiancé had dated her?"

She cringes. "Not really. He was into Lennon, but Len was always into Macon. Eric never stood a chance. When he realized that, we ended up getting into this huge fight and he confessed that he'd never loved me. He just thought I'd bring Lennon back into his life. Then he took back the ring and kicked me out. Kind of set me on this path of self-destruction, I guess. Ended up with pretty bad ulcers in my throat. Had to be hospitalized for a couple days to receive IV fluids." She smirks. "Upside of making myself vomit for over a decade, though, is that I barely have any gag reflex. You're welcome."

I bark out a laugh. "Thank you."

"Anyway, after I was discharged, I checked myself into a treatment facility. Then I got my teeth fixed and moved to New York to start fresh. Met your dad a few months later. Relapsed a couple months after that. And now I'm here. A statistic." She moves her piece, then looks back at me. "Hooray for me."

I shrug. "I'm glad you're here, Claire. Even if you had to fuck my dad to get here, I'm glad for it."

JONAH

Claire sighs. I wait for her to say she's glad, too. That she's happy to be here with me. She doesn't. Her brow furrows as her eyes fall back to the board.

"Something Mabel and Sav said has been sticking with me lately. Sometimes you have to cut away the worn-down parts of yourself so you can move forward."

"What if there's nothing left?"

She flicks wide eyes back to mine. She opens her mouth twice but says nothing.

"What?" I ask, but she shakes her head.

Then she gives me a sad smile and answers on a whisper. "You have to have faith that you'll grow back better."

I glance down at the board. *Grow back better.* I can't even fathom it.

"What if I don't deserve to grow back better?"

Her hand rests gently on my cheek, and she guides my eyes back to hers. She's crying again. So am I.

"You do, Jonah. You do."

THIRTY FOUR

Claire

JONAH FALLS asleep wrapped around me, and his question echoes in my head.

A question I feel so viscerally it's like I asked it myself.

What if I don't deserve to grow back better?

He does.

He does, and so do I.

When I'm sure he won't awaken, I slide out of his hold and take my phone into the main room. It's almost midnight in New York, so my call is forwarded to the office answering system. When it beeps, I take a deep breath and leave a message.

"Hi. This is Claire Davis. I was a patient of Dr. Clay's about a year ago. I was hoping to maybe get back onto her schedule. I, um…well, I've relapsed. If you could call me back, I would appreciate it."

I leave my birthday and phone number, and when I hang up, I feel lighter. I feel like I have a purpose. A plan. I always feel better when I have a plan.

Then, I make a harder decision. I text my brother.

> ME
>
> Hey. It's not an emergency, but I'd like to talk to you when you get a chance.

My phone rings within seconds of hitting send, and my heart starts to race. I want to panic. I want to hit ignore. I answer instead.

"Hey, Macon. I wasn't expecting you to be awake."

He laughs. "Yeah, well, Len wants lemonade Italian ice so I'm driving to the gas station. I don't know if you saw but she's pregnant."

"Yeah." My eyes sting with tears, and I force a swallow. "I saw. Congratulations. Is Gabe excited to be a big brother?"

My brother laughs again. "He's got no idea what's going on, honestly. But we're excited."

"Oh yeah, well, I guess he's still pretty young..."

I trail off, and the music from Macon's car radio floats on the silence. Fleetwood Mac. It causes more tears to well until they're streaming down my cheeks.

"What's up, Claire? It's not like you to call and small talk."

I blink. Straightforward, but not harsh. He's right. We don't small talk. We barely talk at all other than the occasional text, and even then, I've exchanged more texts with Lennon than him. I nod and sit up straighter.

"Right. I, um...Well, I have kind of a personal question, I guess. But I understand if it's not something you want to share with me, so it's okay if you—"

"Just ask it. I'm an open book."

"Right." I inhale and exhale slowly. "Right. Well. When you got sober...what, um...What made you decide to do it? Was it hard?"

"Getting sober was the hardest thing I've ever done, but the easiest decision I've ever made."

"What do you mean?"

He goes quiet for a moment, and I wonder if he'll actually answer, but when he does, it takes my breath away.

"The actual act of getting sober was like being skinned alive. It was a physical, mental, and emotional pain that, at the time, I thought would never end. But I knew that if I didn't do it, I'd never be someone who deserved Lennon."

I bite my cheek and wipe my eyes. "You did it for Lennon."

"Yeah. But for myself, too. I needed to be someone worthy of her even if I didn't think we'd ever be together." He pauses briefly, and I hear the car engine and radio cut off. "I couldn't love myself until I knew I was someone deserving of her love."

I have to choke back a sob, the sound breathy and wet. My inhale is shaky.

"What did that feel like? Falling in love with her. How did you know?"

He hums. There's a tapping sound. His hands on the steering wheel, I realize.

"Falling in love feels like falling to your death."

"Jesus. Then why do people do it?"

"Because it's the revival that feels so sweet."

I can hear the smile in his voice when he responds, and I picture him in my mind. Sitting in his car in the gas station parking lot, smiling softly down at his steering wheel. His curly hair is probably falling into his eyes. He's probably wearing a USMC shirt and sweats. I know he's thinking of Lennon. Lennon, Gabe, and the new baby. His little family.

My brother is happy. He's so happy, and it makes my heart squeeze because I'm happy for him. No jealousy. Nothing toxic. Just happiness.

"I'm glad you found your way back to each other," I say on a whisper. "I'm sorry for ever keeping you apart. I know I've said it before, but I do mean it. I really am so happy for you both."

There's a pause. It's long enough that I have to check my phone to make sure he didn't hang up. The longer it stretches, the more I worry, and then he sighs.

"I know. I know you are, Claire. And in hindsight, Lennon and I needed that space. A lot of pain came out of it, but so did a lot of good. It's not...it's still not okay, you know? But it doesn't feel as terrible as it once did."

I shrug even though he can't see me. "I'm sorry just the same."

"Is everything okay, Claire? You've never asked about my recovery before. You've never asked about any of this before."

Not because I didn't care, I want to say. *Because it wasn't my place*. I swallow down the excuse and force a smile instead, trying my best to sound cheery.

"Yeah. Of course. Everything is fine."

"Are you in trouble? Do you need anything?"

"No." I swallow and sit up straighter, hoping like hell I sound more convincing than I feel. "No, I don't need anything. I was just doing something for work, and I was thinking about it. Thank you for calling me back. I should probably go. I know it's late by you."

"Sure..." He hesitates. I hear his car door open and shut. "Hey. I'm here, so I'm going to have to let you go. But I love you, Hairy Clairy. You'll always be my baby sis, even if...well, I'm always going to love you, okay?"

I press my hand to my mouth and hiccup on a sob. I squeeze my eyes shut and try to catch my breath. I try to hide how hard I'm crying, but I know I fail.

"I love you too, Macon like Bacon."

It's not forgiveness. I may never get that. But he doesn't hate me anymore. I try not to dwell on the hesitation. The sighs. The, *it's still not okay*. He doesn't hate me, and that's better than I could have hoped for.

I have to wait nearly half an hour before I've calmed enough to climb back into bed with Jonah, but the moment my body hits the mattress, he's pulling me against his chest. I snuggle into him, and he hums.

"You're here."

His voice is low and sleepy. His breathing is deep enough that I'm not sure he's awake. I press my ear to his chest and listen to his steady heartbeat.

Falling in love feels like falling to your death.

It's the revival that feels so sweet.

I take my hand and place it on my flat stomach. According to my internet search, it's the size of a sesame seed. One-sixteenth of an inch. So small. So fragile. I listen to Jonah's heartbeat, and I picture the little sesame seed we created in Madrid.

We're two disasters, he and I. Two broken, damaged people who've made so many mistakes. But this sesame seed? Something tells me it's not one of them.

Together, we can grow back better. We *deserve* to grow back better.

The three of us.

It's the revival that feels so sweet.

I press my lips to Jonah's chest, then tilt my face up and kiss his throat.

"I'm here," I whisper against his heart tattoo. "I'm here, and I'm not going anywhere."

HE KISSES ME AWAKE.

I twine my arms around his torso and hide my face in his neck.

"I have morning breath."

He rolls me onto my back, and I wrap my legs around his hips. He presses his erection against me, and I gasp.

"I don't care about morning breath."

Jonah presses hot, open-mouthed kisses to my shoulder. My collarbone. My jaw. The whole time pulsing his hard cock against me. When his lips meet mine, all concerns of morning breath are gone. All I can think about is how badly I want him.

I snake my hand between us and into his boxer briefs. When I grasp him, he groans into my mouth and thrusts into my palm.

"I love having your hands on me."

I squeeze, and he groans again. I stroke him with one hand and use the other to try and push down his underwear. He chuckles.

"In a hurry?"

"Are you feeling better?"

He flexes his hips into my palm. "What do you think?"

"Then yes, I'm in a hurry."

"Too bad." He moves down my body slowly, shoving my pajama top up my torso while kissing and nipping at my skin. He traces the hem of my bottoms with his tongue. "Because I'm not."

Jonah pulls off my pajama bottoms and tosses them to the floor. Then he slides his palms up my thighs, grabs the backs of my knees, and spreads me wide. He stares brazenly at my pussy. He bites his lip, and it's such a sexy look on him that I whimper. He brings his eyes from between my legs to my face and smirks.

"Jesus." He shakes his head, dragging his gaze up and down my body. I'm on total display for him, panting and flushed, and he looks ravenous. "Look at you, Trouble. Mmmm, just fucking look at you."

Without another word, he lies flat on his stomach and covers my pussy with his mouth. I gasp, and he shoves his hands up my body to grip my breasts. He massages them as he sucks on my clit, then tweaks my nipples when he shoves his tongue into me. I moan and try to ride him, but he brings a forearm to my pelvis and holds me down.

"This is my show." His words rumble against me, his hot breath tickling my sensitive skin. "I'm taking my fucking time. Now sit still."

I try my best. I swear I do. But the more he works me with his tongue, the more impossible it becomes. I try to fight against his hold; I *need* to move on him, but he pushes me harder into the mattress. When he releases my breast to shove three fingers into me, I buck and thrash. Then he flicks his tongue against my clit, making me cry out.

"I'm going to come. Let me come," I beg. "Make me come, and then fuck me."

He laughs against me, vibrating over my skin, then hooks his fingers inside my pussy and sucks hard on my clit. My entire body contracts with the orgasm. I practically fold in on myself, locking my legs around Jonah's head. When he doesn't relent, I grab his hair and pull hard.

"Stop. Stop, please God, stop."

He laughs again, then mercifully obeys. He drags his wet mouth up my stomach, stopping to bite one of my nipples before he attacks my mouth. I taste myself. I suck on his tongue and lips, and without hesitation, he pushes his cock into my aching pussy.

"Yes," I gasp into his mouth. "Oh, yes."

I don't waste time. I thrust and move with him as he fucks me. He slides his arms beneath mine and cups my face, kissing me deeply. Desperately. My pajama top is bunched under my armpits so our sweat-slicked bodies glide together, and I drag my hands up and down his back. I feel his muscles move as he flexes and bends. His heartbeat pounds so hard against his chest that I can feel it in mine. I sink my fingers into his hair and pull at the root until he groans.

"You're beautiful," I say between kisses. "I want to touch every part of your body."

"It's yours. You can do whatever you want with it."

His statement makes my heart squeeze and my breath catch. I don't know what to say, so I kiss him again and hope that he's telling the truth. I want it to be the truth. Please let it be the truth.

When Jonah's close to coming, he pushes his hand between us and rubs my clit, bringing me over the edge with him. My orgasm makes me see stars, and I clutch him like a lifeline while I catch my breath. He kisses my cheeks and forehead. My nose and jaw. He kisses the spot where my shoulder and neck meet, then nuzzles me playfully. I giggle, and when he kisses my lips, we're both smiling.

He pulls back and makes eye contact, those brilliant blue irises shimmering, and I'm overwhelmed. By him. By these feelings.

I love him.

The realization shocks me at first, and then I want to laugh. I'm relieved and excited. I'm hopeful. I bite my lip and consider telling him. He's so much more than I thought he was when we first met. He's layered and complex and *more*, and I love him.

"Hey, Jonah," I whisper, my voice shaking with nerves.

"Yeah, Trouble?"

I open my mouth, the confession ready to fall out, when the bedroom door flies open and bangs against the wall. Jonah and I jump and turn toward the doorway. I'm expecting Hammond or José, but my breath is sucked from my lungs when it's Conrad I see. His expression is disgusted as he drags his eyes over us, and then he laughs.

"Well, I wish I could say I was surprised."

THIRTY FIVE

Claire

"FATHER."

Jonah turns his body to make sure mine is shielded, and I'm taken aback by how bored he sounds.

"Would you mind stepping out of the room? I'll be with you in a minute."

"It's Ms. Davis I'm here for."

"It's me you'll get."

"Jonah, I will speak with Ms. Davis." Conrad narrows his eyes at me. "Claire, we need to talk."

Jonah starts to protest, but I place my palm on his chest.

"It's fine," I tell him, and then I look back at Conrad. "I'll be right out."

Jonah's body goes rigid, and it remains so even after his father leaves the room. He rolls off me and goes to his suitcase without a word. I sit up and fix my pajama shirt. We never took it off.

"Are you okay?"

He huffs a laugh, but he doesn't respond, so I get out of the bed and follow his lead. I change into a pair of leggings and a sweatshirt, and I pull my hair back in a claw clip. Jonah leaves the bedroom before I'm finished, but when I step into the main room, neither men are speaking. They're just staring at each other, and I notice José in the corner. I arch an eyebrow in his direction, and he shakes his head.

"Sorry," he mouths to me.

I look away and move to stand next to Jonah. A united front. Us against everything. Then I take a deep breath and look at Conrad.

"Conrad. How did you get in here?"

My words are curt, and I try to appear unfazed. I'm sure he wanted to gain the upper hand by unsettling me. I won't give him that. He narrows his eyes.

"I have connections."

"You mean you bribed some poor hotel employee."

He doesn't respond, which is confirmation enough. Entitled prick.

"What do you need? I'd like to get it over with. We have work to do today."

"You call fucking my son work?"

"Watch it." Jonah takes a step toward his father, but I place my hand on his bicep, stopping him.

"What do you need, Conrad?" I repeat, and I watch as his expression changes.

His face softens. His eyes, eyes so similar yet so different from the ones I've come to love, grow sad. He looks lost, and for a moment, I almost feel for him.

"Tell the muscle to step outside, please. This is a private matter."

I know I'll regret this. I know I will. But I just want to get this over with.

I glance at José. "Can you please wait in the hallway? This won't take long."

José looks between me and Conrad. "Are you sure, Ms. Davis? I think I should stay."

"It's fine." I give him a tight smile. "I'll call for you if you're needed."

José looks at Conrad once more, then nods. "Okay. I'll be right outside."

He walks past Jonah and I slowly but stops briefly in front of Conrad. He doesn't say anything, but from the slight flare in Conrad's eyes, I'm guessing José's expression is less than friendly.

The moment José is out of the room, Conrad smiles at me. It's a playful smile, almost suggestive, and it makes my skin crawl.

"You have quite the command over these men, don't you?"

I ignore his comment and cut to the chase. "What do you need, Conrad?"

"I need you to come back to Innovation."

"No."

"Claire, please."

Conrad takes a step toward me, but Jonah inches his shoulder in front of mine. Not blocking me from his father completely but drawing a very obvious line.

Conrad doesn't even acknowledge him.

"Come back with me, Claire. The department needs you. The campaign needs you." He reaches past Jonah and takes my hand. It's cold and rough. I hate it. "*I* need you."

I pull my hand out of his father's grip, but Jonah still stiffens beside me. I shake my head.

"I'm not going anywhere with you, Conrad. My resignation is final. I'm done with Innovation, and I'm done with you." I glance up at Jonah. He's still staring holes into his father, his jaw tense and hard. "Come on. We have a lot planned today."

I turn to leave, hoping like hell Jonah will follow me, but then Conrad opens his big, stupid, conceited mouth.

"If you're done with me, then you're done in this industry."

I stop in my tracks. That's my first mistake.

"You won't work with a competitor, Claire. I'll make sure of it."

My stomach sinks. This isn't news to me. He's said it before. But hearing it again just serves as a reminder of how much I dread it becoming a reality. I love my job. I love New York. The idea of finding a new career...of starting over...

Every plan and dream I had for my future, everything I'd worked for, would be gone. It would all be for nothing.

"You'll be signing your own name on the industry blacklist."

I turn back around. That's my second mistake.

"You already told me this," I say, my false calm wavering with every

303

word. I can tell by the twinkle in his eye that he knows how affected I am by his threat. "I've made my decision. You can leave now."

My final mistake. I should have kept my mouth shut and continued walking.

Conrad's eyes narrow.

"Do you think fucking my son will get you what you want, you little slut?"

"Motherfucker."

Jonah rushes Conrad. He shoves him, causing him to stumble backward, before I'm able to wrap my arms around Jonah's waist.

"Stop! Stop, Jonah."

"You think she's fucking you because she wants you?" Conrad straightens to his full height and sneers. "I warned you about her, but you never fucking listen."

"Conrad, you need to leave." He flicks angry eyes toward me. I'm still holding on to Jonah's waist, but I don't take my glare off Conrad. "Leave, before I have José call security."

Conrad ignores me. "She just wants your money, Son. She'll get knocked up, take you for all you're worth, and disgrace the family name."

His comment makes me flinch, but I don't have time to dwell on it. Jonah's body vibrates, his muscles so tense that they feel like rocks between my arms, and I know I need to put an end to this before all hell breaks loose.

"Conrad. I'm serious. You need to leave."

He never takes his eyes off Jonah.

"You were a mistake. Worthless. Couldn't even do what you were intended for."

Conrad takes another step toward Jonah, and my blood boils with every word that comes out of his mouth.

"A waste of money. A waste of resources. A waste of time. You're defective, and I'll be damned if I let you fuck up the family name like you fucked up my chance at an heir."

My brows furrow at his last statement. It makes no sense until Jonah speaks.

"It's not my fault Theo died."

Jonah's words are gritted through clenched teeth, and I can tell it's not the first time he's had to say them. Why? Theo had a brain tumor. It doesn't make sense that Jonah would have to defend himself in this way.

I flinch when Conrad laughs. "If you weren't defective, he'd be alive, and so would your mother."

The already tight leash I have on my temper frays, and I have to dig my toes into the floor to keep from launching at him.

"You can't put that on him, Conrad. Jonah had nothing to do with their deaths."

His lip curls in disgust, still not looking away from Jonah. "Your mother never recovered when Theodore died. She'd still be alive if you'd just done what you were intended for."

"That's bullshit, and you know it." Jonah's voice is strained, no doubt trying to keep from shouting. "Even Theo knew it was bullshit."

"Theo would tell you whatever you wanted to hear. You killed him anyway."

"Stop it!" I step in front of Jonah, pressing my back to his front, and square up against Conrad. "That is disgusting. Your son had a brain tumor. How could you possibly blame Jonah?"

"Because he couldn't use me to save him."

"What?" I turn to look up at Jonah. "What does that mean?"

His nostrils flare and his eyes glisten with unshed tears. "Do you know what a savior sibling is, Claire?"

My mouth falls open, and my eyes go wide.

"It's fascinating, really. Controversial, but fascinating." He drops his eyes to me. "Essentially, you have a fatally ill child, so you create a new one in hopes that they can save the sick one. In our case, Theo was the fatally ill child—he was born with a rare blood disorder that caused bone marrow failure—and I was the genetically modified body intended for harvest."

"Thousands of dollars wasted on you."

I gasp, whipping my attention back to Conrad. Rage simmers in my vision, making everything blurry on the edges.

"The kidney?" I whisper, and Jonah huffs a laugh.

"Kidney. Cord blood and bone marrow before that. Too bad I couldn't donate my brain too, right, Dad?"

The men stare at each other, two sides of the same coin. Jonah must look more like his mother, but he and Conrad have the same eyes. The same sharp jaw. The same incinerating wrath.

"You know the sad part?" Jonah blinks, and a single tear rolls down his cheek. "I'd have done it, if I could. If I had to kill myself to save him, I'd have done it. For fucking years, you had me convinced that was all I was good for. That Theo's life was my only purpose. I believed it so strongly that when he died, part of me died, too."

My heart breaks for him. I want to hold him and protect him. To have lived with this his whole life? And his middle name...it seems so sinister now. I reach up and press my hand to Jonah's cheek.

"Hey," I whisper, willing him to look at me, to look away from his father, a man who has never seen his worth, and at me, the woman who loves him. I open my mouth to tell him. *I love you. You matter to me. I love you.* But Conrad speaks, and I snap.

"You should have."

I whirl on him, my open palm landing right on his cheek with a loud crack. I raise my other hand in a fist with every intention of aiming a jab to his nose, but I'm yanked back into Jonah's chest. He wraps firm arms around me and says something, something like *don't*, but I barely hear him through the sound of my racing heart. I thrash against his hold and keep my glare fixed on Conrad as he takes an aggressive step toward me.

"You feral bitch."

"You vile excuse for a human being." I practically growl the insult. "You should be ashamed of yourself. You're disgusting. You disgust me."

His eyes narrow, then he smirks. "You didn't think I was disgusting when you were in my bed moaning my name."

The comment makes my stomach roil and stokes my rage. I want to rip that smirk off his face and shove it down his throat.

"Not a single one of those moans were real," I say with a sneer. "You're just as pathetic a lay as you are a parent."

"Stop, Claire."

Jonah's voice is a whisper in my hair as his arms tighten around me, but I can't take my eyes off Conrad.

"I'm so pathetic that you move on to my disgrace of a son? It just serves as proof that you're looking for a payout. Even if you get yourself pregnant or cry sexual harassment, you'll get no money from this family."

I give Conrad a grin so maniacal, I'm sure I look psychotic.

"I didn't move on to your son for his money, Conrad. I did it because he has a bigger dick and actually knows how to make me come, you selfish, arrogant, evil, tiny little excuse for a man."

His nostrils flare, and his entire face flushes so crimson, the handprint from my slap disappears.

"I will ruin you."

"Fucking try it. I'll tell everyone how you prey on new hires. How you manipulated me and lied to me. Every dirty detail, every damning thing I know, I'll tell all of it to everyone who will listen."

"No one will believe you. Especially not when they learn you're a gold-digging whore who fucked my son when you realized I wouldn't marry you. Your reputation will be ruined. You'll never be able to show your face in New York City again."

Jesus Christ, what is it about these men and calling me a whore? I bark out a laugh.

"I don't care what lies you try to sell about me. I'll take a torch to my whole fucking life if it means you'll burn with it."

When he doesn't respond right away, I know I've won. He's terrified. The only thing Conrad Henderson cares about is his reputation. Bad press? He'd never let that happen. It's the whole reason he asked me to come work with Jonah. Not because he was worried about his son. Because he was worried about himself.

I hate him.

I lean into that hatred and force a smile.

"Get the fuck out of here, or I'll start calling every news station in New York."

Conrad shakes his head and takes one step backward.

"You're fucking crazy."

"Women do these things when they've been scorned, right?" I point to the door. "Contact us again and you will regret it. Get out."

He flicks his eyes over my head to Jonah.

"You're cut off. Next time you're arrested, don't call me."

Jonah scoffs, but says nothing, and I don't stop glaring at Conrad until he's in the hallway and the door has shut on his back.

I release a sigh of relief, then twist in Jonah's hold, looping my arms around his neck in a hug.

"I'm so sorry, Jonah. I had no idea."

I stand on my tiptoes and kiss his lips, but he doesn't kiss me back. He's not holding me anymore either.

"Jonah?"

I drop my arms and survey his face, his body language. His muscles are just as tense as they were moments ago. His jaw is just as tight. His eyes are clamped shut, and his chest is heaving.

"Jonah, what's wrong?"

He takes a step away from me, putting distance between us, and then he opens his eyes. The look he gives me chills my blood. I can feel my heart start to race for a new reason.

"Jonah."

"Was that the truth? Did you want to marry him?"

"No." I shake my head. "Absolutely not. I told you, I was wanting to end th—"

"But you still fucked him."

I flinch like I've been slapped. "Jonah."

"You fucked my dad, Claire." He gestures forcefully to the door his father just vacated. "I hate him with every fiber of my being, and you fucked him. You fucked him for months. Worse still, you dated him. You called him your boyfriend. He's one of the worst people I've ever met, and you fucked him."

My mouth drops open twice to defend myself, but both times, I can say nothing. I just stand there and watch as he shoves his hands into his hair and completely unravels. I try to walk closer, but he backs away, and it's like a punch to the stomach.

"Jonah...I'm sorry," I say softly. "I am. I can't change it, but it's over now. It doesn't matter."

"It does matter."

"Why? I didn't know you. I didn't even know him. It was a mistake."

"I can't do this right now." He drops to the couch and puts his head in his hands. "I can't do this right now."

I shake my head. "What do you mean?"

"I mean I can't handle this right now." He stands again and starts to pace. "Fuck, I just keep picturing you with him. And now—" He shoves his palms into his eyes and groans. "God, what if you'd stayed with him? What if you loved him? What if you did get engaged? What if I fucking met you at your fucking wedding to my father?"

"Jonah. You're spiraling." I fist my trembling hands at my sides and try to keep my voice even. "None of that is real. It never would have happened."

"I know! Fuck, I know. But Claire..."

He sits again, propping his elbows on his knees, and I take the opportunity to sit beside him. His back rises and falls with his quickened breaths, and when I place my hand on it to soothe him, I can feel his rapid heartbeat.

"I'm sorry," I say softly. "I am. But I'm here with you. I *want* to be here with you. I want nothing at all to do with your father."

He rocks his head back and forth on his fists then sits up quickly.

"Why are you here?"

I frown. "What do you mean?"

"I mean why the fuck are you here with me, Claire? I'm an addict, remember? You called it. I've said terrible shit to you. I fucked you just to turn around and call you a home-wrecking whore."

I flinch again. I feel like I'm getting my ass kicked.

"I know but it's different now."

I shake my head and take his hand in mine. When he pulls it from my grip, my stomach clenches. No. No, this isn't happening.

"Jonah. Everything that happened before is over. We both said some terrible things, but we're past that. I'm with you because I want to be."

"Is it the money?"

My jaw drops. "Excuse me?"

"He's got a point, Claire. You went from him to me, and we have nothing *good* in common. Just the money."

My mouth drops open. I'm blindsided.

"Jonah, I do not want your money. I don't care about it at all. If I wanted money, I'd have stayed with your dad."

"But he wouldn't marry you."

"Are you fucking kidding me right now?" I stand from the couch and fold my arms over my chest. "After everything, you think I'm here because of money? Because, I swear to God, Jonah, there are much easier ways to make money than putting up with you and your fucking father."

He huffs out a laugh, even though I wasn't joking, then he shakes his head.

"I meant it when I said I wouldn't care. You want to get knocked up and take me for all I'm worth? I don't care. I just want to know."

My jaw drops, and I have to blink away the sting of tears. I resist the urge to put my hand on my stomach. How can I tell him now? *Oh, by the way, I am knocked up, but I swear it's not for your money despite what you and your father have both said multiple times.* And after last night when he said how glad he is that he doesn't have kids.

I don't want to think of all the ways I could fuck them up.

I try to force away any regrets, any thoughts of mistakes, but I can't.

Nothing good came out of that bedroom in Madrid. Nothing.

"Fuck you, Jonah."

I turn to walk away, to go I don't even know where, but he stands and grabs my arm to stop me.

"I'm sorry. I'm sorry. My head's just...My head's a fucking mess, Claire. I'm overwhelmed and not thinking clearly, and I just..."

He pulls me into a hug, and I let him. I sink into his hold and press my ear to his chest. I listen to his heartbeat. Everything is going to be fine. I love him. I know he loves me. It's all just happening at once, and it's overwhelming. We're broken, but we'll heal together.

We're going to be fine.

"I just need some space."

I freeze, then step back. I hold his eyes. The sadness in them guts me.

CLAIRE

He looks tortured. I can't even imagine how painful this has been for him. For someone who keeps so much to himself, he's been completely exposed in a gruesome way.

I think back to what Macon said this morning.

Getting sober was like being skinned alive.

A physical, mental, and emotional pain.

Compound that with everything that's happened over the last few days, and I'm surprised he's even standing here talking to me. I'm surprised he's not ripping the bedroom apart or running off to find some other way to silence reality.

I want to hug him again, but I don't.

I know where this is headed, and I know there's nothing I can do to stop it. It takes everything in me not to cry. And even though I already know what he's going to say, I ask anyway.

"What does that mean?"

"I think you were right. I think I just need a break."

THIRTY SIX

Claire

"ARE YOU NERVOUS?"

I nod and blow out a slow breath. I'm naked from the waist down and wrapped in some sort of bedsheet, plus it's cold in here. Why is it so cold in here?

"Yeah. I'm nervous."

"Me too."

I smirk at Mabel. "What are you nervous for?"

"I mean, I'm kind of the daddy in this scenario, so that's nerve-wracking enough as it is. Plus, I was curious and did an internet search on what to expect. That doctor is going to shove some kind of dildo-shaped camera up your vag." She throws her hand over her mouth. "Sorry if you didn't know. Surprise!"

"I know," I tell her, flaring my eyes. "They told me when I made the appointment."

"Do you get to find out the sex today? I think if it's a girl, you should name it Mabel."

"Not today. It's too early." I smile and grab her hand. "Thank you for coming so last minute. I just..." I shrug. "I got scared, I guess."

"Thank you for asking me to come." She squeezes my fingers and lowers her voice. "Have you talked to him at all?"

"Not since I left Amsterdam." I purse my lips and shake my head, a mixture of anger and hurt swell in my chest. "Not for lack of trying, though. I've texted and called. Nothing."

"Damn." Mabel drags concerned, sympathetic eyes over my face. "For what it's worth, from what I've heard, he's not back to his usual bullshit. He's spent the last two and a half weeks with Sav at her place in North Carolina." She pulls out her phone, scrolls, then holds up a picture. "They took him kayaking."

I can't help but smile. He looks happy. He's grinning in a two-person kayak with Brynn and wearing a blue life jacket. My heart hurts. I want to see that grin in real life, but he "needed a break."

I try not to dwell on the fact that I don't know how long his "break" will last, or how angry I am that he's found me so easy to discard. For all his blustering of love, he certainly doesn't seem to be able to forgive my past. It didn't take much convincing for him to believe the worst of me, either.

Why are you here?

Is it the money?

Maybe he thought he loved me, but if that love is conditional, I don't want it.

"Are you going to tell him?"

I blink out of my thoughts, look back at Mabel, and nod.

"Yeah," I say on an exhale. "He deserves to know."

But I just keep hearing his voice over and over.

I'm glad I don't have kids.

I'm glad I don't have kids.

I'm glad I don't have kids.

I'm not looking forward to telling him, but I know it's something I have to do, even if just the idea of it makes my stomach churn. How will I convince him that I didn't do this on purpose? I don't want his money. This isn't some nefarious plan to trap him or whatever other bullshit his father has him believing.

God, this is such a mess, but I almost want to laugh. He did say he'd want to know.

You want to get knocked up and take me for all I'm worth? I don't care. I just want to know.

Well, I'd definitely let him know if he'd just return a fucking text. Asshole.

"You don't have to answer this if it's too personal, but..." She drops her voice lower. "Are you going to keep it?"

"Honestly?" I chew on my lip and fidget with my fingers, then I shrug. "I don't know yet. I just...I don't know that I trust myself as a mom. It's never been something I wanted. And Jonah...he's so..."

I drop my head in my hands, visions of that last day in the hotel swarming my mind. I'd left within the hour. He didn't want me there anymore, and it wouldn't be good for him if I tried to stay. I had so much hope after talking to Macon, but hope's never gotten me anywhere but hopeless.

"He's so volatile, Mabel. I can't expect anything from him. And as much as I want to, as much as I've *tried* to, I don't even know if I can trust him. I've been trying to convince myself that this wasn't a mistake...but what if it was?"

Fuck, what if it was?

She nods. "I get that. I do. I think you'd be a great mom, though."

"Sure." I snort a laugh. "No offense, but you haven't known me that long."

"True, but I watched what you did for Jonah play out in real time, Claire. I know for a fact it wasn't easy. There's something to be said for that."

"I mean...how much of that was because I was sleeping with him, though?"

Mabel rolls her eyes with a grin.

"Shut up. You single-handedly whipped his ass into shape *and* rehabbed his image in the media. When he canceled on the children's hospital, tabloids actually believed he had food poisoning; when six months ago, they all would have been speculating it was drug-related. That was all you. To accomplish something like that, you have to be determined and compassionate. You have to be a problem-solver *and* have empathy." She shrugs. "I don't know, babe. I think that means you'd be a pretty kick-ass mom."

"Thanks," I whisper. Tears sting my eyes, and I wipe them away quickly with a laugh. "Sorry. I've been such a crybaby lately."

"Hormones are a bitch."

"Yeah. Anyway, let's just get through this appointment, okay? For all I know, it's not even a viable pregnancy."

I try to stay neutral about it, but it's hard. I can't even meet Mabel's eyes. I've gone through every possible emotion leading up to this appointment, and the only consistent one has been fear.

I could have miscarried. It could be nonviable. Or I could be really, truly pregnant.

At this moment, sitting half-naked in a sterile, unfamiliar doctor's office, I honestly don't know which is more terrifying.

I don't have a job. I don't have a family. I don't even have a partner to help me through this. I'm alone, and even my lowest low points in life don't compare to this. I was alone when my eating disorder was at its worst, but I was also the only person to worry about. I had no one depending on me. It's different now. So very different.

I tried to prepare myself for all outcomes. I thought I was ready, but I woke up early this morning and realized that I wasn't. I don't know what's going to happen next. I don't know what I want or what I'll do. I don't know anything.

The only certainties in this moment are that I am terrified, and I am so grateful Mabel answered my 2 a.m. text.

A knock on the door has us both turning toward it.

"Come in," I call, and it opens to reveal a woman I've not met. I raise my hand awkwardly and smile. "Hi."

"Hi, Ms. Davis." She crosses the room and offers me her hand. "I'm Dr. Giles. It's nice to meet you." She turns to Mabel and shakes her hand too. "Are you emotional support today?"

"Life partner, but unfortunately not the daddy."

I laugh as Mabel grins.

"Well, congratulations to you both!" Mabel sends me a wink that has me rolling my eyes as Dr. Giles washes her hands. "So, it looks like you're almost nine weeks along. Is that right?"

"Yeah, that's what they tell me."

Dr. Giles scrolls on a tablet. "We were able to get records from the hospital in Cardiff. It looks like you'd had a fall from dehydration and dizziness." She looks up at me. "Have you been having any trouble with that since?"

"No. I've been making sure to stay very hydrated. Switched up my diet so I'm eating all the nutrient-rich foods, and I'm taking prenatal vitamins."

Just saying the words has me swelling with pride. It's been a much easier transition than I was worried it would be. I know it's not like this for everyone. Restarting my therapy sessions with Dr. Clay has helped immensely. She says I'm likely doing well because my concern and attention is on the pregnancy instead of myself. I still have a long way to go, but this is something.

Dr. Giles asks me about any symptoms I've been having. No real nausea, but extreme fatigue, some weird cravings, and really lucid, abstract dreams. The questions have me feeling good. Everything is normal. I'm doing a great job. But when the ultrasound tech comes in, guilt starts to creep in.

Jonah should be here for this.

I should have just told him through text. It's a delicate topic, and at the time, I didn't want to spring it on him like that, but now I'm worrying that I was wrong.

There's no guarantee he'd even want to be here, but he should have at least had the option. Instead, I kept it from him.

"Hey." Mabel puts a hand on my arm. "You okay? You freaking out?"

I shrug, fighting off more tears. "I feel bad. I feel like he should be here. Like, I should have just told him through text or something."

She smiles softly. "I can record it?"

That perks me up a little. "Yeah. Yeah, thanks. That would be great."

The tech introduces herself and explains what she's going to do. I take a deep breath and reach for Mabel's hand.

"Okay. I'm ready."

She turns on a monitor, rolls what looks like a giant condom down the ultrasound wand, and then she does what she said she was going to do. It's...weird. I'm uncomfortable. But when she turns the monitor to me, all of that disappears.

"There you go," the tech says with a smile.

I stare at the screen, a strange tingling sensation spreading over my body. It's not a sesame seed anymore. I read it's the size of a strawberry now. The tech says it's looking right on track for a nine-week fetus, and I just...

I can't look away.

My jaw drops. I start to cry again, a mixture of sadness and awe. Jonah should be here. Even if I'm mad at him, he should be seeing this, too. This tiny product of Madrid. The thoughts overwhelm me. Everything is so overwhelming, and my tears fall faster.

Then Mabel squeezes my hand.

"One time, when I was in, like, second grade, my hamster had babies. It looks kind of like that."

The tech and I both start laughing, and I look at Mabel.

"Thank you," I whisper, and she winks at me.

"I got you."

I believe her.

I feel like I have someone in my corner, and words can't express just what that means to me. I look back at the monitor, blinking away more tears so I can see the screen clearly, and place my free hand on my stomach.

It's going to be okay, little strawberry.
We're going to be okay.

THIRTY SEVEN

Claire

"THIS PLACE IS NICE."

"Right." I smirk at her as I kick off my shoes. "I'm sure my postage stamp of an apartment really measures up to a world-famous rock star."

Mabel sits on my couch and grins up at me. "I wasn't always a world-famous rock star. I used to be just another unwanted foster kid runaway who disappeared into the system, never to be seen or heard from again."

I raise my eyebrows in surprise, then take the seat next to her. I rest my head on the back cushion and close my eyes. I'm always so tired these days.

"When I was hired to do Jonah's PR, I tried to do as much research on you guys as I could." I raise a hand to stifle a yawn. "I found very little about you."

"One of the few good things the label's done for us."

"What do you mean?"

"They scrubbed us from the internet."

"Really? Why?"

"Less mess, I suppose. Less chance anyone from our pasts would come knocking. We were young and aside from Jonah, we didn't have stable upbringings. Sav was a runaway. I was a runaway. Torren should have just run away. The label didn't want any surprises, so a cursory internet search won't tell you much of anything before we became The Hometown Heartless." She laughs. "Well, except Sav and Torren, now. They've blown their own shit wide open."

I laugh with her. "Yeah, I noticed that."

"Everything in my past is a lot more boring than theirs, honestly. I doubt anyone would care even if they did find it."

I turn my head so I can look at her. Her pink-highlighted hair is perfectly styled. Her winged eyeliner is sharp and precise. Her pink lips are curled into a subtle perma-smile as she thumbs through a design magazine I had sitting on the coffee table.

Mabel's been nothing but kind to me from the beginning. Always happy. Always smiling. Always quick to toss out a snarky-yet-good-humored joke. I realize now that the bubbly exterior could very well be a survival tactic. A protective armor of some sort.

No one ever looks too long at the happy ones. It's the broody, angry, mysterious ones that tend to draw attention.

Mabel is the only bandmember who doesn't have a permanent residence in the media. I run through my memories and can't recall a single headline about her. How much of that is intentional?

"What *is* in your past, Mabel?"

"Just another sad orphan backstory to tug on the heartstrings, Claire." Her lips turn up in a grin, and she arches a brow. "Think it's enough to make a main character?"

"Probably."

"God, I hope not." She laughs and rolls her eyes, then pulls her phone out of her pocket. Whatever she reads has the smile wiped from her face. She turns to face me. "Let me preface this by saying I'm sorry."

I sit up straight. "What?"

"Sav and Callie are coming over."

"What? Why? I thought Sav was in North Carolina, and Callie was in LA?"

"They were, but Caveat had some studio time in the city, so Sav came with. Sorry. I told them I was meeting up with you, but I didn't think she'd just swing by." Mabel winces. "In hindsight, I probably should have seen it as a possibility."

"How does she even know where I live?"

"She's Sav. She knows everything."

A knock rings through my apartment, and I sigh, pushing myself from the couch.

"Sorry," Mabel whispers, and I wave her off.

"Do I look pregnant?"

She snorts. "No."

"Phew."

I mime wiping my forehead with my hand and head to the door. I take a deep breath, count to ten, then force a smile and open the door.

"Hi! Come on in!" I take turns pulling Sav and Callie into hugs as they walk into my apartment. "It's good to see you guys."

Sav moves toward Mabel and leans on the wall next to the couch. "Sorry for just dropping in unannounced."

"Are you really?" Mabel asks with a smirk.

"Yes, I am." Sav flips Mabel off playfully before returning her attention to me. "We finished up at the studio a little early, and I'd been meaning to meet up with you anyway. Since I knew you were with Mabes, I figured now was as good a time as any."

"It's fine, really. It's nice to see you. Though, if I'd known, I'd have had us try to meet somewhere else." I gesture awkwardly. "Sorry it's so tiny. Just, um, sit wherever? It's not the best space for gathering."

Callie laughs and takes a seat on the floor, crossing her legs in front of her. "I grew up in Santa Monica and shared a place not much bigger than this with my mom *and* sister. You don't have to apologize."

"Well, that's one perk of moving back home. I'm likely to have more space." I open the fridge and glance over my shoulder. "I have lemonade? Or I can make some coffee?"

"Lemonade is great," Callie says. "Why are you moving back home?"

"Oh, right." I huff a laugh as I pull four glasses from the cabinet and fill them with lemonade. "Well, I'm not sure how much you guys know, but I quit my job at Innovation, and it's unlikely I'll get hired anywhere else."

Sav's moved to the floor next to Callie, so I hand them their glasses, then grab mine and Mabel's before taking my seat back on the couch.

"My lease is up in a month, so I'm just cutting my losses and moving back to Virginia. I don't really want to drain my savings trying to stay in this shoebox, anyway."

I try to sound lighthearted, but I can tell I fail. I love this city. I love this apartment. I loved my job. Now, everything is changing rapidly, and I'm just trying desperately to stay upright.

"I heard about your job, actually." Sav gives me a sympathetic smile. "I'm sorry to hear about it. I'm surprised Jo's dad didn't offer to triple your salary to get you to stay after you did such great work with Jo."

I force a laugh. "Yeah, well, when you date your boss, things like this happen."

Sav spits out her lemonade as Callie chokes on hers.

"What?" Sav gasps out. She reaches over and pats Callie on the back. "You dated Jo's dad?"

The shock in her voice has me laughing, and I flick my eyes to Mabel and find her staring at me too. I wince.

"Sorry for not telling you sooner."

Mabel huffs out a laugh and shakes her head. "It's fine, babe. It's your trauma to tell."

I laugh again, louder this time. Trauma is right.

"I dated him for almost a year before I ended things and quit Innovation. He didn't take it well, hence, I won't get hired anywhere else."

"Bastard," Sav growls. "That's illegal."

"His word against mine." I shrug and force myself to sound more positive than I feel. "I could fight it, but it would be a huge pain in the ass. Costly and a lot of media attention. It's the last thing I want to deal with. It's fine. Virginia isn't bad."

"That's so shitty, Claire. Seriously. I'm so sorry."

I give Callie a smile. "It is, yeah. Thanks."

Callie looks tentatively at Sav, then Sav flicks her eyes to Mabel before looking back at me. She smiles brightly, making my neck prickle with awareness. Sav's up to something. I can tell.

CLAIRE

"Well, I have something to discuss with you. But can I use your bathroom first? I can feel lemonade pooling in my bra."

"Yeah, of course." I point to the clearly visible bathroom door.

"Thanks."

When the faucet turns on in the bathroom, I bounce my eyes between Callie and Mabel.

"What is she up to? And don't say nothing. I can tell it's something."

Mabel and Callie share a glance, and then Mabel gives me a small smile. "Just hear her out. It's nothing bad, I promise."

I open my mouth to argue, but the bathroom door opens and Sav reappears.

"So much better," she says on a sigh before plopping down on the floor next to Callie. "Anyway, as I was saying, I have something I'd like to discuss with you."

I arch a brow. "Okay. What is it?"

"I'd like you to come work for me."

My jaw drops. "What?"

"At the end of the European tour, we'll be out of the contract with our label—thanks in large part to the way you were able to turn things around with Jonah—and then I'm going to launch my new record label, Rock Loveless Records. I'd like to hire you."

"As what?"

"Marketing and communications director. Rock Loveless needs branding and a marketing plan, and then you'd be overseeing the PR and marketing plans for any bands we sign. At present, we only have one band."

She hooks a thumb toward Callie, and Callie smiles brightly, putting her hands under her chin and fluttering her eyelashes.

"That would be me and my band of idiots."

I laugh and shake my head, then look back at Sav.

"Next year, I'll be bringing on more, so you'll be able to hire people to work under you. The job would require some traveling, though, especially at first. You might have to do some tour stops, if that's okay."

When I don't respond, her smile turns playful.

"Have I rendered you speechless?"

"I mean...I...I'm flattered, but..." I give my head a shake, then narrow my eyes. "Why me? You have no idea if I can do this level of work. You don't want to at least put me through an interview or ask for references or my portfolio or something?"

Sav shrugs. "You've basically been doing a working interview since Stockholm. And Crue's brother owns MixMosaic, so he works as a reference. He said your design presentation was the only reason they hired Innovation to help with their rebrand. He vouches for you."

My eyes widen. "MixMosaic is owned by Crue's brother? Like, Caveat Lover Crue? *That* Crue? *He's* related to a successful art broker?"

"I know, right?" Callie laughs. "I was shocked to hear it, too, but yep, our little baby Crue is from a *very* cultured bloodline, and his family is loaded."

"I never would have guessed." I look back at Sav. "So, you've just been checking up on me? For how long?"

She smirks. "Since about five minutes after we learned Jo's dad was sending you as his babysitter. But it wasn't until after you set up Jonah's social media that the idea of hiring you came to me."

I breathe slowly and drop my attention to my battered wood floor. I do love the floors in this apartment. The building is old, and the floors are original. It's another thing I'll miss when I move.

My mind starts to swirl with possibilities.

Working for Sav would mean I could stay in this industry. I don't know what she'd pay me yet, but I'm certain it'd be enough that I wouldn't have to leave the city. I wouldn't have to switch careers. I wouldn't have to uproot my life and change everything.

Change.

My eyes flutter shut on the word.

Everything is changing.

I make eye contact with Sav again. I give her a sad smile.

"Thank you, Sav, really. I appreciate the offer. But I'm going to have to turn it down."

"Why?"

My brows jump. "I'm moving back to Virginia."

"So?"

I chew my cheek, then shrug. "I just don't think working in the music industry is for me, and I can't commit to travel or touring at the moment."

She smiles. "Is it because you're pregnant?"

I gasp and whip wide eyes at Mabel. She throws up her palms.

"Don't look at me! I'm a vault!"

I turn back to Sav, my eyebrows nearly hitting my hairline. "How?"

"You have prenatal vitamins on your sink."

Callie laughs, then slaps a hand over her mouth, and I drop my forehead in my palm with a groan. Mabel drops her hand on my shoulder and rubs.

"If being pregnant is why you don't want to accept the job offer, we can do most everything remotely," Sav continues. "We can do video conferences, and I can come to you. I'll even pay you maternity leave, Claire."

I groan again. "It's not that."

"Well, if it's about Conrad Henderson, I'm not afraid of him. He might be able to scare all these other companies out of hiring you, but I don't give two fucks what he has to say. Honestly, it's disgusting that he would treat the mother of his kid this way, but I guess I'm not surprised. What an asshole."

A giggle bubbles out of me. I sit up and look at Sav and Callie. They're so confused, and that just makes me giggle more. My emotions are such a rollercoaster, but I turn to Mabel and find her trying her best not to laugh, too.

Oh God, what a mess.

"Conrad Henderson isn't the father," I say slowly, bouncing my eyes between Sav and Callie. I don't say anything else, but when Sav's eyes widen, I know she's figured it out.

"Oh shit, Claire."

"Oh shit is right."

"What?" Callie asks. "What am I missing?"

Sav arches a brow but doesn't speak, so I give Callie the truth.

"Jonah's the father."

Her jaw drops. "Oh shit."

I nod. "Yep."

"Does he know? How far along are you? What are you going to do?"

"One question at a time, Cal," Mabel says, but I wave her off.

"It's fine. No, he doesn't know. I'm about nine weeks. And I have no fucking idea."

The room falls silent, and I feel the sting of tears once more.

"Sorry," I say on a small laugh, running my fingers under my eyes. "Sorry, I'm really hormonal right now."

"Babe, stop apologizing. We're all a bunch of crybaby bitches here. You cry all you need." Mabel throws her arm over my shoulders, and I lean into her before looking back at Sav.

"So, while I'm beyond flattered, now you know why working for Rock Loveless Records would be a bad idea."

Sav purses her lips. "I think we need ice cream."

She pushes to standing and crosses to my kitchen in four strides, then pulls open the freezer.

"Claire!" She turns back to me. "You have no ice cream?"

"I'm not an ice cream craving kind of pregnant person."

She curls her upper lip. "Please don't tell me you're a pickle craving kind of pregnant person."

"Pickles and mayonnaise. And those ranch flavored crinkly potato chips."

Sav pauses, tilts her head to the side in consideration, and then shrugs. "I don't hate it." She ducks into the fridge. "Claire!" She turns around and holds up an empty pickle jar. "Claire Davis, you have no pickles."

I laugh. "I know. I ran out this morning. I need to get to the store."

"There's a little bodega down the street, right?"

I glance at Callie and nod. "Yeah. Two blocks."

She stands and walks to the door. "I'll go with Red."

"Red's here? Where's Red?" I look around the apartment as if that giant man could have gone undetected.

"He's just downstairs," Sav tells me, her voice muffled as she opens each of my cabinets. Then she turns to Callie. "Get some ice cream, too. And those ranch chips."

"The crinkly ones!" I add quickly. "Only the crinkly ones. The others taste burnt."

"On it. Be right back."

CLAIRE

After raiding my kitchen for bowls, spoons, and paper towels, then connecting her phone to my Bluetooth speaker to play her, as she put it, "happy bitch playlist," Sav turns to study me with her hands on her hips. I sigh dramatically, then stand from the couch and take off the sweatshirt I was wearing. I turn to the side, lift my shirt, and smooth a hand down my stomach for good measure.

"Well, I'll be damned." Sav grins at me. "Your boobs got bigger, but you still have abs."

I laugh. "My boobs hurt like hell, actually, but I probably won't show at all for a few more weeks. Oh, but..." I walk to the table and dig through my purse. "I have photo evidence."

I wave the strip of ultrasound images in the air, and Sav grabs them from me. She studies each one, turning the photos around and tilting her head.

"What exactly am I looking at?"

Mabel laughs. "I said it looked like when my hamster had babies."

"I'm told it's a healthy nine-week-old *human* fetus, but honestly, who knows at this point." I lift my shirt and flatten my palms on my stomach. "Could it be a hamster? A burrito? An alien? I have no idea."

Mabel leans closer to my stomach, then looks up at me. "Can it hear me?"

I shake my head. "It cannot."

"Can you feel it move?"

"I cannot."

"So right now all you get is exhaustion, sore boobs, and pickles?"

I laugh and nod. "And crinkly ranch potato chips."

"Which end is the head on this one?" I glance over and find Sav holding one of the ultrasound images close to her face. "I can't tell, and it's not labeled."

She turns the image to me and points just as Callie knocks on the door.

"Come in," I call out, and then I go back to studying the ultrasound picture. "Oh, that's the head." I frown. "I think." I take the ultrasound and study it. I barely register the sound of the door opening and closing. "Oh yeah, that's the head. See right here? It's a little arm."

"What?"

There's a collective, sharp intake of breath, and I clamp my eyes shut.

No. This isn't happening.

My fingers tighten on the ultrasound picture. I flex my toes into the floor, then slowly open my eyes and lift them to the doorway.

Jonah's face is pale, his attention stuck on the strip of ultrasound pictures in my hand.

"Who's pregnant?"

No one answers. I feel Sav and Mabel's eyes on me, and just as I open my mouth to confess, the door behind Jonah opens.

"The guy behind the counter knew exactly what I meant when I said *ranch crinkly chips,* Claire." Callie laughs as she steps into the apartment. "Seems your pregnancy cravings are famous in that bodega—"

She freezes as soon as she sees Jonah, but Jonah doesn't take his attention off me. His jaw pops and his nostrils flare as he drops his gaze down to my exposed, still-flat stomach. He swallows twice, that heart tattoo beating with the movement, then locks eyes with mine.

"Are you pregnant, Trouble?"

Slowly, I nod. "Yeah. I am."

THIRTY EIGHT

Claire

HE STARES at me until Sav, Callie, and Mabel leave.

Sav tells me she'll call tonight. Mabel says she'll see me tomorrow. I nod and say thank you, but I don't look away from Jonah.

When the door shuts, signaling that we're alone, I brace myself for whatever comes next. This isn't the way I wanted to have this conversation, but it's a conversation that needs to be had. Might as well be now.

I give him a tight smile and gesture to the couch.

"Do you want to sit?"

"Is it mine?"

My eyes widen, and I wince at the question. "Yes, Jonah. It's yours."

"Are you sure?"

"Yes, I'm sure."

He narrows his eyes slightly, and I grit my teeth, anger heating my blood. He's skeptical, and it makes me want to punch him.

"How far along are you?"

I huff a laugh. "Why? You don't believe me?" I march toward him and slap the ultrasound pictures on his chest. "I'm nine weeks. Madrid resulted in a pregnancy. Surprise, asshole. Now I have a souvenir to go with that pleasant memory."

His hand covers mine, holding my palm to his chest, but I pull away from him. Slowly, he drags his eyes from my face to the strip of ultrasound pictures. He blinks, and as his face softens, so does mine.

"How long have you known?"

My brows furrow as I'm hit with a wave of guilt. "Since Cardiff."

"The hospital," he says quietly, almost as an afterthought.

When he finally brings his eyes back to mine, they're hard again. Emotionless. Giving nothing away. It just makes me more agitated.

"Why didn't you tell me?"

My guilt morphs into anger. I grow defensive. I think I hear a hint of accusation in his tone. He has no right.

"Gee, I don't know, Jonah. When do you think I should have told you? When you were buying drugs from the roadie? When you told me you were glad you didn't have kids? Oh, I know, how about when both you *and* your father said I would get knocked up on purpose and take all your money? You said you needed a break, sent me back to New York, and haven't returned a call or text since. When the fuck should I have told you?"

His eyes bounce between mine as I seethe. My heart is pounding, and my chest is heaving, and he's just...cold. Again.

"So it was an accident?"

"Jesus Christ." My jaw drops and angry tears surge to my eyes. "I sure as fuck didn't do it on purpose. Rest assured, Jonah, I don't want anything from you. No money. No commitments. Nothing. You can leave now."

I turn and walk quickly into my bedroom, but when I try to shut the door, his boot stops it.

"Go away."

"No."

"I don't want you here, Jonah! I don't need you here. You're absolved of any responsibility, and you never have to see me again."

He grabs my wrist and pulls it to his chest again. I flex my fingers into the fabric of his cotton T-shirt. His heart is beating so fast.

"Don't say that, Claire. That's not what I want."

"Well, it's what I want."

"It's not."

"It is."

"It's not!" He takes a step closer and cups my neck with his other hand. "You don't want me to leave. You don't want to do this alone."

"You think I want to do it with you? You think I would trap you. You asked me if I got pregnant on purpose. Fuck, you thought I was lying that it was even yours! I don't want to do anything with you."

I pull away from him and put as much distance between us as possible.

"God, I'm such an idiot. You've showed me time and time again what you think of me, and I just ignored it. I ignored it when I should have sprinted in the opposite direction, and now…"

I press my fingers to my temples and tilt my face to the ceiling.

Now I'm fucked.

"I want to do this with you."

"We're not *doing* anything."

"What do you mean? You're pregnant. You're having my kid."

I sigh and look back at him.

"Jonah, I need you to really think about this for a moment, okay? You and me? We would be terrible parents. You said it yourself—you don't want to think about all the ways you could fuck a kid up."

He shakes his head. "No. We can do this. We can do this together."

"Me being pregnant isn't going to just erase all our issues. I'm still going to have slept with your dad, remember? That was a huge trigger for you. I'm still going to be me, and you're still going to be you. You're an addict, Jonah, and I've relapsed with my eating disorder. We both hate ourselves. We can't even get our own shit together. How can we coparent a child?"

"I don't want to coparent with you, Trouble. I want to do this with you. Together. Me and you. Mom and Dad."

I shake my head and bite the inside of my cheek. He's not getting it.

"I didn't get pregnant to trap you into being my baby's daddy, Jonah. That's not what I'm trying to do, okay? I'm not going to force you into a situation you don't want to be in, especially when I don't know what I want either."

He tilts his head, then lowers his voice to a whisper.

"What are you saying? Are you saying you want an abortion?"

"No," I whisper back. "I considered it, but no."

All the fears that have been building inside me bubble over and spill out of my mouth as anxiety wraps around my chest.

"But how can I be a parent? How can I be a mom when I can't even take care of myself? What if I fuck it up? What if I make all the wrong decisions? How can I do that to a baby? I don't want to saddle a child with my baggage. I don't want to fuck it up the way we're fucked up. It didn't ask for that."

I squeeze my eyes shut against the tears, and not for the first time since discovering this pregnancy, my stomach swirls with anxious nausea. My body wants to vomit, and it just makes everything worse. It just confirms all of my fears. I place a hand on my abdomen and breathe through it. I picture the little strawberry, and I breathe.

As soon as I think I can open my mouth without throwing up, I try again. I speak more calmly, but my voice still shakes. My words are still cloaked in despair.

There is no hope here.

"I watched my mom struggle after finally getting away from my father. She tried her best, but the damage was done. Macon turned to alcohol and drugs. I started purging. If I try to be a parent, I'm going to fail. I'm going to fail, and this baby is going to pay the price. I'm not cut out for this. I can't do it. I'm going to fail."

Calloused hands cup my cheeks as I'm engulfed in the scent of Jonah's bodywash.

"Listen to me, Trouble. I love you."

I shake my head, opening my mouth to protest, but two fingers press against my lips.

"The only person in this room down on you is you. You're so busy beating yourself up that you can't understand why anyone would love you, but I do. I'm sorry I made you doubt it. I did and said stupid fucking things because I was afraid of how I felt. Even today, when you said you were pregnant, I thought it was too good to be true. I fucking love you. I've never felt so connected to another person like I do to you. You are the strongest, smartest, most caring person I've ever met, Claire Davis, and I want to have this baby with you."

Tears stream down my face as his words settle in, but I don't speak. I don't move. I barely breathe. Then he presses his forehead to mine and threads his fingers through my hair.

"Tell me you haven't thought of it. Tell me you can't see it, Claire. Me and you and this baby. Happy and together. If you haven't thought of it, if you've never once wanted it, tell me, and I won't bring it up again. But if you have, even just once, I'm begging you to do this with me. I'll even be the more loving one. *If equal affection cannot be, Let the more loving one be me.* I don't mind. If it means I get to keep you, I don't mind. Tell me, Claire."

I force a swallow and shake my head, and I feel his body droop in defeat. His breath hitches, his fingers loosen in my hair, but just as he starts to pull away, I grab his shirt. I keep him close to me.

"I've thought of it," I confess. "I have."

I don't say any more. I don't tell him that I've dreamt of it. I've seen it so vividly that I've woken up in tears, longing for him. Mourning that life I thought I'd never have.

And yet...

I keep going back to him in that hallway with the roadie. Him in the hotel room digging through my suitcase in search of my prescription. Spiraling over things I can't change.

Checkmate, Trouble. Pack your shit and get out of my life.
You're cute thinking I talk to my therapist about anything of importance.
The only thing I learned in rehab is how to be a better liar.

"Jonah," I say on an exhale. "I can't be with an addict. I have my own shit to work out. It's not good for either of us, and it's certainly not good for a baby. I can't be wor—"

"I'll play you for it."

I pull back and look at him. "What?"

"The chess board I got you is set up in the corner. You've even got the queen from Stockholm on the board. I'll play you for it."

"For what?"

"For us. If I win, we do this. I'll go back to rehab. I'll complete the program for real this time. I'll take it seriously, and then we give it our all. You, me, and this baby."

Macon's words play over in my head.

Getting sober was the hardest thing I've ever done, but the easiest decision I've ever made.

I start to want things. To imagine things. My stomach flips as hope blooms in my chest, but I shove it down. Not yet. I can't do this to myself again.

"And if I win?"

He shrugs. "Then I step back. We do it your way."

"We can't play a chess game to decide that."

"Why not? You've thought of us together as a family. You're not completely against it. If you were, you never would have admitted to it. We're not making the decision any other way, so why not this way?"

Something in me knows this is ridiculous, but another part of me, that stupid hopeful part of me, wants to try. I'm exhausted and emotional. My brain is foggy. I can't settle on a decision on my own, and he's right. I've thought of us as a family. I'm not completely against it.

It's the absolute worst thing to leave to chance.

I shake my head again.

"I'll beat you, Jonah."

"Maybe not. I've been practicing over the last few weeks. It helped with my detox."

Detox.

It helped with his detox. That stupid feeling of hope grows.

"Have you used anything?"

I ask the question tentatively, but he answers immediately. No hesitation. I know it's the truth.

"No. Hardest thing I've done is this nasty ass mocktail Sav made for me."

I close my eyes and try to bite my tongue. I try to force myself to turn him down, but when I open my mouth, I say the opposite.

"Fine. One game."

Jonah grabs the chess board, walking carefully so as not to tip over the pieces, and takes it into the living room. He sets it on the table, then sits himself behind the white pieces, so I take my place behind the black pieces.

"Ready?"

I nod, and then he moves his king pawn two squares. I arch a brow.

"You have been practicing."

"Told you."

I move my piece and wait as he studies the board again. He takes a long time before making his move. Every turn of his is carefully considered, and it's obvious he's taking it seriously.

He doesn't want to lose. It makes my heart hurt, but it also has me hoping he wins. I want him to beat me. I want to do this with him.

But then, in fifteen moves, I see a pathway to checkmate him with my queen. That blue wooden queen he made for me in Stockholm. I flick my eyes to him and find him staring at it. He can see it, too, and he knows he's about to lose.

It's almost poetic that my queen, the queen he made for me, would be the piece to win it for me.

But what would I be winning?

My fingers tremble as I reach for the queen. I rest my forefinger and thumb on it and look at him once more. His blue eyes shimmer with unshed tears. He swallows roughly, and I watch that heart on his throat beat with the movement.

"Just do it, Trouble."

God, his voice is so strained, like he's holding back a sob. His breaths are ragged. His chest is heaving. Tears well in my own eyes. I won't do it. I *can't* do it. Even if I wanted to, I couldn't, and I don't want to.

Without a second thought, I lay my queen on its side, forfeiting the game.

His eyes lock on mine. He blinks, causing those unshed tears to fall. He swallows again and his brows furrow in question.

I give him a small smile.

"Okay, Jonah. Okay."

He blows out a puff of breath, then lunges over the chess board. I barely register the pieces falling to the ground as he cradles my face in his hands and presses his forehead to mine.

"Thank you. Thank you. I won't let us down. I swear it. You won't regret this."

I nod, but I can't speak, and when he kisses me, I let him.

I'm so scared. I'm so fucking scared, but just having him here makes me feel better. Even knowing he's leaving on Monday to finish the tour my nerves have calmed a little. I wrap my arms around his neck and deepen our kiss, finally letting myself admit how much I've missed him. When he finally breaks away from me, it takes all my self-restraint not to pull him back.

"I came to tell you I'm going to rehab. I leave tomorrow."

My eyes widen. "What? What do you mean?"

"I mean, at the advice of my therapist, I've admitted myself into a ninety-day residential program. I won't have access to my phone or internet—no outside contact at all unless it's an emergency—so you won't hear from me until I'm out. I leave tomorrow."

"You're supposed to leave for the last leg of the tour on Monday."

"Rock's playing the rest of the tour for me."

"You can't...you can't do that. What about the contract?"

"Nowhere in the contract does it say we can't bring in musicians to fill in for us. Torren did it after Callie's accident. I'm doing it now."

"But the morality clause?"

"That was added as a gotcha. The label expected one of us to fuck up and for the tabloids to run with it, but Hammond's already gotten ahead of this story. He's reached out to the big media outlets, and they'll be printing that I've been admitted for *rest and recovery*. Now that you've made me a media darling, they were nothing but supportive, so we're expecting the same reaction from the public. *And* Hammond already told the label that if they try to say we're in violation of the morality clause, we won't finish the tour. They'll be out a lot of money, and let's be honest, that's all those fuckers care about."

I don't know what to say. I just wipe at my tears and shake my head. How is this happening? Is this real? Can I trust this?

"You already set this up?" I ask, bouncing my eyes between his, searching for the lie. The trick. "Even before the chess game, you were going to do it anyway?"

CLAIRE

He nods slowly and traces his knuckles over my jaw.

"That's what I came to tell you. I came to beg for your forgiveness and prove that I won't fuck up again. I don't want to lose you, Claire. I'll do anything to keep that from happening."

He reaches up and fingers one of my loose curls, tugging it down before letting it spring back up, and then he smiles.

"I want to be able to do that for the rest of my life, Trouble. I want to travel with you. I want to get my ass kicked in the gym with you. I want to play chess with you. I want to teach our baby to play. I want everything with you, and I'm going to earn it. I swear to God, Claire, I will. Let me."

My breath hitches as I swallow back a sob. I believe him. I can see it. I want it so badly that it's a physical ache in my chest.

"Okay." I nod, pressing a quick kiss to his lips. "Okay, Jonah Hendrix. I love you too, so let's earn it together."

THIRTY NINE

Jonah

THREE MONTHS LATER

MY KNEE BOUNCES up and down as I sit in the lobby.

I stare at the *Welcome to Tranquil Waters* sign on the reception desk while I wait. The first time I stayed here, I laughed at that sign. White lotuses floating on a clear blue stream under a red and purple sunrise, the slogan *from struggle to strength, your rebirth awaits* written in flowing script underneath. I thought it was cliché and tacky. I thought it was too much symbolism. I thought it was trying too hard.

Now I might get part of it tattooed on my neck.

I check my watch again, then I check the clock on the wall.

This fucker is late.

I wait ten more minutes, then pull my phone out of my pocket and call him. It starts to ring just as Torren walks through the door. He hits me with a grin.

"Impatient?"

"You're forty-five minutes late." I stand, shove my phone back into my pocket, and haul my duffle bag over my shoulder. "I think that warrants a phone call."

"Sorry. Traffic."

I shake my head, but I don't bother fighting the slight upturn of my lips as he pulls me in for a hug, patting my back the way a big brother would.

"Good to see you." He releases me and looks me over. "You look about a hundred times better than you did last time I picked you up from this place."

"I'd hope so. I was high when you picked me up last time."

Torren's eyes widen. "You dickhead. You were lying to all of us."

I shrug. "If it's any consolation, I'm not high *now*. It's going to stick this time."

"Thank God." Torren smirks and turns toward the door. "This place is the most expensive treatment center on the West Coast. Wouldn't want you to have to go through it a third time."

"Right," I deadpan. "Thank God."

"Still surly, huh? Sobriety hasn't perked you up any?"

Torren climbs into the driver's seat of my sports car as I slide into the passenger seat. He starts the engine, then waits until I've done my seat belt to put the car in drive. I'm glad he's driving. My head is spinning too much to focus on the road, and since Callie's accident, he prefers to be behind the wheel whenever possible.

"Sorry." I release a slow exhale. "I'm nervous."

Torren hums, and I glance at his profile. I'm grateful he's not making a bigger deal of this, and he's not treating me with kid gloves, either. I don't know which would bother me more.

I just want to feel normal again, but I don't know what that means anymore. I have to discover it as I go, and that task feels daunting.

I flex my fingers into my thigh.

From struggle to strength. One day at a time.

"I wanted to talk to you about something."

Torren pulls me from my thoughts, and I glance at him.

"Is it something I want to hear?"

He smirks. "I'm going to say it regardless."

I wave my hand in the air. "Carry on."

He swallows and purses his lips, pausing for a moment as if collecting his thoughts. He never takes his eyes off the road or his hands off the wheel while speaking, but I feel every word as sincerely as if he were making eye contact.

"I'm sorry. I should have recognized that you were struggling. I should have seen it when I picked you up the first time, and I sure as fuck should have seen it since then. I let myself be naïve and saw only what I wanted to see, especially after Callie came along. I dropped you, and even though I could tell it bothered you, I ignored it. I'm sorry. It was fucked up, and you deserved a better friend. I won't let it happen again."

I exhale slowly, my forehead creasing as his message sinks in. Then I huff a small laugh.

"You didn't see what *you* wanted to see, Tor. You saw what *I* wanted you to see. I've spent my entire life observing and analyzing people, then over a decade perfecting how to use what I learn to my advantage. I didn't want your help. I didn't want *anyone's* help, and that's on me, not you."

Torren shakes his head. "No, Jo. You're my best friend. You're my brother. I should have been paying better attention."

"You can't put that on yourself, Torren. You all tried your best. But until I wanted it, it wouldn't have mattered."

Briefly, he flicks his eyes to me. "But you want it now?"

"More than fucking anything."

He smiles. "Good. I'm really glad. We want it for you, too."

I nod, then turn my attention back out the window and sit with that truth. I do want it more than anything. I want it for me. For Claire. For our baby. I want sobriety for *us*, and I want it so badly that I'm terrified I'm going to lose it.

What if she's changed her mind?

I thought about it a lot in rehab. If Claire changed her mind, if she doesn't want to do this with me, it will absolutely crush me. I'll have to go through every raw emotion without a chemical crutch because I refuse to backslide again. I meant what I said to Torren. It's going to stick this time. I'm staying clean, and so I'm preparing myself for the worst. It will be a heartbreak like I've never known. Worse than Theo. Worse than learning that my existence was solely for the purpose of keeping him alive. Worse than failing.

Worse than anything.

I flex my fingers into my thigh again. I focus on my breathing. On my heart rate. For the first time in a long time, my experience of the world is untainted. That fills me with just as much fear as it does pride.

I just have to take it one day at a fucking time.

I break the silence with a question. "She here?"

"Been here, actually."

"What do you mean?"

"She's been staying at Mabel's place since her lease ended."

I turn and face him. "One of Mabel's places on the East Coast?"

"Nope. Mabel's place down the street from Sav's right here in LA."

Excitement stirs in my stomach. I didn't think she'd leave New York. Not without me having to beg, which I was fully prepared to do. This is a good sign, but I try not to get too hopeful.

"Did she take the job offer from Sav?"

"She did. She's already drawn up marketing plans for Rock Loveless and Caveat. She's really fucking smart."

I smile at that. "She is."

She's working for Sav now, so the move could have been work-related. But she's here. She's here in LA, and that's one obstacle I no longer have to clear.

"And what about the other thing? Does she know?"

"It's done, and as far as I know, she has no idea. The girls can keep secrets when they want to."

I drum my fingers on my leg. "Okay." I nod. "Okay. Good."

"I know this isn't going to help anything, but you don't have to be nervous. She's excited to see you. Everything is going to be fine."

I don't respond. Instead, I mentally run through every scenario.

I haven't spoken to her in ninety days. I have no idea where her head is. I don't even know if she still feels the way she did when I left her in New York. I begged her to give me another chance, and then I left her for three months.

A lot can change in three months.

JONAH

I know because *I've* changed a lot in three months.

I told her she wouldn't have to go through any of this alone, and then I left. I've missed so much already.

I'm sure I made the right choice for myself in going back to Tranquil Waters. I'm anxious and afraid, but I'm not running. I'm *feeling,* and that's huge. If I didn't fix *me*, I could never deserve *her*. I would never be worthy of *us*.

It was the right choice. I know it. I just hope Claire believes it, too. Ninety days ago, she said she loved me. I just keep replaying those words over and over in my head.

I love you, too.

Let's earn it together.

She loves me. Ninety days wouldn't undo that.

I glance at the GPS on the dash and my shoulders drop when I see a red line indicating stopped traffic on the freeway.

"Told you. I left at 8 a.m."

Torren points to the ETA on the screen. Four hours. I groan and fix my eyes out the window. I don't even have a book to read.

"Want me to tell you about it?"

"No," I answer immediately. "I trust the girls."

I see him glance at me from my periphery.

"You want to talk at all?"

I think it over. Would I have wanted to talk three months ago? A year ago? Should I want to talk now? Do I?

My lips curve into a small smile when I realize that I do.

"How'd the tour go?"

Torren returns my smile. "It went good. No issues. People were upset you weren't there, but everyone for the most part understood. Ham's been a puppet master with the media, thanks in large part to the groundwork Claire laid out. And it doesn't hurt that Rock's gotten himself a bit of a fan following. It's that glittery pink Fender, I swear. People are obsessed with it."

I arch a brow. "Is this where you tell me that you're replacing me with Rocky Halstrom?"

He barks out a laugh. "Want me to tell you all the times he fucked up to make you feel better?"

"Hell yeah, I do," I say on a laugh, and then I grin. A real, full-faced smile, and I feel lighter. I feel hopeful.

This. Speaking with Torren freely without having to worry about hiding my addiction. Laughing with him. Joking. This will be part of my new normal. I'll create it myself. I'll collect moments, piece them together, and rebuild my life from the ground up.

From the ground up, one day at a time, and with Claire front and center.

WE PULL up to Sav's just before 5 p.m.

When Torren turns off the car, we climb out, but I don't move toward the house.

"Are you going to come in?"

I shake my head. "No. Not yet."

"I'll send her out, then." He holds the keys out for me, jangling them a few times before dropping them into my palm with a smirk. "It's the new one."

"No shit."

Just before Torren reaches the door, he turns back around.

"Hey, at the risk of sounding like a complete asshole and making you extremely uncomfortable again..."

"Don't do it," I warn, but he doesn't listen.

"I'm really fucking proud of you, Jo. I'm proud, and I believe you. I know it's going to stick this time. You deserve happiness."

I pause. I needed to hear that, and surprisingly, I believe them.

"Thanks, Tor."

He nods once, then turns and disappears into Sav's house. When the door closes, I stare at it and start to count. At eighty-five, the door opens, and I hold my breath as she steps out onto the stoop.

She's beautiful, and I lose my breath. Her curly brown hair is down, falling just past her collarbone. She's in a plain black T-shirt and leggings, and when my eyes fall on her stomach, I start to cry.

JONAH

Tears fall silently as she closes the distance between us. I dreamt of that beautiful smile every night since I left her in New York, but nothing compares to seeing it in person.

I expect her to stop when she reaches me, but she doesn't. Thank God, she doesn't. Instead, Claire wraps her arms around my waist and hugs me tightly. I pull her against my body and bury my face in her hair. I inhale deeply, filling my lungs with her. Lavender and sugar. It calms me immediately. She lifts on her tiptoes and lays her head on my shoulder.

"I missed you." Her lips tickle my neck as she speaks, and my shirt dampens with her tears. "I missed you so much."

The relief those words give me is unmatched. I've never felt relief like this. She's not angry. She doesn't hate me. I force a swallow and pull her closer.

"Do you still love me, Trouble?"

"Yes. Do you still love me?"

"Endlessly." I pull back and kiss her lips, tasting her tears as they mix with mine. "I love you endlessly."

She laughs lightly and kisses me again. She missed me. She loves me. She's still mine.

I cup her face in my hands, deepening our kiss. I don't want to let her go. I want to stand in this driveway forever with her in my arms.

"You're still mine."

She nods, then wraps her hands around my wrists and guides them down her body.

"*We're* still yours. Both of us."

The moment my hands are on her rounded stomach, my tears come faster. I press my forehead to hers, kiss her once more, then lean back and look. Her small hands top my larger ones as she gently presses my palms into her skin, and I'm in awe. It's not a very large bump; my splayed hands cover it almost entirely, but it's noticeable. It's beautiful.

Then her breath hitches, and her eyes connect with mine.

"Are you okay? Did I hurt you?"

She smiles and shakes her head. "No...it's..."

Her eyes flutter shut for a moment, and then her breath hitches again. Her shimmering gaze locks with mine once more, and she smiles brightly.

"It says hello, Daddy."

"Did you feel it move?" I swallow back a sob and blink away more tears when she nods. "What's it feel like?"

"Like a little flutter. Like a stomach flip." She kisses me again. "Say something. Talk to it."

I step back then kneel in front of her, putting my face level with her stomach. I don't take my hands off her, though. I just lean in close and say the first thing that comes to mind.

"Hey there, baby Trouble."

Claire laughs. "It likes you. It's flipping around like a little fish."

"Yeah?" I rest my forehead on her stomach. "I like you too."

Claire takes one hand off mine and threads it into my hair. I tilt into her touch, then kiss her little bump.

"I love you, baby Trouble," I whisper. "You and your mommy. I love you."

This feeling. This absolute, unconditional feeling of love. Me and Claire and this baby. This will be part of my new normal. This will be my every day from now on.

"I won't miss anything else," I say against her. "Never again. I promise."

"I know. I believe you."

She takes a step back and then gives my hand a soft tug. I stand up as she reaches into her pocket and pulls out her phone.

"Actually, I have something for you." Claire glances down at the screen and scrolls before handing the phone to me. "It's a little album. Some videos and pictures. Mabel flew home every other week between shows, so she was able to film the appointments. It was her idea, and I know it's not the same, but I wanted you to have something."

I hold my breath as I flip through the album, blinking rapidly to clear my vision so I can see through the tears.

There's a short video of her first ultrasound. I saw the ultrasound images, but this video is a different experience. Then there's a video of Claire and Mabel in a doctor's office hearing the heartbeat. I play that video three times, closing my eyes so I can hear it better. So I can commit it to memory. There are pictures of Claire from the side with a progressively growing belly, each one labeled by the week of pregnancy, but it stops at twenty-one.

"Where's twenty-two?"

She shrugs. "I wanted to take it with you."

I hiccup on another sob and pull her back into my arms. "Thank you. Thank you so much." I hold her until I catch my breath, then I step back and smile down at her. "I have something for you, too. Want to come with me to my place?"

She smirks and arches a brow. "Are you going to take your dick out?"

"Only if you want me to, but no, this isn't code for let's go have sex."

"Okay," she says with a playful smile. "I suppose I can go with you."

FORTY

Jonah

GETTING to the address Torren programmed into my GPS takes three minutes.

I knew it was close to Sav's, but I didn't realize it was just down the street.

When we pull up to the gate, I punch in the code—which happens to be Mabel's birthday because she thinks she's hilarious—and drive up the brick driveway. When I stop in front of the two-story Mediterranean-style estate, I try not to be obvious about how I watch Claire's expression, but I fail. She turns wide eyes on me and smiles.

"This is gorgeous. The courtyard and the ivy? Talk about curb appeal."

"Come on. Let's check it out."

We climb out of the car and make our way up to the door. I flip through the keys, then smile when I see a queen chess piece on a keychain. I'll have to commend Mabel for that one.

"I'm honestly surprised," Claire says as I unlock the door.

"Why's that?"

"I expected you to live in some sort of penthouse bachelor pad downtown with minimal furniture and a fully stocked bar."

I swing the door wide, and we step into the foyer, and I watch her face go slack. It's the perfect view of the open-concept first floor.

"What do you think?"

She laughs and flicks her eyes to me before she goes back to staring.

"Good lord, Jonah. This is beautiful."

I drag my eyes away from her and take it in for myself. She's right. It's beautiful.

I'm met with vaulted ceilings that must reach about thirty feet and an elegantly crafted staircase leading to the second floor. Then there's an expansive living room, highlighted by a stone fireplace, and a dining and family room with views of a pool and landscaped gardens. The real jaw-dropper, though, is the panoramic view of Downtown Los Angeles offered through the floor-to-ceiling windows. Even Sav's house doesn't have a view like this.

Claire kicks off her shoes, so I do the same, and then I follow her through the first floor.

"I was right about one thing," she says with a laugh.

"What's that?"

"Minimal furnishings."

I glance around. "Oh, yeah." I tap on the back of a cream-colored sofa. "I think these actually came with the house."

She laughs again. "What?"

I smirk. "I bought some of the staging furniture. You know. So, it wasn't totally empty."

Claire shakes her head and walks into the kitchen, then whistles.

"Do you even cook?"

"I could learn." I glance around the space. It's a gourmet kitchen. Granite countertops, six-burner stove, massive refrigerator, dual ovens. I hum. "Looks like I'm going to have to learn."

"Can I go outside?"

"You can go wherever you want."

I follow her through French doors that lead to a BBQ patio. The patio wraps around the house and has access to the pool and spa.

"Whoa." She cups her hand over her eyes and peers out into the distance. "Is that the ocean?"

JONAH

I follow her eyes. "Yep. I bet we get some pretty sunsets."

"You bet?" She turns and grins at me. "You've never seen it?"

"Can't say that I have."

She laughs and shakes her head, then turns around and looks up at the second-story patio. "Can I go upstairs?"

"Already told you, Trouble. You can go where you want."

I follow her back inside and up a staircase to the second floor, where she wanders in and out of three sparsely furnished bedrooms and a few elegant bathrooms.

"How many bedrooms and bathrooms are in this place?"

I purse my lips. "Five and eight?"

"Are you sure?" she asks, her voice teasing. "You sound like you don't know."

I just smile and stay quiet. She walks into the primary bedroom and hums when she sees a California king bed.

"Oh, thank God you at least have a bed." She turns to me and wiggles her eyebrows. "Do I get to sleep in it?"

"I hope so." I chuckle. "Maybe we can do more than sleep."

"Play your board right, and maybe..."

She trails off with a wink, then saunters out of the room. I'm a few steps behind her, but she gasps when she walks into the next bedroom. When I step up behind her, I know why.

This room is almost empty except for one thing.

A crib.

I hear her breath hitch, and I wrap my arms around her from behind, placing my hands on her stomach and resting my cheek against her head.

"They did good putting it next to our bedroom," I whisper.

"They?"

"The girls. Mabel, Callie, and Sav."

She turns a little and looks up at me with teary eyes. "What do you mean?"

"Well, they picked out the house and stuff. I'm guessing it was their idea to put the crib in this room."

She blinks at me. "They what? What do you mean?"

Gently, I turn her around so we're facing each other. "Do you like the house, Trouble?"

She nods. "Yes. I love it."

"Do you want it?"

Her mouth drops open, her next word escaping on an exhale. "What?"

"I bought it for us if you want it. Just in case you were open to leaving New York City. I'm sure it will sell quickly if you don't like it. But I'd like to be wherever you are if you're okay with it. I'd like us to be together."

I cup her cheek in my palm and wipe at one of her tears.

"Want to move in with me, Trouble? I'll learn how to cook. I'll let you decorate. We can do whatever you want, however you want. What do you think?"

She kisses me, wrapping her arms around my neck and holding me to her. She peppers kisses on my lips, jaw, and neck, and I laugh.

"Is this a yes?"

"Mmhmm. It's a yes. It's a hell yes."

I pick her up and spin her once, then softly set her back on her feet.

"Thank God," I joke. "Think how pissed Mabes would be if we didn't like it."

She laughs, then shakes her head. "When can we move in?"

I reach into my back pocket for the keys, then press the keychain with the queen on it into her palm.

"Now. It all starts now."

IT DOESN'T TAKE LONG to move Claire's things from Mabel's house to ours, and within an hour, I have a moving company bring my stuff out of storage.

Neither of us has much, and I'm grateful for it. As far as I'm concerned, the only things that matter moving forward are the things we'll have together.

I text Mabel to thank her and ask her to tell Callie and Sav that Claire loves the house. Then, instead of driving back to Sav's so they can all welcome me home from my second stint in rehab, we plan to have a housewarming cookout next weekend.

JONAH

Then something dawns on me.

"We don't have groceries."

"Oh." Claire laughs. "Can we order something to be delivered?"

"Pizza?"

"Pizza."

I pull up the closest pizza delivery place, click on the online ordering page, then pause. I have no idea how her recovery has been going. I glance at her and try to read her body language. Try to determine if the topic of food has made her uncomfortable or anxious, but she looks unbothered.

I almost let that be enough, but I can't. I can't, and I shouldn't. That's something I'm learning. Communication is essential in relationships and crucial for recovery.

"Trouble. How are you doing?"

She looks up from her phone. "What do you mean?"

"With your recovery. With your eating disorder. We didn't talk about it in New York, and I should have checked in with you sooner. How are you?"

"Oh." She clicks her phone off and drops it in her lap. "I haven't purged at all, so that's good. But somedays are harder than others."

"How so?"

"It's been difficult seeing these changes in my body. Stepping on a scale at the doctor's office. Buying bigger clothes. Having to scale back my workouts. It's all been, well, hard. That trauma doesn't heal overnight, you know? And throwing in these pregnancy hormones and crazy cravings doesn't make it any easier to manage. But I've been meeting with my therapist weekly, and knowing that any relapse could have a negative impact on the baby has helped with making healthy decisions, too."

My brow furrows. "What about the negative impacts it could have on you?"

"I'm getting there. Right now, though, I'm proud of the progress I've made." She places a hand on her stomach. "And I'm really proud of what my body is accomplishing. I'm confident I'll get to where I need to be. I promise."

"I'm proud of you, too, Claire."

"Thank you." She smiles. "We both have a lot to be proud of."

My lips curve into a smile that matches hers, and our gazes hold long enough that my skin starts to heat. Then I drop my eyes back to my phone.

"Okay, then. Pizza. What do you like? I have no idea."

"Whatever. I'm easy."

I tilt my head to the side and look her over. "Liar. You like something weird, don't you?"

"Well..." Claire scrunches up her nose. "I have these cravings, so..."

"What is it? Just tell me. We'll get whatever you want."

"Banana peppers, black olives, and barbeque chicken." I scrunch up my nose, and she smirks. "I'll also eat pepperoni, though."

"Nope." I shake my head and start selecting ingredients. "Banana peppers, black olives, and barbeque chicken it is. Gotta keep my babies fed."

Her smile is wide, and her cheeks tint pink before she sits up straighter. "Oh! And fried pickles for an appetizer, too, if they have them. Please."

I chuckle and hit submit on my order, then drop my phone onto the couch cushion beside me. "An hour. What should we do until then?"

"Hmm." Claire's eyes grow heated, and she smirks in a way that hits me right in the groin. "I can think of something."

Slowly, she climbs onto her knees and crawls toward me.

"So, the thing about pregnancy is that, along with the strange cravings, I'm also really horny."

"Yeah?" I grab her thighs as she moves to straddle me, my cock growing hard beneath her. I wrap my hand around the back of her neck and pull her mouth to mine. "Do you want me to take care of that for you?"

"Yes, please." She kisses me, then smiles against my lips. "But if you want to fuck me, you only have this hour window." She moves her hips, pressing down on my dick, and I groan. "Because after I eat, I'm going to get really tired and pass out until morning."

I don't need any more explanation. I lift her shirt over her head and toss it on the ground, but when I go for her bra, she stops me.

"That stays on." I poke my lip out in a pout, and she laughs. "They're really sore."

JONAH

"Okay." I press a soft kiss to the swell of each breast, then nip lightly at her. "I don't want to hurt you."

I smack her ass lightly, then lean back and spread my arms over the back of the couch. "Stand up for me, Trouble. Let me look at you."

Hesitantly, she obeys, and fuck me, the sight of her. I squeeze my aching cock, then lean forward and tug her pants down. She steps out of them and kicks them to the side, and I can't stop staring.

She's in a simple blue cotton underwear and bra set, and I've never seen anything sexier. Her belly rounded with my child, a baby we made together, and I'm filled with this primal sense of pride. She's mine. This gorgeous, intelligent, strong woman is mine, and she's pregnant with my child.

"There are a lot of changes."

Her whispered words and nervous expression have me sitting up straighter. I glance at her hands and find them closed into fists. I can tell she wants to cover herself. She initiated, but now she's second-guessing herself. She's uncomfortable, and it concerns me as much as it hurts me.

That trauma doesn't heal over overnight.

"My body...it's a lot different now than it was. It will, well, it will probably be different for a while. Maybe forever."

It's a warning. She thinks she has to warn me. Slowly, I slide off the couch onto my knees in front of her. I kiss her stomach, then take her hands, making sure to hold eye contact as I speak.

"You are the most beautiful woman I have ever seen. Seeing you like this..." I shake my head, and I can't help but smile. "This is my new favorite sight. My new favorite version of you. And after you have this baby, *our* baby, no matter how you've changed, that will be my new favorite version of you. You just keep getting better, Claire. The more I learn, the more I look at you and talk to you, I fall harder. You'll always be beautiful to me."

Her mouth turns up into a small, soft smile. "Are you just buttering me up so we can get on with the sex?"

I check my watch. "I mean, we do only have forty-five minutes now."

She rolls her eyes, and I laugh, squeezing her hands.

"I mean every single word. I would never lie to you about something like that. Now." I stand back up and pull on one of the loose curls framing her face. "I want to take you to bed. You go first so I can watch your ass on the way up those stairs, and then I'm stripping you naked and laying you flat so I can fuck you while staring at this sexy fucking pregnancy belly."

I splay my palms out on her stomach. "I want to watch my cock slide in and out of your pussy while touching this. Fuck, I'm going to come so hard. You have no idea how many times I jerked off in rehab thinking about it."

Her smile grows. "Are you going to make me come first, at least?"

"Always, Trouble. You will *always* come first."

Claire turns with her hand in mine and leads me to the staircase, but then I stop and release her. She looks over her shoulder at me, and I smirk and gesture to the staircase.

"Go on, baby. I've got the best seat in the house."

Her blush stretches to her chest, but her eyes sparkle, and slowly—ever so slowly—she walks up the spiral staircase. The way her thighs and ass flex shoot right to my dick. Fuck me, it's like porn. Ninety days without Trouble was too fucking long.

The moment she's at the top, I climb after her. "I want you on your knees on that bed. I'll make you come first, but I'm doing it my way."

I round the corner into the bedroom and groan when I find her exactly where I want her. I step up behind her and run my hand down her sloped back.

"Are you comfortable like this?"

She nods. "Yes."

I hook my fingers into her underwear and pull them to her knees. When she's bare, I groan and grab her perfect ass cheeks. I squeeze, then spread her wider, and she gasps.

"Are you still comfortable?"

I sound damn near feral in my own ears. Even the simplest sentence comes out desperate and ravenous, my voice sounds like it's been dragged over gravel. This is what she does to me. She makes me fucking insane.

"Yes." She presses back into my hands. "But I'm impatient."

I smirk and swipe my fingers through her pussy lips, making her hum.

"Sensitive?"

"Mmhmm. Very."

"Good."

I spit on her ass and watch as it drips to her pussy, then slowly slip one finger into her.

"Oh, yes. Yes, Jonah."

Fuck, hearing her say my name. It lights me up. I've never wanted something so bad in my entire life. I don't wait. I drop to my knees and cover her pussy with my mouth.

She moans and pushes against me, and I wrap my hands around her thighs and pull her in closer. I shove my tongue into her, then flatten it over her swollen clit and massage, humming against her.

"Mmmm, I missed the way you taste, Trouble." I spread her wider and suck on her clit.

"Oh God." She drops to her forearms, resting her face on the mattress. Her breath comes in pants, and her whole body trembles. "It's so sensitive."

I lean back just to look at her. I'm so hard that I'm almost lightheaded.

"It's not going to take much, is it?"

"No."

Thank God. If I have to wait much longer, I'll lose my mind.

I use two fingers to stroke her inner walls in the way I know she likes and tend to her clit with my tongue. I alternate flicking and sucking until I feel her pulsing around me.

"That's it, baby. Give it to me."

She comes hard, her body shaking and her muscles contracting. Her moan is muffled by the mattress, and as much as I want to hear it, I don't take my face out from between her thighs—don't stop sucking her swollen little clit—until she's shoving me away from her.

I chuckle as I rise to my full height. I can feel her arousal coating my face, and I lick my lips, savoring it.

"Roll over, Trouble. Spread your legs wide open for me."

Slowly, she does, and the sight of her is intoxicating. I take off my own shirt and jeans as I drag my eyes down her body. Skin flushed, chest heaving, full breasts straining against her bra. And that sexy fucking belly bump. God, I can't get enough of it. Then my eyes drop to her pink, swollen pussy, glistening and inviting me in.

"You are the sexiest thing I have ever seen in my entire life." I climb onto the bed and kneel between her thighs. I want to savor this. I want to take my time, but the urge to fuck her senseless is nearly impossible to ignore. "I will never forget this moment."

"Stop talking and fuck me."

Her panted, breathy words snap my restraint. I grab her hips and lift her, then shove a pillow under her lower back. It gives me the perfect angle as I line my cock up and thrust into her in one steady motion.

"Oh fuck, Trouble."

My hand is no comparison to her pussy. Three months without her, and I'm a fucking wreck. I haven't even moved yet, and my eyes are sparking white. Slowly, I move in and out of her, pulling my dick all the way out before pushing back in. I try to hold back. I try to get myself under control, but she whimpers, and my body tingles. It's a lethal combination. I bounce my eyes from her face to her pregnant belly to her pussy, where my cock slides in and out. It's too much. It's too fucking much. It's too good.

I push in deep and stop moving. I close my eyes and breathe. I try to regain some composure, but then she flexes around me, and I choke on a moan.

"Baby, don't. I'm going to come."

She does it again, and I open my eyes to find her eyes sparkling and her mouth open on a whimper. She flexes, pulsing around my aching cock, whimpering with each contraction of her muscles.

"You're going to make me come," I rasp out. "If you want me to last—"

"Rub my clit."

Goddamn it, this is going to be over in seconds. I suck on my thumb and rub circles on her clit, then she speeds up, tightening around my cock, then relaxing, over and over.

"Oh fuck. Claire. Claire." I growl and rub her clit faster. I clench my teeth, breathe through my nose, and grit out my next words. "Trouble, I'm about to fill you so fucking full with my cum, and you better fucking come with me. I want you to orgasm so hard my cum drips down your ass cheeks. You understand me?"

She nods frantically, her mouth opening on a silent cry right before I lose it with her. Her pussy clenches with her orgasm, and I can't avoid mine anymore.

I come with a rumbling moan, thrusting deeper until I've spilled every last drop of cum into her. Then, when I pull out slowly, I rub her clit again, making her tense up so I can watch my cum seep from her. I rub my fingers through it and shove them back into her, keeping it there until her pussy stops fluttering around me.

When our orgasms have passed, I drop down beside her. I rub my hand up and down her stomach and kiss her deeply. My heart swells, and my stomach flips.

"I've never been this happy," I confess. "I'm so fucking in love with you that I'm borderline obsessive."

Claire smiles and laughs softly. "Kegels make you euphoric, hm?"

"*You* make me euphoric. This makes me euphoric. The fact that this is my life now, this is my normal, makes me fucking euphoric." I slide my hand to her throat and rest it there. Her eyes flare, and I smirk. "I hope you're prepared. I'm going to love you so fucking hard, you won't know what hit you."

She mimics my move, resting her hand on the base of my throat. I picture her holding my heart in her palm.

"Is that so?"

"Mhmm." I kiss her. "Checkmate, Trouble. This win is all mine."

FORTY ONE

Jonah

"HOW ARE YOU FEELING?"

I look at Claire and raise my eyebrows, then nod to my rapidly bouncing leg.

"I'm so fucking nervous I might explode." Claire laughs and squeezes my hand. "Can't they make it a little warmer in here, though?"

"I know, right? It's always so cold."

"It's been like this every time?"

"Yeah."

"I'll go get someone to turn the heat up."

I spring from my chair, but she grabs my arm, stopping me. "Sit down. It's fine."

I sit like she asked, then reach in my pocket for my gum. I pop a piece in my mouth and chew. It's a piss-poor substitute for smoking, especially in moments like this. A few months ago, I'd have needed a pack of cigarettes and a trusty prescription cocktail just to get through it. Now, I'm relying on gum and willpower.

Sobriety is fucking hard. It gives me more respect for Sav. Everything is still so raw that even the smallest things feel huge at first. I made it through the first ninety days, though, and I'm proud of that. I didn't even try the first time around. They tell you the first ninety days are the hardest part, but that doesn't mean that the rest is a walk in the park.

Just one day at a fucking time. One foot in front of the other. Bit by bit, building a new normal. I inhale and exhale, chew on my gum, and shove my hand under my thigh so I don't pick at my thumb. Then I smile. It's going to stick this time.

"Oh, can I have a piece?"

Claire reaches her hand out, pulling me from my thoughts, but I shake my head.

"Nah, not this. It's nicotine gum."

"Nicotine gum? Why?"

"Smoking is bad for you and the baby."

Her brows shoot up. "You quit smoking for me and the baby?"

I almost want to laugh at the disbelief in her tone, but it makes my chest tighten with sadness. I hope that someday she can see herself the way I do. I lean in close and take her hand.

"There isn't a fucking thing on Earth that I wouldn't do for you."

She gazes at me, eyes bouncing between mine, searching. Always searching. It's automatic for her. To look for the lie. To prepare for pain. She still doesn't feel worthy of love. It's going to take a while to heal that part of her, but I'm here for the long haul, and I'll make sure she sees how sincere I am.

"Not a fucking thing," I say again before kissing her knuckles.

She smiles and nods, and it will have to be enough for now.

We break apart when someone knocks on the door, and the doctor walks in. She says hello to Claire, looks at me with a smile, and then her eyes flare wide. She recognizes me, and apparently, it's caught her off guard enough that whatever she was going to say has left her.

"Oh, I'm sorry. This is Jonah. He's the baby's father."

"Jonah Hendrix." I stick my hand out for the doctor to shake. "I'm Claire's boyfriend."

I hear Claire's breath hitch, so I send her a smirk and mouth the word again— *Boyfriend*—making her blush. I grin and look back at the doctor. "It's nice to meet you."

JONAH

By then, the doc has regained her composure and continues like nothing happened. She asks Claire questions. How she's been feeling. Any concerns or new symptoms. Any questions today, et cetera. When she's determined all is well, she leaves and sends the ultrasound technician in.

My leg starts bouncing again, and Claire reaches over and takes my hand. We share a smile, then the tech gets to work. She squirts a blue gel on Claire's stomach, positions a wand-type thing on the gel, and then there is a sound that resembles a heartbeat. I heard it once on the video that Mabel took, but this is closer. More real. It gives me goosebumps.

"Is that what I think it is?" I look between Claire and the tech. "Is that the heartbeat?"

"That's right. A healthy heartbeat."

I can't contain my smile. I don't think I can smile any bigger. But then something comes on the screen, and my own pulse speeds up.

"Is that...?"

"That's your baby."

I look at Claire and find her smiling at me.

"That's our baby," I whisper, then my eyes are pulled back to the screen as the tech speaks.

"I'm just going to be taking some measurements and pictures, but let's get you a good profile image first."

I'm in awe. She moves the wand, giving us a side view of the baby, and I can see a little nose and mouth. Arms and legs. The tech points everything out as she measures it, and I can't look away. I just run my thumb back and forth over Claire's hand and try my best to commit all of this to memory.

I'm overwhelmed with emotions. They fill me up until I swear I'll burst. Sobriety means I'm not numb anymore. These emotions aren't dulled. Reality isn't foggy.

I feel *everything*, and I'm grateful for it.

"Do you want to know the sex?"

I whip my head to Claire, and she nods. "It's up to you. I scheduled this one so you'd be here for it."

I answer immediately. "Yes. Yes, we do."

I can't wait. I'm too excited. I want to know now.

The tech moves the wand around and then smiles. "You're having a little baby girl."

"A girl." Tears fill my eyes and stream down my cheeks. I look at Claire. "We're having a little girl."

"Our little girl."

I bring her hand to my lips and kiss it. "A little baby Trouble. My favorite girls."

After the appointment, we're given some ultrasound images, and Claire is scheduled for another appointment in a few weeks. The doc discusses some routine tests, then talks about what to expect as Claire gets closer to the third trimester.

That catches my attention, and as soon as we're in the car, I bring it up.

"When's that start? The third trimester?"

"Twenty-eight weeks."

"And pregnancy is forty weeks?"

"Yep. Usually about that."

I do some mental math and then it hits me. "We're halfway."

Claire smiles. "Yeah, we are." She puts a hand on her stomach. "Baby girl will be here before we know it."

The excitement that bubbles up inside of me is almost unbearable, and instead of driving home, I call José and ask if he can meet us at the nearest store that sells baby stuff.

"What are we doing?"

I program the GPS, then wink at her. "We're going shopping for our baby, baby. We've got a nursery to fill."

MY PHONE BUZZES in my pocket as I'm folding tiny baby clothes and setting them neatly in a brand-new handcrafted dresser.

I had it custom-made. Little queen and king chess pieces are carved into each drawer, and the knobs are shaped like pawns. Claire got misty-eyed when it was delivered, so I'm pretty proud of it.

I pull my phone out of my pocket and sigh when I see the caller ID.

JONAH

Conrad Henderson.

Of course.

I knew it'd been too quiet for too long. My father never relinquishes control without a fight, and with both Claire and me disappearing, it was only a matter of time before he reached out.

I silence the call, then peek into our bedroom. Claire is still fast asleep, so I pull the door closed and head down to the pool deck. I don't want to wake her, especially not for this. She needs her rest. Growing a human is hard work.

Once the glass door is closed behind me, I call my dad back. He answers on the first ring.

"Jonah."

"Conrad. You called?"

"I'm Conrad now?"

"That's your name."

My father huffs, perpetually annoyed by me. "I'll cut to the chase. You have to cut ties with that woman."

I shake my head. "Yeah, okay, Conrad. If that's all you wanted—"

"Jonah, she is a pariah in this city, so she's latched on to you for financial stability."

I close my eyes and breathe, wishing I had a pack of cigarettes. Instead, I reach into my pocket, pull out some fucking gum, and pretend it does the trick.

"I bet that baby isn't even yours, and now you're all over the tabloids with her. They'll make a mockery of our family when they find out she's made a cuckold out of you."

I snort a laugh. "A cuckold? Really."

"This isn't some joke, Jonah. This is serious."

I drag a hand down my face and pinch the bridge of my nose. I was over this conversation before it began, but it has to be had. My therapist will be so proud.

"Look, I'm not some stupid, naïve child anymore. I know you have zero interest in my well-being or my reputation. You never cared what stories were printed about me until the mausoleum, and that was only because that shit would have tied me to you. That's the only reason you didn't press charges, too.

It wasn't because you didn't want me to go to prison. It was because the whole thing would reflect poorly on you. You've successfully kept your youngest son a secret for over a decade. How dare I come in and try to fuck it all up, right?"

My father grumbles. "Jonah, this is completely unnecessary."

I can practically see his patronizing expression. He feels zero shame for any of the truths I just laid out. He thinks I'm wasting his time. I sigh.

"The only reason you're concerned about my relationship with Claire is because you don't want people to learn of *your* relationship with her. If I were having a child with a random groupie, you wouldn't care. You only care because if it gets out that you dated her, it could make you look bad."

"You don't think it would make you look bad?"

"If you think I care about what the media thinks of me, you're an idiot."

"What about your record label? The morality clause. If you get more bad press—"

"We're out of our contract. Have been since the last Warsaw show. It just hasn't become public knowledge."

Likely because the label doesn't want to be humiliated, but I don't really care. Right now, all people care about is the romantic little love story they've created, circulating my *rest and recovery* stay at Tranquil Waters and my girlfriend's cute little belly bump.

I smile.

My girlfriend.

My smile disappears when I realize my father has fallen silent. I roll my eyes.

"I know it's hard for you to hear that there is literally nothing you can hold over either of our heads, but I think you need to sit with that discomfort. Embrace it. This is real life, Conrad. You can't manipulate everyone to get what you want."

"That is not what I'm doing. I am looking out for both of us."

His barked, defensive tone says otherwise. I have to stifle a laugh.

"Look. I'm going to put you out of your misery so you can go back to your self-absorbed life fucking new hires to feed your ego, hoarding your millions while underpaying your employees, and building yourself up by putting others down, okay? We want nothing from you. I never have. My name is Hendrix. My daughter's name will be Hendrix. And when I marry Claire, her name will be Hendrix. You don't have to lose sleep over it anymore, because as far as we're concerned, you don't exist, so you can go back to acting like I don't exist either. Is that clear?"

He's quiet for a moment before clearing his throat and once again saying something that doesn't surprise me.

"I want it in writing that you relinquish any claim you have to the Henderson fortune and business."

This time, I don't bother hiding my laughter.

"Because you want to be buried with it? It's not like you have any kids or grandkids to carry on your legacy."

"Jonah—"

"I don't want your money, Conrad. I don't want your business empire. I've already said I want nothing from you. If you're okay having that paper trail, have your lawyers draw up a contract and send it over. I'll sign it, and you never have to hear from me again."

"Consider it done."

He hangs up without saying goodbye, and though I know it's likely the last time I'll ever hear my father's voice, I can't find even a sliver of sadness. I laugh and push my phone back into my pocket. What a relief.

I head back upstairs, check on Claire once more, then finish with the baby clothes. I can't get over how tiny they are. The size of my forearm, and every time I fold one, I picture our daughter in it.

I keep wanting to pinch myself. I can't get over how lucky I am. My life was on a very different trajectory. I was destined for destruction, and I didn't care.

I could have died and never known this kind of happiness.

What if they couldn't revive me after the overdose? What if Sav had never sent me to rehab the first time? What if I'd never toned down my drug use so I wouldn't get caught again?

Fuck.

What if she'd never dated my father, and he'd never sent her to be my babysitter?

Anything, any split-second decision, could have kept me from her. Just the thought overwhelms me with an onslaught of raw, visceral emotions.

Grief for what I could have lost. Anger for how stupid I'd been. Determination to never fuck it up again.

For years, I let my wrath and self-loathing fuel my every move. I hurt people. I said and did terrible things. I pushed myself to the brink of death over and over. I'm not proud of the person I was, but it was that chaotic maelstrom of mistakes that lead me to her, so I can't regret it entirely. All I can do is vow to be better moving forward. To spend every day earning her love, earning this happiness, and to never take any of it for granted.

I smile.

From struggle to strength.

Fucking Tranquil Waters had it right. I'm definitely getting it tattooed on my neck.

When the last tiny onesie is folded in the dresser, I make my way to the bedroom.

I strip out of my clothes and climb into bed next to the woman I love. And just as I gently wrap my arms around her, she stirs awake.

"Go back to sleep," I whisper into her hair.

Claire hums and turns in my arms, so she's facing me.

"I had a dream."

"A good dream or bad dream?"

"A good one."

"Yeah? What was it about?"

Claire gives me a soft smile. "Names."

I pull her closer, so her head is tucked under my chin, and I can feel her breath on my neck. I just want to touch her. I want to smell her.

"What have you come up with?"

She presses a kiss to my throat, right on my heart tattoo.

"What about Theodora? After your brother Theo. We could call her Teddy for short."

The breath is pulled from my lungs, and my next exhale is shaky. I'm once again blinking against the sting of tears. I hadn't cried in years before breaking into that mausoleum. Now, I can't seem to stop. The difference now is they've been tears of happiness. Not anger. Not dread or despair. Just happiness. I don't know if I'll ever get used to it.

"Really? You don't think it's too old-fashioned?"

"No. If you like it, then I think it's perfect."

I force a swallow. "I love it."

She presses another kiss to my throat before pulling back just enough to kiss my lips.

"I love you."

I smile, finally letting the tears roll down my cheeks.

"I love you, Trouble. Endlessly."

FORTY TWO

Claire

"YOU KNOW, you could start calling before you just come over."

Sav smirks as she and Mabel push past Jonah into the house. Jonah sighs and follows them, but he can't hide the small smile on his face. He likes to act as if he doesn't like having his bandmates show up unannounced, but he's not fooling anyone. He loves it, and so do I.

"How you feeling, mama?" Sav grins, dropping onto the couch beside me and putting a gift bag at her feet.

"I'm feeling large," I say honestly.

I do feel very large. And as uncomfortable as I am, I smile. The statement doesn't impact me the way it once would have. No shame. No self-loathing. No anxiety. Just *large*, and that means I'm healing.

Mabel laughs. "I hear that's what happens when you're over nine months pregnant."

She grabs my almost empty glass of lemonade and takes it into the kitchen to refill it without my having to ask.

I arch a brow at the gift bag they brought.

"What's that?"

Sav shrugs. "You wouldn't let us throw you a baby shower."

"Savannah. One of you has brought a gift every day for the last four months."

She arches a brow back. "She's our first niece. What else would you expect?"

"I don't know," I answer honestly, laughing it off like it doesn't make me want to cry.

It happens every time one of them calls this baby their niece or refers to themselves as her aunt or uncle. The first time it happened, I was so shocked that I didn't process it until later. When it finally sunk in, I sobbed.

My daughter is going to have a family. She's going to have aunts and uncles. A cousin. Even potential grandparents, since Sav has started referring to both Red and Hammond as *Gramps*. Neither has objected. Even Sav's mother has offered to babysit anytime she visits from North Carolina. I've met her twice now, and she's wonderful.

My own mom has started calling me every week. She heard about my pregnancy in the media, and she and my stepfather have been supportive from afar. I've gotten a few texts from Macon and Lennon, and I try not to overthink them. I try not to spiral on the lack of them in this huge part of my life, nor obsess over the hope that I might have redeemed myself enough to earn a spot in theirs.

The important thing is that I've redeemed myself in my own eyes. I've earned a spot in my own happiness, and that's more than I could have ever hoped for. There's a chance that family will start feeling like my own again someday, but if it doesn't, I know I have one here that I can rely on.

I replay Sav's words from all those months ago often.

You have to forgive yourself, even if they can't.

She was right. Even my therapist agrees. Regret was eating at me, destroying me from the inside out, to the point where I wasn't living. I wasn't growing. I wasn't allowing myself to. I had to move on. I owed it to Jonah and to our baby. I owed it to myself.

Mabel hands me a fresh glass of lemonade, and then wiggles her fingers at me.

"May I?"

"Of course."

She kneels in front of me and puts her hands on my stomach.

"Hey there, Teddy girl. I know I said this yesterday, but you're late, and we'd love it if you could stop dillydallying and grace us with your presence now."

The baby kicks right at Mabel's hand, and I gasp just as Mabel laughs. She lifts her eyes to mine with a smirk. "She's going to be sassy."

"Trouble." Jonah bends down and kisses the top of my head. "She's going to be trouble for sure."

"Well, she's got four more days to show up on her own before they're going to induce me." I look down at my stomach. "I'd really like to avoid that, so anytime is a good time for me."

"That kid is going to do what she wants, when she wants," Sav adds with a laugh. "I have a feeling our world is about to become Teddy's world, and we'll all just be existing in it."

I laugh with her, and I don't miss that she said *our*. *Our* world. So loved. This baby is already so loved. I glance up at Jonah, and the way he looks at me...

I feel loved, too.

He reaches down and pulls on one of my curls before letting it spring back, then he winks and moves to one of the overstuffed chairs. Out of habit, I drop my eyes to his thumbs. They're healed. He still picks at them, but he hasn't done it recently, and that brings a smile to my face.

"So what kind of things are supposed to bring on a pregnancy?" I open my mouth to answer Mabel, but she's already scrolling her phone looking for the answer. "It says here that long walks could do it."

"I've taken two already today."

"Sex."

"Did that already, too," Jonah adds with a smirk. Mabel rolls her eyes but keeps reading.

"Oh, what about spicy foods?"

"That's the plan for dinner."

"The rest of this stuff is weird." She drops her phone back on the cushion beside her. "Fingers crossed the spicy food does the trick."

I cross my fingers and hold them up.

Fingers crossed.

Mabel and Sav stay for a few more hours before putting their newest gift in the nursery and heading home. They've gone a little overboard since we found out the sex. We have a closet full of outfits, another closet full of diapers, a bookshelf teeming with books, and every developmental toy a baby could want for their first year of life.

I've found myself frequently hoping that Macon and Lennon have people like this around them. Friends and family who love their babies like their own. They deserve it.

Jonah makes Jamaican curry chicken for dinner, and despite ramping up the spice level, I don't go straight into labor. We had unrealistic expectations, I know, but my false hope is fueled by my growing discomfort.

"She's just taking her time," Jonah muses as he washes dishes.

"Yes, well, I've served her an eviction notice. Her time is up."

He spins and leans back on the sink, folding his arms against his naked chest. His tattooed biceps bulge as he shrugs, then hits me with a suggestive smirk.

"I stay inside you for as long as possible, too."

I tip my head to the ceiling with a laugh. "You're ridiculous."

He crosses the floor and wraps his arms around me, then presses a soft kiss to my lips.

"I know this hasn't been easy, and it's come with a lot of changes that you probably never wanted, but I'm grateful every day that you're doing it with me. I love you. I love this baby. I love the life we're building. Thank you."

I run my eyes over his face. His eyes are so much brighter blue than they were when we first met almost a year ago. He's cut his hair, getting rid of the bleached blond and returning to his natural dark brown. He's even sporting a bit of a tan thanks to our pool. Jonah Hendrix looks healthier and happier than I've ever seen him, and it brings me happiness in return.

"I love you," I say honestly. "But I should be thanking you. What you've done…what you've accomplished in such a short time. I know it was hard…" I shake my head. "My brother said that the act of getting sober felt like being skinned alive. He said it was a physical, mental, and emotional pain that he thought would never end."

CLAIRE

Jonah huffs a small laugh and jerks out a nod in agreement.

"To see you now, to know what you went through...I'm so proud of you, Jonah. I'm so grateful for your strength and bravery. We're here because of you. I wouldn't want to do it with anyone else."

"You've been strong and brave, too, Claire. Your recovery hasn't been easy, either. Be proud of yourself. I am."

I smile. "We're earning it together, right?"

"Together. One day at a time."

I WAKE from a pain in my lower back.

It happens all the time now. One of the joys of late-stage pregnancy. I stand and stretch, and it lessens the pain, but it doesn't subside. Quietly, I walk from one side of the room to the other and breathe through the aches. At times like this, I find Jonah's deep, undisturbed sleep almost annoying. I haven't been able to sleep through the night for weeks, and here he is, slumbering away without a tiny human beating him up from the inside.

I put a hand on my stomach and exhale slowly as another pain tightens in my abdomen. Braxton-Hicks contractions are no joke. There's been more than one time where I thought I might be in active labor, but nope. It was just "practice contractions."

For practice, though, they really fucking suck.

When walking the room doesn't work, I move quietly into the en suite to draw a bath. I turn on the tap, sprinkle in some bath salts, and then shrug out of my clothes. I'm dropping my shirt into the hamper when another cramp hits in my abdomen that's so sharp, my body bows and I gasp.

"Ow, fuck," I grumble. "Take it easy."

I brace myself on the bathroom counter with one hand while the other rests on my lower stomach, and another sharp pain shoots through me. I hiss through my teeth and exhale slowly.

Fuck me. I'll be glad when this is all over.

I stand back up and walk toward the tub, but halfway there, water trickles down my inner thigh. I stop walking and look down. When tightening my muscles doesn't stop the trickle, my pulse starts to race, and I call for Jonah.

"Hey, babe?"

To his credit, I don't have to call for him twice. I hear the blankets rustle and the bed shift, and almost immediately he appears in the bathroom doorway. He drags concerned eyes down my naked body, surveying me for harm.

"Is everything okay? What can I do?"

"Well," I say with a forced smile. "I think my water broke."

His brows shoot to his hairline. "Your water broke?"

"That or I peed myself, but I'm pretty sure I didn't pee myself."

"Your water broke." He drops his eyes to the tile floor under my feet. "Your water broke."

"Yes. It did."

"She's coming?" He looks back at me with wide, excited eyes and a smile blooming across his beautiful face. "Our daughter is coming?"

Love and adoration pour from him in waves. Anything else I might have felt, any fear or anxiety that was building inside me, is diluted enough that his love is all I can focus on. He's been an amazing partner, but I think he's going to be an even more amazing father. I am so lucky that I get to witness it play out in real time.

I nod and smile back.

"Yeah, Jonah. Our daughter is coming."

FORTY THREE

Jonah

I'M in awe of her.

Her ten little fingers and ten little toes. Her head full of dark curls. Her button nose and cherubic cheeks. As she sleeps snuggled up on Claire's chest, I've never seen anything more perfect. I just sit beside the hospital bed rubbing my thumb back and forth over Claire's forearm and staring.

"I can't believe it," I say on a whisper. "I can't believe it."

Claire hums, the tired sound drawing my attention back to her face. She's smiling softly and her blue eyes glitter, but her blinks are slow. Sixteen hours of labor, and she was brilliant through all of it.

"You were amazing, you know?" I cup her cheek. "I don't know how you did it. I don't even have the words. I'm just...I'm in awe."

She looks down at our baby, and her smile grows. "She's beautiful, isn't she?"

"*You're* beautiful, and she looks just like you." Claire rests her head back on the pillow and closes her eyes. She's understandably exhausted, and if anyone deserves rest, it's her. "Do you need anything? Can I get you anything?"

She shakes her head. "No. I promise I'll tell you if I need anything."

"Do you want me to take Teddy so you can get some sleep?"

She turns her head toward me, then winces slightly as she scoots over and pats the mattress. Something about the movement catapults me back in time.

A different room. A different bed. A different person.

A different feeling entirely.

"Climb in here."

"I'm too big. I don't want to hurt you."

The words are pulled from my lips before I think them, and tears form in my eyes. Irrationally, my body braces for what comes next. Theo's voice floats in my memory, a harrowing response echoing in my head.

"You won't hurt us." She pats the mattress again, but when I don't move, she arches a playful brow. "Jonah Theodore Hendrix, you're not paying four grand a night for this boujee maternity suite to sit in that armchair. You won't use the other bedroom, so get into this bed and hold your girls."

Hold your girls.

My girls.

I laugh and wipe away a stray tear, then I gently get into the bed beside her. I slide one arm under her and lay the other over her, carefully resting my hand on Teddy's back.

"Thank you."

Claire's voice is a whisper, content but tired, and slowly her breathing deepens until she's sleeping peacefully. And still, all I can do is stare. My eyes bounce from Claire to Teddy and back. The two loves of my life, and not for the first time, I'm so grateful that I'm experiencing these emotions unhindered. Raw and real and overwhelming in the best, most moving of ways. In this moment, I can't bring myself to regret any decision I've made, no matter how reckless, because it brought me to her. To here. To them.

This is healing. They are my purpose.

This right here.

This is my redemption.

JONAH

"ARE you sure you want to let them in? We can tell them to fuck off until next week."

Claire laughs. "I'm sure. I want to see them. And don't try to act like you don't want to show Teddy off. You've already targeted every nurse in the maternity ward, José, and the grocery delivery guy. You need a new audience."

I smirk. "I'm telling you, she's the smartest three-day-old baby in the state. Maybe the country."

She looks down at Teddy and smiles. "Your daddy is your second biggest fan."

"Well, before they come disrupt our peace, I have a gift for you. I'll be right back."

I run up the stairs, taking two at a time, and grab the gift box off my dresser. I meant to bring it to the hospital, but I was so excited that I'd forgotten to bring my overnight bag. When I get back to the living room, she narrows her eyes at me with a small smile.

"You didn't have to get me a gift."

"I know." I cross the floor to the couch and hand her the box. "But I have plans to give you a lot of them, so you might as well get used to it."

She drops her eyes to the gift box, and her cheeks heat with a small blush that fills me with pride.

"Well...Thank you." She whispers the words before taking a deep breath, then raises her gaze back to mine. "Can you take her?"

"Absolutely." I bend down and scoop Teddy up carefully. It blows me away how perfectly she fits cradled in my arms. I run my eyes over her for the millionth time, and I laugh, then drop my voice to a whisper. "I didn't know I could love someone so much so quickly in such a new way. It's like...it's like a new part of me was born with her. Created *for* her. Does that make sense?"

I look back at Claire and find her smiling softly, and she nods.

"Yeah. It makes perfect sense."

Something passes between us that emboldens me. It bolsters my confidence in us. In myself. In this new normal we're crafting.

"Open it," I urge, nodding to the box, then I hold my breath as she does. Her gasp is a good sign. Her sniffle is another. "Do you like it?"

"I love it."

I watch as she takes the rose gold bangle out of the box and studies it. Two small stones, her birthstone and Teddy's, are the only embellishments. Classy and elegant.

"Thank you. I love it so much."

"Check the inside."

She does, and when she reads the inscription, she starts to cry, then huffs out a small laugh. It's a single word, but it holds more weight than she'll ever know.

Endlessly.

"It's perfect."

"I mean it."

"I know."

As if on cue, the gate buzzer sounds through the house, announcing that my bandmates have arrived. I give Teddy back to Claire, then walk to the door to let them in.

Sav's got a bag of food, Torren's holding a vase of flowers, and Mabel's got a little gift bag. I can't help but smile.

"Hey, Daddy," Sav says to me with a smirk.

I arch a brow, and she manages to hold a straight face for a few seconds before sticking out her tongue on a dramatic gag.

"Can't do it."

"Thank God," I say with a laugh, pulling her in for a hug before doing the same with Torren and Mabel. Then I gesture into the house. "Come meet the newest member of the band."

They walk quietly into the living room, set their gifts on the coffee table, and greet Claire with smiles.

"You look good," Mabel says to Claire. "How are you feeling? Jo texted us that everything went well, you know, all things considered."

She flares her eyes, and Claire laughs.

"Yeah. I'm okay. Tired and sore, but stupidly happy."

"Well, if you need anything, we're just right down the street," Sav adds. "Seriously. Anything at all, just call."

"Thank you." Claire turns her arms to show Teddy to the room. "Now, why you're all here. The girl of the hour. Meet Theodora Andrea Hendrix."

"She's absolutely beautiful," Sav says. "Look at that head of hair."

Mabel smiles at Claire. "She's going to look just like you."

"Thank God," Torren says with a grin.

I shake my head and bite back my smile. He's an ass, but I don't exactly disagree with him on this one.

"So where did you come up with the name?" Sav asks, and I decide to answer.

"Theodora after my brother, and Andrea after Claire's mom."

"Well, it's beautiful."

"You know I love an old-fashioned name," Mabel chimes in with a waggle of her brows. "That's why I picked mine."

Claire's jaw drops. "Mabel isn't your real name?" Mabes shakes her head slowly. "What is it?"

Mabes sighs dramatically, then lies. "It's been so long that I've forgotten it."

Claire looks at me, and I throw up my palms. "Don't look at me. She's been Mabel since I've known her."

"Do you know?" Claire asks Sav, and Sav shrugs.

"I know everything."

Mabel laughs, then changes the subject. "Anyway, we brought you a few things."

"You guys don't have to keep bringing me stuff."

"To be fair, only the food is from us," Torren adds.

I tilt my head. "What?"

"We brought sushi because we knew Claire was craving it for the last month of her pregnancy," Sav says, pulling sushi rolls out of the insulated cold bag.

"Oh yum." Claire looks up at me. "Can you put Teddy in her bassinette?"

I take my daughter and put her in the bassinette. We've only been home a day and a half, but we've basically been moving the bassinette wherever we go. Kitchen for cooking. Dining room for eating. Living room for lounging. Where we go, Teddy goes.

Claire is surveying the sushi when Mabel slides the vase of flowers in front of her.

"This and the gift bag are a special delivery."

"From who?" Claire asks, reaching slowly for the bag.

She holds Mabel's eyes, and Mabel gives her a small smile. "Open it."

Claire hesitates, and I watch as goosebumps rise on her forearms. I think I see a slight tremble in her fingers as she reaches into the bag, and when she pulls out the gift, tears well in her eyes.

It's a little orange sleeper with dinosaurs on it. It's obviously used. The color is faded and there's fraying on the hems, but I can tell it means something to Claire. Tears stream down her face as she flips over a little notecard, and I read it over her shoulder.

> ***Gabe and Charlotte have outgrown it.***
> ***It's your turn now.***
> ***-Lennon***

Claire laughs and glances up at me.

"This was mine. Well, Macon's first, and then mine. My, um..." She sucks in a shaky breath and laughs again. "Nephew and my niece wore it when they were infants, too. I guess...Well, I guess Lennon wants me to have it now."

I put my hand on her shoulder and smile. I know what this means to her. I can only imagine what she's feeling. I don't even know her brother and stepsister, but I almost want to cry too.

"It's a good gift," I whisper to her, and she nods.

"Yeah. It's a great gift."

"That's not all," Mabel says, and Claire looks back at her. "The flowers."

She gestures to the vase of flowers on the counter, and Claire studies it. At first, it's just a bouquet of flowers, but then she realizes something. Once again, with trembling fingers, she reaches for the flowers. She pulls them closer, then spins them on the tabletop.

JONAH

Then it dawns on me.

She's not looking at the flowers. She's looking at the vase. So I do, too.

It's ceramic. Handmade, I realize. And hand-painted from the looks of it. It's decorated with lots of little images resembling something out of a Rockwell painting. Street signs and small-town businesses. A grocery store. A hardware store. A youth center. A public school. Two houses.

"It's my hometown," she whispers. "She painted my hometown."

"Who did?"

"Lennon." Claire smiles at me then looks at Mabel. "Did Macon make the vase?"

Mabel nods. "Yeah."

"How? How did you get it?"

"She emailed the label, the label forwarded it to Hammond, and Hammond sent it to me."

"What did she say?"

Mabel nods again. "She asked if she could send me a gift to give you when the baby came. She wanted it to be a surprise."

Claire nods, her attention falling back to the vase as she clutches the sleeper to her chest. She doesn't say anything for a long time, and we sit in the silence with her. Teddy's soft breathing and Claire's quiet tears are all I focus on. I rub her shoulder, a silent gesture to let her know that I'm here, and I wait.

When she's processed it all, she tells Mabel thank you, then changes the subject. We spend the next few hours talking about nothing in particular and laughing about everything, and it feels good.

Torren, Sav, and Mabel are my oldest friends. They were my first example of what a family should be. My proof that people could love me for who I was without pretense or condition. It got fucked up for a while, convoluted as we each fought with our demons, but they never gave up on me. Not even when they probably should have. They have always been there boosting me up when I was drowning, forcing breath into my lungs when I was suffocating. Keeping me alive when all I wanted was to disappear. To have them still here, after everything, feels like a miracle.

Later that night, Claire and I lie in bed with our daughter between us. We're both on our sides, splitting time between gazing at each other and at her. At this little amazing bundle of life that we created together. The light Claire brought to my darkness. I take Teddy's small hand, and she wraps it around one of my fingers.

I don't know how I got here. I'm still not sure I deserve it. But I know I won't fuck it up again.

Of all the raw emotions swirling in my chest right now, the strongest one is gratitude.

"Trouble?"

"Hmm?"

"Thank you."

She raises her eyes from Teddy and locks them with mine. "For what?"

"For seeing my ugliest parts and loving me anyway."

"Every part of you is beautiful to me." She smiles softly, then reaches up and cups my cheek. "I love you, Jonah Theodore Hendrix. I love you endlessly."

EPILOGUE

Claire

ONE YEAR LATER

"THIS WAS SUPPOSED TO BE SMALL."

I look between all four members of The Hometown Heartless and wave my hand around Sav's backyard.

"This is not small."

They all turn faux-innocent smiles on me. I'm not fooled. There's not an ounce of contrition to be found between the four of them.

"Technically, going off the guest list, this is small," Sav says, batting her eyelashes at me. I scowl, and she sighs. "We went a little overboard, but it's not a big deal. It will be fun!"

"Savannah. There's a pony in your back yard. This is a first birthday party, not a county fair."

"Wait until you see the manicurist."

I turn around and find Ezra, the guitarist for Caveat Lover wiggling his fingers at me. They're pink with purple gemstones on them. I only have seconds to admire them, though, because his outfit has me raising an eyebrow.

"Ezra. What are you wearing?"

"Oh." He grins and spins in a circle. "Two of the princesses had to cancel, so I stepped up. My wig and heels are over there."

My jaw drops, his pink ball gown forgotten as I whip back around to face the *other* bandmembers.

"*Two* of the princesses? How many are there?"

"Just four," Mabel says, and Jonah steps in front of me with his hands folded under his chin.

"Don't be mad, Trouble. Teddy's only going to turn one once. I wanted to give her the best birthday party."

I laugh, my irritation already disappearing. "She won't even remember this, Jo."

"But we will."

"Yeah, especially because he's hired a photographer and a videographer," Torren cuts.

Jonah shoots him a scowl and Torren laughs. I take a deep breath and look back at Jonah.

"Why didn't you at least tell me?"

"You've been working your ass off with Rock Loveless, and since I'm returning to Heartless next weekend, I didn't want to add any more stress to your plate."

"I told you not to worry about that. I'm excited for you to go back. I thought you should have gone back six weeks ago when they started the new tour."

He shakes his head.

"Hell no. I would have missed Teddy's first steps. Her first words. I'm already having separation anxiety, and I haven't even started yet."

I smirk. "It's not like we won't be right there with you."

"I know." Jonah wraps his arms around me and pulls me in for a hug. "I'm sorry the party is bigger than I said it would be. It's going to be fun. I promise."

I sink into his hold. "Ezra Hawke is dressed like a princess."

His rumbling laugh vibrates against me. "Crue is dressed like a princess too."

I pull back and stare at him.

EPILOGUE

"Fifty percent of the princesses are Caveat boys?" Jonah smirks, and I roll my eyes. "You better get them on that video."

"Already on it."

I lean into his hold for a few more breaths, then I step back and look toward Sav, Mabel, and Torren.

"Okay. Do your thing." They whoop and clap as if they had any doubts, and I shake my head with a laugh. "You're all incorrigible."

Jonah presses a kiss to my head, and then I leave him and his bandmates to go back to whatever mischief they were making before I interrupted. I walk back to the living room where I left Teddy coloring with Brynn, Red, and Sav's mom.

I bounce my eyes between the three of them.

"Did you all also know that this first birthday party was going to be a veritable three-ring circus?"

Red and Brynn both nod, but Sav's mom Sharon throws up her hands.

"I knew, but I didn't know until last night when my flight got in."

Brynn grins. "But if Gram did know, she'd have supported it."

I arch a brow at Sharon, and she smiles in a way that makes her look a lot like Sav. "You do only turn one once."

I shake my head and take a seat on the couch. I watch as Brynn helps Teddy color in a book full of puppies, and then I look back at Sharon.

"Are you coming with to the Art Fusion show?"

"I'm not sure yet," she says with a shrug. "I know it's the ten-year anniversary, but I'm not the biggest fan of music festivals, to be honest. I might come for a few of the shows in Asia, though."

Sav's mom lives on the coast in North Carolina and visits once a month or so. From what I understand, she and Sav only reconnected a few years ago, but her relationship with Sav is a good one. It gives me hope for my own family.

My mom and stepfather have been out to visit a few times in the last year, but I haven't had a chance to go home. I've been busy, yes. Having a baby and starting a new job is time-consuming. That's not the only reason I haven't returned to that small town on the East Coast I used to call home, though. It's also because I haven't wanted to. Not because of guilt or regret, but because of trauma. That town holds a lot of bad memories for me, and while I'm healing more every day, I'm not in a place to subject myself to a town full of triggers.

I watched my mom and brother be abused in that town. I was emotionally manipulated by their abuser in that town. I was so lost and confused as a kid in that town that I started purging. I was taken advantage of by a boy I thought loved me. I lost my best friend in a way that, at the time, felt like the worst kind of betrayal.

That town helped create the ugliest parts of me, and I'm not ready to face it.

For now, I'm more than happy in LA with Jonah and Teddy. I look forward to our weekly dinners with Sav, Mabel, Torren, and their families. I enjoy working for Rock Loveless Records. I even like helping wrangle the Caveat Lover boys, despite the headaches they cause me. I honestly don't know how Callie puts up with them.

I love my life and the people in it, and it's honestly the first time I've ever been able to say that. Maybe someday I'll be able to go back home, but not yet, and I'm in no hurry.

I pull myself from my thoughts and smile at Sharon.

"Well, I'm glad you're here now. Thank you for making the trip for Teddy's birthday."

Sharon smiles. "Honey, I wouldn't miss it."

After a few minutes, Mabel pops back inside and claps her hands.

"Everyone! The party is starting. If you'll all follow me out to the yard, we can begin the festivities."

I laugh and stand, then pick up Teddy.

"Alright, Teddy girl," I say with a smile. "Let's go see your very first circus."

"First of many if Jonah has anything to say about it."

I flick my eyes to Brynn and find her grinning. She's not wrong, but I don't really understand the extent of it until we step foot in the backyard.

It's not just a pony.

It's a magician, a DJ, a guy making balloon animals, a tower of cupcakes, and, yes, two princesses and two Caveat boys in drag.

"Good Lord," I say on an exhale, scanning the yard for more surprises.

EPILOGUE

I have to blink several times when I find another one. "Is that...is that a Wiggle?"

Brynn follows my line of sight and then snorts. "Yep. That is a Wiggle."

"Good Lord."

"Look on the bright side, Aunt Claire. At least you don't have to do any of the cleanup."

I laugh and nod. "At least there's that."

As soon as Jonah spots me, he practically sprints to my side. He kisses me, kisses Teddy, then flares his eyes.

"Isn't this the best?"

I smile and nod. "The best."

"Hammond got a Wiggle. Did you see the Wiggle?"

"I did. I did see the Wiggle."

He kisses me again, then scoops our daughter into his arms. "C'mon, Teddy baby. Let's go ride a pony."

After a few minutes of observing, I have to admit that this party is pretty great. They were all right. It's fun. It's a lot of fun, and the best part is seeing Teddy have fun. She's nothing but giggles and smiles as she's passed among all of these people who love her, and seeing her with Ezra, Crue, and the other two princesses is something I will never forget.

By the time we get to cake and presents, my cheeks hurt from all the smiling I've done. But then the mountain of gifts is revealed, and my smile falls.

So much for "nothing big or extravagant."

My eyes find the Caveat boys in the crowd, and I march over to them, stopping in front of Ezra.

"Did you get her a drum set?"

"How'd you know?"

He's playing dumb. He's good at that. I gesture to what is obviously a drum set with each individual drum and cymbal wrapped in wrapping paper.

"What does that look like to you?" I ask with an arched brow, and he grins.

"Okay, you got me. But I had to upstage Rock."

I turn to Rocky. "What did you get her?"

"A guitar."

I laugh. "Let me guess. It's a bedazzled pink Fender."

He doesn't answer, but he smiles, and that's all the confirmation I need.

"Guys. She can barely walk."

"Don't worry, Claire Bear. I'll keep the drums until Ted's old enough."

"Yeah, and then I'll teach her how to play the Fender."

A familiar tattooed arm drops onto my shoulder, and I'm awash in Jonah's clean, woodsy scent.

"If anyone is going to teach my daughter how to play guitar, Halstrom, it will be me."

"You'll have arthritis in your hands by then, old man."

"An old man who can still outplay you."

I roll my eyes and step out of Jo's hold, leaving him and Rocky to their competitive banter. I take Teddy to the birthday girl chair, Mabel gives her a little birthday crown, and Callie places a cupcake in front of her. We sing Happy Birthday and laugh as she demolishes her cupcake and opens her gifts. The whole time, I'm grateful Jonah thought to hire people to document it all, and when we finally get into the car to head back home, I'm on cloud nine.

"You were right. That was fun, and I'm glad you guys did it."

He leans over the gear shift and kisses me. "I'm glad you had fun."

I'm ready for bed when we pull up to the house, but there's a package on our porch.

"Another surprise?" I ask him, and he shakes his head as he turns off the car.

"This one wasn't me."

He picks up the package and carries it into the house while I carry a sleeping Teddy in her car seat, and then we put both down when we reach the living room.

"It's addressed to Teddy. Return address is from Virginia."

I furrow my brow. "My mom and stepdad already sent their gift."

That leaves one other possibility.

I open the package slowly. I find a gift-wrapped box inside so I open that too.

EPILOGUE

And then I smile.

"A little pottery wheel?"

Jonah sounds confused, but I don't explain right away. Instead, I find a birthday card and open it.

Happy 1st Birthday, Theodora.
Love, Macon, Lennon, Gabe, and Charlotte

"That was nice of them," Jonah says. I nod.

"Yeah. Macon throws pottery. Remember that vase?"

"Oh, that's right." Jonah drags his hand up and down my back slowly. "I think someday, whenever you're ready, Teddy is going to love meeting her cousins."

I lean into his hold and flick my eyes back to where our daughter is fast asleep.

Jonah and I are determined to make sure that the traumas of our past will never touch her. She will grow up knowing that she matters. She will never have to doubt if her parents love her without condition. She will never have to look at herself and question if she's enough. He and I have made so many mistakes, but she's not one of them.

I love this life. I love Jonah. I love our daughter. I love the people we spend our days with. And for the first time in my entire life, I love who I've become.

I'm content. I'm happy.

I'm healing.

I look up into Jonah's eyes and smile.

"I think she will, too."

The End

EXTENDED EPILOGUE

Claire

ONE YEAR LATER

Jonah's hand covers mine to stop my wringing.

"We're good, babe. Deep breaths."

I inhale and exhale slowly, then nod.

"We're good."

"We were invited. Your parents are excited. This is going to be good."

I nod again.

"I'm just nervous. I haven't seen Macon and Lennon in years. And the last time was *not* a good time."

Jonah turns and puts his fingers under my chin, then locks his eyes with mine.

"We can turn around and leave, if you want. We don't have to do this. We can try again next year."

I think about it briefly, then flick my eyes to the rearview mirror. Teddy is sitting quietly in her car seat with a board book in her lap. She has no idea the turmoil thrashing about in my stomach, or the way I've oscillated between anxious and excited for the last month.

EXTENDED EPILOGUE

All she knows is that we spent a week with Sav, Levi, Brynn, Papa Red, and Nana Sharon at the beach, then borrowed Nana's car to go on a little road trip. I want to keep it that way. This will be good for her. This will be good for all of us.

I shake my head and look back at Jonah.

"No. No, this is fine. I've turned down every invite for the last two years. Let's just rip the band-aid off. I want Teddy to know her cousins."

"Your brother and stepsister want that, too."

I laugh. "Less keen on sparking up a relationship with me, though."

He takes my hand and squeezes it. "This is a good start, though. Neutral ground. No big obligations. If you're feeling too much, you can take a break. You can hang out with Andrea and Trent. You don't owe anyone anything."

"Except Teddy."

He gives me a half smile. "Only what you can handle."

I turn and look at the aquarium. Nice, neutral ground with the kids as the focus. Better than Thanksgiving or Christmas. Better than a birthday. No obligations.

"It's going to be harder in person. Texts and packages are easy. But this...I just want it to go well for Teddy."

"I know. But I'm here. Mabel's here. The offer to rent the aquarium still stands, too. We can cancel and reschedule for after hours. Sav'll make the call if you need."

I laugh. "That's overkill, even for you."

He smirks. "Nothing is overkill when it comes to my girls."

"I love you," I whisper, then lean in to kiss him.

"I love you."

I run back over my last conversation with Dr. Clay. I've accepted my relationship with my brother and ex-best friend as is. I occasionally still long for more, and I likely still will, but I don't harbor extensive feelings of self-loathing anymore. I no longer beat myself up over the past.

Forgive yourself, even if they can't.

I have.

I look back at Jonah, scanning my eyes over his face. It's only been three years, but we've weathered so many storms. We've conquered moun-

EXTENDED EPILOGUE

tains and come out stronger. For ourselves. For each other. For our daughter.

"Thank you for doing this with me."

"Trouble, there is nothing I wouldn't do with you."

I wait for another moment, take another deep breath, and then grab my phone. I pull up Mabel's contact and send her a text that we're on the way.

"Alright. Let's do it."

Jonah and I climb out of Sharon's beat-up Toyota, and he rounds the back to grab Teddy.

"Ready to see some sharks, baby girl?"

"Sharks!"

With our daughter perched in one arm and his other hand in mine, Jonah and I walk toward the aquarium entrance. A little of the tension leaves my body when I notice Mabel just inside the doors. I can't help but laugh as we step up beside her.

"I barely recognized you."

She rolls her eyes. "I haven't worn normal tennis shoes in years. I feel like a suburban mom."

I smile and survey her outfit again. She's not wrong. She looks completely different in leggings, tennis shoes, and a sweatshirt, but the baseball hat has to be the funniest part of the whole ensemble.

"I forget how short you are." Jonah smirks and flicks his eyes to her feet. "Without the platform combat boots, you're not much taller than Teddy."

"Ha ha." Mabel scowls playfully, then focuses on my daughter. "What's up, Ted? Want to come to me?"

She holds out her hands, wiggling her fingers. Teddy gladly leans toward her, so Mabes takes her out of Jonah's arms, and Jonah immediately wraps me in them.

"You ready?" Mabel's smile is sympathetic. "I'll cut a bitch if I have to."

"Bitch!"

My jaw drops, and I throw my hands over my mouth to stifle a laugh.

Mabel's eyes go wide. "Whoopsie. That's an auntie word. Are you an auntie?"

EXTENDED EPILOGUE

"Nooo." Teddy giggles and shakes her head.

"Then no bitches for you." Mabel boops her on the nose, then mouths *sorry* to me.

I shake my head. "It's fine. And no cutting is necessary, I promise." I turn my attention to the aquarium. "We're meeting them in the café."

Teddy starts to squirm in Mabel's arms. "Shark! Shark!"

"We'll get you your sharks, LT."

I smile at Jonah. LT. For Little Trouble. I love it so much.

"Alright. Let's go."

Jonah opens the door for us, then he and Mabel flank me as we walk through the aquarium. I keep my back straight and my attention forward. I'm sure Jonah has adoring eyes on him, which is partially my fault. I did my job too well, it seems. Mabel, however, is probably under the radar, especially with the disguise.

I spot Trent first and my mom second. My stepdad towers over everyone, and he has his arm slung over my mother's shoulders. They're basically attached at the hip, and after everything she went through with my father, it makes me happy to see her being loved the way she deserves.

Nervously, I scan the surrounding area. Lennon is chatting with our parents with a toddler on her hip, and after another second, I find Macon at the cashier with their son.

"You're good," Jonah whispers. "But the moment you need a break, let me know. There's no shame in tapping out, okay?"

I smile. "I know."

A few feet from the café entrance, I lock eyes with Lennon, and thankfully, she smiles. It's not a big smile, more tentative than anything else, but it's not forced. More tension leaves my body.

"Claire!" My mom rushes me. "You made it." She pulls me in for a hug before moving on to Jonah. "I'm so glad. How was the drive?"

"It was smooth." Jonah gives my mom a hug, then turns toward Trent. "It's good to see you."

"Mom, Trent, you remember Mabel."

"Mabel, it's so nice to see you again."

Trent shakes Mabel's free hand, then my mom gives her a hug.

"Yes, thank you for coming with today."

"Hey, thanks for the invite. I've actually never been to an aquarium."

I whip my head in her direction. "I'm sorry, what? How did I not know this?"

She winks. "Orphan sob sorry, remember? Not much time to do kid stuff when you're on the run from the foster care system."

"Huh." I nod slowly. "What about the others?"

"I think Sav vandalized that big one when we were in Florida, but she's never actually been inside."

Jonah laughs. "I forgot about that."

"Damn. Maybe we should rent it out tonight."

"She'd be down," Jo says with a nod, and Mabel smirks.

"But tell her to leave the spray paint at home."

"This doesn't surprise me. She is quite a spirited individual."

I look at Trent and flare my eyes. "She definitely is."

I glance between my mom and Trent when Macon steps up beside Lennon. I give them both a smile.

"Macon. Lennon. This is my friend Mabel."

Mabel waves. "Hey y'all."

Jonah snorts a laugh, and I elbow him. "And this is Jonah. Jo, Mabel, meet my brother Macon and my stepsister, Lennon."

Macon nods, shaking Jonah's hand before doing the same with Mabel.

"Nice to meet you both. My friend's sister is a huge fan."

"Yeah? We could sign something for her?"

Lennon smiles at Mabel. "That would be great. She'd love that."

I bounce my eyes between my two families, chosen and chosen for me, and the tightness around my chest loosens a bit more. Then I glance at the toddler in Lennon's arms and the boy at Macon's feet, and the nerves amp up again. My niece and nephew.

"Hey there," I say softly. "I'm Claire."

The little boy smiles. "I'm Gabriel Christopher Davis, and that's my sister Charlotte Grace Davis. Mommy says you send Christmas and birthday presents but I can't 'member what you send but she says I need to say thank you anyway so thank you anyway."

Lennon and I share an amused glance, but Gabe just continues on, unfazed. He points his little finger as Teddy.

EXTENDED EPILOGUE

"Who's that?"

"That's your cousin, Theodora, buddy. Remember?" Macon smiles down at his son. "We said you would meet her today?"

"Yep." Gabe nods. "Does she talk?"

"She does," Jonah says. "She's still little, so she doesn't make a lot of sense sometimes, but she usually talks up a storm."

"Char too." Gabe throws a thumb at his sister. "She makes no sense." He glances up at his Macon. "Can we see the sharks now?"

"Sharks!"

"Oh, you're speaking her love language now," Mabel says with a laugh. "Ted wants to see the sharks, too."

"Welp, c'mon, then."

"Welp," Jonah says seriously, nodding at Gabe. "The man has spoken. Off to the sharks."

"Can Teddy walk?"

"She can."

"I can hold her hand? I hold Char's hand all the time."

My breath hitches, and I glance from Gabe to Lennon and Macon. Lennon smiles and shrugs, then puts Charlotte on her feet. Gabe takes Charlotte's hand, then puts his hand up for Teddy.

"C'mon, then."

Everyone laughs, and with one nod of approval from me, Mabel sets Teddy on her feet too.

"Hello, Teddy," Gabe says, holding his hand out for her.

"Sharks. We go sharks. Come, come!"

She takes Gabe's hand without hesitation, and he sends a big smile to me. I smile back.

"Do you know where you're going?"

"Yes."

"We've come her before," Macon tells me before look back at the kids. "Haven't we, Gabe?"

"Yep."

"Okay, then, Gabriel Christopher Davis." Jonah gestures forward with his hand. "Lead the way."

Then, slowly, holding hands with Charlotte and Teddy, Gabe starts walking. The sight brings a sting of tears to my eyes.

"That's so sweet," Lennon says, and I turn to her. She's watching them, too, a soft smile on her lips. "Five, three, two." She glances at me. "I think they're going to get along."

"Yeah."

I laugh lightly and bring my eyes back to our children, hand in hand, off to see the sharks. Unburdened by their parents' pasts. Not weighed down by anyone's baggage. Completely carefree, accepting of each other with open hearts. Jonah puts his arm around me and presses a kiss to my head, and I look back at Lennon.

"Yeah, I think so, too."

The End

Mental Health Resources

If you are struggling with substance abuse or disordered eating, I encourage you to speak with a mental health professional. Below you will find some resource for the United States, the United Kingdom, and Canada.

You matter. Your health matters. Take care of you.

UNITED STATES

Substance Abuse

The National Drug Helpline at (844) 289-0879
https://drughelpline.org/

Substance Abuse and Mental Health Services Administration's (SAMHSA)
National Helpline
1-800-662-HELP (4357)
https://www.samhsa.gov/find-help/national-helpline

Eating Disorder

National Eating Disorders Association
https://www.nationaleatingdisorders.org/get-help/

ANAD Helpline

MENTAL HEALTH RESOURCES

1 (888) 375-7767
Monday-Friday, 9am-9pm CT
https://anad.org/get-help/eating-disorders-helpline/

National Alliance for Eating Disorders Helpline
: 1 (866) 662-1235
Monday-Friday, 9am-7pm ET
https://www.allianceforeatingdisorders.com/

Diabulimia Helpline:
1 (425) 985-3635
http://www.diabulimiahelpline.org/

24/7 Crisis Help

Suicide and Crisis Lifeline
Call or Text 988
https://988lifeline.org/

Text Crisis Text Line:
"HOME" to 741-741
https://www.crisistextline.org/

UNITED KINGDOM

UK Substance Abuse

Talk to Frank Substance Abuse Hotline
0300 123 6600
www.talktofrank.com

Club Drug Clinic

MENTAL HEALTH RESOURCES

020 3317 3000
clubdrugclinic.cnwl.nhs.uk

DAN 24/7 (also known as Wales Drug & Alcohol Helpline)
0808 808 2234
81066 (text DAN)
dan247.org.uk

UK Eating Disorders

BEAT (Beat Eating Disorders)
0808 801 0677
www.beateatingdisorders.org.uk

Anorexia and Bulimia Care
03000 11 12 13
www.anorexiabulimiacare.org.uk

National Centre for Eating Disorders
0845 838 2040
www.eating-disorders.org.uk

UK 24/7 Crisis Help

Samaritans
general crisis and suicide line
116 123
www.samaritans.org

Shout Crisis Text Line
Text "SHOUT" to 85258
Text "YM" if you're under 19

MENTAL HEALTH RESOURCES

CANADA

CAN Substance Abuse

Drug Rehab Services (DRS) Canada
1-877-254-3348
https://www.drugrehab.ca/

National Overdose Response Service (NORS)
1-888-688-NORS (6677)
https://www.nors.ca/about

Overdose Intervention App
http://stopoverdoseapp.com/

CAN Eating Disorder

National Eating Disorder Information Centre (NEDIC)
Toll-free: 1-866-NEDIC-20
Toronto: 416-340-4156
https://nedic.ca/

Eating Disorders Association of Canada (EDAC)
Email: edac@edac-atac.ca
https://edac-atac.com/

-
Bulimia Anorexia Nervosa Association (BANA)
Office: (519) 969-2112
Intake Requests: 1-855-969-5530
https://bana.ca/

CAN 24/7 Crisis Help

Canadian Suicide Crisis Helpline
Call: 9-8-8

MENTAL HEALTH RESOURCES

Text: 9-8-8
Services in English and French
https://988.ca/

**You matter. Your health matters.
Take care of you.**

Acknowledgments

I love Claire Davis.

I said when I started this book that my goal was not to make you like her, but to at the very least help you understand her. I hope I did that. I really do, because Claire Davis owns my heart, and I think she deserves the world. I never thought I would say that, but here we are. I love her alone. I love her with Jonah. I think they make the perfect pair of broken-and-bruised hearts, and if you don't agree, don't tell me, because I will fight for these characters.

As always, thank you to my **Emotional Support Pirates**, Hales and Jessie. You're always so clutch, and you are wonderful sounding boards.

To **Haley**, who was the inspiration behind *I love you endlessly*. You are in a gem in my life. Love you endlessly.

To **Carrie**, who has been a cheerleader for a Claire redemption arc from the very beginning, thank you for always seeing beauty in the broken. You're a gem of a human, and I am lucky to call you friend. I love you.

To **Sluts4Lyfe**, y'all are unhinged and cause me great stress with the notifications BUT I am so grateful for your advice and support. I appreciate your honesty, your encouragement, and your general tomfoolery. So much love to you.

To **Ashley Carey,** my authenticity and sensitivity reader. You swooped in when I needed you most and I am beyond grateful for your insight and wisdom.

To my editors, **Becky with Fairest Reviews Editing**, **Sarah with All Encompassing Books**, and **Emily with Lawrence Editing**, thank you for polishing this manuscript up and making me look smarter than I am. I appreciate you all so much.

To my super talented cover designer, **Kate with Kate Decided to**

Design, thank you for once again creating magic. These covers have been stunning, and I am forever in awe of your talent.

Shauna and **Becca** at **The Author Agency**, you have no idea how grateful I am for you. You go above and beyond with every release, and I shout from the rooftops how amazing you are. Thank you for the never-ending support and encouragement. I LOVE YOU WITH ALL THE EXCLAMATION POINTS!!!!

To my **Street Team**, I friggen love you all. I would not be here, publishing my TENTH (wtf?) book, if it weren't for you all. You're the best bunch of humans on the internet, and I'm so damn grateful for each and every one of you.

TO THE READERS – there are so many amazing books out there. The fact that you've taken the time to read this one means so much to me. Thank you.

And to Jonathan. You're always the last on these lists, but you're the most important. I couldn't do this without you. Thank you for everything. I love you the biggest.

I love you all!
Until the next one,